KING
OF THE
GREY

RICHARD A. KNAAK

A PERMUTED PRESS BOOK

ISBN: 978-1-68261-228-6

Permuted Press, LLC
permutedpress.com

Published in the United States of America

CHAPTER I

Birds of a feather might flock together, but no one had apparently made mention of this to the huge ebony raven that sidled its way along the Bartlett Station crossing gate, drawing, as it did, the attention of one smoke-haired Jeremiah Todtmann. The last of a long line of lemmings seeking entrance to the tarnished, city-bound commuter train this fall morning, the gray-suited, thirty-something Jeremiah watched with deep detachment the avian's antics. Though he was by no means a scholar when it came to the field of ornitholgy, Jeremiah knew that it was indeed a raven and not a common blackbird. The blackbirds, in point of fact, who did not think of themselves as common in any respect, were keeping a fair distance from the lone refugee from Poe's darksome verses. Even as the mortgage broker put a gloved hand on the car rail and pulled himself up into the belly of the train, he could see how the other birds all watched the raven as if it were some sort of pinioned pariah. The creature in question, oblivious to the cocked eyes of its brethren, turned an orb of its own in the direction of Jeremiah himself.

Jeremiah thought little of the bird's interest in him; what would a raven or any other child of the air want with a single man of narrow build and pale but unremarkable features? Nothing, that was what. It was the place of ravens, robins, and all other birds to fly, lay eggs, eat bugs, and stare at commuters as the latter went on their way to work. Perhaps, Jeremiah thought in retrospect as the outer doors of the car hissed their way closed behind him, they found the very concept of commuting an amusing idiosyncrasy of the wingless ones.

He forgot the feathered misfit as he surveyed the worn and smoke-scented car for a place to sit. Not just any of the cracked vinyl seats would do. Jeremiah always sat at the window and stared out, even if his eyes rarely even saw what lay beyond. It only mattered that he had somewhere to turn his dreaming gaze to other than the bent backs and unsightly faces of his fellow passengers. Since this was one of the first morning stops, his choices were many; only a third of the seats had any occupants. He settled on a place to his right, which would be the left when he turned to face the direction they headed, and quickly made his way to it, only barely beating the train's first jerking movements.

Jeremiah slid toward the scarred window and immediately turned his attention to what little of the town he could see. There was the coffee shop that closed before he returned on the evening train. Across the street from it was a corner bank, tiny, crowded, and built to seem both neighborly and with the times, whatever those times happened to be. A few parked automobiles testified to the early hour. By the coming of the next train, spaces would be a premium worth the gold of princes and the curses of the unfortunates who found themselves forced to take places nearly a quarter of a mile from the station.

Stirring to life, an ancient behemoth prodded into movement, the train snarled, dragging itself forward. The landscape began sliding past Jeremiah's green-tinted window, an emerald realm fraught with the grit and decay of reality. The closer to the city he traveled, the more Jeremiah's view would darken and age until at last the black night announcing the end of the ride, the terminal, would be all that remained. The tunnel always chilled Jeremiah during the first few seconds after the train entered, though he was at a loss to explain why that was so. As with many things, it was one of those mysteries of life that would, for most people, remain a mystery.

For the moment such mysteries meant nothing to him. Already his eyes no longer even paid heed to the world outside. Instead, they stared at themselves, icy blue orbs matching against a pair of ghostly green ones reflected in the window. The coffee shop and the bank vanished from view, to be temporarily replaced by more parked vehicles, then by a few houses, and then briefly an uncared-for field. Jeremiah saw none of that, though he knew all those things were there.

Its trek barely renewed, the train began to slow again, a protesting whine from the engine alerting those within that the next stop and more riders lay just ahead.

The mad, blinking eyes of the crossing gate jarred him from his stupor. Jeremiah frowned, thinking it was not so much the shrieks of the gate but something he had seen perched atop the eyes themselves. As the train commenced a reluctant halt and opened itself up to the newcomers, he twisted around and tried to see what it was that had caught his eye. His efforts were for naught, however, for only the bare tip of the arm could be seen. Jeremiah leaned his body forward, still gazing back.

Was there the flash of something ebony upon the arm of the gate? The answer would forever remain limited to his imagination, for the engine was already struggling on. The crossing gate was left behind almost immediately.

Annoyed with himself, the mortgage broker leaned away from the window, placing his right hand on the seat for balance.

His fingers touched cool, soft flesh.

Jeremiah pulled his hand away as if a leper now sat next to him. So engrossed had he been with the matter of the gate that he had not noticed that someone had chosen to share his seat.

"Sorry!" he spouted, embarrassed at his accidental encounter. He turned, already committed to repeating the apology, and found... no one.

The seat was empty.

He put his hand back on the spot it had vacated and ran his fingers across the fading vinyl. The material felt, as he had expected, exactly like old vinyl and most definitely not like supple human flesh. Jeremiah turned his hand over and studied his fingertips. They revealed no great secrets concerning his vanishing seatmate. It was evident that he must have imagined the other person, but Jeremiah found that hard to accept in light of the sensations he had experienced. How could the harsh, aged material pass for the skin of a young woman? Todtmann was a quiet man who had little contact with the opposite sex outside of the workplace, but even he had tasted the simple pleasure of holding a woman close. Not by any stretch of the imagination could the vinyl play at such a role... yet, it had.

"Too tired; that's it," he muttered. That much was certainly true. Who could say that Jeremiah might not have drifted off a little deeper than normal, entering, without realizing it, the world of dreams?

The number of empty seats quickly dwindled. Most of the tired faces around Todtmann were ones that the mortgage broker saw every silent morning. He perhaps knew the names of a handful and had no desire to make the acquaintance of any more, save perhaps two or three of the female passengers. They, unfortunately, had no such desire concerning Jeremiah and he was not one for forward action. As the last of the train's latest catch found places to sit, Todtmann finally turned his attention back to the dim, emerald world outside and his own private unthoughts.

Given free rein once more, the engine roared anew and lurched into motion. The next leg of Jeremiah's journey went without disturbance. Older, grittier buildings flashed by, ephemeral landscapes that he knew so well yet could not have described if asked to do so. A field eventually slowed into focus, the first sign of yet another pause in the trek. The bitter squeals of the engine as it once more was forced to cease its breathless run shattered the numbness that Todtmann had only just succeeded in recreating.

"Damn!" Jeremiah straightened. No crossing gate screamed dire warnings at this station, but something else had caught his eye. This time, he was certain of what it was he had seen.

A raven. It perched atop a sign that, in letters of authority, announced this as the Schaumburg commuter station. One round eye was cocked in the direction of the train and, if Jeremiah's own eyes could be believed, directly at him.

Mad as the thought seemed to him, Todtmann was almost certain it was the same bird. He fairly pressed his face against the smudged window as he tried to focus on his avian shadow.

To his dismay, the raven winked.

Not winked, but blinked, he corrected, chiding himself for even imagining such a ridiculous notion. Of course the ebony ghost was not winking at him; the only reason it had seemed that way was that due to the peculiar nature of a bird's features, it could only stare at him with one eye. The other had to face the opposite direction.

Still...it had almost seemed like an act with purpose, not an instinctive reaction.

As if to settle the matter, the raven spread its long, sleek wings and took to the sky. Jeremiah smiled in relief and sat back against his seat. As he did, he barely caught sight of a tall, pale woman who, to his startlement, was staring at him as she walked by. No, he corrected himself, pale implied color, however slight, and this woman, both ageless and perfect, had skin that made even the pale of the moon a kaleidoscope of color. She left his view before he could even finish drawing a breath, but every detail concerning her features was already etched into his mind. He turned quickly, hoping for one last glance at her perfection before she sat down behind some dour lemming whose gray form would obstruct his vision, but despite Jeremiah's speed, there was no trace of her when he looked. A few bland faces briefly turned his way and then ignored him.

He blinked and, without pausing to think of the image he projected, stared down into the seats directly behind him. Jeremiah's view brought no new glimpse of his glorious enchantress. The cascades of raven-black hair, the almond-shaped, silver eyes, the arched brows as black as the tresses, and the full, red lips that seemed where all the color of her skin must have gathered...he saw no one who could claim even the weakest reflection of that wondrous visage. A worn old man with tiny brown eyes and a perpetual sneer carved into his features by years of commuting looked up at the younger traveler as if demanding to know why Jeremiah was disturbing his vegetating. With an embarrassed smile, Todtmann whirled about and, trying without success to be nonchalant, commenced to stare out the window with such intensity that one might have thought he were witnessing a cold-blooded murder taking place in the station itself. Crimson embarrassment gave his emerald reflection a Christmassy touch that he failed to appreciate at that moment.

First questing ravens and now dream women who were just that. Jeremiah shook his head, both in disgust at his sorry state and in the wild hope that he might clear his muddled thoughts. Nothing helped. Staring out the window as the train started up again brought no comfort, either. Neither the raven nor the woman would leave his thoughts, and in fact, each passing breath increased their demand for his total attention. Had she run to the following car? Was the raven following him? How could he think it was the same one? Had she been no more than his imagination? Why were such things making his heart beat madly and his forehead perspire? He was not, by nature, a nervous, flighty man. Jeremiah glanced down at his watch, but he already knew that there was at least another half hour's worth of travel ahead of him. It might as well have been an eternity.

When the car jostled and jerked and the engine's roar announced the next pause, Todtmann was already glued to the window seeking his winged nemesis. He had attempted, in the couple minutes between stations, to convince himself of the idiocy of such an act, but he might as well have sought to cease breathing. Still, his initial scan of the station revealed only a handful of weary newcomers, a few of whom looked briefly in his direction and then immediately turned away so as not to draw his attention to themselves. He cared not what his demeanor must have resembled at that point, though, in a saner moment, Jeremiah might have again questioned how a bird and a woman, however goddesslike she might have been, could muddle his mind. The only thing of importance right now, though, was finding or not finding the raven. He looked over the tiny building again. His heartbeat slowed as the first sensations of relief washed over him. There was no raven at the station. As he had thought earlier, it had been mere coincidence. Probably not even the same bird...

"Sonuvabitch!" he whispered, wide-eyed. It was there. Not perched on the arm of a crossing gate or atop the station, but farther back, in the parking lot. It walked serenely on the hood of a brand-new, racing-red sports car, its claws doing untold damage to the paint. Jeremiah almost suspected it enjoyed what it was doing.

As if feeling his eyes upon it, the raven brought one of its own onto the unnerved human. Again, the gaze that met the man spoke of intelligence and understanding...and more than Jeremiah felt he himself contained at this time.

The raven winked again. This time, Jeremiah was certain of it even though the bird was fairly far away. Something in its movements told him it was so. He had never seen another bird that walked and acted the way this one did. Perhaps someone had trained it once and it had escaped. Yet, the ebony nightmare did not walk as a creature trained to mimic men might walk; rather, it stalked across the hood with the evident satisfaction of one who quite revels in the havoc it is wreaking.

Jeremiah fell back against the dusty seat and squeezed his eyes closed. He did not open them again until he felt the car moving and then it was to stare ahead of him, not out the window. Anywhere but the window. Only when the station was far behind did he dare a peek outside.

Transient landscapes once more darted past, racing ever back and out of sight behind the train. Todtmann had never been one who looked at work with overly fond eyes, but this once he dreamed of the office, his cramped cubicle, and the endless stacks of confused and incomplete files with an ardor approaching worship. If there was one thing that could bring him back to the safe world of the mundane, it was the offices of Everlasting Mortgage, Inc. Imagination and the unknown died at the front doors. Everlasting did not permit such things in its daily routine; they interfered with the schedule.

Breathing easier, Jeremiah covertly scanned his fellow passengers, wondering how his peculiar behavior had touched them. Despite his continual bouncing and gasping, however, not one other commuter looked his way. They might have been purposely ignoring him, for fear he would try to make their acquaintance, but everyone appeared too typically disinterested for such pretense to be possible. Even the sour soul who sat behind him and whose attention he had briefly drawn minutes before seemed truly unconcerned with his antics. It was an unwritten rule that those who were only pretending to ignore someone generally tried too hard, making them look more like players in an intense masters' chess tournament than the unconcerned citizens they hoped they appeared to be. Such was not the case with these folk; they were unconcerned...and very much so.

While he was still brooding over this curious little fact, the train slowed yet again. The first half of the daily journey was fraught with pauses, something Jeremiah Todtmann usually paid no heed to. Now, however, he jerked his head up and looked outside, bug-eyed, suddenly atremble with renewed fear, and trying to recall just how many more stations he had to survive before the terminal could claim him.

"Just a bird, damnit," he whispered, his eyes not yet focused on the scene outside. "Just a bird!" Why did the raven unnerve him so each time it appeared? Why had it appeared in the first place?

Slowly, his vision took in everything...the waiting passengers, the graying building behind them, the automobiles lined up like so many pets anxiously awaiting their masters' return. The buildings and streets beyond....

No raven.

He almost laughed out loud, but managed to smother it before it was anything more than "Haulp..." Neither those new internees nor the ones who had boarded from prior stops took notice of Todtmann's peculiar utterings. This early in the morning, he told himself, it would have taken a derailment to even gain the momentary attention of some of his fellows. That was all it was. There was nothing supernatural about it.

Supernatural? Why had he even thought that just now?

The question faded in rapid fashion as Jeremiah drank in the welcome sight of the station, drawing every available second given to him. When the engine finally announced its impatience and began pulling the train along again, Jeremiah twisted around so that he could savor yet another moment or two before the stop vanished behind him. When he leaned back this time, the smile that crossed his face was wide and relaxed.

"Just a bird," he muttered to himself in pleasure.

The stops that followed were so uneventful that Jeremiah almost thought he might dose off. A few familiar sights, such as the old Elmwood Cemetery, garnered a bit of his attention. He had always thought the cemetery had needed a good-sized, old-fashioned mausoleum or two to do it justice. Even that thought, however, was only a drifting one. Yet two things still marred his happiness as the commuter train neared Chicago and its ultimate destination, Union Station. One was that he still desired a second peek at—actually, he wanted to be able to ogle forever—his pale dream. Jeremiah could still not see how he could have imagined so perfect a woman. No one that he had ever met could have been the prototype for such ethereal majesty.

The other thing that disturbed him might have only been the result of his already overworked imagination, but the fact that it existed at all even as such left some doubts in his mind concerning his mental health.

What disturbed him was the empty place to his side. By now, bodies packed the car. That was as it was every day during the workweek. Every seat around had two or three aggravated figures crushed into it. Both levels were full. It was to be expected by this point in the run since not all the cars were open and would not be until the next trip into the city. What was not to be expected was the empty place next to Jeremiah, a place that even at the last stop, more than a dozen oblivious newcomers must have bypassed. They had, as far as he could hazard, traveled on to the next car behind rather than sit down beside him.

The paranoia that lurks within all folk asked, Do they know something?

Even the most unappealing of the other early morning commuters, such as the silent sufferer behind him, had seatmates. Jeremiah had only dust. He would not have normally complained over such luck but now he felt a deep, urgent desire inside to assure himself that he was one of these folk, one of the bored nine-to-fivers to whom nothing out of the ordinary ever occurred. He wanted the gray, uneventful existence to be his once more.

Three stops later, Jeremiah was still alone. There had been no trace of his early companion, the insistent raven, and his phantom love had become just one more lost dream to store in his memory for later sighing over. He had pressed himself against the car wall in an unconscious maneuver to make the seat more inviting, but still no one had joined him. By now he knew one thing was true; everyone who entered ignored the place beside him, almost as if they thought somebody sat there already. Was that an impression in the faded vinyl? Why did he have the unsettling feeling that they saw more than he?

Jeremiah reached out and his hand touched the nothing that his eyes told him was there. He grimaced, folded his arms, and shut his eyes tight again.

Somewhere soon after that, the sands of Hypnos, god of sleep, took him. The next thing Jeremiah knew, his fellow travelers were rising, a revivified line of shuffling corpses. Outside it was dark. Barely visible forms moved about, seeming like lost souls searching for release. He stretched, a bit disconcerted at both his earlier actions and the curious fact that he had actually slept...and saw her again.

It was yet another teasing glimpse. Her eyes were again upon him as she left the car. Completely turned about, Todtmann clambered to a standing position and attempted to thrust himself into the line...but the line was not having any of that and several darkening visages warned him that he should wait his proper turn. Jeremiah studied the snaillike movements of those in the aisle, seeking even the slightest opening. A man paused for a single breath, his briefcase having caught itself on the metal edge of one of the seats. Jeremiah darted forward, his face molded into the same mask of arrogant indifference that the other wore. Behind him, the other man grunted in annoyance at the sudden intrusion, but said nothing more.

Jeremiah allowed himself a tiny, fleeting smile...one that disappeared as someone tripped him and he fell into the man in front of him.

"Watchit!" the passenger in front, a tall, narrow man with a muzzle for a nose, snapped.

Todtmann turned around, causing yet more anger and consternation among his fellow commuters, and sought the culprit who owned the foot.

The seats had all been emptied. The aisle was clear of refuse. There was nothing that could have tripped him, unless someone had left a loose foot lying around and he had kicked it away after stumbling over it.

Just for a moment—only a moment—Jeremiah considered that possibility.

"Excuse me!" growled the man with the briefcase. "Can I get around you if you're gonna stand there all day?"

Without thinking, Jeremiah gripped the other passenger's arm tight and asked, "You didn't trip me, did you?"

"Course not!" The man, a bit older and pudgier than Todtmann and with a face that looked as if someone had tried to squash it, tried desperately to pry the fingers away from his arm, but the newspaper he held in his other hand made that maneuver nearly impossible.

"You...you didn't see a beautiful, black-haired woman leave, did you?" Jeremiah asked in sudden inspiration. To his surprise, it felt good to be noticed by anyone, even if that unfortunate happened to think he was mad.

The man shook his head in vehemence. "Nope. No one. Doya mind, guy?" It was clear he had categorized Jeremiah as one of those unspeakables that haunted Union Station, but generally at night, and who accosted good folk like himself for the oddest and worst reasons. He'd always warned his wife about the dangers of the city.

Jeremiah blinked. Where had that last come from? It was almost as if he had read the other's thoughts.

He released the unnerved man's arm and whirled about, racing down the now-empty aisle to the front of the car and the exit.

"Watch your step," a conductor called out in automatic fashion as Jeremiah fairly leapt out of the car and into the narrow corridor between trains.

The train, the conductor, the swarms of lemmings flowing toward the light at the end of the gate, none of these so much as touched upon Jeremiah Todtmann's senses save as obstacles in his path. He barged past one unsmiling figure after another, his eyes darting this way and that, searching for the raven-tressed figure that would stick out like a rose among weeds in this pedestrian crowd.

From the darkness of the dimly lit terminal, he stepped into the glow of the station itself, seeing yet not seeing the bustling hordes around him, but being pulled along with them all the same. In truth, Jeremiah could have walked the path blindfolded, as could most of the others. Because of that, he was able to continue his search for his shadowy beauty without care for anything else. He did not really question why she had come to obsess him in so quick and stunning a fashion or why there now seemed to be an occasional figure who would not come into focus when his eyes fell upon them. If he found his dream, he would ask her…once he was able to speak in her presence without stuttering, that is.

Would she even deign to speak to him if he did find her, Jeremiah wondered in horror just before the hordes pushed him into the brilliance of the main station. Or would she just see him as some madman?

And why was he so certain that she would be able to answer all of his questions?

Far above Jeremiah's head, perched on a ledge overlooking the vast interior of Chicago's venerable Union Station, the raven surveyed the crowds, a single eye focused on one commuter in particular.

"Merrily, merrily," he said in a voice much too deep and modulated for a bird of any feather, even one as masterful as this. "All things go well for those who wait." He studied the mortal souls below and sought out those who were not mortal and certainly had no souls to call their own. As ever, the dark figures were there in good numbers, flitting through the living as unseen ghosts. In a corner behind one of the gigantic columns and all by herself— naturally—he saw the ivory-skinned object of Jeremiah's obsession. Her expression interested the raven much and made a decision for him.

"All things come to those who wait," he said, then spread his wings. "But he who hesitates is lost, too true."

The huge raven fluttered off to do his work.

CHAPTER II

The king is dead, long live the king.

Haros Aguilana had known the human they called king, known him all too well. Thomas O'Ryan had been a man of great humor, a rare thing for one of his…unique…status, and Haros had thought, very naïvely he now decided, that this reservoir of humor would prove the anchor the Grey had sought so long, the anchor that would allow them the future they deserved.

And then the damned mortal had gone and tried to make a hero of himself.

"Alas, poor Thomas," he muttered as he doused the cigarette in the ashtray. Actually, it was not a true cigarette but only the shadow of one, for that—and it was indeed a regret to Haros, who craved the taste of a real one—was all that a Grey could touch. After all, in many ways he was as insubstantial as the smoke floating free from the dying ash. "Alas poor Thomas. I knew him, Horatio."

The one who sat across from him at the table, a table in a place congregated by the Grey, blinked, the red eyes disappearing and reappearing like the warning lights of a railroad crossing in the dark. There was certainly not much to see of his companion, Haros noted, but then the other had not been so fortunate as to draw the attention of O'Ryan and thereby gain some solidity in existence.

Around them, the specters danced.

They were a contrast, these two, yet also so very similiar. Those unfortunate enough—or fortunate, as Haros considered it—to meet the tall, thin member of the Grey came away, when they were able, with the image of a pipe-thin, elegantly clad member of an old European aristocracy. If he allowed them, they might question his bone-white skin, the immaculate black hair slicked back, and his crimson slash of a mouth. Haros Aguilana had a narrow, vulpine face and eyes that were as black as the shadows from which his kind might be claimed to come. In many ways, he represented the movie and comic book vampire, though he was far more and far less.

His companion was less solid of form, but vaguely resembled an apelike creature. He was one of those fortunate enough to possess some control, which was why Haros dined with him in this place where the shadows of women and men—and others undecided—danced with one another to the silent music only the Grey could appreciate. There were so few with any control, especially during the time after the king's death.

It was the best of times and the worst of times, Aguilana thought. For now was the time when he could work for himself, change what had always been to what it should be.

Aguilana's companion finally stirred himself. "My name isn't Horatio...is it?"

The narrow figure grimaced. It might have been funny at one time, but he felt nothing but sadness for the other. With the anchor dead—so much for O'Ryan's practical joking about heights—even this one was losing himself.

"No, my friend, you have no name. None of the kings ever turned that much of an eye to you."

They were all like that, those humans, he thought. Never had they understood their place among the Grey, which was why he, Haros Aguilana, the Grey's hope, had planned for the next successor. This king, this anchor, would serve his kind the way he was meant to.

A swirl of darkness covered the table and left two glasses filled with drink. The glasses and their contents, of course, were only the memories of drinks drunken. They kept a wisp of their former glory, allowing the Grey to even derive some satisfaction. Nothing of the Grey was truly real when it came down to it, not even Haros Aguilana.

That annoyed him more than anything else.

"Callistra will have him entranced by now," he informed his nebulous companion. "He will follow her and the bending will take place. O'Ryan's chosen successor will be molded to my—our desire."

The other took time to visibly absorb this. Grunting, he finally asked, "Why this man? Why did O'Ryan choose him to be king? Is he special? Is this…a sign?"

"Hardly. The jokester liked his name. Heard it once as he listened in to the world of light." Haros grimaced again. "King O'Ryan said, 'Scarecrow, now there's a man who should be your bloody anchor! Todtmann, get it? Means dead man or something like it in German!' Little did I know that he had this in mind."

"I liked his sense of humor," the apelike thing said, eyeing the phantom drink before him and trying to remember what it was he was supposed to do with it.

"You would." The pale Grey recreated another cigarette. Had he been a human, it was very likely he would have been dead long ago, so like a chimney he smoked. Fortunately, both he and the cigarette were only reflections of the real things. There was not even the smell of smoke in the club, only the mustiness of an empty place.

Still the dancers danced, the players played, and the Grey as a whole tried not to think about what the future held for them.

There were times when Haros Aguilana would have been willing to suffer lung cancer, if only to experience something of life. Such was not the fate of his kind, however, no matter how much he played at living.

"Will he be like O'Ryan?"

"No." He took a puff on the phantasm and glanced at the dancers, who twirled and twirled without hope, for even the pleasure of dance was beyond them. They could only pretend and hope they derived a little something from it. Most of them were no more than shapes, distended shadows of folk and such who were not there. These were his people, such as they were. "Jeremiah Todtmann will know fear by the time his place is ready. I will see to that. This mortal, he will give us substance as we have never had."

"Will we be real then?"

Haros was trying to enjoy his impending triumph, but he could not deny his companion an answer. "As real as the imagination of men can be."

"Not real then."

There is a point when too much is too much and that point had come. He could not sit here anymore. Standing, Haros reached for his cane, a shadow of a piece that had a wolf's head for the handle. There were things to do and he could not trust everything to Callistra even though there was surely nothing to be wary of.

Haros had thought of all circumstances and had, he was proud to tell his listeners now and then, planned accordingly for each. He was thorough, Haros Aguilana was, because there was little else to occupy his time. The plan gave him purpose.

The darklings shifted away from the table, giving him space. So many of the Grey wanted to be where he was, if only because he knew himself, had identity of a sort. To the apelike thing, who was scratching himself in order to think better, Haros said, "I must go now. Have no fear, though. Save that for the mortal man."

He would have stepped away then, left the dimly lit club dubbed The Wasteland by O'Ryan, but his companion was visibly struggling with a thought he wished to express and Haros, however much he wanted now to see his perfect plan come off...perfectly, respected the battle the other member of the Grey was going through.

The eyes of the other lit up in enthusiasm, the thought he wished to convey to Haros finally shaped to his liking. He looked up at the patiently waiting Aguilana and said, "I saw a raven in the moon."

And suddenly Haros Aguilana's perfect plan proved as insubstantial as he.

Was Union Station more crowded than usual? The thought occurred to Jeremiah as he entered. The river of humanity that washed him along had a stronger pull than normal and it seemed determined to drag him to a direction not of his choosing. He had missed his own exit early on, not a care of his at first, but now he went past the escalators and stairs, around the corners and into the main station itself, heading ever farther away from work.

To make matters worse, she was nowhere to be seen. That bothered him much more than it should have, but Jeremiah could not fight his upturned emotions. He started to experience an irrational panic. Union Station in Chicago was a place where people could be separated and never find one another again…at least during the rush hours. Todtmann let his worries concerning the office fade to the back. At that moment there was a greater priority, as far as he was concerned.

As filled with folk as the station generally was, it never seemed completely full. That perhaps was due to the high ceiling, a relic of the earlier days of the twentieth century when architects, on occasion, did not build with optimum office space in mind. In this place, huge columns rose high, one of the romantic touches that the outside of the nearly underground domain did not hint at. There were still marble walls and scrollwork. Row upon row of bench marked the waiting point for those intending travel farther than merely to work. There were always people waiting here, even in the latest hours of the night. Some of those folk even had destinations. Another time, he might have eyed them surreptitiously, his mind filled with fanciful dreams of hopping a northbound train to the wilds of Canada or a northwest-bound one to Alaska. His dreams were the dreams of the weary, the bored—something Jeremiah Todtmann could hardly be called at the moment.

Harried would have been a far better description. The crowd was now proving itself quite reluctant to let him pass through, more so than anytime past that his muddled mind could recall. River of humanity? This was the veritable sea….

"Excuse me!" Jeremiah swam the gauntlet, seeking a place where he could stop and breathe. With no recent sighting of his raven-haired vision to enforce his desire, it began to wane, albeit not completely. The commonsense part of his mind, a part that held great sway with him, pointed out that he would likely never see her again if he started looking for her. In fact, he would likely never see her again, period. Still, Jeremiah had a bit of the dreamer in him, however small that bit might be, so he did not give in immediately. All he asked was a place from which to search…just for a few minutes, the young man promised himself.

There are too many people here, came a sudden, peculiar thought. It was not merely a complaint upon his part at being unable to make real headway, but rather an observation of his subconscious that there were those in the station who should not be here. Yet, every time Jeremiah tried to make out some of those extra bodies, his eyes seemed unwilling to focus. Figures darted in and out of the masses like slippery eels, yet he could not see their faces or forms as more than shadow. Some were so indistinct he wondered if they might just be tricks of his eyes.

"Glasses. I'm going to need glasses before I'm forty," he muttered. A column loomed before him, a haven in the sea. He steered toward it, broke through the throngs, and pressed his back to the cold, dead stone. The flow continued on, oblivious to the loss of one when so many were still caught. Now and then, the same vague figures shifted among the real folk, never seeming to go anywhere, just…mingling.

Should've had more coffee. Just groggy, that's all. Too many late nights during the workweek, even if those nights had only been spent reading. Jeremiah tried to blink away the ghosts he saw, but they chose to be uncooperative, continuing to slip through the herds of solemn lemmings released from the bellies of the trains. Jeremiah grunted; if they would not vanish, he would ignore them. They were only phantasms, after all, the creation of his own overworked mind, no doubt.

Was she also a phantasm? If so, his imagination was wondrous indeed, for he saw her even as he was about to dive his way back into the sea of souls. It was only her back that he saw, but there could be no other back like hers, not on ordinary women. His ardor suddenly reinvigorated, Jeremiah Todtmann began to break his way through the flow, ignoring angry looks and hardy shoves of those whose schedules he had dared to disrupt by so many precious seconds. Jeremiah did not care, automatically mouthing his apologies as he tried to narrow the distance between the ebony-haired enchantress and himself.

Unfortunately, the flow of traffic proved stronger than he. He found himself going too far, being swept toward a brightly lit exit. His subconscious informed him without success that the exit should not be there. Jeremiah, though, focused on the sign above and suddenly saw the exit as his means to an end, for he knew that she, too, had to be seeking an egress. If he could reach the street before her, it might be possible to meet his dream after all. His head filled with hope as he neared the doorway.

The raven laughed as he landed on a ledge overlooking the mortal man and the exit that wasn't, but no one, of course, heard it.

" 'Welcome to my parlor,' said the spider to the fly," he added, hopping about with anticipation. "Enter freely and...be afraid."

What is a tunnel doing in this part of Union Station? a voice in his mind chided Jeremiah. What is so dark and deep a tunnel doing here?

"It's not dark at all!" the mortgage man argued under his breath. What would make him think it was dark when the very light of it was so blinding? Still, there was something dark about the light, if such a thing were possible.

He stepped inside and did not notice the large black bird that swooped in behind and above him.

Light should reveal things, not hide them, but this light made no clearer the tunnel than if Jeremiah had been walking in the midst of a heavy, stifling fog. There was no sign of the exit, no sign of anything.

His feet made no sound nor did even his breathing break the silence. Only when he spoke was there anything and even then his voice seemed muted, as if he were farther away from himself, a tricky concept indeed. There was nothing to do but go on, however, and Todtmann, with the diligence that had got many a home buyer's problem file dealt with in record time, walked with the determination of the righteous. Exits had exits; the logic made complete sense to him. If the powers that managed the daily life of Union Station put in exits, then by God those exits would have endings. They would lead someplace, supposedly outside. It was as natural and proper as a nine-to-five position in life.

As if bowing to his not considerable will, the exit did end…and almost in that very minute, too. Jeremiah was saved a swollen nose or a stubbed toe by the hand that slammed into the doors. First cursing and then thanking his lucky stars, he pushed one of the doors open and stumbled through to the street beyond.

"What the devil?" was the nearest he could come to a succinct remark about his new surroundings. There was, perhaps, a good reason after all for the odd, neglected state of the exit tunnel and that was that the street itself was nothing a commuter or visitor would desire to come upon. It was a shameful embarrassment and though that might seem a redundant turn of phrase, it appeared justified in this case. The street, which he could not readily identify, was awash in shadow despite the dim light of day that should have still burned much of the dark away. Vermin were alive and well, skittering about the area with no concern at all for the large being invading their domain. Big as some of them were, it was Jeremiah Todtmann who thought twice of stepping any farther from the doors. The street also smelled, a euphemistic term in this case, of decay and dampness.

The ground squished beneath Jeremiah's shoes as he stepped out to see which way would lead him to Jackson or Adams Street. All he needed was one of the major streets surrounding the station to put him back on track and those were most likely. Again, the woman of his dreams became little more than just that to him; getting his life back on a steady, undramatic course was the first priority now and the initial step toward that—a careful step, considering the many unmentionables crawling or scuttling around his feet—was to start walking.

The shadows seemed to thicken when Jeremiah turned and tried to make out the street signs on the nearer end. He knew that shadows did not work that way, but still....

Todtmann was left-handed, so he chose to go that way. It seemed as logical as anything else. She should be down that way somewhere, he told himself. If not her, then at least a familiar place.

What was this street? Not one of the ones that he was used to, but streets didn't just sprout from the ground, did they? This one looked to him as if it had not sprouted, but rather spoiled.

He had taken two or three steps forward when the familiar shape, so sharply defined where nothing else here was, alighted onto the vague shadow that was the street sign. It spread its wings and, despite the darkness, eyed him with one sharp, burning orb that he could see and feel all too well.

"No. Nonono. Not you again."

The raven nodded. There was no mistaking the action as there had been no mistaking earlier when Jeremiah had been certain that this refugee from a horror story had been looking at him on the train.

The harried Todtmann began backing up, wondering why he had not heeded his very first thought that morning, the one that had said, Stay in bed; don't go in to work.

Around him, the shadows deepened. A part of his mind registered the fact that he had never seen a deep shadow before, but there was no better way to describe them. They were not just dark; Jeremiah had the peculiar sensation that the blacker they became, the farther one could go inside them...perhaps even beyond the oh-so-solid wall?

The raven spread his wings again and flapped them hard, as if preparing to rise and attack the human. The pale young man stumbled and one of his feet landed in some of the deepest of the shadows, sinking into some muck that the darkness hid.

His eyes on the ebony pariah, Todtmann began pulling his foot free of the muck, only to find it would not give so easily. He turned his attention rather reluctantly to the task...and found the shadows creeping up his leg like a coy but persistent lover.

Jeremiah stifled the scream but not the terror. He grabbed at his leg in desperation and tore it free of the clutching black. The shadows withdrew with a sucking sound.

It occurred to the young, fair-haired broker that he was surrounded by many such shades.

I just wanted to go to work!

Under pressure, he came up with the only viable solution to his predicament.

He turned and ran in the opposite direction from where Poe's pet watched. Jeremiah Todtmann ran as hard as his body would permit, his legs and arms akimbo like some fanciful scarecrow. There was method here, however, for the violent action of his limbs kept any of the deeper shadows from clinging long. They could only pull at his legs and shoes and slurp back in what might have been disappointment. The end of the alley street grew nearer and nearer, but the shadows lengthened and deepened the closer he drew to freedom.

Behind him, laughing as no bird, however masterful a mimic it was, was able, the raven rose from his perch. It was the laugh of a child, but a child with no soul.

"Run wild, run free, all the same to me!" he heard a low, madcap voice call. Todtmann did not turn and look to see who spoke; he knew it would be the raven and he knew that ravens did not speak, at least with such personality.

He was still running when the shadows gave way to streams of pacing pedestrians, many of whom were not in the least pleased when Jeremiah came tumbling into their midst. Their protests, some rather vehement and unprintable to say the least, meant nothing to him as he turned to see if the thing of evil dared to cross the threshold after him.

The raven was not there. The shadows were not there. Truth be told, even the street was not there, though where one could hide a street was a very good question.

Jeremiah stood facing the office building nearest to Union Station. He had, if his eyes swore the truth, walked through the walls of both structures without even noticing what he was doing.

His fear, if not his confusion, momentarily at bay, the hapless figure finally became aware of the discourse of some of those around him.

"Christ!" yelled the nearest, a heavy man who was sweating despite the cool weather. "What the hell's the matter with you?" He did not wait for an answer, but walked briskly along, hoping, perhaps, that someone else would deal with the lunatic. No one seemed to care that he had come through a solid wall that had temporarily been a darkened street occupied by one maniacal black bird and several thousand denizens of the city's earthier side. He wondered what they had seen.

Many faces turned Todtmann's way, but while some contained sympathy, most carried that look that he himself would have worn under the same circumstances. It was the look that said, Poor man, maybe he was mugged but it could be that he's crazy so I better stay away from him and besides someone else will surely handle it before he gets out of hand and why isn't there a policeman around what with all the tax money Chicago takes from the state....

The roar of a city still waking reminded him that this was the reality that he had sought. Everything was solid and as it should be. Angry cars growled their way down the street, reluctantly pausing for those pedestrians daring enough to believe in the "right-of-way" nonsense but who ignored the very legal "don't-cross" signals before them. People were as they were meant to be and no vague specters walked among them. Oh, there might be a few extra shadows on the Sears Tower, which was where he supposedly worked, but they were no doubt the product of scattered clouds. Jeremiah was convinced of this last even though the thin cloud cover made such deep shadows virtually impossible.

He straightened his tie and tucked his escaping shirt back into his still perfectly creased slacks. To his surprise, his shoes were devoid of any lingering mess, making Jeremiah think that at least the deep shadows were easy to clean off.

The bizarre journey had led him to the opposite side of the station, away from the Sears Tower, the building that housed his office. Jeremiah was not yet late, but he wondered about the sensibility of walking through the front doors of Everlasting in his mental condition.

Morgenstrom, his superior, would have a field day with him. "Too much work for you, Jeremiah?" Jeremiah could almost hear his dome-headed superior's high-pitched and grating voice. Even though he preferred "Jerry," everyone insisted on being formal and calling him by his full first name. It had always made him feel like he should have graduated from college with a degree in prophecy or philosophy, rather than business. "Perhaps you should sign up for one of the company's excellent detoxication programs! You were a valuable worker once, and with their help, you can be one again!"

He sighed, putting the sum total of his existence in that sigh. There was no avoiding work, but he could at least call in and say that he had missed the train. That would allow him time to sit down somewhere and let caffeine recharge his overtaxed and under-rested mind.

Jeremiah could not recall crossing the bridge nor passing the street after that. His thoughts demanded too much of his attention and so he allowed his feet, which generally had command at this time in the morning, anyway, to take him toward his place of work. Neither the flowing, odoriferous body of water coursing under the bridge nor the ever-growing leviathan of the shadow-encrusted Sears Tower touched his senses as he tried to sort the events of

morning to his liking. There was a slight tingling, but nothing significant enough to merit more than a flicker of active thought.

Buried within the confines of himself, Todtmann turned at the next corner and crossed another street. He paid no mind to such a minimal event, nor did he think about the second and the third street he crossed soon after.

Only when Jeremiah turned his third corner did the discrepancies begin to penetrate. Only when he was halfway down this latest avenue did it occur to him that he had passed more than half a dozen coffee shops.

Jeremiah Todtmann looked up and wondered where the hell he had walked himself to now. Certainly not in the direction of his office.

There were stores and shops for all the sort of things the lunchtime shopper could desire, but since this was early morning, most were dark and empty and of no use to a man so perplexed that he did not even know the name of the avenue he was traveling. Jeremiah put a gloved hand to his face and tried to wipe the frustration away when a familiar image caught the corner of his eye. It was fortunate indeed that his hand covered his mouth then, for it was the only thing that stifled the yell that escaped his lips.

She was there again, reappearing in his life the same sudden way that she had before and standing no more than a dozen or so yards away from him. For the first time he noticed that she was wearing not a dark suit, as he had vaguely supposed before, but a cloak of all things. It ended just below her tiny waist, from where a long, thin black skirt continued down, billowing in a breeze that had to be much stronger than the weak one touching him. She almost appeared to be floating, which, in truth, would not have surprised

him at this point. The skirt was low, but now and then bits of perfectly contoured leg revealed themselves.

She was turned so that her profile was his to admire for a moment. Her long, elegant fingers closed around a door handle. To Todtmann's surprise, the door was open. She slipped inside while he was still pondering that little fact. Who was open at this time?

Having found her again, Jeremiah could think of nothing else but to follow her. The common sense part of his mind ranted and raged, but he ignored it. Work could wait. He had to follow her.

Jeremiah stalked after her, ignoring the few other passersby, who in turn tried to ignore the wild-eyed man in their midst. It did not take him long to reach the building, but to Jeremiah it was yet another lifetime. He put his hand on the door and pulled.

It was locked.

In point of fact...the building was closed.

The confused broker took a step back and studied the doorway. A sign above read RENOVATIONS UNDER WAY! BUILDING A BETTER CHICAGO FOR YOU!

He peered inside. Nothing but the skinned frame of the structure's interior met his gaze. There was nowhere she could have gone. Todtmann tried the door again, just to be certain. It was a fruitless attempt. He stepped away and stared up the length of the building, as if that might explain to him what had happened.

A flicker of movement caught the corner of his eye, a flicker that his mind registered as rich black hair flowing in the wind. Jeremiah turned, half expecting what he was about to see.

A door in the shop next to the empty one closed.

"Damn!" It was short, succinct, and summed up his twisting emotions as adequately as anything else could have. He rushed after her, hoping it was not too late.

The shop next door proved to be a small café with draped windows, a

café open in the pathetic hope, in his august opinion, of catching the morning traffic. The crowds on this avenue were already thinning to near nothingness, however.

The smell of fresh coffee invaded his nostrils as he opened the door, almost actually making him forget his purpose. Perhaps that could be his opening, the offer of a drink between two waking commuters, two slaves of the city. He took a deep breath, entered, and looked around. This was it at last.

It was a tiny place, little more than a counter and some booths. It had seen better days, but was not in bad shape at all. A handful of patrons sat scattered about the shop. Jeremiah smiled at the normalcy of the place.

The smile died abruptly as he noticed one thing not in place.

She was missing…again.

CHAPTER III

There stirred within Jeremiah Todtmann something that had been buried since almost childhood. It had begun to stir with the coming of the raven and it had increased its efforts to be heard when first the broker had abandoned his routines and chased after beautiful will-o'-the-wisps. It was a way of seeing the world as only a few do, a wakefulness that would never again allow him to return to the numbness in which he had lived his life.

The change went unnoticed by him, though, for other, more earthly needs intruded. With his quest once more at a dead and frustrating end, Jeremiah began to consider his new surroundings and their potential. The sight of someone drinking coffee birthed within Jeremiah a passion for the black nectar such as he had never felt before. There was also a pay phone in the place and it occurred to him that he could call the office from here, making some sort of excuse as to why he was not in yet—once he actually figured out what that excuse would be.

He closed the door behind him. The customers paid him no mind, preferring to huddle around their cups. The man behind

the counter, however, met his eyes squarely, seeming to size up the newcomer to his establishment. Jeremiah swallowed, for some insane reason hoping that he would measure up to the elderly man's standards.

"Welcome, my friend," the other said with a toothy smile. He had a rather lupine face, Jeremiah decided, save that an excess of weight had filled it out, as it had the rest of the man's body. A wolf with a full belly. "Is it coffee you would desire?"

The words were spoken in careful English. Despite the lack of accent, the proprietor—which was who Jeremiah assumed he was—had probably not been born and raised in this country, unless he had been brought up in one of the enclaves that still existed here and there in the city.

"Yes, coffee." Feeling foolish for having stared so long, he quickly looked down as he pulled change from his pocket. "How much?"

"Ten cents will be fine."

"Ten cents?" Even as disheveled as he was, Jeremiah could not help but notice the lunacy of charging only a dime a cup. At those prices, nearly every man and woman who worked in the city would have been down here, taking advantage of the crazy price before the café went out of business.

Yet, they were not.

The wolfish smile lengthened. The man was old, but just how old, Jeremiah could not guess. There was still plenty of strength in that form and the smile was anything but weak. It was downright predatory. "My special for first-time customers."

"Oh." He dropped a dime on the counter and while the old man went for his coffee, Jeremiah walked over to the telephone. Picking up the receiver, he dropped a quarter into the slot and started poking buttons. It occurred to him after the first two that

there was no sound coming from the receiver. He pressed another button. Nothing. Frustrated, he hung up. Typical of his luck, the quarter was not returned. Picking up the receiver again availed him naught; the telephone was dead.

"The telephone is dead. It does not work." A hand thrust a cup of steaming coffee under his nose. For a man of great volume, the proprietor moved with stealth.

"It took my quarter." Once over his initial fright, Jeremiah took the cup eagerly, downing almost half in one swallow.

"I will reimburse you."

Jeremiah set the cup down on the counter and waved him off. "That's okay. Do you have another phone?"

"None."

"What about in back? A private one?"

"This is the only phone here." The robust figure turned and walked toward the far end of the counter. His walk was as silent as a wraith's.

"Where's another?"

Behind the counter again, the lupine café operator shrugged. "I could not say."

"How about—" Jeremiah had been about to ask the nearest of the customers...except that the figure had vanished. There was not even an empty mug to mark his brief stay. Todtmann looked around; only he and the owner still remained.

"Where'd they go?" "Who?"

He waved his arms at the empty establishment. "The people who were sitting in here when I came in."

The elderly man looked around, surveying the place with his narrow yellow eyes. "There is no one here," he finally said. "They departed while you were attempting to use the phone."

"No one went past me."

"But they must have." This time it was the proprietor's turn to indicate the abandoned café. "You see, there is certainly no one here, my friend."

It was happening again. Jeremiah shook his head and backed up to the door. "Forget it. I'll find a phone outside somewhere."

"As you wish."

He stumbled outside and back to the intersection. The street here was empty now, yet another peculiar thing for a city like Chicago. Jeremiah put a hand to his head, wishing he had something to drink so that he could clear his mind a little.

Drink? In his haste, he had forgotten his coffee. However odd the little establishment had been, he wanted that coffee. If he just went in and out, he might not have to deal with the peculiar owner again. If the portly proprietor had already disposed of his drink, Jeremiah would ask for another and pray it arrived without incident.

The empty structure to which he had at first followed his beauteous mirage—Jeremiah could no longer believe she had existed, except in his wishful mind—beckoned to him as he passed it. Todtmann paused briefly, wondering why his mind was playing such foul tricks on him. Everything that had happened to him had to be the product of his own imagination; there was no other way to account for the events. What they meant, he could only guess. Some of those guesses left him uncomfortable, dealing, as they did, with his almost hermitical lifestyle. Had he gone stir-crazy? Not since he had been young and school had not yet dulled his imagination had Jeremiah lived in such a world as he was now. Of course, back then he had enjoyed it. Now, it was making a shambles of his nice, predictable existence.

"Lonely man cracks up, " he muttered, abandoning the building for the one housing the café. Still, his eyes lingered on the edifice even as his hand sought out and caught hold of the other door handle. The harried broker quietly wished that she would reappear, whatever the cost to his questionable sanity.

When the door did not budge after the second attempt to open it, Jeremiah finally turned his attention to what he was doing. The door, he saw, was older than he recalled and obviously stuck. Two hands failed to free it. Irritated, he looked up, wondering why the old man had not yet come to help him. Small wonder that the café had trouble gaining a clientele. No one could get inside.

Jeremiah froze. His mouth dropped open. He stopped struggling with the door, though his grip itself tightened to the point where his hands grew white with the effort. Something like a whimper escaped his cavernous maw.

The café was gone. In fact, there was nothing inside the building at all. Like the first, it was undergoing renovation. A few planks lay stacked in one corner and scraps abandoned by workers lay scattered elsewhere. There was a phone and it was where he remembered it, but the one before him was a battered, dust-enshrouded thing without a receiver.

I went into a café. It was here. I got a coffee. I tried to use a phone, but it didn't work. It was here—wasn't it? The shaking man glanced down at the dirt-encrusted floor inside, then abruptly released his grip on the handle as if it had given him a shock.

Jeremiah knew he had been in the building, then. There were footprints in the dust, recent ones that were the same size as his and led a path to where he recalled the counter being. From there, they doubled back to the damaged telephone. He had been inside; Jeremiah was certain…but where had he been?

A prickling sensation ran down his back and through his system. There was indeed something different about the world around him and he was beginning to realize it on a conscious level now. Jeremiah did not rule out madness, but only in that it was a part of whatever was happening. There was too much going on. It could not be him alone. Someone else had to notice. Someone else had to see.

Yet no one did.

He stumbled back in the direction he had come, determined once and for all to reach the office. It was not because of any dedication to his work, not anymore, but because there he would find people who knew him, who might be open to what he had to say.

People who might not strap him down, tie him up, and call the police to drag him screaming away.

It was at the river that he began to notice a subtle change in the crowds. Perhaps it was his eyes, but among the throngs there were those who seemed…out of focus. Almost like the customers at the café—providing there had ever been such a place. They were gray figures among the gray suits, folk who were there and were not, depending on when he looked. Faint recollections of Union Station rose up from the depths of his mired memory. Jeremiah pulled his suit coat tighter, not certain as to what to make of them. Another figment? Another bit of madness? Something more?

I take back all the wishes I might've ever made, he silently called out to the heavens. *I want my life quiet and singular again.*

If those above heard him, they made no response. At this point, if they had replied, Todtmann would not have been at all surprised.

Crossing the river, Jeremiah was struck with a sudden sense of intense dread. He looked down at the cloudy water flowing

beneath the bridge. A black form that could have been part of an abandoned tire rose above the surface just long enough to grab his attention, disappearing into the murky depths again when the fearful watcher leaned closer to study it. There were fish in the river, he supposed, and the occasional ton or two of trash, but....

"It's nothing," he muttered at last. "Nothing." The sensation did not ease, however.

Harder to ignore were the shadows. Like the alley of the raven, they grew darker, deeper, as he neared the vicinity of his place of work. There were always a few of the gray figures near them, though they never seemed to actually walk through the shadows. Always around. Jeremiah surreptitiously watched the dark places formed by the tall towers of Chicago, for he knew now that one could not trust the shadows to stay where they were. Some of them were hungry and not for rats, more the pity.

The sense of dread grew stronger with every breath. The shadows clung to the buildings as they had never done in his memory. Instead of a proud leviathan, the Sears Tower, now looming over him, looked more like a demonic castle from which the sorcerer of the city would survey his terrified subjects. The glass and metal structure was dark and overcast even where the shadows did not drape it.

He stopped. Another block and he would be there. One block to people who knew him, who would listen—he hoped. Yet, staring at the tower made him want to do nothing more than curl up somewhere and pray the day would pass. The shadows moved along the sides of the structure, almost as if they were living, thinking creatures. There were clouds in the sky, but nothing that would explain, as far as he could see, any of the patterns of darkness dancing about the cityscape.

"Jeremiah!" The shadows had come for him. Death clutched his shoulder....

Only it was not Death. The man who Todtmann nearly swung at was simply a fellow employee and one he knew well.

The slightly balding black man easily ducked the aborted attack. About the same age, he dressed and looked as if he had been enjoying life a little more than Jeremiah Todtmann. His suit was more expensive and neatly pressed, while the body beneath it was obviously the result of continuous workouts. The black man smiled and laughed. "Man, I promise I won't be sneaking up behind you no more, Jeremiah! Though it might be worth it to see that look on your puss, buddy!"

Jeremiah stared at the newcomer, the name coming to him with the speed of frozen molasses. "Hector?"

His friend and coworker looked him over with a critical-but-amused eye, then shook his head. "Man, what have you been doing to yourself? The rumpled look is definitely not you."

"I—" How many words would escape Jeremiah's lips before Hector would decide that his friend was mad? Best, he thought, to wait. Let things settle down. He and Hector had worked together for the past couple years and were as close friends as Jeremiah permitted himself, which was to say that they had lunch on occasion, a drink or two sometimes after quitting, and a very rare get-together at Wrigley Field during the baseball season. The black man had invited him to tag along on other things, but those other things generally involved groups. Groups generally involved couples, which Todtmann rarely was. Despite Jeremiah's idiosyncrasies, however, Hector never faulted him. He was glad. The other man's friendship meant a lot to him. Unlike with most people, he had not had to work for it with Hector, who just accepted folk the way

they were. "I slipped on something on the sidewalk back…back by the station."

"Morgenstrom's gonna love you, Mr. Tidiness."

Was Hector always like this? For the life of him, Todtmann could not recall the other man ever being this jovial. Was this yet another change or had he simply never noticed before?

Hector checked his watch. "We're both gonna be late, Jeremiah. You better start work and then, first chance you get, head to the restroom. You've gotta clean up your act."

"Late? But it's—" He checked his watch and saw that somehow he had lost an hour. Jeremiah bit his lower lip and said nothing more. To him, perhaps fifteen minutes had passed, but certainly not an hour, no indeed.

The black man turned him around and started to guide him to the front entrance, but Jeremiah found his feet reluctant to be of service. The shadows still clung in possessive ways to the steel leviathan and to his eye they grew by the second. Such cloud cover as Chicago faced this day should not have allowed the spawning of such deep shadows.

"Man, you need a heavy dose of caffeine this morning!" His coworker tugged on his arm. Todtmann reluctantly followed. "Come on! We mustn't upset Morgenstrom, must we? Geez, talk about your zombies…."

Into the dark tower they journeyed. Jeremiah Todtmann braced himself for the shadows, phantoms, and creatures of his nightmares. Yet, when the doors were breached and he found himself at last in the lobby, only the everyday hustle and bustle of Midwest business life greeted his eyes. A smile, tentative at first, spread across his weary features. Jeremiah straightened and increased his pace. He was safe. In work, there was always safety. He should have known that from

the beginning. If she had not steered him astray, Todtmann would have this minute been perusing his third or fourth file.

Following Hector, Jeremiah crossed the vast lobby, passed through the narrow halls, and joined the masses filing toward the elevators. The mortgage company's headquarters were about midway up the vast length of the tower, but at that moment, they were the top of the world to him. Nowhere was safer than the mazes of Everlasting.

Lost in thought, Jeremiah wandered to an open spot in front of one of the elevators and waited for it to arrive.

Hector came up beside him. "You are out of it this morning, man! You want this one, you're gonna have to wait a long while!"

The bedraggled Todtmann frowned, wondering what his companion meant, then took a second look at the elevator.

The very insistent words OUT OF ORDER glared at him.

"You should've stayed home, buddy." Hector glanced to their left. "Come on; here's one that'll get us to where we need to go."

"Sorry," Jeremiah managed. *What is happening to me?*

"Come on, Jeremiah!" From within the lift, the black man reached out and dragged his coworker inside. If there was one benefit to his condition, it was that Jeremiah paid no attention to his fellow occupants and therefore was spared the mass glower that they, who were late for no good reason, cast upon him as he joined Hector. He took up a position next to the other man and stared without seeing.

Only when the elevator closed did he begin to relax.

As the elevator swallowed up the smoke-haired figure and his companion, a winged visitor alighted on a ledge outside of the very

doors by which Todtmann had entered the Sears Tower. The pigeons below scattered, not trusting the hunger of such vile company as this. The raven paid them no mind.

"Up, up, and away," the black bird chortled, his voice unnoticed by the humans around him. "To your home away from home have you flown...but more accidents happen in the home, alas and alack for you."

Spreading his wings, the raven rose from his perch. He circled once, then began a slow but steady ascent. The shadows of the tower, knowing their place, retreated whenever he grew near. Higher and higher the raven climbed, his destination a point about midway up the steel behemoth.

All the while he laughed.

Across the street, she now watched her adversary. It was not a role Callistra desired, for by no means was her power any match for the avian's. His untimely appearance made a shambles out of the plan and she was not one gifted with the initiative needed to plot against the raven. A frown marred her otherwise ethereal beauty.

"Haros, what do I do now?" she whispered. He was not here, however, and so Callistra knew that it would be up to her and her alone to lead the mortal back on the proper path.

That was, if they both survived the raven.

His pleasure at being returned to the routine of life was so immense that Jeremiah Todtmann passed approval on the first four files almost without reading them. Mortgage approval was not supposed to be part of his job description as broker, but in

Everlasting the title was whatever Morgenstrom decided it was. Morgenstrom, who considered these offices his private kingdom, had decided that his brokers, Todtmann in particular, needed to understand or refresh their memories concerning this aspect of the business and so that was what they were doing. No one questioned it; they were, after all, on salary.

Lost in the joy of his work, a change that Hector at least had found amusing, he did not think again of his unkempt appearance until Morgenstrom himself happened to walk by. Not a hair atop the supervisor's head had survived his long-past thirtieth birthday and some thought that was when his mood had permanently soured. No one in recent memory could recall a day when his demeanor had been anything approaching reasonable.

Today was not to break that streak. Jeremiah's peace was shattered by a tirade concerning the reputation and appearance of the company, a tirade that anyone in the next forty cubicles could not help but overhear. When it was all said and done, Jeremiah was dismissed to the restroom, there to make better his image. He was not to come back until he was presentable.

Todtmann watched his superior stalk off, likely to find someone else not up to the standards of perfection Morgenstrom had set. From the cubicle next to him rolled out Hector in his chair. The black man surveyed the damage. "He was pretty light on you, buddy. Must be mellowing in his old age."

"I've never seen him this bad." Jeremiah felt like a child reprimanded at Sunday school.

"You been sleeping the past few years?" Hector looked truly surprised by the statement. "This is one of his better days."

"Well, he's always been touchy...."

"You have been asleep. After you clean yourself up, you better get more coffee, man. Wake up before he takes a bite out of you!" Grinning like a hungry shark, his friend rolled back into his own cubicle.

Todtmann's brow furrowed. Jeremiah did recall that Morgenstrom had a temper, but this bad? All the time? He glanced Hector's way. It was not just Morgenstrom. He had wondered about Hector earlier, someone he knew much better than anyone else he worked with. In fact, everyone that Jeremiah had run across since entering the office doors was more vivid than he recalled. The receptionist's voice grated on him as even Morgenstrom's could not. Ben Willard, a loan purchaser for the company, was a tall man, but he was taller today. Things like that didn't just happen, did they?

Hector had told him to wake up. He was beginning to think that he finally had…and was none too pleased about it.

Abandoning his work, Jeremiah slithered his way through the office maze toward the restroom. He passed the employees' snack room and almost paused for coffee, but thought about what Morgenstrom would do if the supervisor caught him pouring a cup while still disheveled. That encouraged renewed haste to his original destination.

There was no one in the restroom, for which he was both grateful and disappointed. Another soul in the place would have given him an anchor of sorts to lean on, yet, in his present mood Jeremiah knew he was just as likely to frighten that soul away.

There are things that mortal men are not meant to see and Jeremiah's first glimpse in the mirror was almost too much for the quiet man. No wonder Morgenstrom's after my hide. His suit looked like it had been driven over by the train and his hair bore a close resemblance to a nuclear mushroom. Jeremiah's eyes wore

sacks. He could have sworn that he had shaved, but the stubble on his pale face was advanced. There was nothing Todtmann could do about that, but he at least knew he had a chance against the hair. Pulling out a comb, Jeremiah battled against the wild cowlicks and wavy locks that on Jose Ramirez, the senior processor of the office, would have looked dashing but on Todtmann simply looked dashed.

The duel ended a few minutes later in what was at best a draw. Scowling, he thrust the comb back into his pocket and simply stared at himself. There was really not much he could do about his clothing save for trying to straighten it a bit. Jeremiah studied his face again and decided to try rinsing with cold water. What good that would do him he could not say, but people in movies and novels were always rinsing their faces after exhausting and frightening situations. At this point, he was willing to try anything. Turning on the water, Jeremiah leaned forward and cupped his hands.

"Urk!" The water was indeed cold, far colder than he had wanted. In his hands it had not felt so chilling, but once on his face it was like trying on a mask of ice. Shivering and now very much awake, the wet broker backed away. As he shook off his damp hands, Todtmann glanced up.

There were faces in the mirror. They were little more than shadows, but just distinct enough that he could make them out as what they were. Distorted. Pleading. Demanding. Human. Inhuman.

Soulless.

His mouth gaped. Without realizing what he was doing, Jeremiah blinked...and saw only himself in the mirror when his eyes opened. The faces had literally vanished in that blink.

"Oooh, God...." he muttered. Fearful yet driven, Jeremiah turned around and surveyed the room. As he had both hoped and expected, the room was empty save for himself. He searched carefully, making certain that none of the shadows hid more than they were supposed to hide. The shadows here, however, were extremely ordinary. Todtmann exhaled, but did not relax. He glanced at the mirror, ignoring both the fact that the water still ran and that his hands still dripped.

There were ripples in the mirror, a manufacturer's fault, making it possible, just possible, that the angle that he had stood at plus the water in his face had distorted his vision.

He didn't believe that, but he nonetheless accepted the answer. The other choice in no way appealed to him.

A harsh laugh shook his already-fragile being to the core, but after a brief shock, Jeremiah recognized it as the laugh of a coworker outside.

"Pull yourself together." Now he was talking to himself on a regular basis. Although he had lived alone most of his life, Jeremiah had never developed the habit that many folk in his position do, to wit, putting voice to his thoughts. Until now, he had considered such people a bit addled; now he was certain of it.

Coffee. I need some coffee. It was beginning to sound like a litany, but he did not care.

As he turned off the water and dried his hands, Jeremiah wondered not for the first time just what was happening to him. His efforts, though, drew naught but a blank. Nothing in his rather limited experience could put sense to his delusions save some sort of growing madness...and that was not the case, he quietly insisted.

Somehow, Todtmann had trouble believing himself. What was it if not insanity?

Maybe I'm just overworked. That was true enough, but was it enough to cause this?

Jeremiah departed the restroom, his eyes never once returning to the mirror. The last thing he needed to see was the mirror. If the faces were there...

Coffee. I need coffee.

He could smell the wondrous aroma even from outside of the restroom. It did not have the delectable smell of the coffee Jeremiah had purchased earlier, or imagined he had purchased, but it was enticing. Jeremiah worked his way through the maze to the employee snack room, nostrils flaring. Yes, a cup of unsweetened, undiluted black tar would put an end to the day's transgressions against him.

One of the secretaries departed just as he reached the snack room, a steaming cup cradled gently in her hands. He watched the mug jiggle as she walked and especially enjoyed how the curves of smoke swayed back and forth above it. Jeremiah stared at the enticing cup until the young woman's slim backside blocked his view.

There was half a pot of coffee sitting on the burner when he entered. Jeremiah started toward it, skirting around a small table accompanied by four plastic chairs, the combination of which was, so management seemed to think, supposed to serve fifty-plus people. Belatedly, he recalled that he had left his own mug back at his desk. He looked around, his gaze finally fixing on the water cooler. The small paper cups were not the best thing for hot liquids, but there were napkins nearby that if wrapped around the cup a few times would prevent him from burning his fingers.

At last ready, Todtmann walked over to the coffeepot. It was ironic, he thought, that his entire day now revolved around a single

cup of coffee. His life was often like that, a slow, methodical thing fixed on certain events and duties. Rarely people, though. He knew too little about people to allow his existence to be threatened by them very often.

The contents of the pot still bubbled as his hand neared the handle. That meant the coffee was fresh, almost new. He sniffed the air and drank in the delicious aroma.

The coffee began to boil over.

"Damnit!" He backed away as a sea of black ink poured over the rim. *Just what I need! Morgenstrom will string me up!* Forget that he had not had a thing to do with the spill; the surly supervisor would only care that Jeremiah Todtmann had been standing there when it had happened. To Morgenstrom, that was guilt enough.

Dropping the cup, the smoke-haired man knelt down and tried to clean up some of the liquid that had reached the floor. When he attempted to put the napkins in his hand to use, however, the growing puddle spread away from him. He reached over and tried to wipe it up from the other side, but once more the expanding puddle shifted in the opposite direction.

Jeremiah dropped the napkins and, still on his knees, scrambled back several feet. He shook his head, muttering, "Not again...."

The napkins fell into the puddle and sank instantly, accompanied by a horrible sucking sound. There was already enough coffee on the floor to fill three pots, but still it flowed from the container. Oddly, the coffee machine did not short-circuit despite being drenched.

There is a limit to what the normal mind will tolerate and although Jeremiah Todtmann had long thought he had reached that limit, the part of human nature that keeps most folks sane through denial had each time pulled him back.

Not this time.

He screamed...and screamed louder when he saw that the coffee was now flowing toward him. The puddle had split into four separate appendages, which to his eyes resembled the fingers of an immense hand. They crept closer and closer, growing wider as they moved. A veritable sea of coffee had now claimed most of the snack-room floor and yet still the pot overflowed.

Jeremiah screamed again. Only after he finished did he begin to wonder why no one was heeding his cries. At the very least, Morgenstrom should have come running to see who was disturbing his kingdom. Where was

everyone? Was he now alone in the office?

The protean fingers stretched and oozed, surrounding Jeremiah even as they surged toward him. One tendril flowed around the legs of a nearby chair and to Todtmann's horror, the chair began to go the way of the napkins. The legs started to sink into the quagmire, disappearing in rapid fashion into a puddle that, to the naked eye, was only a fraction of an inch deep.

Primal instinct at last stirred him to action. As the fingers neared his feet, Jeremiah leapt for the chair, the closest free spot he could not reach. He landed with one foot upon the still-visible plastic seat, which sank perceptively faster with the addition of his weight, and then fell across the table. No sooner did Jeremiah steady himself when he felt the table begin to shift. The side nearest to the ever-growing pool sank lower.

Scrambling over the other edge, Jeremiah Todtmann threw himself to the floor. Harsh linoleum slapped him in the face and shoulder, but such pain was laughable at the moment. With the coffee in pursuit, he dared not think of anything else but flight.

A quick glance back showed him his fears were justified. Vastly unperturbed by his escape, the coffee was already hot on his trail.

The old tendrils were withdrawing into the main body and new ones now directed his way were reaching forth. The chair was gone and two of its mates were about to join it. The table had tipped over and more than half of it was now lost somewhere within the horrific puddle, a grim reminder of what he could expect. This was hungry coffee, indeed.

Crawling on hands and knees, he abandoned the snack room. The office he entered, however, was still and silent. Not even the sounds of the heating system touched his ears. It was not yet lunch hour, although the steaming liquid pursuing him obviously did not care about that fact, but even if it had been, there was always someone at work. Telephones should have been ringing, employees should have been grumbling, and Morgenstrom, who never left the office until the end of the day, should have been haranguing someone for a task not performed to perfection. None of those sounds assailed Jeremiah, however, and he suddenly grew cold with the notion that perhaps the coffee had saved him for last. Everyone else had filled their mugs long ago.

A menacing gurgle warned him just in time. The pool, now an inky ocean, was fairly nipping at his heels. Rising to his feet, Jeremiah reentered the maze of cubicles. His movements were slow, though, and each one was a strain. He might have been trying to run against the Chicago winds, so little progress did he seem to be making.

"Jeremiahhhhh…"

It was Hector who had called his name. Hector, standing no more than a few yards from him. If his own steps seemed leaden, his friend's were almost so slow that the black man might have been posing.

"Hector?" Todtmann's own voice sounded normal enough, but normal was not the norm now. Savage, seeking seas of coffee and surreal visages in the restroom mirrors were, it seemed.

"Jeremiahhhhh?"

The other man was staring past him. Fearing that the coffee was following, Jeremiah glanced over his shoulder, but the aisle was devoid of even a drop of the pursuing puddle. He turned his attention back to Hector, who had shifted slightly but still stared past his friend.

"Hector?" He started forward.

The shape that crossed between the two was nearly human in outline, but of detail there was little to see. It moved with a speed that made Todtmann feel as still as Hector, flitting past and darting around a corner before Jeremiah could even gasp. He looked at the black man's visage, but it was clear that for Hector the sinewy shape—and Jeremiah, for that matter—did not exist.

Out of the corner of his eye, Todtmann caught sight of another, similar shape. It, too, darted out of sight, almost as if it had suddenly noticed him watching.

He began to notice other forms, less distinct, that almost appeared to occupy the same space as cubicle walls or office furniture. It was as if Jeremiah were seeing two worlds transposed upon one another. The notion disturbed him, not only for the truth he knew it to be, but also because it was not something that should have come to mind. Not his well-dulled mind, at least.

Hector was opening his mouth to speak again. His movements continued to grow even slower. Jeremiah could not find it within himself to be as concerned for his friend as he was for himself. He suspected that for Hector and everyone else in the office, all things

were as they were meant to be. Only he, Jeremiah Todtmann, had anything to fear. Only he saw the things that infested the office.

Only he saw the raven that suddenly fluttered outside one of the windows.

Even through the reinforced panes, Todtmann could hear the insidious-yet-childlike laughter...or perhaps he heard only the memory of that past time in the alley. Jeremiah did not know which, but he knew that if the raven was here, up here, then the situation was going to get worse yet.

He pushed past Hector, who might have been chiseled from marble so little did he shift at the touch, and ran for the doors leading to the elevators and stairwell. In his haste, Jeremiah nearly crossed paths with one of the shadow figures, but the unfocused thing suddenly backed away, almost as if frightened of him. Jeremiah would have laughed had he seen that, but his attention was on the corridor just outside the entrance.

His luck had changed. An elevator, an open elevator, waited just beyond the glass doors. Thankyouthankyouthankyou...he silently chanted, inanely hoping that his unheard-yet-effusive gratitude would keep the elevator open just long enough for him to reach it. The thought of all those flights of stairs....

To the receptionist, adrift in a telephone conversation with her mother concerning the low pay she was receiving for the exceptional work she was giving in return, the doors of Everlasting simply flung themselves open, swinging with such intensity that they nearly broke off the hinges. Out of the corner of her eye, she thought she saw someone she knew, but there was no one in sight

when she looked again. The incident would raise some talk for the afternoon, but by quitting time would be forgotten. The routine was all that truly mattered at Everlasting Mortgage.

Unmindful of the doors and the extraordinary push he had given them, Jeremiah stumbled the last few feet toward the beckoning elevator. It was still open, but any moment, he was certain it would—

She stood in the corner of the elevator, both alluring and unnerving. If anything, she was more ethereal than he remembered. Almost she was a ghost, yet at the same time she was so real. Jeremiah Todtmann stopped at the edge of the lift and hesitated, not certain whether her abrupt presence meant him good or ill.

"Enter freely and unafraid." Her voice was a caressing wind, yet a wind that also chilled. It put one to mind of cemeteries or buildings left abandoned and wasting away. "I come in peace."

To which Jeremiah succinctly replied, "I—"

His ears filled with the beating of great wings. Glancing back at the office he had abandoned, he thought he saw an avian shadow nearing the receptionist's desk.

"Please...come...with...me!" She fought for each word. Her hand was stretched out to him, but to take it he would have to cross the line between corridor and elevator. Cross from what little reality he had left to him to...what?

The choice was no choice, in the end. The lady or the raven. Todtmann knew what the black bird wanted, at least to some extent, which in his opinion meant that whatever the pale enchantress desired of him, it could only be an improvement.

He jumped into the elevator. She took him by the arm and dragged him into the corner with her, keeping his back to the open doorway. The peal of laughter from outside made him shiver.

Then, the mocking laugh was cut off as the door closed.

She continued to hold him, something Todtmann did not argue against although at the moment romance was the least of things on his mind. Her skin was cold against his, but soft. She was so slight to his touch a part of him was afraid she would break. Yet, despite all that, in her arms Jeremiah felt safe for the first time since leaving the train station.

He might not have felt so secure had he seen the sign that was posted on the outer side of the elevator door. It was an exact duplicate of another sign he had seen only a short while before and like that other sign it consisted of three simple words.

OUT OF ORDER.

CHAPTER IV

"She has him," Haros Aguilana said to no one in particular. He wanted to exhale in relief, but since he did not breathe, the act would have been superfluous and yet another reminder of what he was. Instead, the elegantly clad Grey put another lit cigarette to his thin, scarlet mouth. Pretending to smoke was even more superfluous, but like all Grey, Haros Aguilana was not constant in his choices.

He stood alone in one shadow-strewn corner of a rank graveyard of broken chassis and years-old seas of oil and grease. The yard was farther away than he would have liked, but it offered him the best of the city's abandoned. No matter how dire the situation, Haros tried to have his standards. It was another game he played, but since such an affectation was a human quality, it was also a quality of the Grey. A tainted reflection of the original, but still a quality.

His gaze alighted on the rusting vision of a vehicle whose only remaining identifiable feature was a small winged figure above the grill. He could see that it had once been silver, appropriate for the

- 56 -

name the makers had given it and even more appropriate now that he needed the poor skeleton for his own uses.

Haros removed the cigarette from his lips and threw it to the ground. No longer held together by his will, the narrow cylinder dissipated into the smoke it was before it could even touch the grimy dirt. The Grey allowed himself a thin-lipped smile as he inspected the vehicle of his choice.

"Gentlemen, start your engines."

With some doing, Jeremiah at last garnered the wherewithal to separate himself from his savior. She remained in the corner, allowing him to back away as far as he desired. What she thought, he could not tell; her face was an enigma in shadow. There were moments when her entire form was vague or perhaps out of focus.

Yet, she had saved him from the bird. "I suppose…I suppose I should thank you…."

She remained a silent statue.

Jeremiah pressed on. "But should I?"

"Perhaps," was all she said. Her arresting eyes shifted from his face to the array of buttons.

He followed suit and noticed that despite the movement of the elevator, none of the buttons was aglow. "Where are we going? Where are you taking me?"

"Somewhere under the rainbow."

"That's not how it—" Jeremiah paused. The bittersweet smile she wore was proof that she had meant the sentence as she had spoken it. He ran a hand back through sweat-soaked hair and finally asked the question that, for some reason, had been hardest to free. "Who are you?"

She continued to watch the unlit panel. "Wystan dubbed me Callistra. Vachel dubbed me Munro. What's in a name?"

"Callistra Munro." She was speaking with much more ease, yet her manner of speech bothered him. In many ways, Callistra sounded much like the raven. *But she doesn't work with him. It. The raven.*

He noticed that she smiled as he spoke her name. That brought an unconscious smile to his own features. "What do you want with me?"

That made her smile fade. "Harps will explain, but first we must leave this building. Hell hath no fury like a raven scorned."

"But what about—"

The elevator came to a stop. The door slid aside.

Jeremiah could see nothing but darkness. "Where are we?"

"The bird didn't know about the elevator."

A singularly unhelpful response, but it was clear that this was the best Callistra would offer to him. She stepped easily into the blackness, then beckoned Todtmann to join her. He tried, but his feet would not move. The dark recalled the hungry pool of coffee. Jeremiah knew that Callistra was not leading him into such a trap—actually, he hoped that was true—but still the image remained with him.

"Please, Jeremiah Todtmann, walk this way."

There was nowhere else to go. The only other direction was up and there the raven gleefully awaited him.

He stepped out of the elevator.

It's not so dark after all was his first thought. Actually, it was more like the first glimmer of light before the rise of the sun, that moment when the world is visible but seems washed of all color.

A slender, flawless hand touched his. "The raven is no slow fool; hurry, lest you desire to be his tool."

Once more her manner of speech reminded him of the madcap bird. Both of them slipped into twisted cliché and rhyme without hesitation. Where were they from? Whatever did they want with someone like him?

He gasped as a slim, almost shapeless form swirled between the two of them. It was a shadow, much like those he had witnessed in the office. This one, though, tried to stay with him. Jeremiah backed away, but the shadow clung to him like a hungry child. He was awash with a sense of need, of the same sort of pleading he had read in some of the faces in the mirror. It wanted something from him, wanted something that only Jeremiah Todtmann could give it.

Knowing that, he lost all fear of it.

Callistra's hand cut a swath through the shadow. It reformed, but then fled from her in terror. Jeremiah began to protest, but stopped when he saw the sorrow in her visage. She held out her hand to him.

Jeremiah took it. The tall, pale woman pulled him along, guiding him through the gray enshrouded place. He looked this way and that, trying to decide where they were, but could make out no sign of walls or ceiling. Even the ground beneath his feet was shrouded.

"Where are we? The sub-basement?"

"Yes," was her sole reply, but her tone hinted at something more. He did not press.

The place they traveled through was silent, but that did not mean that they were alone. Although he could not see them, Jeremiah became aware of more things like the shadow. They were

all around the due, but keeping a respectable distance. Now and then, the man thought he caught sight of one out of the corner of his eye, but there was nothing when he glanced that way. Callistra, if she saw them, said nothing. There was that about the shadows that appeared to annoy, worry, and sadden her, all at the same time.

They're almost like lost children. Then, he recalled the raven's laughter and amended the thought. *Feral children.*

"Freedom rings," the enchantress whispered. She pointed ahead.

If this was the way to freedom, it had a most contradictory look to it. The door that stood before them, almost as much a shadow as the creatures to their sides, was tall, rounded on top, and metallic. Jeremiah recalled such doors from movies like *The Adventures of Robin Hood* or some other fantasy. Ever such doors led to the dungeons, not freedom. Almost he wondered what sort of whimsical turn had caused the architects of the Sears Tower to put something like this in the sub-basement.

The mocking laugh that he had come to know as well as himself cut through the silence. The shadows dispersed in obvious fright. Callistra's face was a study in dismay.

"Empty faces, empty sighs, empty arms outstretched..." the bird babbled from the grayness. "Empty places, empty hope!"

If he had been told that the sun had just been dropped into the sub-basement of the Sears Tower, Todtmann would not have disbelieved. The grayness was burned away without fanfare as a brilliance both burning and cold overtook all. Callistra did not scream, but the strength in her hand almost crushed his. Oddly, it was Jeremiah who now was the protector; she turned to him and tried to bury herself in his suit coat.

Callistra was as afraid of the light as he was of the grayness, more so even.

Jeremiah Todtmann's eyes slowly recovered. He realized that the light was not so brilliant, not once he was accustomed to it. Actually, there was a touch of the gray on it as well.

It was also moving.

"And I said, 'Let there be light'..." the infernal avian cackled. "And there was..."

"Callistra?" Jeremiah whispered. She was silent, almost catatonic, he thought.

Most folk like to consider themselves brave to a point, but Jeremiah had never been one who had subscribed to that notion. He had always been certain that come the time, it was more likely he would run. The raven had already proven the truth of that to him several times. Yet, with Callistra in his arms, he found himself thinking very disturbing thoughts. Disturbing thoughts dealing with standing up to the menace and defending the damsel in distress.

And how am I supposed to do that? the rational part demanded of him. *Even if I had a sword and knew how to use it, it wouldn't do much good against light, now would it? I can't very well cut light, can I?*

It was too bad that this was not really the sub-basement, assuming the skyscraper had one. Perhaps then there would have been a fire extinguisher or sprinkler system he could have turned on the blazing menace. Or the flood waters from spring of 1992, he added. The tower, like many buildings in the area, had suffered damage when careless city maintenance had allowed the river to break through and spill into the city. Some buildings had even reported fish in their main lobbies. Jeremiah could not recall how much damage the Sears Tower had suffered, only that Everlasting had actually been closed down for a day.

A flood would be nice. Where was one when he needed it?

Callistra suddenly looked up, her eyes wide with renewed fear. "No! Don't!"

The light ceased moving. He had the oddest feeling that it was hesitating because of him.

The mortgage broker heard a trickle of water, as if someone had forgotten to turn off the tap in one of the restrooms. Then, the trickle grew to a steady shower and the shower almost immediately became a torrential downpour. Jeremiah twisted this way and that, but there was no sign of water.

The thing of light faded away, but any notion of safety was shattered by the raven's chuckle and the ominous words that followed. "Float upon the river of his thoughts…but 'ware sharks, Callistra!"

An ocean fell upon them.

The dry nothingness of the gray world became a violent maelstrom, a tidal wave, with the two in its midst. Jeremiah barely had time to take a breath before he and Callistra were swept under. He lost his grip on her, but she managed to hold on to his arm.

Todtmann's head broke the surface. He gasped and drew in moist air. The Chicago flood had never touched the tower like this! Jeremiah had wanted water, but not the entire river. How would that look, to drown in the depths of the steel-and-glass leviathan?

A huge and very hard shape bumped against his leg.

'Ware sharks! the Stygian songbird had warned. But there are no sharks in the river…are there? Yet, now he recalled the moving form that had briefly risen from the river while Jeremiah had been crossing the bridge. It might have been more than just some floating trash.

Another wave buried Jeremiah again. Callistra still clung to him, but the turbulence was threatening that grip. This was all insane, he knew, but it was occurring nonetheless. He was also certain that no one else in the building was aware of what was happening, just as no one in the office had heard his cries for help or had noticed the gray shapes flittering about.

"Unngh!" His shoulder struck a bracketed surface just as he broke through to the open air again. Reacting instinctively, Todtmann took hold of it. Only when his eyes had cleared did he see that he had a grip on the massive door that Callistra had been leading him toward before the raven's latest assault.

Callistra! Momentarily secure, Jeremiah only now had the time to consider her fate. Not once could he recall seeing her surface. He began to fear that the reason for her tenacious grip was that she was already dead. A death grip was supposed to be strong, sometimes stronger than any such hold in life.

"Callistra!" Shouting was useless, but Jeremiah, being very human, shouted over and over. He felt with his free hand for the mysterious woman's arm and found it. A shiver ran through him. She was cold, very cold, but he convinced himself that it might only be the water making her feel so frigid.

Her other hand caught his wrist. The half-drowned Todtmann was so relieved that at first he did not catch sight of the massive shadow rising from the water. He did not, in fact, acknowledge it until the shadow let loose with a rumbling roar.

His eyes traced the shape even as he continued to pull his companion to him. Jeremiah stared in disbelief, an almost common emotion for him of late, at the three humps and tall, narrow serpent neck jutting from the miniature sea.

The Loch Ness Monster is swimming in the basement of the Sears Tower. He had seen the fuzzy photograph in a fair enough number of news articles and television specials over the years to recognize it. It looked exactly as it did in that photograph, even down to the fuzziness.

Callistra's head broke the surface. Had his attention not been so occupied by larger, toothier matters, Jeremiah Todtmann might have wondered why her hair and face were dry and immaculate. As it was, he could only gape, sputter, and try to make her look behind her.

She had other ideas, though. Leaning close, the raven-haired woman shouted, "You must open the door!"

Open the door? He was having enough trouble just keeping hold. If he tried to open it, he was more likely to send both of them flailing back into the maelstrom…where a legend was waiting to nibble on their soaked bodies.

The out-of-focus leviathan moved toward them, rumbling again.

Gasping more wet air, Jeremiah dragged Callistra close enough so that she could take hold of his waist. Seeing that she was secure, he twisted around so that he faced the door. Much to his dismay, though, the designers, in their whimsy, had not seen fit to put in any sort of knob or turning handle. The only handle was the one he had managed to grab and that, Jeremiah already knew, did nothing.

"Be open to new experiences!" she called back.

He tried to hide the grimace on his face. Half of what Callistra said sounded like television or an old book. If she was trying to be of aid, she was failing miserably. Jeremiah ran his hand over the door. Still he felt nothing. Frustration fueled by fear that in turn was fueled by the unhappy knowledge that a sea monster was breathing down his neck made him finally pound his fist against the door. "Open up, damn you!" he roared. "What the hell am I supposed to do, yell 'Open Sesame'?"

Jeremiah, Callistra, and several hundred tons of water poured through the suddenly open doorway. Todtmann thought he heard the Loch Ness Monster rumble in disappointment. Then...

He was kneeling on a sidewalk outside the skyscraper. The sounds and smells of the city assailed him, but just this once he welcomed their intrusion. Jeremiah Todtmann studied the sidewalk with care. It was dry, as he was, he noticed a moment later. His suit was rumpled, but nothing more.

"Stand and be counted, Jeremiah Todtmann." Callistra was beside him, but where he had fallen she had somehow landed on her feet. The ethereal enchantress might have been patiently waiting for a taxi or so her appearance suggested. Everything was in place and perfectly so.

People passed them from both sides, but no one seemed at all perturbed by the sight of a man in a rumpled suit kneeling on the pavement. Lines of traffic edged their way along the street that Todtmann belatedly recognized as Adams. He slowly rose, as of yet unable to accept that they were safe on the street. All the water that had poured through the door was gone, and twisting his head, he saw that the doorway itself was no more. Jeremiah found he was not a bit surprised at the latter, which worried him. He did not like the thought of accepting the raven's world as commonplace.

The raven.

Jeremiah spun around and eyed the side of the office building. As with his escape from the alley, there was no sign of any exit. The door did not exist on this side of the wall.

That did not mean the danger was past. "What about—"

"Into shadow, into light, from—" she began.

"I'd like something that makes sense, please." His irritation surprised him. He had not thought it would be possible for him to be angry with her.

Callistra paused. She regarded him, a look that might have been hope briefly lighting her face. One hand stretched out to touch his cheek. "Do you...believe in me?"

At least it was a properly formed question, albeit a bit vague. " 'Believe in me?' "

"Am...I real...to you?"

Considering the world he had just passed through, he was not at all certain he liked the question. It stirred up connotations Todtmann did not want to consider. Still, he felt safe in answering her. "Yes. If there's anything that seems real to me right now, it's you." He shook his head. "I'm not sure about much else, though."

That brought a delicate smile. She looked beyond him and whispered, "To dream the impossible dream..."

"What about the raven?"

Returning her attention to Jeremiah, she gestured at the street. "The ghastly grim and ancient raven will not face Haros. Not yet."

He leaned forward, looking for any sign of who or what she was pointing toward. " 'Haros'?"

Callistra pointed at the traffic and at a vehicle that even obscured in part by the others, he should have seen the first time and yet had not. There were not that many sleek, gleaming Rolls-Royces in Chicago—not in the Loop, anyway— and certainly not many as elegant as the silver automobile that somehow was managing to wend its way toward them despite the heavy, slow traffic.

"Haros," Callistra repeated, this time with more confidence.

It was not one of the older vehicles that the venerable automobile manufacturer was best known for, but still there was that mystique.

This model looked a few years old in design, yet Jeremiah could not spot a single blemish on it, almost as if someone had kept it locked up since its creation. How any vehicle could manage to look like that after even a day in city traffic was almost as astounding as sea monsters swimming in skyscrapers. Only vaguely did Jeremiah consider the fact that the Rolls gleamed despite the overcast sky.

The windows were mirrors, hiding the identities of both the driver and whatever passenger sat in the back. Jeremiah backed up as the intrepid Rolls maneuvered its way to the curb. The vehicle came to rest directly in front of them.

"Safe and sound, Jeremiah Todtmann," Callistra commented. "You're in good hands with Haros."

The rear passenger door opened, but nobody disembarked. He glanced at Callistra, who beckoned him inside. Jeremiah sighed and, with one last, nervous look back at the shadowy tower, entered the sleek automobile. The interior had the same murkiness about it that the basement had suffered from. Jeremiah sat down on a plush seat and admired what he could see of the car's insides. That was not much.

"I much prefer the Phantom VI to the present Silver Spirit," a cultured voice beside him commented.

Had not Callistra chosen that moment to sit down beside him, Jeremiah Todtmann would have fled from the vehicle right there and then. Only now did he make out the stick-thin figure on his other side. A faint smell of old smoke tickled his nose. The shadowy interior kept him from making out much detail, but he was certain that the regally clad man was even paler than the woman.

"The Silver Spirit," the shadow man continued as the Rolls-Royce reentered traffic—a partition made it impossible to see who was driving—"while an exceptional vehicle, bares just a bit too much of a resemblance to something put out by Detroit." He leaned forward, letting what little light there was at last play on his features. "Do you like automobiles, Jeremiah Todtmann?"

Gasping, Jeremiah slid away from him. Callistra patted his knee in sympathy. "Haros is your friend."

"Friend?" He had fled the black bird only to give himself into the custody of an anorexic Dracula. Why had he assumed that since one side wanted to do him ill, the other side wanted to help him? Haros and the raven might simply be rivals with similar goals.

The chalk-colored figure put a lit cigarette in his mouth. Jeremiah had not seen him pull it out, much less light it. Haros leaned back again, but now, despite the shadows, the macabre figure's eyes remained visible. "Forgive and forget, Jeremiah Todtmann. Allow me to introduce myself in a proper manner. I am Haros Aguilana. I am here to guide you through this travail."

After the raven's insane commentary and Callistra's half-undecipherable explanations, it was a pleasure to hear a voice that spoke not only with authority, but intelligibly as well. Almost it made up for the fact that Jeremiah was certain he was a prisoner of some refugee from Night of the Living Dead or The House of Dracula, except that in the latter, John Carradine had still looked human. Haros Aguilana literally looked like death warmed over. Especially when he smiled.

Haros leaned forward and smiled. "I apologize for not coming sooner. I had to locate proper transportation. So many vehicles these days are little more than junk."

For reasons he could not fathom, Jeremiah was certain that he was supposed to find this funny. Perhaps there would come a time when he would look back and laugh at all of this, but now only one thing concerned him. "What's happening to me, Mr. Aguilana? Do you know? What do you and…he…want?"

The stick man looked aghast. He took the cigarette from his mouth and threw it aside. Out of the corner of his eye, Jeremiah watched it fade in mid-fall.

"Callistra!" The well-groomed ghoul shook a finger at his underling, sounding all the while like a father lecturing a neglectful child. "Ignorance is bliss, but a mind is a terrible thing to waste!"

God! Not him, too! Just when he had hoped for some answers. Where were these characters coming from?

"Time was precious, Haros."

"Yes, so a little bird told me." The stick man caught the look on his guest's worn visage. "But that is neither here nor there. You are deserving of an explanation, of course. You, of all people. We should wait, however, until we reach our destination. I think the proof is in the pudding and the Wasteland is certainly that. If anything can convince you of the truth of my words, it will be when you see the club. Anything I say beforehand might not make sense enough…and please, call me Haros. I insist."

Even as addled as he was, Todtmann knew that his host was stalling. At this point, Jeremiah had nothing left to lose. He was already their prisoner, despite their friendly tones. "I don't want to wait. Why don't you tell me what you want from me? Maybe I might be more agreeable if I understand something of why you want me."

Haros sighed in defeat, yet something in that sigh did not ring true with Jeremiah. "You have me. I can really keep nothing from you if you so desire. Your cooperation and good will are paramount to us."

At last stirring, a worried Callistra asked, "Haros, are you certain?"

The vampirish creature shrugged his bony shoulders. "Why not? It is not every day a man assumes the mantle of Ozymandias, is it?"

Jeremiah felt no closer to the truth. "Who is or was…the name you said."

Another cigarette appeared. They seemed to materialize in Haros Aguilana's hands whenever he desired a puff. "Ozymandias, Jeremiah Todtmann. King of Kings." He smiled. "Just as you will soon be."

The pigeon was mindful of nothing around it save the discarded candy wrapper a negligent passerby had dropped a few minutes prior. The gray-and-white bird pecked hopefully at the wrapper, knowing that at one point there had been something edible within, but not intelligent enough to immediately discern that only a few slight crumbs, too small even for it, were all that remained.

A flurry of black feathers, jagged talons, and wicked beak fell upon the occupied avian.

The pigeon flapped wildly about, struggling to free itself. Its attacker fought to hold on to it, but the pigeon persevered, pulling loose despite claws that should have held it in a grip of death. All thought of candy wrappers vanished as it soared into the darkening sky and raced away in a panic.

The raven, his claws scratching marks in the sidewalk, contemplated pursuit, but he knew that the result would remain the same. He was not yet strong enough to take on life. His failure with the human should have told him that. The pigeon had not actually broken free from his claws but rather had struggled right through them. Both pigeons, he amended.

"Subtle demonisms of life," cursed the black bird. "Seeing must be believing! Belief must help create the fact!" He flapped his wings, sending forth a gust of wind that was ignored by passersby, who were accustomed to such blasts here in the heart of the Windy City. "I will be fact, not fiction!"

The human was in the care of the pompous Haros Aguilana now. Haros, who would play at savior for his own ends. They were ends not too different from the raven's own.

Not too different from his own....

"Too many cooks spoil the broth." A plan was forming. "Best for now to let the stick man lead and the king follow; Haros will still find his dreams turn hollow."

Several pigeons landed nearby and began searching along the pavement for edible refuse. The ebony specter contemplated them with a hunger not borne from a lack of food, but was aware that he would have no better success with these. Besides, why dream of pigeon feed when one could soon look forward to a kingly feast?

Or feasting on a king.

Some children grow up dreaming they will be president. Others grow up hearing that they will be president. Jeremiah recalled his own parents, long passed on, telling him that. Like most youngsters, he had outgrown the notion, believing it beyond his reach and, after a time, not even being concerned about it.

No one had ever suggested to him that someday he might be king.

" 'King'?" had been the sum total response he could muster.

"King," was Haros Aguilana's just as short reply. After that, the emaciated corpse refused to speak further on the subject save to promise once again that all would be made clear when they arrived at the Wasteland.

The name of this mysterious club did nothing to assuage the new monarch's apprehensions. Haros, unfortunately, considered his announcement sufficient and this time would not give in to Jeremiah's prodding.

Unwilling to ride the rest of the way in silence, Jeremiah wracked his mangled mind for questions that might yet elicit some response. There were few, but one did leap to the forefront.

"What about work? They'll be missing me." The smile. "Will they?"

So ended the questioning. Much to his chagrin, Jeremiah knew very well what his host meant. Oh, a few individuals like Hector would personally miss him, but Todtmann had chosen a position and life that made him an unimportant cog in the scheme of things. It had seemed most suitable at the time, a way to get through existence in a decent but not spectacular manner. Until today, Jeremiah Todtmann had been perfectly satisfied.

Callistra's hand touched his. She said nothing, perhaps concerned that her words would only annoy him, but her manner soothed him. He began to recall how he had first felt around her. While Jeremiah was suspicious that the dark-haired woman had somehow engineered that original obsession, he knew that what he felt now was more real, more his own interest. Callistra did not want to hurt him; she cared at least a little bit about his well-being and that was all he could ask for now.

Of course, she might simply be an exceptionally talented actress.

"We are here," Haros announced.

Jeremiah, who had just been settling in, sat up in some confusion. As best as he could estimate it, they had only been in traffic for a short time. He looked at his watch, which only added to his bewilderment. According to the timepiece, which the manufacturer's commercials had assured him would keep good accuracy for years to come, it was past four in the afternoon.

Had it gotten waterlogged? Nothing else had.

Haros was watching him with avid interest. Todtmann pushed his cuff back into place.

The door on Haros Aguilana's side opened. The gaunt figure stepped out. Steeling himself, Jeremiah slid across and followed. Haros was waiting for him, one hand proffered in case the man who was to be king needed it. Jeremiah managed without his aid, not wanting to touch the chalky skin. He was certain that where Callistra's skin felt merely cool, the flesh of Haros would chill his fingers. Avoiding his host, he glanced around, looking for the driver or anyone who might have opened the door for them. Only Haros Aguilana was visible.

Automatic doors, he reluctantly decided. After all, it was a Rolls-Royce.

It proved to be much more challenging to find a reasonable explanation for the rest of his surroundings.

The Chicago that Jeremiah saw as he stepped out of the Rolls was not the one of memory. First and foremost was the impression that night was descending, for not only were the massive buildings locked in shadow, but the sky was becoming darker. With the clouds obscuring the sun, Jeremiah could not verify his suspicions about the time indicated on his watch, but he was growing to believe that the timepiece was not in error.

Then there was the city itself. He blinked, trying to clear his vision. Nothing changed.

Callistra was beside him. "Come along, Jeremiah."

"Everything's...wavering." He spotted the John Hancock Building, once the reigning monarch of the city, but it was tilted and swaying back and forth with the wind. Skyscrapers are supposed to sway, that much Jeremiah Todtmann knew, but not at such severe angles. They would have had to bolt down the furniture and put seat belts on all of the people. The Hancock rocked like a blade of grass during a thunderstorm, looking more a thing of rubber than steel.

Haros was on his other side. "They're waiting for you, your majesty."

The stick man took him by the arm and although Jeremiah's fear concerning Haros Aguilana's touch proved to have some merit, Jeremiah did not notice. He was still trying to refocus his eyes in the hope that eventually the vast metropolis would cease resembling some swaying city seen through a fish bowl and instead return to the rigid solidity it had once had.

"You are exhausted, that's all," Haros kindly whispered.

Jeremiah gave up. He shook his head. "Take me back. Take me back to work."

Callistra gasped and raised a hand toward him. "Jeremiah, no, don't say—"

Twisting, the reluctant monarch-elect started back to the Rolls...and froze. The elegant vehicle was still parked by the curb, but was it fading?

Aguilana and his companion whirled him about and renewed their holds on him. In most suave tones, the angular ghoul said, "Even the best memories fade with time."

They led him up some steps to a darkened doorway. It was indeed a club, but Jeremiah was almost certain a name other than the one Haros had mentioned hung above the entrance. The name was unlit, however, and what with the speed with which the duo walked him to the doors, he was unable to read it. The rest of the exterior was a mass of shadows that barely hinted at a style reminiscent of the twenties. While not one who frequented such entertainment often, Jeremiah could not recall anyone in the office mentioning such an establishment. There was no doorman. Haros released Jeremiah, but even if he had contemplated running, Callistra's sudden iron grip on his other arm would have belayed that possibility. Opening the door wide, Haros Aguilana bowed to his guest and said, "Enter, 0 seeker of knowledge." With Callistra at his side—and pulling him along—he had no choice.

Dry, dust-ridden air made him cough as he stepped past the makeshift doorman and into the dark entrance. The unilluminated approach took him by surprise. Unlike the basement and the automobile, it was simply dark. Not shadowy, but dark. He was almost tempted to ask Callistra if they had come to the wrong destination, but both she and Haros, who once more resided next to him, acted as if all was as it should be.

"And here we are!" Haros announced a moment later. A single, dim bulb flickered to life, unveiling the interior.

Here was not by any means impressive, especially not after the Rolls-Royce. Here was an empty, half-dismantled lounge that those tearing it apart had evidently forgotten about. Tables were clumsily stacked in one corner with chairs next to them. A long, mirrored bar lined the far wall, but there was no place to set the drinks, for the top of the counter was missing as were most of the stools. A number of light fixtures were missing, as was evidenced by the empty sockets and such that marked their former places. The mirror was streaked and warped making the newcomers as twisted as Jeremiah's last view of the city had been.

"Home is where you hang your hat," Aguilana quipped.

"There's no place like home," Jeremiah muttered.

Both of them glanced at him as if he had just spouted the secret of life. After too long a scrutiny, Haros finally released him. The B-movie vampire walked slowly across the deserted chamber, gazing around at things that, for Jeremiah Todtmann's eyes, were evidently not there. When he had reached the bar, he turned back and smiled at the new king.

"I would recommend a tall, cool one, but then, you already have the lovely and talented Callistra by your side."

Jeremiah started to smile, but stopped when the raven-crested woman stiffened. Haros, ignoring her, reached behind the bar and pulled forth, much to Todtmann's disbelief, a bottle of whiskey and three shot glasses. He lined the glasses on the edge of the counter frame and managed to pour three drinks without so much as making one container wobble.

Replacing the bottle, he signaled to Callistra. She separated from Jeremiah with evident reluctance and walked over to Haros, who handed her two of the shot glasses. As the slim woman returned to Todtmann, Haros picked up the remaining glass and sipped from it.

"You may find it a bit dry," he chuckled.

Callistra reached one of the drinks toward Jeremiah. He took the glass from her but did not immediately sip from it, choosing first to study her face. He was not adept at reading people, but Callistra was at times such a novice at hiding her emotions that it was hard to believe she could be real. Now the would-be monarch read concern and hope, all of which appeared to rest on his drinking the whiskey. Glancing beyond her to his peculiar host, who was sipping the contents of his tiny container as if it were the finest champagne, Jeremiah Todtmann saw just a glimmer of eagerness and hunger… all of which also appeared to rest on his drinking.

He hesitated, but reminded himself once more that these two could have easily done away with him. They seemed absolutely serious about this king business, which would make for an interesting story when Jeremiah tried to explain to Morgenstrom where he had been all this time. *Have you met my kingdom, Mr. Morgenstrom? They're a bit peculiar, but they seem like a nice pair.*

Jeremiah shrugged and downed the drink. He was not much of a drinker—actually, he was beginning to realize he had never been much of anything—but Jeremiah was certain that this was the smoothest whiskey in the world. There was not even any of the aftertaste that usually sent him looking for a glass of water.

Both Callistra and Haros were beaming.

If the reward for drinking was always being ensnared in the arms of a stunning woman, alcoholics would run rampant. Jeremiah forced himself to endure the sweet-smelling, snug torture for as long as Callistra was willing, even barring the chance that she might spill the drink she held down the back of his much wrinkled coat. The only drawback to the situation was Haros Aguilana, who Jeremiah could see through her hair. The stick man was looking pleased, but with himself, if anybody.

"Congratulations, your majesty," he said. One of his magical cigarettes materialized.

As if struck, Callistra moved away. She did not look at either of her companions. Todtmann realized she was embarrassed again. It was a strange sensation to realize that he was the cause of her embarrassment. The only prior embarrassment he had ever caused women had been being with them in the first place.

Aguilana took a puff from his cigarette, then dismissed it to whatever netherworld he had summoned it from. Jeremiah squinted. Either Haros was an excellent stage magician, or the cigarettes faded the same way the Rolls-Royce had...and how had that happened?

How did sea monsters get into the Sears Tower?

"Well, as I said, the proof is in the pudding, isn't it? You are very, very ready."

That had the most ominous overtones he had heard so far. "I don't understand. Ready for what?"

"They've held back, not wanting to press you too soon. We know how it can be. The crossover is difficult for some, impossible for many others, and for everything to be dropped on you at once... well, that can be the straw that breaks the king's back."

He wished Haros would have used a less disagreeable allusion, preferably something not involving maiming or killing. "Who are 'they'?"

"You met some of them, the least of them, the poor huddled masses one might call the ephemerals." Haros Aguilana stepped slowly toward him and as he walked, the empty club took on the gray, predawn light that Jeremiah had come to know and dread. Dim shapes began to gather behind the pipe-stem thin cadaver. Haros spread his arms wide as he continued. "Mere shadows, mere wastrels, mere hangers-on. Here but not here...and in great numbers." He smiled wider, revealing overly long canines. "But the others are here as well, as many as the grains of sand in all the world, with your permission."

The other day 1 met a man who was not there. When 1 returned the next day, he was not there again. Jeremiah Todtmann's recollection of the old rhyme was faulty at best, but his own version felt very apt at the moment. Very apt, that is, for describing Haros Aguilana. He began edging backward. If what Jeremiah suspected was true, this was one crown he could do without.

"Please do not, Jeremiah," Callistra whispered from behind his right shoulder. He started, then glanced at where she had previously stood. She could not have gotten behind him without him knowing, but then how often had she been able to elude him both on the train and in the city?

"Heavy on the head lies the crown, Jeremiah Todtmann," Haros continued, not missing a beat. The gray light now encompassed all of the interior save where the reluctant monarch stood. "You have nothing to fear but fear itself, your majesty. We are but your humble servants."

Callistra stepped to the side and curtsied. Haros bowed. "We are…" he concluded with a dramatic flourish, "the Grey."

The club interior was suddenly filled with every nightmare Jeremiah Todtmann had ever had or ever would have…or even would not. The sea monster, by comparison, was nothing, a simplistic shadow. What surrounded him now, edging ever closer, brought new meaning to the word fear.

These, according to Haros Aguilana, were his subjects.

Faced with what he saw, with what desired to be a part of his life forever, the new king of the Grey did what he had to do.

He fainted.

CHAPTER V

"Snug as a bug in a rug," Haros Aguilana said quietly, peering down at the resting form of his chosen monarch. Jeremiah Todtmann lay on an elaborate but aged couch, his arms crossed over his chest and a pillow behind his head.

"He looks so lifelike, I almost want to touch him to see if he'll awaken."

Haros shifted his gaze to the woman standing on the other side of the bed. "He will, Callistra, and I do not desire that just yet. Let our king rest until he chooses to wake."

She pouted. It was well done, a credit to his training.

"I know you like the back of my hand, dear one," he intoned. "And I suspect that your heart is not in your work."

"I want to live life to the fullest, Haros. What we do to him... will the end justify the means?"

They locked eyes across the inert body. With the exception of where the trio themselves were, the entire area was shadow. Not the shadows that were the Grey, but rather simply darkness that Haros

Aguilana had chosen to allow to enter the club for the time. The other Grey would have to wait. There were priorities, after all.

"Do you want to see the sun, feel the wind, and sing in the rain, Callistra? Do you want to sleep, perchance to dream?" His eyes grew cold. "I do."

She stretched forth a hand toward Jeremiah, but was careful not to touch him. Her eyes lingered first over his calm face, then the rise and fall of his chest as he breathed. "That and more."

"Then you must make him believe in you so very much that there is no living without you. You must make him believe that you are life itself for him."

"Believe strong enough and anything can happen," she whispered in growing hope. To say that Callistra glowed would have been a literal description.

"Yes…" The stick man began backing away into the darkness. "Life is what the king makes of it, dear one. Remember that."

Callistra nodded. She shifted then, taking up a position that would guarantee that the first thing the new monarch saw when he woke was her face. Not able to tire, she would simply stand there until he noticed her. It was one of the few benefits, such as it was, of being one of the Grey.

"Faith, Callistra," came the voice of Haros from the blackness. "It moves mountains."

She folded her hands and nodded, her gaze still locked on Jererniah's peaceful visage.

"But not the Grey," she whispered.

A part of Jeremiah Todtmann desired to wake; another part of him did not. He heard the buzz of voices, but was not conscious of what they said. In his mind, he struggled to move aside a huge veil, but though it gave way, it did so with only great effort.

At last, Jeremiah succeeded in opening his eyes, which were immediately filled by the wondrous sight of Callistra's fearful yet caring features peering down. He wondered how long she had been hovering there.

"You are well?"

"What happened to me?"

"Fell you into a faint, for Haros—" she began.

"If it's going to rhyme, please stop now." He winced as pain abruptly attacked the right side of his head. Jeremiah rubbed it, then noticed that Callistra was silent. When he looked at her, he saw that she had her mouth clamped tight, making her resemble a petulant child. Immediately Todtmann regretted his words. "I'm sorry. I didn't mean it the way it sounded. I was just afraid that with the way I feel, I wouldn't have understood you. I know I've asked this before, but why do you talk like that?"

"I speak in the shadow of the manner of men." Seeing him grimace, Callistra paused, then added, "Old habits die hard."

It was still a cliché, but at least an understandable one. Jeremiah continued to rub his head as he looked around. Other than the couch and the woman by his side, he saw nothing. Darkness surrounded them, but at least it was a darkness Jeremiah was used to seeing. There was no sign of the grayness that the shadows inhabited. "Are we still in the club?"

"Yes." A smile accompanied the short response. Callistra was visibly pleased by the succinct answer.

The pain would not go away. "What happened to my head?"

Her smile faltered, yet, with effort, she was able to say, "You struck your head when you fainted."

"Some great king you've chosen."

"Yes." This time, her smile had nothing to do with her answer. He saw that Callistra was simply agreeing with his statement. Sarcasm appeared lost on her.

The pain lessened, but now Jeremiah tasted the dust in his mouth. Small wonder, considering the condition of this place. He felt as if he had not had a drink in weeks. "Do you have any water? I'll even settle for more of that whiskey."

The ethereal enchantress shifted, but did not act on his request. She looked to be at a loss.

Not understanding her confusion—his own being more than enough for him to handle—Jeremiah added, "The bottle was behind the bar." He started to point, but could not locate the proper direction in the darkness. "Wherever that is."

Callistra finally acted, turning from him and heading toward the inkiness to his right. The black void swallowed her up in so swift a fashion that memories of the hungry coffee bubbled to the surface again. Todtmann started to wrap himself into a ball. The coffee, in turn, was dragging along the unwanted memories of just what had made him faint in the first place.

Suddenly the darkness was no longer comforting. The shadows, the Grey, as Haros had termed them, might not need the dimness to move about. Had they not been in Union Station and the office? They might be watching him even now …

He jolted as something emerged, but it was only Callistra. She paid no attention to his reaction, instead staring intently at the shot glass in her left hand. In her other hand, partially hidden by her body, was the bottle. For the first time, Jeremiah noticed that she was not dressed as she had been before he had fainted. Now Callistra wore a more modern outfit, a black-and-white woman's business suit, but one tailored to accent her exceptional femininity. What was unsettling was that he was certain that she had been wearing the other outfit when she had gone in search of his drink. Perception was a questionable thing in this place.

Then the thing that Jeremiah Todtmann had been secretly denying to himself became clear.

She really is one of the Grey....His hand shook as he accepted the glass from her. Callistra smiled, but her eyes were downcast. Did she realize what he had been thinking? Feeling guilty, he swallowed the contents of the shot glass without looking

...And promptly spit out a mouthful of dust. A very Greyish thought concerning the proverbial Sahara came to mind, but he stifled it before it could escape his lips.

She backed away. The bottle slipped from her hand and shattered on the floor. Instead of a spreading puddle, a small cloud blossomed from the long-empty vessel.

You may find it rather dry...

"Why's there—?"

"Callistra." Haros Aguilana's quiet voice somehow silenced all else. Callistra, crestfallen, retreated into the nothingness. As she vanished, the stick man materialized. He bowed to Jeremiah, then shook his head. "You must forgive her. Her heart is in...the right place. She is in dire straits, I imagine, over what she has done."

"Why—" Todtmann coughed. "Why would she give me this dusty glass instead of the whiskey?"

"She lacked insight. She only followed what had been done before, which is not uncommon among us." "I don't understand."

Haros beckoned him to rise. "To understand Callistra you must understand the Grey. Come. Join me."

Jeremiah walked over to the lanky figure, who pulled out one of his magical cigarettes and offered it to him. Jeremiah turned him down. Haros did not seem displeased.

"Let me show you something." He took a puff from the cigarette, then blew into his monarch's countenance. The would-be king sniffed and coughed. Haros smiled briefly, then held out the lit stick again. "Take hold of this."

Reaching out, Jeremiah took hold of the cigarette...or at least tried to do so. Try as he might, he could not touch it. His fingers went through it. Even when the tips of his fingers should have grazed the glowing end, Todtmann felt no heat, nothing. The cigarette was more insubstantial than the smoke rising from it.

"How do you do that?" "Illusion."

"So you are a magician?" Hope swelled within. "This is all just illusion?"

The reoccurring smile had a bittersweet cast to it. "In one respect this is all illusion, including me."

"You?" Unable to resist, he reached toward the macabre figure. His fingers felt the material of the jacket and the solidity of Aguilana's torso. A quite formidable illusion. "You're real enough."

"Thank you." Haros was genuinely pleased by the compliment. He dropped the cigarette, which faded, and took Jeremiah by the arm. "I think a tour is in order. It's time to put my money where my mouth is and explain to you a little of the world of the Grey... and, coincidentally, why you have been chosen."

Jeremiah tried to pull away. "I just want to go back to work, unless it's too late for that. If it is, then just bring me back to Union Station."

"It's later than you think. A day late and a dollar short, in fact." The chalky face screwed up in self-annoyance.

"A day late and...are you trying to tell me I was unconscious for an entire day?"

"By your reckoning, not by ours." In more soothing tones, Haros added, "It really would be better if you allowed me to show you your kingdom."

"I...don't...want...to...see...it!" He tried pulling away again, but the stick man, despite his appearance, held him in a grip that made Callistra's weak in comparison.

"I insist." Haros Aguilana snapped his fingers.

A chair coalesced before them. Not any ordinary chair, either, but a tall, elaborate throne of the likes that Jeremiah imagined the Queen of England sat upon. Even standing, he was shorter than the backrest. Scrollwork dominated all but those parts padded for his comfort, scrollwork carved into the fanciful forms of dragons and knights and creatures of legend, most of whom Jeremiah only vaguely recalled from childhood. He could not say for certain whether the chair was carved from some hard wood or was made of stone, for it was surrounded by a misty glow, an aura, that made it impossible to focus long.

Callistra stepped out from behind the throne, all traces of her embarrassment gone. She was as he first recalled her, perhaps even more vivid in some undefinable way, and the sight was enough to make him almost forget the throne.

"Walk this way," Haros politely commanded. He led Jeremiah to the throne, where Callistra helped turn the new monarch about so that he could sit down. She said nothing, but smiled. Todtmann could not help but smile back. Haros Aguilana he might have trouble trusting, but there was something about her that made it impossible for him to not want to believe in her.

"A throne fit for a king!" the stick man proclaimed, ending his statement with a bow. On Jeremiah's other side, Callistra curtsied.

For the first time, he almost forgot his objections to this scheme. The throne fit him perfectly and the dazzling glow made him feel…radiant. What did he have to look forward to back in his old life? Work? Solitude? There were few who would not have been tempted with the thought of being a king and Jeremiah Todtmann was certainly not one of those.

"There is so much that is offered you, your majesty." Haros waved a hand at the darkness.

Music surrounded them. It was lighter fare but played rather mournfully, as if the orchestra had come to the concert after a night of depression. Jeremiah recognized the tune as French, but that was the extent of his knowledge.

"You can be anywhere you want to be, go anywhere you want to go. The world of the Grey has no boundaries." The French music became Oriental, then distinctly African, followed by Spanish, and on and on. If not for the orchestra playing, it all would have sounded delightful. Instead, the music had the opposite effect than what Haros Aguilana likely desired. It dampened rather than raised Jeremiah Todtmann's enthusiasm.

Callistra leaned toward him, her nearer presence pushing back the doubts. "Paris is lovely in the springtime."

The way she said it was enough to make any man's face redden, excepting Haros Aguilana's, that is.

The gaunt vampire pointed at the darkness. Materializing before them was a vast pile of treasure surrounded by a glow that nearly competed with the aura about the throne. There were diamonds, gold, silver, works of art, dollar bills, furs…the pile grew and changed with each passing breath. Everything that people valued, on a monetary basis, that is, appeared in the pile. Wines, jewelry, even electronic equipment of the likes that Todtmann had been dreaming of buying someday. It was a cornucopia of material wealth.

All of which made him at last ask, "Why me? Why all of this for me?"

The incredible mountain of valuables faded. Haros summoned up a cigarette. "Because you are the king."

With that statement, the world turned Grey.

Jeremiah Todtmann found his throne perched atop a tall dais and the dais, in turn, positioned in the midst of the strangest celebration he had ever witnessed.

Shadows danced, vague shapes resembling women and men. They spun around and around with a frenzy not quite synchronized to the music, which while gay on the surface was much like the earlier tunes. Instead of pleasure, it was more reminiscent of sadness.

There were now tables and chairs spread all around the club, a night spot resembling one of the speakeasies he had seen in countless gangster films. There was light, too. Not bright light, but more than just the dim grayness. Just enough to see that while the club might resemble a mobster's hidden pleasure palace, the denizens were more out of a café from a Rod Serling film.

While the maddening nightmares of his first encounter were nowhere to be seen, those Grey gathered were by no means ordinary to the eye. A thing with a neck like a giraffe but a head almost human watched the dancers from the corners. Almost next to the dais, an apelike creature sat alone at a table where a drink suddenly materialized before it. Its eyes glowed when it saw the glass but it did not attempt to reach for the glass. Instead, it continued to stare.

Batlike forms hung from the rafters. There was now a bar and behind it stood a familiar figure, the heavy, lupine man from the coffee shop. There were others who looked even more human. Not all of the Grey were evidently indistinct forms or horrid monsters. Several figures sitting in the suddenly decorated club had a look that reminded Jeremiah of the elves of myth. Other characters—some squat, some narrow, and some dressed like punkers—wandered around the club. Much of the room looked like a fantasy novel gone bad.

Not all of the Grey were monsters, but many were. A trollish creature shambled back and forth for no visible reason, which, judging by others in the club, was a popular pastime among the shadow folk. A thing too close in resemblance to the deadly coffee flowed to one of the natural shadows, where it vanished. There were shapes that Jeremiah had only seen in works by Dali or Escher. Horrific creatures out of legend appeared and disappeared in the blink of an eye. The cast of the club changed so often that Todtmann soon gave up trying to keep track of what lurked around him. He only hoped that none of them would take too much interest in a simple mortal man.

A man who happened to be their king.

Music continued to play and although it sounded live, not recorded, there was no band. Each tune attempted to be merry, but there were always overtones that made it, in the end, mournful and without hope. Despite that, the dancers continued to dance and the others drank or stared in front of them at nothing at all. There was very little conversation.

It was, Jeremiah thought, a dismal night's entertainment. No one was truly enjoying themselves. They were going through the motions like folk who did not understand what it was they were doing.

"Welcome to the Wasteland. So dubbed by Master Thomas O'Ryan, but what's in a name? A club still as dark—"

For what seemed the thousandth time to him, the newly crowned monarch asked, "Why do you—you, Callistra, the raven—talk like that?"

"Rhyme, not reason? Cliché, not thought?" The cadaverous figure stepped in front of Jeremiah and indicated himself. "We are parodies par excellence, Jeremiah Todtmann! We are your thoughts, your dreams, your nightmares come into existence. We are your fads and fantasies. We are your id and your ego. Poor reflections of the way you are, were, and will be." He pointed at the dancers, then at other Grey in the room. "Your kind have created us and shaped us through the millennia, constantly rearranging us as you change yourself. We are puppets and because we are puppets, your words fill our mouths." Haros stalked up to Jeremiah, his death's-mask visage coming within a few inches of the man's. "We are the Grey, the accumulation of thousands of years of Mankind's conscious and subconscious." His arm came around Todtmann's shoulder. The stick man smiled. "You made us what we are today."

It took Jeremiah several seconds to wend his way through his host's words and even when he had translated them into his own, more simplistic terms, he could still not believe it. "Are you saying that you are all products of the imagination of people throughout history?"

"Give the man a cigar," the apelike creature intoned solemnly.

"We are as real as your dreams, you might say."

Around them, the dancers continued their whirlwind efforts, never slowing or speeding up but simply repeating the same movements at the same pace without stop. The music had changed, but once again to no avail. Shadow couples merged with other shadow couples, then broke apart with neither group seeming to notice. They were desperate to be enjoying themselves. Todtmann could sense that. He could also sense that they were failing.

Despite Callistra's soothing presence beside him, Jeremiah had just about had all he could take. Fainting was a good possibility. Many of the more ungodly members of Aguilana's people were conspicuously missing from sight, but the club and its paradoxical patrons were still making him tense and more than a bit frightened. How could he not be? Subjects or not, and that was still something open to debate as far as he was concerned, many of the Grey harkened back to his childhood fears.

As much as he feared them, the strange thing was that he also pitied them. The shadows he had seen earlier had been sad enough, but now, watching the Grey gathered together in this place of supposed amusement, Jeremiah wondered how they could exist so.

"And exist is all we do, Jeremiah Todtmann." Haros surveyed his folk. "Drawn into creation some time far past from the shared dreams and beliefs of your kind. The human mind is a stronger thing than most imagine. Your thoughts, your perceptions, shape the world. Working in unknowing concert, those beliefs drew upon the natural forces of the world and shaped us. We have existed from shortly after men first became aware all the way to the present. Ever-changing form and mind but never changing in what we are."

Jeremiah looked around and saw the wolfman behind the counter. "What about him? Or you for that matter? You both seem fairly…fairly…"

"*Real* is the word I think you look for." Haros Aguilana disposed of his cigarette. "Vulfgang and I have had the benefit of being recognized by kings for some time back. Recognition gives us strength, identity—to a point—and the longer we are locked into that identity, the longer we may maintain it. My poor unfortunate friend at the table has never been one who was granted more than passing favor by the kings. Thomas O'Ryan acknowledged him, gave him some substance, but he was always more of a pet to dear Doubting Thomas." A trace of bitterness accented the last statement.

Jeremiah briefly watched the hapless dancers dance on and thought of how similar his life was to theirs. "You mentioned this O'Ryan before."

"Thomas O'Ryan!" Jeremiah Todtmann jumped. The shout silenced the denizens of the Wasteland. Haros Aguilana faced them. "Thomas O'Ryan! Eat, drink, and be merry, for tomorrow we will start all over again! That was Thomas, wasn't it? He was our friend, was he not?"

The music began anew. The rest of the Grey slowly returned to their false merrymaking.

"You can see the legacy he left behind." Haros snorted. "We were the fairies and little people to him. It was Thomas who found and created this place for us. The Wasteland, he dubbed it, for Thomas was fond of poetry from many ages and thought that one piece particularly appropriate for us."

Although his attention was certainly with Haros, Jeremiah Todtmann could hardly be blamed for continually glancing around. Out of the corner of his eye, Todtmann thought he saw a very familiar figure. Still listening to Haros, he shifted his gaze in the direction the white-clad person had headed. There was, of course, no one to be seen—that was the way of the Grey, he was discovering—but Jeremiah was almost certain he had just spotted the passing figure of...Elvis?

*We are your thoughts, your dreams, your nightmares come into existence. We are your fads and fantasies...*Those were the words his macabre host had used, but just what that encompassed he was just beginning to understand. *How many sightings of Elvis have there been? Of the Loch Ness Monster? Of...UFOs?*

Were they all the Grey?

"Was O'Ryan also king?"

"King of all you survey; King O'Ryan ruled the Grey." Haros actually shivered after spouting the rhyming answer. He glared at Callistra, as if expecting her to laugh, but she looked away.

Jeremiah decided it was best to make nothing of the nonsensical rhyme. "What happened to him?"

"As with all kings, he passed on. We do not offer immortality, Jeremiah Todtmann. Merely a stretching of the years."

Some of the Grey were finding it impossible to hide their interest in their new monarch. Some of the shadows danced closer. Several shapes passed just beyond the edge of the dais. A few of the more human-looking Grey began to watch from their seats. One woman who bore a close resemblance to Marilyn Monroe winked at him. Beside him, Jeremiah felt Callistra shift. The woman turned quickly away.

"A favorite of Master Thomas's." The stick man's tone dismissed her as any subject of interest. "Understand that he was a good man at heart, but he was frivolous in many ways. In the end, he left only one worthy legacy. You." "Why me?"

"Strength is in the eye of the beholder," Callistra replied before Haros could. She had evidently tired of being simply an ornament in this conversation. "Thomas said, Haros! There's the man for you!' "

The macabre mannequin was silent for a moment, but then nodded. "Yesss…that's the way it was. He looked out over the world and there he found you."

It must be said that no one had ever looked upon Jeremiah Todtmann and found him so worthy. Not even his folks. Certainly not Morgenstrom or any of the women Jeremiah had dated. He could not help but swell a little in pride.

"What does it mean to be king?"

"Aaah, if I were king of the world…" Haros summoned another cigarette. Jeremiah noticed that sometimes he did not even pretend to smoke them but merely held them. Haros was as addicted to his phantasms as many humans were to the real thing. Did he really feel more human pretending to smoke or was he no different from the shadows, who went through the motions but did not enjoy or even understand what they were attempting?

"Though drawn forth from the minds of men, we still have some semblance of will, Jeremiah Todtmann. Shaped to be men's elves and fairies and the like, we could not help but become what we were expected to be. Clever and worldly wise. In some ways, almost superior to our creators…almost." Haros took a puff. "We could never truly be cleverer, could we? After all, we are only poor copies."

The resentment in his voice was obvious to the new ruler, but evidently the stick man did not realize that. Jeremiah could understand that resentment and so let it pass.

"We understood ourselves a little better than men understood us, that much credit is ours. Given by men's myths and beliefs minds somewhat of their own, a few came to realize our tragic existence.

As men changed, so, too, did we. Gone were the memories of what we had become, only to be replaced by what would come next. We were literally mercurial creatures, altering to suit whatever people believed. Sometimes day by day and night by night. Immortal we were, but forever slaves of others' whims."

An eternity of being shaped to suit the fantasies of others would not be a very delightful existence for anyone. Jeremiah tried to imagine how he would feel in the place of the Grey. Still, what did that have to do with him? How did he as king make some difference? Jeremiah Todtmann was not always the swiftest of men, but he was beginning to have an inkling of his place here. He kept silent, however, wanting to hear the answer that Haros would give him.

"The world holds more power than humans imagine. Power that in the ancient days of your folk would have been called magic. You, in your more enlightened times, would think of it more as a variable field of energy that can be tapped by the right mind."

Actually, Todtmann was fairly certain that he would still have called it magic. Science had never been one of his strengths.

"Combined, a number of Grey found that they could also manipulate this natural power. We could perform magic of our own. Not enough to give us what we wanted, but enough so that we could bring to us one who could."

"Like you," whispered Callistra in his ear.

He looked out at the world of the Grey, seeing them struggling to maintain some self. Even the most horrid of those in the club did not look so horrid when viewed that way. They could not help what they were. They were trying to change things.

Haros Aguilana's latest phantasm vanished in a puff of smoke. The gaunt Grey had his hands clasped together, making him resemble a televangelist. Jeremiah, understanding that even Haros was a creature of Mankind's foibles, did not hold the posturing against him.

"Like you, yes. We exist in a world somewhat loosely overlapping your own. The world of dreams, it seems. A world not in light but also not in darkness. It was one of the early humans who gave us our name, one of the few things that is truly ours. He was one of our kings."

People had gone missing throughout time. Most of them were simply the victims of treachery or accidents and eventually some of their bodies would be discovered. A few, though, sensitive to the world in a way that most folk were not, stumbled into the dim places inhabited by the Grey. Some of these humans were what would have been known as sorcerers by their fellows; others were simply considered madmen.

From what happened when those people became trapped in the Grey's world came the solution to the phantoms' problem of consistency in mind and form. Humans, being ofttimes fixed in their ways, did not truly understand the malleability of the Grey and so the shapes they saw were the shapes they believed the spectral denizens wore all the time. The Grey found, to their surprise, that those humans trapped in their world had a stronger impact on their forms than almost the sum total of the many who existed only in the true Earth.

Of course, the Grey were many times not pleased with those choices given them. The spell they worked upon was one that would better protect their realm by finding for them a single man or woman of more noble mind, someone with the ability to understand and work with the Grey as they were. They could not help but be molded, for that was their way, but at least under the one human chosen, they would have a greater stability and the opportunity to expand in directions that in the past had been beyond them.

The Grey could almost be real. "We could create a society of our own that borrows from only the best humanity can offer," Haros added. "And put an end to the kind of empty play you see around us."

The best laid plans of mice, men, and the Grey, however, do not always turn out the desired way. The spell did work in the beginning, to a point, calling to the shadow world select folk. Yet, each time there was more variance in the type chosen, a variance that grew alarmingly out of control. The Grey were left with human kings who did not always care for their ways, kings who often found them repulsive or interesting playthings…and the shadow folk did not consider themselves toys.

"What happened?" Jeremiah asked when Haros paused too long. Shapes kept moving just at the edge of his field of vision. Little rats wearing armor and carrying lances. A figure clad in bloodied overalls and a hockey mask who might have been staring at Jeremiah a moment before. A pointy-headed child who reminded him of some cartoon.

A pink rabbit beating on drums?

The twentieth century was likely to give the Grey some of their most peculiar shapes yet.

"It was the kings themselves, of course. Being human, they influenced us and, of course, the spell itself. It changed, became a thing of its own, yet also a thing of those it had chosen. Once more the decision was taken from us; it was now up to the whims of the kings and the unpredictability of the spell as to who would next come to us. It has been that way ever since."

There seemed to be no more, for Haros Aguilana then bowed. Callistra clapped her hands, but other than a brief nod by the apelike thing, none of the other Grey appeared to have noticed the end. Most of them had probably not even noticed the beginning. A few probably noticed nothing at all.

"And I'm the chosen one. What I think is what you become?"

Callistra touched his shoulder. "You have it in you to make us more than we have ever been. You can make us be all we can be."

"Which is why we came to you rather than let you stumble through to us." Haros tilted his head. "And you would have, too. Once touched by the power, you could not help but be drawn to us."

As before, Jeremiah Todtmann was certain that his host had not told him of everything. Haros was a creature of secrets. Many secrets. "And you? You're my guide?"

"I am here to show you the ropes, yes." Haros was clearly pleased with how he thought Jeremiah was taking all of this. He turned toward the bar. "Vulfgang! A drink!"

Recalling his last one, Todtmann tried to decline.

"You must forgive Callistra her effort, my lord. She did the best she could, but she did know the way. In truth, the first glass you drank...was just as dry."

While Jeremiah was no drinker, he was sure that he knew the difference between whiskey and dust. One was wet. Seeing his disbelief, Haros explained, "There is no real food here. What we drink and eat—and smoke—are the memories of things that have already...passed on. The first drink was a test; if you saw, felt, and tasted the whiskey, then you had safely passed into our world."

"And the second time?"

"A misjudgment of her skills. She did not reach far enough. To summon the memories, we reach out and feel the history, the ghosts of its past, if you will."

"I have much to learn," the pale beauty added.

A shadow passed across the stick man's empty hand. A glass materialized. Haros offered it to Jeremiah. "Trust in me. You'll find this quite smooth."

He took the glass and, still recalling the first time, swirled the contents. The maelstrom reminded him of the basement and the Loch Ness Monster. Jeremiah looked up again, surveying the Grey. They drank freely, for shadows no doubt did not suffer from hangovers or dying livers.

I wonder if there are really pink elephants here. The possibility was absurd enough to allow him to sip without thinking too much about the mouthful of dust Callistra's offering had contained.

It was every bit as good as the last whiskey Haros had brought him, save that this time there was no accompanying grapple with the raven-haired enchantress at his side.

He swallowed the last of it and as he did, the tempo of the music changed. For the first time, it was almost upbeat, hopeful. The dancers moved just a little livelier and conversation grew among the Grey. Some of them began to boldly approach the throne, bowing or curtsying or simply bending if their bodies would permit nothing else. Those whose semblance was most human began to dance near his throne, but their eyes were ever on him, not their partners. The Grey resembling Marilyn Monroe was especially attentive and despite his attraction to Callistra, Jeremiah could not help basking in the other woman's attentiveness.

He reminded himself that both women were not real, not even living as humans judged, but humans were also creatures of the senses and his told him that both Callistra and the Marilyn were very, very feminine, indeed.

All of which made what he had to tell Haros even more difficult. "Listen—"

"Callistra! He should be dancing!"

He was. Without rising from the throne or descending the dais, Jeremiah Todtmann was dancing with Callistra. He blinked and stumbled against her. She slowed in order to allow him to get back in step.

"Could I have some warning?" he sputtered, trying not to step on her feet.

She smelled of fresh lilies. Her smile threatened to dazzle him. "I was afraid you might ask her for your first dance." There was no need to ask who her was. "You would've been the one I asked, but that's—"

Her cheek pressed against his, stifling, for a moment, both his words and his thoughts. The two of them twirled through the crowd. Caught up as he was, it was probably best that Jeremiah did not notice that several times his path literally took him through the shadow couples. He only knew that he held the woman of his dreams.

It was that which finally reminded him of what he had wanted to say. "Callistra, we have to stop dancing."

Her eyes were needles piercing him. "You want to dance with her?"

"No, it's just that..." He twisted around, looking over the heads of the other revelers. "Where's Haros?"

"He is readying your residence for you. Don't you know that a king needs a residence?"

Todtmann paused for a second, noticing how her manner of speech had altered to something more what he was used to hearing. She even looked a bit different…more substantial. Real. It was not something specific he could have pointed at. She simply seemed more real than at any other time he had seen her, even including the past few moments prior to their dance. Callistra was, in fact, more real to him at that moment than anything else in his rather tedious life had ever been.

Nonetheless, he refused to continue the dance. "Call or bring him back. I have to talk to him."

Slender arms held him close. "Talk is cheap. It can wait."

"No it can't. He's the one I have to tell; I know that. I'm sorry, really I am, but I don't want to be king." He expected many expressions to pass across Callistra's perfect face, most of them related to surprise or incredulity, but certainly Jeremiah did not think to see the look of pleasure that formed immediately following his refusal of the crown. "Is something I said funny?"

Now her features formed into the incredulous expression he had first been prepared for. "You were not making a joke? You actually meant what you said?"

"Of course I did."

"But this is an offer you can't refuse!" She held him at arm's length, looking him over as if seeing him for the first time. "It just isn't done!"

He folded his arms. The music faded, but did not stop. The dancers still danced, but now they gave the two a berth wide enough for the Loch Ness Monster to swim through. "I'm doing it. I'm sorry, Callistra. I can't be a part of this world."

"But you are!" She reached down, took his hands in her own, and leaned closer. "This is a one-way ticket! You've passed the point of no return! There's no going back...even if you want to!"

"No going—" Jeremiah Todtmann shivered. She could not mean what she said. "Are you saying that I have to stay here? That I'm not allowed to return?"

"That's the writing on the wall," Callistra returned, looking down. The sultry Grey's speech pattern had completely backtracked. "You can't get there from here."

You can't get there from here...He was king of the Grey, but he was also a prisoner, an exile from the world of men. He could assume the role that had been chosen for him or be nothing.

Worse than nothing. A shadow of nothing.

In his mind, Jeremiah Todtmann could hear the raven's laughter.

CHAPTER VI

Few folk are comfortable talking to the police for any reason and Hector was finding out that he was not one of those few. Even though his reasons for calling were quite legitimate, the black man felt ill at ease, as if he had committed a crime and were trying to keep it a secret. The only person with less to hide would have been Jeremiah. Granted, the Chicago police sometimes had a rocky reputation, but the officer on the line had been very pleasant and erstwhile. She had been so the three times he had talked to her.

The pleasantry was wasted, though. They still had no word on Jeremiah Todtmann. Hector had been prepared for such lack of news, but it was still worrisome to hear.

"Well, thanks a lot. I appreciate it. You'll let me know, right? Thanks again." He hung up the phone and stood up. In all of the maze, only he and a couple of others still remained at work. Only he evidently was concerned over Jeremiah's lengthening disappearance. Morgenstrom was only concerned that Todtmann's work was having to be divided between two other people, one himself.

There was no sense hanging around any longer. The police had his home phone number. He reached for his coat, which hung from a small hook he had installed in the removable wall of his cubicle, and readied himself for the walk to the station. Thanks to being put on hold for the first ten minutes, Hector had already missed one train. Now he would also have to walk to Union Station in the dark. At least it was a short trek.

Something large fluttered outside. Hector sensed more than heard it and quickly turned around. For some reason, he thought of Jeremiah, an absurd notion, obviously. Unless his friend had learned to fly, there was little chance of seeing him outside of Everlasting's window.

"Jeremiah," he muttered, staring at the darkness outside. "You are turning me into a bundle of nerves, man! Where the hell have you gotten yourself?" He had been pretty much out of it that day, Hector realized. "You get yourself back here."

Tossing two trouble files into his briefcase, the mortgage man started for the foyer. If he hurried, he knew he could catch the next train out to the suburbs.

Hector reached the glass doors without incident and while he had not expected anything to happen, a sense of relief nonetheless washed over him. He started to reach for a door handle when a reflection in the glass caught his eye.

It was a bird, but not just any bird. It was a tremendous black bird and it appeared to be perched on one of the stiff little chairs set up for visitors doing business with Everlasting.

He gazed over his shoulder.

There was no bird, black or otherwise, perched anywhere.

"Geez, I have got to get out of this place!" he whispered, both bemused and bothered by his own imagination. Jeremiah's disappearance was taking a toll on him. He was a good friend, even if a little clueless about life outside of work. Hector knew Jeremiah well enough to know that vanishing was not like him—on most days. That particular day, though…

Shrugging, Hector opened the door. There was nothing to keep him here. He could continue his worrying on the train. It was all Hector could do for Jeremiah now. The police had the situation covered and he still had a date tonight…he hoped.

As worried as he was about Jeremiah, the departing Hector could not help thinking that at least it, whatever it was, had happened to someone else and not him. That was always a thought to keep one going. However terrible things were, if they happened to another person they were not quite as terrible as if they had happened to oneself. At least his own life was safe and secure.

Turned as he was toward the elevators he did not, of course, see the shadow of a bird that crossed his backside.

It is ever a human trait that even when a person is told something cannot be done, more often than not the person told will have some misgivings about the absoluteness of that answer. A stubborn streak arises in some that further deflects any attempts to reinforce the impossibility of the situation discussed. Such was now the case with Jeremiah Todtmann. This was, after all, his life they were discussing. To tell him that he had only one path open to him would have meant little to him when he had worked at Everlasting, but to say the same now, in the world of the Grey, was unpardonable.

"I don't believe you!"

"It's too true, Jeremiah!" Callistra held him by the arm. Her grip would have rivaled a wrestler's. "There's nothing you can do!"

No way back....."I want out of this place!"

The two of them were suddenly standing in an alley in the midst of a darkening Chicago.

"Jeremiah, you have to be more careful! You go where angels fear to tread!"

"Angels or just Grey?" He had never been so upset in his life and while on one level Todtmann knew he was being unfair to take it out on Callistra, he couldn't help himself.

She released him. Her tone was softer and her eyes were averted. "I only want you safe."

That cooled his anger a bit. He still refused to believe in the inevitability of the Grey path, but Jeremiah doubted that it was the woman before him who was responsible for any of the troubles concerning the crown he had been given. Such blame likely fell on one particular head. Haros Aguilana. Callistra seemed merely to be his puppet, mouthing his words and believing them because she knew no better. *How often have I been like that?* Only in the short period since becoming involved in all this madness had Jeremiah himself become more than Callistra was.

He exhaled. "I believe you, but I don't think I believe Haros. He told you all of this, right?"

"Yes, but Haros is strong. Haros is never wrong."

"Everyone's wrong...Lord knows, I've been again and again." He took hold of her, somewhat surprised by his own aggressiveness. What Todtmann really wanted to do was hold her tight, but she was not only a puppet of Haros but also a Grey. His conflicting thoughts served only to confuse him further, the last thing he needed now. Jeremiah managed to push his growing interest in

Callistra to the side, but could not bury it. With her so close, that was impossible. "I'm not cut out for this. That much I do know. I still haven't figured out whether this is some bizarre dream or psychosis. For all I know, the train derailed and I'm in some hospital, my head knocked around, hallucinating."

"This is no dream." As he calmed, so did she. The shadowy woman seemed to reflect his own moods. Jeremiah was not certain he liked that. What was the real, if he could use the word real, Callistra?

"You're right; it's a damn nightmare!" It was just occurring to him that it must be evening. The only illumination came from either the streetlights or the fleeting gleams from headlights as cars and buses scurried past. The eerie grayness that he had come to associate with his unwanted subjects enveloped Chicago, allowing him to see where normally the night would not permit. That was small satisfaction, however.

"I am sorry, but there is nothing I can do."

He believed her, which made it no more easy to accept. Haros was lying to her; the stick man had to be. There was always a way out. Allowing the Grey to lead him into their world had brought him to this predicament. What would happen if Jeremiah rejected the shadow people entirely? What would happen if he made the conscious effort to return to his life?

"I've got to go, Callistra." "Jeremiah—"

How many men have wanted to play Rick in the movie Casablanca? Jeremiah wished he had watched the movie more often so that he could have said something clever. Rick, however, had been played by Bogart while Jeremiah Todtmann was being played by himself. Not very good casting for the role he had been thrust into, he decided. That was the crux of the situation. "I'm just not cut out for this insanity! I just want to get back to work and live out my dull life!"

"And forever keep an eye out for ravens," she returned.

Ravens. The reluctant monarch's chest sank. "That's one of the biggest reasons for me to give this up! I don't know what that bird wants out of this and I doubt you can give me the answer I need. Haros wouldn't. What would you do in my place?"

"Take the mantle of king."

Wrong question to ask one of the Grey, obviously. Todtmann made his way out of the alley and over to the curb. He shivered as he studied the area. The world still wavered, still suffered from that fish-bowl effect, yet, Jeremiah was fairly certain that he did not recognize this part of the city. The buildings here also loomed too tall for him to be able to see even the Sears Tower. Still, Jeremiah was fairly certain that he was not too far from the Loop. One of the CTA buses would certainly take him within the vicinity of Union Station. Failing that, he still had a chance of hailing a taxi. Given a choice of the two, Jeremiah found himself for the first time since he had started working in Chicago desiring the bus. Buses in Chicago were not designed for comfort. They were heated in the summertime and air-conditioned in the winter. The seats were vinyl wrapped around wood or metal, the padding having long been pressed into disservice.

It was the people, the passengers, that he craved. Their presence would jar him back to reality. Other than work, nothing was more daunting than riding Chicago mass transit.

I need a bus stop, he started to think.

"Damn!" His surroundings had shifted again. He was standing on a different curb. There was illumination, just enough to create shadows and allow him to make out objects. The sidewalk had a peculiar softness to it that made each step an adventure. The buildings around him were jagged and bent. They did not sway as much as the others had, but that made them no less fearsome. Jeremiah was minded of an old, silent German horror film he had once watched. The area was silent, too. All the scene needed was organ music.

Out of the corner of his eye, he caught a flash of movement. Todtmann whirled, expecting perhaps the Loch Ness Monster rising from a manhole, but found instead a rather lively, serpentine signpost facing him. It twisted with an eagerness lacking in the buildings, behaving in many ways like a puppy just reunited with its master. Although not in the least bit interested in petting it, he moved closer and tried to read it. After some struggle to maintain focus on the constantly shifting sign, Jeremiah saw that on it were words announcing this location as a stop for one of the city bus routes.

"Jeremiah! Take heed! The merest thought can be the most dangerous deed!"

Callistra was behind him, every bit as beautiful and frantic as when he had left her, but his thoughts were elsewhere. Slowly comes the dawn to some men, but in this case Jeremiah Todtmann was at last beginning to perceive the truth about his swift hops around the city.

It's me! I'm doing this! There were some benefits to this insane proposal, then. He did not need a bus or train after all. With one simple desire, Jeremiah could transport himself anywhere he wished. Anywhere…

The temptation to cross oceans using only a single thought was great, but doing so could only enmesh him deeper into the world of the Grey. Haros and the raven would like that. So long as he was a part of their realm, they could abuse and manipulate him. Only if he found the way back to the human world would he be safe from them. There, they would only be illusions, true shadows with no depth.

Even Callistra.

He was not forced to follow the last thought further, for at that moment a bus turned around a darkened street corner and headed toward the stop. While travel via the Grey path was much quicker, the human thing was to take the bus. Jeremiah stood on the edge of the curb and waved at the driver. The massive vehicle began to slow.

"You don't know what you're doing!" Callistra called out. She reached for him, but he evaded her grasp.

Jeremiah continued to wave to the driver. The brown-haired, overweight woman at the wheel was still driving too fast for his liking. The staring headlights of the snarling behemoth looked past the waving figure.

"What the hell is she doing?" It looked like the bus driver had no intention of stopping. She was, if his eyes did not lie, beginning to speed up.

A slender but powerful hand caught his shoulder. "Jeremiah, what you see is not what you get! You can't—"

He struggled out of her grip, but in doing so stumbled back over the curb and onto the street.

Todtmann looked up into the uncaring eyes of the bus as it roared down on him. He yelped and covered his face, hoping the end would be swift, if not painless. Jeremiah doubted that being struck by a moving bus could ever be called painless.

The roar of the engine was all he heard as the bus reached him. There was no sound of squealing brakes, no horn. The driver had never even seen him. He was destined to become another traffic statistic—

As he thought the last, the snarl of the engine diminished.

Jeremiah uncovered his eyes. The bus was no longer in front of him. In fact, it took him a few seconds to realize that the sound was now coming from behind him. The grumbling leviathan was already two blocks down the street and dwindling fast.

His body still aquiver, he looked at Callistra for an explanation.

"We are the stuff that dreams are made of," the ghostly beauty reminded him, her expression solemn. "Shadows. No substance."

"But I'm not one of you!" Jeremiah returned to the safety of the sidewalk. "I'm human! I'm real!" He tapped his chest. "I breathe! I live!" Actually, for most of his life he had simply existed, but even that was better than the alternative being offered to him. "I'm not like you at all!" The last words were out of his mouth before he could realize their implications. Jeremiah swallowed and tried to think of some sort of apology, but nothing sufficient came to mind.

"But you are part of our world now," Callistra returned. There was nothing to indicate any hurt or indignation on her part. Once more she stretched out her hand to him. "And that is all that matters in the end…"

"There's got to be a way back!"

"Do not dwell upon it, Jeremiah," she beseeched, taking a step toward him. Whatever her task, whatever her mood, her beauty was unparalleled. That was almost enough to make him come to her, that and the nagging notion that behind the beauty was something more. Something not Grey.

"Take my hand, Jeremiah…"

He reached for her.

As Jeremiah did, he became aware of the fact that the shadows behind Callistra had deepened and were now beginning to move toward the duo.

With an eloquent grunt of dismay, Jeremiah seized Callistra's wrist and pulled her to him. At the same time, he tried to think of some place safe—and far away—for them to be.

On retrospect, the offices of Everlasting would not have been his first choice, but old routines die hard and so he found himself in the midst of the maze of cubicles clutching the night-tressed enchantress as if a host of ravens were about to descend upon them. The office was brightly lit, yet not one of the cubicles was occupied. Jeremiah glanced up at a wall clock and saw that it was almost an hour past quitting time. Somehow he had missed yet another day...or more...

Callistra, making no attempt to break his hold and looking much too much like a Hollywood starlet, breathed, "I didn't think you cared."

He untangled himself. "There were shadows...deep ones...that were right behind you."

"Shadows shadowing." Her expression was more bemused than worried. "Something wicked this way flies. The raven is keeping an eye peeled for you. The shadows are his running dogs."

"No one's told me much about the raven yet."

"Another of us. That's all. His deeds are darksome, Jeremiah."

"So I noticed." Todtmann began searching the office for some overworked soul. *The lights are on but no one's home.*

He cringed at yet his latest Greyish thought. If this went on much longer, he would look and sound like one of them.

As Jeremiah searched, he became aware that the office was empty not only of his coworkers, but also of the shadow figures.

It was doubtful that the Grey kept business hours, although being derived from humanity perhaps that wasn't so farfetched, so where were they? For that matter, the street had been fairly empty. Only the hungry shadows lingered.

Someone in one of the management offices cursed. A drawer slammed and what was likely a chair collided with a wall.

They might call the wind Mariah, but a tempest would certainly be christened Morgenstrom if Jeremiah Todtmann had any say in the naming. His face buried in a file that Todtmann somehow knew was one of the ones he had abandoned, the supervisor stalked toward a series of tall, brown cabinets in which normally were stored files not yet given the grand approval of Everlasting.

Jeremiah had never been so happy to see him in all the time he had worked for the company. "Mr. Morgenstrom!"

Morgenstrom paused and looked up.

Morgenstrom looked down and continued his trek to the file cabinets.

Unable to accept what had happened, Jeremiah rushed his superior. "Mr. Morgenstrom! Sir! It's me! Jeremiah Todtmann!"

"Hmm?" Again, the other man looked up and again he looked away, this time with an even more disgruntled expression.

"He looks but he cannot see," Callistra called out from behind him. "He hears but he does not listen."

"He heard me!"

Still engrossed in the papers before him, Morgenstrom opened one of the massive drawers. He put the open file on top, read a line on one page, then mumbled something that sounded like "Katzgilberg." The supervisor began pushing one stored file after another aside in what was obviously a search for some item of importance to this "Katzgilberg." All the while he was totally oblivious to the shouting figure nearly at his back.

"We ride the peripheral, Jeremiah. A touch, a glance, that's all we can have in the world of men." Despite her continued verbal attempts to dissuade him, Callistra made no more physical efforts to pull Jeremiah back.

"I'm not one of you!" he snapped in what once would have been very un-Jeremiah Todtmann-like behavior. Some things will change a man, though…like becoming monarch to a world of bad dreams. Defying Callistra's words, the unwilling shadow ruler reached out and tried to seize hold of Morgenstrom's shoulder.

He made contact, but his grip proved tenuous and momentary. Morgenstrom's shoulder was a well-oiled surface, slick and smooth. The bald man jumped, then quickly straightened and looked around. His gaze went quickly past his still-hopeful subordinate and continued on for almost a complete circle. Frowning, the supervisor brushed his shoulder off, apparently thinking that something had landed on it. He glanced around one more time, his eyes brushing past Jeremiah with no more interest than earlier.

As his supervisor returned to the files, Jeremiah tried to seize him with both hands. Morgenstrom, seemingly unaware of what he himself was doing, twisted just enough to escape the desperate grapple. Again Jeremiah Todtmann's hands encountered a slickness that made it impossible to keep hold. He stared at the other man as Morgenstrom continued his task uninterrupted by his presence.

"I'm a ghost…" He leaned forward so that his face was beside the supervisor. "I'm a goddamn ghost, Mr. Morgenstrom! Do you hear me?"

As before, the older man looked up, his expression indicating that he had heard something. Yet, when he looked in Jeremiah

Todtmann's direction, Morgenstrom evidently saw nothing of interest, not even the curvaceous form of Callistra standing behind her reluctant monarch. The narrow man muttered under his breath and dug into the files with renewed determination.

Jeremiah straightened, defeated. Callistra came to his side and put her hand on his shoulder. He vaguely wondered whether she kept doing that because she cared for him, had been ordered to by Haros Aguilana, or simply was acting like a Grey. Was she sympathetic because he needed sympathy? Did he really care anymore? His world was beyond his reach now. Oh, Jeremiah could touch it, but only for the briefest of moments. That was not the same as being a part of reality; that was the same as being part of a macabre game of torture. Look but don't try to touch, that was his fate.

"Time marches on, Jeremiah, and so should we."

He was too depleted to even respond to her Greyish turn of phrase. Why bother? If he was part of their world, it was he who had to change.

Morgenstrom pulled out a pen. A spark of life returned to Todtmann's eyes. To some extent, the Grey could manipulate inanimate objects. Surely, he could, too.

"What are you doing?" Callistra's voice was on the cautious side of fear.

"Haunting." Jeremiah reached for the pen. If he could seize hold of so small and simple an object, then he could prove to Morgenstrom that he was real.

His fingers touched solid plastic. Jeremiah's heart was a madman's drum. With deft and determined movements, he slowly pulled the pen away. Jeremiah trembled in triumph, but his success was swiftly shattered by what he saw in Morgenstrom's hand once his own was out of the way.

There was another pen, identical to the first, in the supervisor's grip. Jeremiah released his and watched in horror as it faded before falling even halfway to the floor. He remembered the cigarettes of Haros Aguilana.

"We summon the memories," Callistra gently reminded him, pulling him away. "We summon the ghosts of the past. Everything has a past and, therefore, memories and ghosts."

Something's wrong...it has to be.... Despite the silent denial, however, he could find nothing wrong with her explanation. Now he was truly defeated. Now he had no hope. He had only the Grey.

Callistra leaned close, but instead of words, she kissed him on the cheek. The full lips were soft, desirable, and every bit as real as Everlasting once had been. "Judge not the Grey by its cover, my lord. There is a world of beauty you have not seen yet." She glanced at the unknowing Morgenstrom. "Come. There's nothing more to be gained from this."

He was only half with her, but still he did not resist this time when she pulled him away. His gaze bolted to the bent figure of his supervisor, Jeremiah listlessly asked, "Where are we going? Back to Haros?"

"Not yet." With that short, unenlightening reply, Callistra brought them elsewhere.

It was still Chicago, for Jeremiah could make out dim glimpses of the city, but other things were now transposed over it. Older, archaic buildings and tall wild grass. There was wildlife, including a few large shadows of beasts not seen in this world for thousands of years. Contrary to most of the world of the Grey, there was much light here...but much dark as well. Slowly, he came to the conclusion that what he was seeing was the memories—or ghosts, perhaps— of each night and day since men had first come to this region.

These were the pages of Chicago's history, all overlapping one another yet still distinct.

He had become, as anyone would have under the same circumstances he had suffered through, more than a bit fearful of birds. Thus it was that when an avian shape darted over him, Todtmann desperately tried to hide. As there was no nearby cover, his escape attempt turned into a myriad array of dance steps that ended up looking quite like a combination of the fox-trot and slam-dancing. Only when Jeremiah saw that his companion made no move to escape did he calm.

The bird alighted on the index finger of Callistra's free hand. It was a cardinal with majestic red plumage and did not look in the least like the raven. Callistra politely said nothing. She simply swung the hand and bird toward him so that he could see the cardinal up close.

"Is it one of you?" The Grey could assume just about any shape.

"Say rather that it comes from the same place that we do. It doesn't understand what it is; it simply is."

She smiled at the bird, then let it fly away again. Once more in her own element, Callistra's confidence had returned. It was generally when she had to cope with his human weaknesses that the ghostly enchantress lost her composure.

"Come look at this," she whispered, wandering to her right.

He followed her a step or two, but stopped when he noticed the moist sound his shoes made on the dry street. Jeremiah lifted his foot so that he could see the underside of one shoe; it was wet, yet there was no source.

Callistra enjoyed his befuddlement. "Look past the street. Look to what was before."

Jeremiah tried...and saw the street fade a little. Now he also saw tall wild grass and damp, almost swampy soil. Chicago before there was a Chicago.... Todtmann had little knowledge of the old history of the city other than the great fire and the fixed elections. He was ignorant of what the area must have looked like during the time of the first settlers or, going further back, the first nomads and hunters.

"Look there, Jeremiah." Callistra pointed ahead of them.

It had been a massive, vague form the first time he had seen it, but this time Jeremiah Todtmann was able to recognize the animal. A mastodon. Newspapers printed articles about the discovery of their fossilized bones now and then. Chicago had been a fairly popular stop for the beasts at one point in time. The mastodon moved slowly, an image caught in molasses. Unlike most of the other things, it remained faded at the edges, giving it an even more dreamlike quality. He questioned Callistra as to the reason why.

"Even the best memories fade with time," she responded. Haros had said the same thing earlier. "They are the true ghosts. We...we are not even that."

"You're more."

"And less." The images around them dwindled away, once more leaving them in the midst of modern Chicago. Modern Chicago as the Grey saw it, that is. Jeremiah quickly looked around for deep shadows.

"We are safe and sound here."

Even without the hungry shadows or the mocking raven, this was not a place that Jeremiah Todtmann would have ever called safe. The buildings around them were desolate even when considered without the warped view created by the world of the Grey. Some of them were so dilapidated it was a wonder that they still stood, let alone that people still inhabited them.

They were inhabited; there was no doubt about that. Lights shone behind worn curtains. The sounds of television and conversation, the latter sometimes raised to high, shrill levels, reverberated through the street.

This was also a part of what had once been Jeremiah's reality.

"Look here. Someone once had a garden here."

He looked at the spot Callistra was pointing at, but saw nothing but a cracked walkway. "Doesn't look like it's doing too well these days."

"Now, yes, but let me take you back to those days of yesteryear…"

*The Lone Ranger rides again…*finished Jeremiah. He was feeling quite Greyish. What else was there for him?

"It was a beautiful garden."

"Was—" The retort died as a cornucopia of blazing color and shape sprouted before his eyes.

There were flowers, large and small, sometimes from bushes and sometimes simply bursting from the ground. They were red, yellow, blue, pink…the flowers changed with each passing second. Bushes sometimes offset them, but were now and then replaced by rock gardens, tiny picket fences no more than half a foot high, and small statuettes of birds, animals, and even a figure of the Virgin Mary. It was a fireworks display unparalleled, save that instead of raucous explosions of light there was the silent blossoming of flowers.

When she was satisfied that he had seen enough, Callistra put an end to the wondrous exhibition. "Even in the worst of places there has been beauty…and that beauty is a thing forever in our world."

"It's beautiful," he agreed, but the sense of wonder was fading, "for ghosts."

"You have it in you to make it more. Haros—" Callistra closed her mouth, at the same time looking very vexed with herself.

"Haros what?"

She snared his arm. "Haros has the utmost confidence in you. Would you like to see something else or shall we return to the club?"

"What choice do I have? They say you can never go home, right? That leaves me the Grey."

"I understand some of your pain, Jeremiah," Callistra breathed, her face close to his, "but I can't say that I regret the power that chose you for the role of king."

"Welcome back, your majesty."

Welcome back? Todtmann blinked, breaking whatever glamour Callistra's words and presence had cast upon him.

Welcome back?

He was back in the Wasteland, seated on the throne, with the dark, shapely witch before him and Haros Aguilana, who had been the one to greet him, standing on the steps of the dais. The gaunt Grey, a hat in one hand, was bent forward in a half bow. Once more, the deserted nightclub was filled with the dream denizens. Shadow couples danced and danced, whirling in false abandon. Other, more solid creatures sat at the tables while many more moved about.

In many respects, Jeremiah noted, it was almost a complete duplication of the earlier tableau he had witnessed. The Grey even stood or sat in the same places they had inhabited the first time. They were creatures of the imagination, but among themselves it was clear that few had more than a spark of imagination to call their own.

Jeremiah Todtmann found himself wondering if he could possibly change that. Could he make them more than what they were? That was within the realm of power of a king, wasn't it?

"You must be exhausted, your majesty." Haros remained on the steps, a position that forced him to look up to the human.

He was. Until now he had not noticed it. Jeremiah yawned and felt his eyes droop. Sleep sounded very delicious right now. Perhaps a good rest would enable him to mull over the change in his life with a bit more optimism. Jeremiah hoped it might. Still, there was one problem; he certainly had nowhere to sleep in the club. For that matter, the would-be monarch doubted he could have ever slept in the club even if a plush bed had been provided. Knowing one was literally surrounded by one's worst nightmares was not conducive to rest. Or maybe it was in a perverse sort of way, if he didn't mind falling asleep each time by way of fainting in fright first.

"Would you like to retire, my liege?" The polite ghoul took a step up, bringing him almost eye level with the seated figure.

Jeremiah would have liked to retire permanently, but that was evidently not to be. "Yes."

"Fine. Callistra, would you please show his highness to his quarters? I think, your majesty, that you will find this one very positive aspect of your rule."

"Are you ready, Jeremiah?" Callistra asked. "Ready?"

"To depart, of course."

"Oh…" He tried to clear his head, but it refused to be anything other than muddled. Sleep would be a pleasant thing. Jeremiah was faintly aware of having just slept only a few hours ago, at least by his reckoning, but time was a quicksilver thing in the realm of the

Grey. Based on what Haros and Callistra had said earlier, he had been missing from work for two days, maybe more. "I'm ready."

"Then let me show you to your room."

Around him, the Wasteland simply ceased to be.

Haros Aguilana remained where he was until the duo was gone, then ascended the rest of the way to the throne. The human would sleep for quite some time, in part due to a little persuasion from Haros himself. That would allow time for dealing with a few other matters.

The new king was coming along quite well, even barring the infernal avian's intrusion. Where he had come from this time, the stick man did not know. He had thought the raven no more after the incident with Thomas O'Ryan.

"Bad pennies will keep turning up," Haros whispered, not noticing the Greyish turn of his words. Everything else was secondary to seeing that Jeremiah Todtmann did exactly what he was supposed to do.

"I like him. Will he stay?"

The apelike shadow formed beside him. Haros eyed his counterpart. While no more stable in form than he had been the last time they had discussed kings, the other Grey was also no less stable. The presence of the human was already enough to cause balance for at least some of the shadow folk. "Of course he'll stay. He has no choice."

For the space of several breaths, a measurement of time used in purely arbitrary fashion by the non-breathing Grey, the squat, murky form contemplated the response. Crossing gate eyes flashed on and off. Then, in an apologetic manner, he returned, "I thought that there was always a choice. That was the way it was before. Always…"

A bit infuriated, and not for the first time, that no one— no one—in this place shared his genius, his creativity, Haros struck out at the throne. His hand and arm cut through the high backside of the chair without slowing. The throne dissipated even as his arm passed, momentarily shrouding the limb in a haze.

He stared pointedly at the apelike creature, whose own eyes were wide and still. "For Jeremiah Todtmann, my dear friend, there is no choice. None."

The other Grey remained wisely silent after that.

CHAPTER VII

Fit for a king, Callistra had said when they had first materialized here. Too exhausted to appreciate his surroundings then, Jeremiah woke up filled with awe. He had seen photographs of the interiors of both the castle of Mad Ludwig in Germany and the stately if a bit battle-wrought palace of the British royals, and found himself now thinking of the two as somewhat lacking in comparison to the opulence now surrounding him. Nowhere could he recall ever seeing so vast a chandelier, save perhaps in one of the Phantom of the Opera movies on late-night television. The ceiling from which it hung, not to mention the walls, was done in a majestic red with gold trim forming patterns throughout. Ceiling-high mirrors dotted the walls. There were dressers, a desk, bookcases, and a nightstand, all carved from a rose-colored wood.

The bed he lay in was large enough for a family of ten, including pets if they so desired. It was the softest bed imaginable and Jeremiah was tempted just to lie in it until his term as king was at an end. Like the rest of the furniture, the wood frame, including the part upon which hung the canopy overhead, was of the finest workmanship.

Jeremiah had worked with high six-figure mortgages involving elegant North Shore homes that were smaller and dingier than this one bedroom.

He stared skyward at the canopy, drinking in the illustrations that decorated it. There were scenes from Greek myth, centaurs, goatmen, and nubile ladies all at play. Other illustrations involved heroes in epic battle and images of love that might have been taken directly from the works of Shakespeare, which was probably the case. Some of the characters in the scenes looked unsettlingly familiar, but each time he focused on one of those, it appeared to shift. Despite being unable to confirm his suspicions, Todtmann was certain that at least a couple resembled him and more than a few resembled Callistra, Haros, and a few other faces he knew, both Grey and human.

By no means ready to confront Haros, the reluctant monarch let the images entertain him. The more he stared, the more lifelike they became. Jeremiah watched as the goatmen chased the nymphs through the field, both groups laughing in merriment. A hero who must have been Hercules but who definitely bore a resemblance to a certain movie star famous for such roles did battle with a savage lion. To the combatants' right, two lovers, the woman on a balcony and the man below her, shared words of worship. The woman's face kept changing, but now and then he was certain that she looked like Callistra.

Jeremiah's eyes slowly closed as he began imagining himself in the role of the man. It was not an unpleasant thought. He pictured poetic words flowing from his lips, a feat only possible in his dreams, of course, and the look on her face as she drank in his impassioned speech. Then, her lips caressing his ...

The kiss was passionate, lingering...and very, very real. So was the sudden weight atop him.

His eyes flew open, but where Jeremiah expected to see Callistra, perhaps drawn to him by his imagination, there instead hovered another beautiful visage. A haunting, well-known visage surrounded by bleached-blond hair.

"Hi, lover," the Marilyn murmured in that husky, arousing voice heard in movie after movie. She was without a single thread of clothing and so, Jeremiah discovered, was he. "Eeexcuse me!" he babbled, sliding her off of him. It was an effort that required both strength and will, to be sure, for even though this was one of the Grey and not the original, the flesh felt very soft, indeed.

"Where're you going, lover?" Her grip was tenacious. She nearly pulled him back into the bed, a place Jeremiah doubted he would have the wherewithal to escape from a second time. As much as it was Callistra who fascinated him, she was not his and might never be. The interest seemed there, but part of him wondered if he might not be better off taking what was now being offered instead of hoping for what might come later.

"I'm sorry, but you've made a mistake!" Where were his clothes? He could not even recall taking them off, especially his shorts.

"But all men want me, honey! Thomas did...so do you!" She turned on her side to better show him what she had to offer. It was monumental.

Thomas did... Haros had said earlier that she had been one of his predecessor's favorites. Not for the first time, Jeremiah wished he knew more about Thomas O'Ryan.

Was that why she had come to him now? Because of a different desire than she believed?

"You're right; I do want you." As she smiled—that Marilyn smile—and started to pull him back to her, he shook his head. Straining, Jeremiah won the freedom of his hand. "Not like that. I want to talk to you about a few things."

"Talk?" He truly had her puzzled. If she was a reflection of the ardor and obsession of her millions of fans, then it was not surprising that talk was not something she was normally asked for. How many fans saw only the legend, the screen presence? There was little of the true Marilyn Monroe before him; what Jeremiah faced was the Hollywood-created seductress.

Yet, she had known Thomas O'Ryan. She could tell him much about his predecessor.

"Yes, talk. You knew Thomas, right?"

The Marilyn drew patterns on the mattress. "Intimately."

He was yet again reminded of their nakedness. Jeremiah looked past the provocative offering in his bed, no easy feat, and tried to measure the distance from where he stood to the closets. There were races run that covered less mileage than he would have to in order to reach the wardrobe closet. *You'd think that here I could just wish for my clothes and then they'd materialize around me—*

Just like that, he was clothed. The suit was cleaned and pressed, yet. It was not exactly the suit he had worn earlier, either. There were changes in the design, small but essential ones, that turned his off-the-rack quick buy into something more appropriate for....well, for a king, he finally admitted.

"Yummm...I love a man who can wear a suit, but that can wait until later, sugar."

"I'd prefer you wore something, too."

"How's this?" She was now wearing material, but Jeremiah would have been hard-pressed to call it clothes. That term usually indicated the material covered parts of the body. This did not.

"How about a dress?"

The Marilyn pouted, those full, scarlet lips making him glad he was now clothed. "Party pooper."

This time, she did as he requested, sort of. Todtmann could not recall which movie the original Marilyn Monroe had worn this particular red dress in, but it looked very familiar. Molded to accent every generous curve to its utmost and with a front that plunged to stunning depths, it did little to diminish her sensuality. "Is that better?"

A nod was the best he could do. Jeremiah walked around to the other side of the vast bed, using the time to regroup. The Marilyn rolled over, somehow turning the simple movement into another seduction. He kept reminding himself that this was not the original Marilyn Monroe; this was one of the shadow folk, one of the Grey, who only wore the form because the dreams and memories of humans forced the creature to do so.

Knowing that made it no easier. He doubted it ever would. "Tell me about Thomas."

"I'd rather talk about us, lover." The neckline threatened him again.

"Tell me about Thomas." He folded his arms and tried to be commanding.

"Oh, very well." The Marilyn rolled onto her back. "Thomas wasn't so formal, that's for sure. He knew what he wanted and what he wanted was me." She giggled. "He liked to read me poetry and he had a great sense of humor." Her smile grew coy. "He had lots of great qualities."

The redness was creeping up his face, Jeremiah was certain of that. "That's not what I meant. What was he like as king? What did he do?"

"I just told you, sugar. Can I take this off now?"

"No!" When she still remained clothed after several seconds, he breathed a sigh of relief and said, "But that can't be all he did. What about his duties?"

"He traveled a lot. We went to Paris, Hong Kong, Rio." She slowly licked her lips. "Thomas liked adventure."

He was still getting nowhere. "How did he govern? How did he rule?"

For the first time, the Marilyn broke away from her expected role. Her eyes moistened a little. Whether a practiced affectation or not, it was effective. "Thomas kept us stable. Thomas tried to give us pleasure. Better than Martine or Chin Ho. They simply went to pieces."

"Those names. Tell me about them?"

The blond bombshell giggled again. "What's in a name? A king by any name would still taste as sweet!" She stretched, raising the hemline of her dress to even more dangerous heights. Jeremiah turned his gaze away. "Enough chitchat, lover!"

Still keeping his eyes averted, the reluctant monarch was once more forced to sort through his thoughts. To a certain extent, the Marilyn looked and talked like a true human, but it was clear now that there were other limitations she suffered that Grey like Callistra and Haros did not. The other two might more often talk in muddled cliché and rhyme, but they could talk about most subjects. The Marilyn could only be the Marilyn of the movies. Take her too far from her role as filmland seductress, a role created more by her still-avid fans, and she faltered.

Still, there were some things every Grey seemed to know. If he was going to get only small talk concerning Thomas O'Ryan and the earlier kings, then it was time to try asking about the one subject that was certain to get a reaction from her. "Did Thomas ever meet the raven?"

Her eyes wide in stage fright, she rolled back into a sitting position. "Don't frighten me with talk like that, sugar! Talk of ravens is for the birds, not us!"

Evidently she did talk in cliché. Unwilling to give in just yet, Jeremiah repeated his question, then added, "Did the raven have anything to do with his accident?"

"I —"

"Tell me!" The force of his words stunned him almost as much as it did the Grey, but even at his most shocked, Jeremiah could not have reacted as she did. The Marilyn quite literally wavered, momentarily becoming one of those blurred forms that old and portable television sets transmit when their antennae are twisted the wrong direction. Todtmann blanched and stepped back.

She reshaped a moment later, looking none the worse for her ordeal. Todtmann supposed that Grey did not feel pain when they altered form, but just seeing it happen had almost been too much for his stomach.

"Thomas got a bird's-eye view of the situation," she whispered, making even that ominous and enigmatic statement sexy. "He saw the light, but only just in time, hon. The black bird almost had him but Thomas had a leap of faith." She raised one perfect, manicured hand high, then let it drop like a stone. As her palm struck the bed, Jeremiah Todtmann's insides quivered.

"The raven killed him?" Every time he thought that being king of the Grey could not be any worse, some new dimension was added.

The Marilyn shook her head. "Thomas did it himself. It was the only way, he said. The wolves were at the gate, sugar, and the bird was tapping, not so gently tapping, on the true world's chamber door."

"What does that mean?"

"He wants one life to live. Flesh and blood. The raven dreams the impossible dream, lover, but maybe for him it isn't, hmmm?" She leaned back, visibly becoming the temptress again.

To dream the impossible dream.... For the Grey that meant living as humans lived. He had heard Callistra use the phrase, but to think that the raven desired the same thing was horrific. What could the raven do if unleashed upon the true world? Jeremiah could not, in truth, blame his bedroom companion for wanting to put an end to the conversation; the bird's desires were not something he himself wanted to ponder.

The Marilyn stretched again. "I've played your game, honey, now how about playing mine?"

"I'm...sorry...believe me, I am...but I'd like to be alone right now. Thanks...thank you, anyway." Jeremiah Todtmann hated sounding like a tongue-tied teenager, but just how did one properly reject such an offer from a Marilyn Monroe look-alike? Even knowing what the stunning form actually hid made it no less painful. What made it worse was that he was also feeling guilty about having any desire for her at all; if anyone had a hold on his heart it was Callistra.

A horrible notion rocked him. Was Callistra close to him because she, too, only desired the chance to be real?

"Do you really mean that?" The Grey rose, her glamorous features twisted into a combination of puzzlement and disappointment.

"Unless you have something to add about the ra—"

"Nothing," she insisted. Then, with arms that almost seemed to stretch to suit her needs, the Marilyn caught him in an unbreakable hug and pulled his face to hers. Her kiss was not the kiss of the true Marilyn Monroe, but, again, that of the silver screen persona, the culmination of all her roles and her fans' interpretation of those roles.

Which is to say, it took his breath away and left him a dazed, moonstruck fool.

The blond bombshell released him and breathed into his ear, "Thomas never liked a shy woman, but to each his own, I suppose. At least I hope you'll think of me now and then, Jeremiah Todtmann. That's what counts in the end, right, lover?"

He was still trying to untie his tongue when she vanished in that abrupt manner the Grey seemed to enjoy.

The recalcitrant monarch gradually found the wherewithal to rerun the short and typically muddled conversation in his head in the hopes that there might yet be something of value he had missed. Thomas O'Ryan had encountered the raven, probably more than once. Those confrontations had eventually led Thomas, carefree soul, if the Marilyn's words were true, to sacrifice his life in order to prevent the awful avian from achieving his goal. If the raven escaped to the waking world, there would be hell to pay.

But Thomas was king.... That appeared not to have staved off the black bird's advances. It also appeared not to have helped the other man in the least. Jeremiah tugged at the collar of his shirt.

From what little he had picked up on his predecessor, the man had not been cowardly. Could he say the same?

I've either got to find some way out of this or I have to learn to protect myself! Jeremiah the Bold did not suit him as a name, especially if carved on his tombstone. What had O'Ryan been thinking when he had chosen him to be his successor? What had he seen in one Jeremiah Todtmann, mortgage man unextraordinaire?

"I could always try to make the bird a deal on a good rate on his nest," he muttered, trying to lighten his mood. The joke fell flat, much the way Thomas O'Ryan had ended up.

There was no way back. Callistra and the visit to the office had made that ever so clear. That meant he had to discover a way to defend himself. He had to become the avenger of O'Ryan, the masterful monarch of the Grey, a champion who could rally his subjects against the winged terror.

He had to become, quite frankly, someone other than Jeremiah Todtmann.

Well, if I'm king of the Grey, I should have some sort of wonderful powers, shouldn't I? That was the way it was in movies and books, but in real life, monarchs were these days more likely to be powerless figureheads and not commanding rulers with great forces at their beck and call. He'd been able to clothe himself, thankfully, but did he have any other skill other than that? There was his ability to go wherever he desired just by thinking of that place, but as inviting as flight was, Jeremiah doubted he could run forever.

"Only one way to find out, I suppose." Life had been so much simpler when all he had really had to worry about was missing trains and facing the wrath of Morgenstrom. Those were the days.

One should start small, that was how the saying went, and if there was one place where sayings held sway, it was the realm of the shadow folk. The novice monarch tried to recall some of the movies and books he had read over the years. There were plenty of tales involving kings and magic; surely he could finally get some use out of those stories. Jeremiah was aware that while he was not totally unimaginative, his resourcefulness had grown stunted after years of little use.

I could try the light saber trick... His lavish apartment was sorely lacking in light sabers, however, and so he focused instead on a small statuette perched atop one of the chests. Jeremiah stretched out a hand and summoned the sculpture to him using only his thoughts.

It refused to come. He tried again, putting much urgency into the demand. *Come to me, damnit! This is my life we're dealing with now!*

The statuette remained indifferent to his pleas.

Please?

The statuette was steadfast.

Jeremiah Todtmann was dead. If he could not even summon a small figurine to him, what sort of defense could he devise against something as old, wily, and mobile as the raven?

The role of king was very limited. Much too limited for his tastes. He was beginning to see that he was a figurehead. No, that was wrong; not a figurehead, but not a leader, either. His presence gave the Grey something they could not give themselves or else they would certainly not have wanted him.

Thomas kept us stable, the Marilyn had said. Was that where his greatest strength lay...in strengthening the stability of the dream folk? *But that's what the raven wants, isn't it?*

The grim Grey also wanted something from him, but could not simply snatch it from his tattered body. It was clear even to

Jeremiah Todtmann that the feathered horror could have taken him in the alley and, the more he thought about it, the office, too. His bedroom companion had said that the raven wanted to be real, truly real, but there was more to it than that. The bird was intent on...on...

His thoughts grew tangled again, causing his head to pound. He had to leave this place, get out and see something else, even if it was a murky world full of shadows, nightmares, and things that went bump in the night. Maybe, he thought, he might even find out more about his place in the scheme of things.

And maybe I'll still find out I'm asleep on the train and this is all just an indigestion nightmare. Not at all likely at this point, but the slim hope helped keep his much-abused sanity in line. He sighed and looked around for an exit.

It dawned on him then that he had never noticed a door during his initial scan. There was a good reason for that, the reason being, of course, that the designer had not seen fit to include one. Other than the occasional patches of wall blockaded by the furniture, his suite was lined with mirrors and little else. Very decorative and very tasteful, but useless as ways out of this elegant cell.

Then again...

He walked up to the nearest one and touched it. It was as solid as anything else he had encountered here, including the Marilyn. Jeremiah pressed hard, trying to force his hand through the mirror. Lewis Carroll evidently held no great influence here; the looking glass remained that. He tried three other mirrors with the same results.

"You're thinking like a human," he suddenly snapped at himself. A reasonable mistake, to be sure, but still a mistake. This was the world of dreams, of the imagination. This was the world of the

Grey. Todtmann was still trying to take everything at face value even though he had the means of escape already in his grasp. Summoning objects to him might be beyond his abilities, but not traveling.

"I want out of here!" Likely he didn't have to say it, but it felt better to do so.

The results were not, however, what Jeremiah had expected. He did not vanish from the suite and materialize in, say, the Wasteland. Instead, the walls, the ceiling, even the floor, rumbled in ominous fashion. The wall before him broke free of the ceiling and fell back like a domino, taking with it whatever bits of furniture had stood propped against it. The furniture might have been glued to the wall, so perfectly did they remain in place. Beyond the wall was the dim light of the Grey realm. There was no hallway, no immense palace, merely the light.

The rest of the suite continued to shake. Jeremiah heard the wall far to his left also break free. With it not only went the chest, but the closets...which, strangely, proved to have no depth. Only the furniture prevented the walls from looking completely flat.

It was when the wall to his far right began to break free that he considered the hazard posed by the ceiling. With a yelp most definitely unregal in tone, the would-be king darted for the relative if a bit nebulous safety of the nothingness beyond his suite. Running up the wall was a strange sensation, but Jeremiah only had to remind himself of the danger behind him to keep his feet moving. He jumped the last yard of wall and, to his relief, landed. It had occurred to him as he leapt that there might be no surface beyond.

He turned in time to see his earlier fear realized. With only one wall still supporting it, the ceiling swung down. The massive chandelier, entirely ignoring the accepted effects of either the sudden motion or the change in gravity, thrust toward the wall, a glittering battering ram. Jeremiah braced himself for not only that collision, but what would happen when the ceiling met the vast, canopied bed he had only been sleeping on a few minutes ago.

Ceiling and wall met without any resistance. From what little he could see from his angle, Todtmann was almost ready to swear that the chandelier and the furniture, including the bed, had simply melted away.

The remaining wall fell forward, obliterating the carpeted floor. The other three walls suddenly broke free of the floor and plummeted into the misty darkness below, entirely ignoring the fact that there had been some sort of surface under them just a moment prior. Jeremiah swallowed, leery now of his own footing. He could see no difference between the areas where the walls had fallen and his own location, yet he had solid footing while they had suddenly had nothing. As if to verify that, the ceiling/wall/ floor also broke free, swinging momentarily from one side like a loose hinge, then plummeting into the same dark emptiness that by rights should not have existed.

The Grey's new lord found himself now alone in the middle of nowhere. Not a trace of his room remained. He even dared carefully edge toward where it had been, searching for the hole into which the pieces had just fallen. It did not surprise him as much as it once might have to discover that there was no hole. For him, there was nothing but solid surface wherever he put his foot.

I must be mad. I can't think of any other reason why I find this at all acceptable. This alone should be enough to drive me over the edge. Maybe I've always been insane, though, and just finally entered a new stage.

Jeremiah was still debating his sanity when he realized that he was no longer alone.

The shadows were gathering. Not the deep, hungry shadows of the raven, but the flittering, ofttimes humanish shapes that inhabited Union Station and the Sears Tower. The first were tentative, almost frightened. He could sense that just by the way they moved. To them, Jeremiah Todtmann was something more than a king; he was their existence. Haros talked about that, but Jeremiah was aware that for the gaunt Grey, he was less a king and more a necessary means to some end. Haros and the raven had much more in common with one another than with these poor things.

More and more of them swarmed around him. They almost seemed to be begging for his touch, but when the would-be lord tried, they skittered away. It was as if they were as in the dark about what they wanted as he was.

Still, he could not help asking, "What do you want?"

His very words stirred them to frenzied activity. He repeated the question. That drew more of the shapes. A few bore remote resemblance to things he recognized. One looked a bit like a woman in a long dress. Another bore similarities to the outline of a dog. He thought a couple had wings.

The one that vaguely resembled a dog moved within reach. Not knowing how else to react, Jeremiah leaned over and stretched out his hand the way he would to a collie or shepherd. To his delight and relief, the latter because he knew from his experience in the flooded basement of the Sears Tower that the Grey might bite the hand that leads them, the canine shape moved closer.

It was definitely a dog or wolf of sorts. Up close, the shape was a bit more distinct. Jeremiah liked dogs; dogs were man's best friend while cats just made him sneeze. Wolves were interesting, too. He wondered what it would be like having a pet wolf.

A cold nose rubbed against his palm. He almost pulled his hand away but thought better of it. Squinting, Jeremiah was now able to say without much doubt that here was a wolf. A silver-gray one at that. Majestic, intelligent, loyal...the traits just seemed to make themselves known to him.

The wolf looked up and wagged its tail.

There and then Jeremiah Todtmann understood why the shadows flocked around him so. He had made the wolf. His tastes, his choices. There had been no trick of the light; the animal before him had been nothing but a vague shape before his interaction with it.

Thomas gave us stability. That was an understatement. Haros had hinted to him what the king was capable of doing, but Jeremiah had not really understood until now. He could literally change them, especially those with no real form to call their own. Given time, he might even be able to affect Haros or the raven.

Affect Haros or the raven! For Jeremiah, the pieces of the puzzle were beginning to come together. Was it possible they worked to manipulate him now in part because when he grew into his powers enough, even they would not be safe? If they allowed him to progress too far without their influence, what might happen? What had happened to his predecessors?

The wolf was licking his palm. There was pure pleasure in those eyes. Any stability, even in the form of a simple animal, brought pleasure to the Grey. With so many minds in the true world affecting them, he realized that they were almost constantly forced to shift. Small wonder they ended up often being simply flittering shadows. Too many minds meant no one shape dominating. Only when enough folk dreamed or believed in the same thing, like the Loch Ness Monster or Marilyn Monroe, did they keep one form. It must have been easier in the earlier days, when people had less images assaulting them. The Grey had been elves, dwarfs, ghosts, and dragons. Now they suffered more minds, minds that were filled with information and image overload. Imagination might be a rare commodity in the present, but that was more than made up by the choice of stimuli a person had. Movies, books, games, news …

The Grey must feel torn apart most of the time.

"Hello."

The wolf bounded to Jeremiah's side and snarled at the newcomer. It was the apelike thing from the Wasteland.

"Haros…I think…is looking for you."

Jeremiah was in no hurry to rejoin the cadaverous Grey just yet and so tried to change the subject. "Who are you?"

The red eyes flashed on and off. After some hesitation, the creature replied, "I'm not Horatio."

"Do you have a name?"

"I…don't think so." The eyes performed Morse code patterns. "Could I…have one?"

Could you have one? "A name? You want me to give you a name?"

"You are the only one."

Jeremiah could not hold back a brief smile. One of his tasks was supposed to be to name them? "What sort of name would you like?"

The blazing orbs flashed. Jeremiah could see that his new companion was seriously trying to consider the matter. It looked to be a struggle, too. Was this what the Marilyn had said about stability? Was his presence that necessary to the Grey after all?

"Any name," the apelike Grey finally uttered. The eyes dimmed.

Any name...*He wants one that bad. I could call him Morgenstrom and he wouldn't care.* That was one appellation, though, that Todtmann would not have wished on anybody.

Having lived his entire life in the Chicago area, Jeremiah Todtmann had been to both the Lincoln Park Zoological Gardens and the Brookfield Zoo more than once during his childhood. The Grey's shape stirred memories of the ape houses and some of the magnificent beasts that young Jeremiah had seen. What was that one that had fascinated him so? It had a German name. He recalled that the animal had died several years back. What was he called...

"Otto?"

"Is that my name?" The orbs flickered to new life.

"Uhhh...do you want that to be your name?" Maybe there was a better one. Otto was not quite what Jeremiah would have chosen, given the chance to think things through.

"Otto!" the Grey roared. The other shadows, including the wolf, scattered into the mists. "Otto!"

"If you don't like it—"

The apelike shade moved closer. His form was just a bit more distinct. It was not surprising to Jeremiah Todtmann that the simian characteristics were stronger than before. "My name is Otto."

"You like it, then." To each their own, it seemed.

"Yes." The newly christened Otto tilted his head. "But Haros is looking for you."

Haros. Jeremiah was not particularly interested in seeing that particular Grey now, but sooner or later there would be no choice. "Doesn't Haros know where I am?"

"Not always."

Now that was something he had not known. It had come to the point where Jeremiah had been thinking of the narrow Grey in terms of Santa Claus. *He sees you when you're sleeping; he knows when you're awake*...That was not the case after all. Haros was limited.

A change that went beyond appearance had come over his simian companion. Otto tilted his head the other way and added, "Haros would like to be perfect, but nobody's perfect. He tries... to do what he thinks is right, but the end does not...always justify the means."

"What does that mean?"

The eyes suddenly shifted to the right side of Otto's murky countenance. "Haros is coming."

"Haros?" He looked around but there was no sign of the other Grey.

"There is always a way out," the creature finished. He evaporated before Jeremiah could say anything else.

Then, there was Haros Aguilana standing before him. The switch was so closely timed that to the human eye it was as if Otto had become the stick man.

"Aaah, there you are! I hope you slept well, your majesty?"

"Yes." He chose not to mention his bedroom visitor.

"Excellent!" The smile was there, a smile that was a far cry from the one the Marilyn/Grey had worn. "There is much more that we need to do! Much more that must be understood before you are truly at home in your position!"

At this point, the unwilling monarch doubted he would ever be "truly at home" in the role chosen for him, especially not with Haros Aguilana acting as his adviser and the raven out to continue something that had begun with Thomas O'Ryan or perhaps an even earlier predecessor. "Where are we going this time?"

"Why, to a ball game, I think."

They vanished before Jeremiah even had time to be perplexed.

Callistra sat at a table in the corner of the Wasteland, sipping the memory of an expensive Chablis that someone had first sipped years ago. It was as tasteless as everything else that was served here, at least to her. If she had been real, she knew, the Chablis would have been heavenly; instead, it simply reminded her of the chasm between herself and Jeremiah Todtmann.

"Hello, Callistra."

She tore her gaze from the dancers, among whom she had been picturing the new king and herself, and turned to the source of the voice. It was the apish thing that kept company with Haros on occasion. He sat across from her, the blinking lights he saw were almost keeping time with the music. There was something different about her new companion, but at the moment she could not stir herself to decipher just what that difference was.

"What do you want? Haros isn't here."

"Haros is with the man who would not be king."

"I know." She took another sip, ready to dismiss the other if this was the extent of his conversation. Conversation had never been his strongpoint, but then, none of the other kings had ever looked at him long enough. He had become, for most, something of a pet. No more. Not like Callistra. She had been given a form that the kings, for the most part, found appealing.

*And I, too, was thought of as a pet....*At least she was not like the Marilyn, who was so locked into her role she knew nothing else. At least Callistra could pretend to be someone unique, someone almost human.

"I worry about Haros," her table mate declared.

"Do you? He has everything under control." She was a little startled at the sarcasm in her voice. It was so human a thing she smiled.

"You are afraid for our king; you think Haros doesn't plan the honorable thing."

Callistra put her glass down and stared at her companion. His eyes had stopped alternating and were now matching her gaze.

"What are you saying?"

"What you are thinking. What I am fearing."

He was more distinct now, she noticed for the first time. There was less of the rough, unfinished quality about him. "You talked to him…Jeremiah."

The apelike Grey straightened with what could only be considered pride. "My name is Otto."

He's given out a name! Jeremiah has given out a name! To a Grey, a name was the most precious thing they could have. It, above all else, allowed one of the shadow folk to develop a core identity. A name gave a Grey a chance to become something more than the whims of waking and sleeping Mankind.

"He made a wolf, too. It was very happy."

"But Haros tried to keep him from discovering that! A little knowledge is a dangerous thing!" It was for Jeremiah's best, the gaunt Grey had told her, and who knew better than Haros Aguilana? He had assured her that once it was time, he would reveal these skills to the king. It was all a matter of proper timing.

"Things happen. People change. Grey change more often. This thing is bigger than all of us, Callistra. Even Haros."

Around them, the dancers danced, the music played, and the other Grey pretended lives, but Callistra no longer even noticed them. "Why are you here?"

The eyes alternated once or twice, then focused on her again. "Why are any of us here? I like him, Callistra. I like our new king."

She leaned back, still staring at her companion and the startling changes already wrought on him by Jeremiah's brief contact. "So do I, Otto. So do I."

"I like Haros, too."

"I'm sure you do."

Otto nodded. "I wanted you to know." He faded away without warning.

Callistra took her drink in her hands but did not sip. In what was very human behavior, especially because she did not realize that it was, she wondered, What was that all about?

Then Callistra wondered if she really wanted to know.

CHAPTER VIII

Among the baseball stadiums of the world, Wrigley Field was the unchallenged grandfather of them all. It was not quite the eldest, but there was a sense of tradition inherent in Wrigley that no other stadium could match. Harkening back to the early part of the twentieth century, it was a landmark. From the old-fashioned, hand-changed scoreboard to the ivy-covered outfield walls where more than one ball had been lost during a game, the venerable stadium was a symbol of what baseball was meant to be.

Jeremiah Todtmann had only been to Wrigley Field once or twice in his life, but he had watched thousands of games on television. The Chicago Cubs still played here, a team with a history more venerable than the legendary field they played on. While there were times when the team did play like it was over a hundred years old, both club and stadium had etched themselves a place in the hearts of Chicago...with perhaps the exception of the South Side, where the city rivals, the White Sox, played. Chicago, however, was a big city and so it supported both teams, but Jeremiah's first loyalty was always to the Cubs.

The season was over though and while most folk, Todtmann included, were waiting for next year, some players, evidently, had decided to continue the great game. There was, however, something unique about the game Haros had brought him to this day.

Tinkers, Evers, and Chance were playing their old positions in the infield. Hack Wilson was up to bat, with Rogers Hornsby on deck. Gabby Hartnett was catching. In the outfield, Ernie Banks was waiting, a smile on his face. Ryne Sandberg was on first and leaning toward second. Charlie Root was pitching. Andre Dawson was leaning out of the dugout and Cap Anson was stalking back and forth inside like an angry bull.

There were other players. Some Jeremiah recognized, some he did not, despite his avid interest in the team and its history. Many of them were or would be Hall of Famers. Most of them were also dead.

Around them, the crowds silently roared. Jeremiah tried to focus on individuals but found that impossible. The crowds at Wrigley Field were one massive memory, one ghost formed of millions of bits of the past. They were an important but secondary part of the game.

Haros disturbed his thoughts by suddenly leaning over his shoulder. The Grey had insisted on sitting behind him so that Jeremiah could enjoy the unusual game. "They play every day, your majesty. That's the way baseball was meant to be played, isn't it? You could come here whenever you like."

Hack Wilson smashed a screaming liner into the bleachers. The shadow crowd rose to its feet. Jeremiah fought back the temptation to join them. It was a thrill to see the greatest players of the Cubs compete with one another, even if they were Grey-wrought copies.

The legends of baseball were meant to be bigger than life and now they were.

Yet, something that had been eating at him since they had first materialized here finally demanded to be heard. He turned away as Rogers Hornsby came to the plate and Charlie Root became Fergie Jenkins. "I thought I was here to learn more about what it means to be king of the Grey."

The stick man smiled and materialized next to him. "And you are. Do you know what is really happening in this stadium? You are stirring the memories to renewed life. The games are ever played strongest when the king is there. It's the same wherever you go. Be it as recent as Wrigley Field or as ancient as the Valley of Kings in Egypt, you stir the memories by walking among them...and by doing so, you stir the memories anew in Mankind."

"I what?"

"If I may show you a less distracting example?"

There was not one true Cub fan who would not have wanted to follow this game to the end, but Jeremiah knew that there would be other contests and right now he needed to hear more about what his host had just said. The idea of being king still did not set well with him, but if there was no other choice..."Show me."

They vanished just as Hornsby began his swing—

—And reappeared as a man in armor who looked like a soldier from an old Hercules movie thrust a short sword through an opponent. All around them, a pitched battle was taking place. No one side seemed to be moving forward; they simply fought where they stood, man after man dropping.

"The Trojan War," Haros Aguilana announced as a dying warrior fell through him.

This was a less distracting example? His wits finally returning, Jeremiah asked, "The real war?"

"A bit of both. The war of memory and legend."

Looking around, Todtmann saw the city. It was little more than a high wall from this angle and the image of glory was dimmed some by the true ruins he could see through the wall. It was much like the scene of Chicago that he had shared with Callistra.

There was a surge in the fighting, as if both sides had received some new encouragement.

Haros leaned close again. "We are your imagination and we are your memories, I've said, and when the king walks, the latter wakes. That, in turn, stirs the former."

"Then what happens? How does that affect people?"

"When memories awake, they touch the subconscious of Humanity. The memories of Troy stirred the imagination of some men and they wrote of that wondrous city and its fall. Other men dreamed of finding that city and did."

Jeremiah's brow furrowed. "What you're saying is that I have some affect on the way the real world thinks …"

"History has always been guided by dreams and imagination. Mankind has always been guided by history." The ghoulish Grey summoned one of his cigarettes and took a puff on it. "And the king may sometimes guide their dreams and imagination."

I'd be able to influence the world? Both worlds? It was daunting enough to think of trying to cope with the Grey, but now Haros was telling him that his actions would touch his own world. Jeremiah was so dizzied by the prospect he failed to even notice the spear that passed through him.

"A truly daunting task for anyone, my lord."

The Grey's comment was possibly the greatest understatement in history, Jeremiah noted when he was at last able to think somewhat clearly. *I'd have the most influence that any man alive has ever had!*

Haros Aguilana, looking gravely concerned, took hold of him just before his legs gave out. "Careful, your majesty!"

Jeremiah managed to straighten. "You don't mean what you said, do you?"

"I am afraid I do. It's all too true." The chalky features twisted into a grimace.

"True…" Each time Jeremiah thought that he had overcome the fantastic obstacles set before him, another one, larger than its predecessors, reared its ugly head.

"I think it might be good if we returned to the club, don't you think?"

The now very reluctant monarch nodded his agreement.

"Good," was all Haros said before the scene around them once more became the interior of the Wasteland.

The throne was there and Jeremiah, who had been standing, was now sitting. It was almost disconcerting enough to make him briefly forget what had just been revealed to him. Almost but not quite. It is very difficult to forget that one has just been informed that one has the power to influence, even in a limited way, the minds of every man, woman, child, and politicians all over the world.

Haros dismissed his cigarette, then snapped his fingers. A light, almost nonexistent shadow passed across Todtmann's hand, leaving in its wake a small glass of dark brown liquid. Jeremiah hoped it was something much stronger than whiskey.

Callistra stood before him, forming in that abrupt way the Grey tended to, and curtsied. Like Haros earlier, she took a position midway up the dais, forcing her to look up into his eyes. Jeremiah was thrilled to see her.

Positioned as he was beside his monarch, Haros Aguilana's widening smile went unnoticed by the novice king.

"Callistra, would you be so kind as to take his majesty to some quiet, pleasant place and see to his needs?"

"Yes, Haros."

Jeremiah took her proffered hand, smiling more in relief now than pleasure. Anywhere where he would not have to think too hard about what he had just learned would have suited him fine. Being there in the company of the tall, dark enchantress instead of the skeletal, smiling Haros suited him even more.

In less than the blink of an eye, he and Callistra were elsewhere again. It was almost becoming routine. Jeremiah took in his surroundings and was tempted to ask her to find some new location, for she had chosen to return him to the vast bedroom that at last recollection had fallen into nothing. Now here it was again, whole once more, but for all he knew it was still falling or might fall again at any moment.

She led him to a chair. "I know it's all so difficult to take in, Jeremiah, but you can't make an omelette without breaking a few eggs. Haros is trying to show you everything as quickly as he can without showing you too much at once."

"The only thing I want to see is a way out of this." "But there is—"

"There is no way. I know that. You said that and by this point I think I can at least believe you, if not Haros."

Callistra turned away in order to find a second chair. "I am always here for you, Jeremiah."

He paused in his contemplation of his misery to ponder that. "Why are you, Callistra?" A week ago, he would have never been so blunt, especially to a woman whose looks were virtually without comparison yet who seemed to find him of interest. It was ironic how a little thing like becoming king of a dream world could change a man so quickly. "Is it by choice or is it by function?"

Extravagantly long tresses flew as she turned back and stared at him. There was no anger, as he first feared, just simple regret. "I am not like her, Jeremiah."

He found himself trying to sink deeper into the chair. There was no need to define who her was. The words were out of his mouth before he could stop himself. "Nothing happened—"

"I know." She did not explain how she knew nor did he ask. "I was like her, but like Haros, I was given a name, something to fix upon. A name is worth more to us than gold is to your kind, Jeremiah. It is a key that opens a new door, a door that can lead a Grey to as close to life as it can come. You have a friend forever in Otto."

"You know about that, too?" How close was he watched? Did the proverbial Big Brother really exist here? Why not?

"I know because he came to me. The change is quick when a name is given. There is one who will never betray you."

"A king gave you your name?"

"Two kings, but the second thought he was giving me a new one. He wanted no memory of his predecessor to remain, but he did not understand that I was already Callistra and I would be as long as I could fight. I simply added the new name to the first, which bound me tighter to who I had become."

"You make it sound as if you've been around for centuries. I thought you were fairly recent."

"Time is relative."

Jeremiah shook his head. "I don't think I want you to try to explain that. Not now, anyway." What she had said, about namings, made him think of something else. "Callistra, who named Haros?"

"Haros has been for as long as I can remember."

Meaning that she did not know. Jeremiah slumped back in his chair, groaning. "Maybe I've watched too many late-night movies." A frustrated chuckle escaped him. "Hell, I live in one, though!"

Callistra stood by the other chair, her slim fingers stroking the back. "I'm sorry for what we've done to you, Jeremiah."

He looked at her, all levity dead. "I'm sorry I'm not what you wanted. Somewhere out there is someone who would've made a far better king than I can ever be. Somewhere there's someone who could face up to Haros and the raven and make himself a hero." The frustration grew. Jeremiah leaned forward, his hands spread almost in pleading. "Callistra, a few days ago I was nothing! I went to work, went home, slept, and started all over. I was happy! What kind of man is that for this? What did Thomas O'Ryan see in me that I still haven't seen? Why was I so special? Can you tell me that?"

"I can tell you," she responded after a lengthy pause, "but the truth hurts, Jeremiah. You won't like it."

At this point, he had no doubt about that. Still, it no longer seemed to matter. Feeling rather Greyish, he replied, "Hit me with your best shot."

Callistra winced, which made him feel worse. "Thomas chose you because he liked your name."

He was not sure he had heard right. "He liked my name? O'Ryan liked the name Jeremiah?"

"Not your first name; your last is your claim to fame." The hauntingly beautiful Grey grimaced the way Haros did when he fell into rhyme or cliché. It was one of the first times, if not the very first, that he had seen her react so. "Todtmann? It's German or something." Jeremiah was about seventh-generation American; he had no idea where his ancestors had come from or what the origins of the family name were.

"Thomas thought it was funny; he said it meant something like dead man in English."

Dead man? "You're...kidding." "No."

"Dead man..." Jeremiah chuckled again, this time with more than a touch of surrender in his voice. "Talk about living up to the family name..."

"Jeremiah, that was why Thomas chose you, but what's in a name? You're more than he could have imagined, much more."

It just continued to get more and more insane, the novice king thought. *Dead man. How appropriate.* "God, I wish I could go back!"

Again there was a lengthy pause. Then..."Jeremiah, there... there is a way."

"Don't play that game with me, Callistra." Yet, there was just enough of a spark left within him to make him listen.

"There is a way back." It was clear she did not relish telling him this. He thought he knew why or perhaps only hoped he did. "Haros wanted me to convince you otherwise, but..." She abandoned the chair that she had never gotten around to sitting in and stood before him. "I cannot do this to you

anymore, Jeremiah." One hand touched his cheek. "I could never do this to you again."

"Callistra—" Human or Grey, Jeremiah Todtmann was finally able to admit to himself just what the enchanting shadow meant to him. Now he wanted to tell her as well.

It might be that she knew what he was going to say, for the hand slid from his cheek to his mouth, cutting off his words. The pale woman continued on as if she had not seen the look in his eyes. "A way does exist. You must go back to your roots. You must go back to where you belong. You must go back home."

"Home?"

"The key to returning to the true world lies in returning to what you know and becoming part of it again. Your home is your strongest link to your old life. To live there, to remember, is the path you need to take."

Without realizing what he was doing, Jeremiah grabbed Callistra by her arms. He stood, still gripping her, and whispered, "Are you telling me the truth?"

"I will not lie to you now."

Her eyes were moist. He wanted to believe her, but after everything else, after all Haros had thrust upon him, it was hard to get up too much hope. The smiling ghoul had a habit of coming along and crushing those hopes before they even had time to take root. "What about...what about being king? What happens to that? Where does it go?"

"I do not know. Another should be chosen, but you are supposed to be involved in that choice. The spell of kingship may choose on its own as it once was supposed to do."

"Well, if I have any choice in the matter, I want it to go to someone more worthy. Someone who can cope with it. Me, I just want to go home."

He blinked, fully expecting the two of them to be in the living room of his unit. Instead, they still remained in the opulent suite Haros had designed for him. Callistra did not seem to notice the discrepancy; in fact, she did not seem to notice much more than Jeremiah himself. He temporarily put aside the puzzle of why they had not vanished and, with great trepidation and not a little expectation of the worst, asked, "Will you come with me?"

"I will guide you as best as I can; you need have no fear of that."

"That's not what I meant." Todtmann steeled himself for a second try. Women, Grey or otherwise, would forever be a daunting experience for him. "What I want is for you to come with me. Come back to my world."

"I can—" she began, then shut her mouth. After too lengthy a hesitation for Jeremiah's heart, the raven-tressed enchantress nodded. If the Grey were not capable of tears, then Callistra was performing an admirable imitation.

Jeremiah braced himself this time. "Then, I really want to go home now!"

Still nothing happened.

"Why haven't we moved?" "I...don't know."

The novice ruler tried twice more with just as fascinating a lack of results. He released Callistra and looked around the suite in the vague hope of finding some reason for their still being there. When he had wished to be away, the power of the kingship had tossed him into an alley of Chicago. When he had desired a bus stop, the same power had brought him to one. Why could it not do the same now?

Haros? Why not? Who else would have an interest in keeping him here? Jeremiah suggested this to his companion.

She did not like the thought, but she nodded in agreement at the plausibility of his notion. "I cannot deny that it would be something Haros would try. He does not watch you now, but there are methods…"

"Is there another way to get where we have to go?"

Callistra pondered. "There may be one, but it is slower and more dangerous, Jeremiah. We must walk among shadows and that way leads to ravens."

"There's no other way?" Of course not, he thought. It couldn't be easy!

Her response was what he expected. It was a jaunt through the shadow world or stay here and assume his royal duties.

"Jeremiah, the raven may not cease his work even if the kingship you shirk." A touch of color spread across her ivory cheeks. "I didn't mean—"

"I know." He thought he understood enough about Greyish speech to know that the rhymes were rarely by choice. Yet, her words still struck him like a well-thrust blade in the hands of Errol Flynn or Tyrone Power. Jeremiah Todtmann simply reminded himself that he was not Robin Hood, Zorro, or even the actors who had played them just as he had not been Bogart earlier. He was Jeremiah Todtmann, who was handier with a pen that, contrary to that particular cliché, was not mightier than the sword. Had it been, he might have been willing to stay and try to make something of the role.

No, that still would not do. Haros wanted a puppet; that was why he was so pleased with Jeremiah. Then, of course, there was always the raven and whatever he wanted, which seemed to just be Todtmann's sanity.

"Let's get out of here. I'll take my chances back in the real world."

She took his hand and without warning they were suddenly back in the misty, dimly lit region that was much of the realm of the Grey. Callistra did not pause, immediately pulling Jeremiah along in one particular direction. He was glad that she was leading; as far as he could see, which wasn't that far, the same nothing existed in every direction.

"How long will this take?" he whispered. Jeremiah was not certain he had to whisper; his surroundings just encouraged the action.

In a voice that was not a whisper, Callistra replied, "Longer than we would like."

A Greyish answer for a Greyish situation. He should have known better. Besides, time was relative, as she had mentioned earlier. What might seem hours might actually only be minutes. Of course, it might also be days.

He tried not to think about that aspect too much.

They had barely begun their journey when he noticed shapes flickering into and out of existence. At first Jeremiah thought they were shadow folk, but these shapes were more defined and more familiar. They were scenes he might have been a part of had he never been touched by the Grey and scenes he might yet be a part of again if he had his way. Callistra was bringing him back to the borderlands between Grey and reality.

That was not to say that there were not shadow folk, too. Jeremiah's mere presence drew them. Few ventured close enough to even give him some idea of their vague shapes, but he recognized one or two that had somewhat human shapes and a couple that definitely did not. Knowing what he could do for them, the reluctant king almost wanted to stop. Callistra, however, waved them away before the desire to help could take root. Todtmann watched the shadows vanish with a twinge of guilt. He consoled himself with the thought that the next king, a far better man than he, would do what was right for the Grey.

Jeremiah only wished he could be certain of that, but unless he chose the man himself, he would never know.

The world of Humanity, his world, he reminded himself, formed around the duo.

No one paid direct attention to them, of course, although one sandy-haired woman in a blue suit did glance their way for the blink of an eye. Jeremiah was still part of the Grey's realm, however, and so the woman moved on, likely thinking that she had been imagining the harried-looking couple who had appeared out of nowhere.

It was daylight for a change, but daylight surrendering to darkness. Another day lost to the domain of the Grey. Jeremiah had hope that it would be the last. "Why here?"

"Because of that."

He looked to where she was pointing and discovered the Jackson Street entrance to Union Station. "We're…taking the train?"

"It's the path least likely to be noticed by Haros and the others who matter. It's the path your mortal life knows best. We have to draw on your memories now, Jeremiah. We have to follow your path of life back to your own domain."

Todtmann ignored the last part. "You said 'Haros and the others.' There are others?"

She did not want to spend time talking, but evidently understood that Jeremiah would not be satisfied until she answered him. "The others, like myself, who followed Haros in his plan. He is the one to worry about. Come now. There will be a train leaving soon."

The surrealistic landscape of the Grey's realm continued to play some havoc with the city. While Jeremiah and Callistra struggled across a tilted, soft sidewalk over which the Sears Tower and neighboring giants leaned like hungry, striking serpents, the stream of commuters walked along at their normal paces, blind to the madness their minds were in part responsible for. Despite the troublesome footpath, however, the two still moved with much more swiftness and dexterity than those around them. Todtmann saw other shadows also darting in and around the hordes and now understood what it was like doing that.

He doubted that he would ever be able to complete the commute to work again without always trying to watch for vague figures maneuvering around him.

With some effort, they wound their way down the stairs, into the station, and toward the trains. Callistra did not have to ask which route led to Jeremiah's home. Not needed as a guide, the runaway king contented himself with keeping an eye out for any sign that either Haros Aguilana or the raven had discovered their escape. Of course, he had no idea what he would do if one or both of them had given pursuit, but like most people it made him feel better that he was at least able to keep watch.

Some of the shadows followed them toward the train. He tapped Callistra on the shoulder and pointed them out. She shook her head at his concern.

"They follow because you are you. You would know the dogs of war if they were at our heels. Even those of Haros."

"What will he do if he catches us?"

"Take you back; Haros does not want to hurt you. I was told to lie simply to keep you here. That was his desire. If you did not believe enough in the possibility of a way back, then so it would be. Your belief in escape had to be strong enough."

They reached the train. "So why can't I go back to my place now?"

"I still have no answer to that."

He hesitated before the steps, recalling what had happened with the bus. Callistra encouraged him forward, but Jeremiah could not help remembering the roaring goliath bearing down upon him. Jeremiah gingerly reached for the handrail and was surprised at the solid feel to it.

Callistra, at last understanding his fears, quickly explained, "The bus could have been real for you, if you had desired it to be. At the time, you had lost all such desire and so it passed through you. We can be anywhere humans are."

"What would've happened if the bus had been solid?"

She glanced away in guilt. "You would have simply found yourself on it, probably standing in the aisle."

He could have taken the bus, but his own, still-human perceptions had betrayed him…and so had she. "That's not exactly what you told me then."

"Then, I was simply obeying Haros and he did not want you leaving, of course. Even despite his orders, I almost told you the truth afterward. I can only say again that I'm sorry."

His briefly resurging anger faded the longer he looked at her. She could not help what she had been any more than Jeremiah could help be what he had been. More, even. "Forget it. We have a train to catch."

It was peculiar boarding the car. Jeremiah had never had such an easy time getting on, but once aboard, the fact that no one really saw him made it almost seem…well, normal. Ignoring one's fellow riders was almost standard among commuters the world over.

There were only a few open seats left, making Jeremiah wonder if they would have to stand. He had never seen a Grey and a human actually occupy the same space, except fleetingly. There was contact, sometimes, and now and then he was certain a shoulder or leg momentarily merged with one of the shadow folk, but Jeremiah now wondered if such was possible. If so, would it also apply to him?

A swarthy man of Hispanic descent prepared to sit down in an empty seat just before them. Callistra reached out with her free hand and, using a touch that Todtmann would have thought delicate, pushed against the man's back. Grunting, the man abruptly ceased what he was doing and moved on to another seat already in part occupied by a husky, blond youth.

"Sit," she whispered to Jeremiah. Still a bit mystified by what the shadowy enchantress had done, the hapless monarch slid into the empty seat. Callistra joined him.

"No one will sit here?"

"No one. This seat was once torn apart and unusable for a week."

Jeremiah studied it. Other than being typically uncomfortable, it was not in terrible condition. "Why will that stop them now?"

"Because that's the memory they'll see. We could occupy the same space as someone in the real world, but I thought you would prefer not to. It is not a comfortable thing."

"Was that why no one sat next to me on the trip in?"

Callistra gave him her most dazzling smile. "I wanted to give us some privacy."

"But I saw you walk past."

"Yes, you did," was the only answer she would give him on that subject.

The train began to rumble and shake as it stirred to waking. Jeremiah Todtmann, long used to the sensation, kept his mind on more important matters. Callistra's ability to keep the seat empty disturbed him, hinting, as it did, of even greater skills he might not be familiar with just yet. "Just how much can the Grey influence us? Just what hasn't Haros thought of telling me yet? What haven't you remembered?"

She took his hands in hers. "We can't influence your kind the way you are fearing, Jeremiah. Only men can influence men that way."

"Which is why Haros and the raven need me pliable." "Haros does not work that way."

"No?"

"No." She was not as adamant about that as she once might have been. "But the raven might. What else could he want?"

The train squealed and grunted, dragging itself from the lair it shared with the others of its kind. Jeremiah turned and stared out at the scratchy, emerald darkness beyond, thinking much over. As turned around as he was, his mind still functioned better than it had for the past several years. He had never been so alive before and he wanted now to stay that way...but in the true world. "You do believe that I can help you become real, don't you?"

She did not answer immediately, which made him turn to her. Callistra's gaze was on those shadows that were on the train. One would venture closer, but the moment her eyes fell upon it, the shadow would retreat. "That was what Haros first offered me. It was how he first drew me to his cause." Callistra bit her lower lip, a human action that surprised him. "I came to want more, though."

"Is it...just because I'm human?"

"I've seen many humans, Jeremiah. I liked what I saw in you. I say again that I think that Thomas made a better choice than he ever imagined."

Callistra leaned over and kissed him. Jeremiah surprised himself by kissing back.

"Am I real to you?" she asked, not for the first time. More than ever, his answer was, "Yes."

She blossomed. "Thank you." Her hand stroked his cheek. "I think you should rest."

He was about to tell her that he was not tired, but a yawn suddenly escaped him. Surprised, Jeremiah struggled briefly with consciousness, then slumped against the seat.

Callistra regarded him. Haros had lied to her when he had said that becoming close to the new king would give her the chance to become human. She knew more about what Haros planned now and what she knew was enough to convince her that the promise had been as transparent as...as her world. All she could do was aid Jeremiah in his desperate attempt to return to the home he had been so unjustly torn from. Let Haros and the bird fight over shadows. Jeremiah, whatever his faults, deserved better.

She kissed him lightly on the lips and smiled when his mouth curved upward. He had brought her as close to life as any of the human anchors had done. His belief in her had given her a stability that would outlast the next human chosen and the one after that. That was all she could ask for.

Well, perhaps not all, but Callistra would at least be able to watch and remember Jeremiah. She had that.

Sitting straight, the alluring Grey once more stared away the shadows, who had taken her interest in the human anchor as an opportunity to sneak closer. Once satisfied that they would remain distant, Callistra turned her attention to the windows, alternating between the two directions. She wanted to be ready, just in case. The first stop was still a few minutes away, but Callistra wanted to take no chances.

One never knew where a raven might pop up.

"They said it couldn't be done, my friends!" Haros shouted to an empty club. He raised the memory of a dusty shot glass and altered it to the memory of one filled with the finest whiskey it had ever contained. The gaunt shadow man leaned against the bar, a cigarette in his other hand. "But they never counted on Haros Aguilana!"

He swallowed the tasteless memory and threw away the glass, which faded almost the moment it was released.

A flutter of wings disturbed his reverie. The stick man turned to the darkness and bowed. "You are late for a very important date, my friend."

"Better late than never."

A piece of the darkness broke away and became the raven. The malevolent avian alighted onto a dusty, very real chair across from his adversary.

"You still wish to go through with this? You would not prefer to surrender?"

"Look before you leap," mocked the raven. "Don't count your kings before they're crowned."

Haros Aguilana summoned up his cane, the head of which he pointed toward the black bird. The head snarled and snapped at the winged Grey, who took no notice of it. "You are pathetic, my ebony-colored friend! Existing for so long and still speaking like one of those timid shades! It's no wonder you fail and fail."

"If at first you don't succeed, try, try again, scarecrow."

The raven fluttered his wings violently, causing Haros to start and the bird, in turn, to laugh. "I speak true, scarecrow; the mynah bird is you! We are Grey; throw the mask of humanity away!"

"We are a part of them!"

"Would that I could bite the hand that forms us."

Haros leaned on his cane. "You will fail this time as you failed with Thomas…and this time will be the last chance."

"Last chance for gas," the raven agreed, nodding his head in case his words did not make clear that agreement. His claws played at the chair. "But the reports of my failure have been greatly exaggerated."

"What does that mean?" Something in the bird's tone made the stick man stiffen.

"Never send to know for whom the bell tolls; it tolls for thee…"

The bird laughed and ran his claws over the back of the chair again. Only then did Haros Aguilana see the scars the raven's sinister talons were making in the wood, but by the time he was able to speak, the bird was no longer there. The mocking laugh lingered long after, though.

Haros stared at the ravaged chair, the chair that a Grey, that Grey, had actually damaged.

How long has he been able to do that? How real has he become? Is that what he has planned? "Impossible!"

Was it? The raven thought not and it seemed he was…living… proof.

"But I still have a king up my sleeve!" "Haros?"

A sense of dread, or the shadow of the emotion at least, engulfed the cadaverous Grey. He turned and saw that his apelike companion had appeared. That in itself was a thing of wonder; the others feared the raven too much to be this close to where he had perched even if the bird himself was already gone. "We will talk later, my friend. Time stands still for no Grey and I must—"

"The king is gone with the wind, Haros." With that statement, the other Grey faded away.

"Gone?" He stared into the emptiness for a moment, then his eyes narrowed and the slit of a mouth curled. "Callistra! Come here!"

She did not materialize, as he had feared. "Not gone with the wind, then, but gone with you."

Never send to know for whom the bell tolls...the raven had said. Now he understood what that pinioned plague meant. The black bird knew of his loss and how, combined with the bird's startling metamorphosis, it might mean the end of all Haros had planned.

Might. The raven suffered from overconfidence himself. He thought this plan meant all or nothing for Haros and that any deviation meant the black bird's victory. He was wrong, of course. Haros had contingencies plotted for almost every situation, including this one.

After all, as any Grey knew, one never put all one's eggs in one basket.

CHAPTER IX

"Wake, Jeremiah. We have arrived."

The slumbering king opened bleary eyes. "Arrived?"

Callistra leaned over him, a dark angel come to take him away to peace. Jeremiah Todtmann blinked, recalling only then where they were and where they had been going. When he had drifted off to sleep, he could not say. The last few moments before his unexpected slumber were a blur. He gave up trying to recall, figuring it was hardly worth his worrying. There was more than enough to worry about. "We're at the stop?"

"Yes. Come along. The train desires to leave." Without the slightest strain, she pulled him to his feet and began dragging him toward the end of the car. As Callistra reached the door leading to the ramps, it slid open. A man getting on the train passed by, but his action left the door open just long enough for the twosome. It was not the first time he had noticed such a coincidence when a Grey was around. He wondered if there was a reason for it; certainly the Grey seemed to be able to come and go as they pleased. They did not need doorways. Perhaps they were compelled to use them the same way they copied so much else from Mankind.

Of course, Callistra might have used the doorway for his sake. Jeremiah's collision with the bus had certainly turned him from the idea of going through walls and such. The very idea sent shivers through him.

Callistra was the first to exit the train. She released his hand and stepped back as he descended. "Be it ever so humble, there's no place like home."

At last getting his first good glimpse of the area, Todtmann would have agreed with the last part of the statement if not the first. There certainly was no place like home...although Chicago was close now.

For some reason, Jeremiah had continued to think of his hometown of Bartlett in the same quiet light he had left it in. In retrospect, it was a naïve thought. The world of the Grey extended to wherever people had been or were now.

Bartlett was a small but by no less sinister version of the city he had just left behind. The buildings were distorted, twisted, and the same wavering, fish-bowl effect blanketed the town. The bank in front of them was twice as tall as it should have been, but narrow in the center, as if someone had tried to squeeze it. The small row of buildings across the street were half-melted globs covered in shadow. As for the streets themselves, they sagged and turned like softening gum. To Jeremiah's eye, the cars that traversed them just barely stayed on the path. It was peculiar to think that to other people the streets were straight and even.

Among the commuters a few shadow folk darted. Some followed specific travelers with an eagerness that made them resemble puppies. *Puppies from hell, maybe.*

"We should not stay here too long. Your presence will draw others and we have no time for that."

"My car is here." Todtmann looked around. The morning of his last commute into the city, he had been fortunate enough to find a space near the station itself. At the time, Jeremiah had been unable to believe his luck. "At least, I left it here."

Left it here he had, but that was days before, he finally realized. In the place of the…the dark blue Dodge, he finally forced from his reluctant memory…that Jeremiah drove was a charcoal-gray Jeep. They had towed his car away, probably the same day he had vanished. Jeremiah hoped it would be safe until his return to reality.

"We do not need your automobile." Callistra took his hand, but this time not because of any sentiment. "This close, we are only a hop, skip, and a jump away. I would prefer another way, but beggars can't be choosers."

She was nervous…or at least as nervous as the Grey could be. *Every time she gets this way, she slips back into the clichés and rhymes.* It had taken him a long time to notice the tendency, but now some of the shifts made sense. It also gave him yet another method by which to read her. Even though Callistra insisted she was with him in all things, there were still secrets that she had not shared with him. Possibly that was the influence of Haros Aguilana or simply a part of being a Grey. He did not think that she was capable of betraying him; rather, Todtmann just assumed that Callistra did not deem it necessary to tell him everything. To be sure, most of her secrets were likely ones Jeremiah did not want to hear.

"Hold tight!"

Her warning barely came in time. Jeremiah had just tightened his grip on her hand when the world became a whirling blur. He caught glimpses of the town hall and the fire station, but as he focused on them, they became a row of shops and then a bank.

Then, the scene froze into stability again. The duo now stood in a parking lot by a food store, a location that Jeremiah recognized as roughly halfway from the station to his home.

"Faster than a speeding bullet," he finally managed. His stomach arrived a moment later, a bit put out at being left behind. "What did you do?"

"It would not be wise to simply appear in your home. There may be someone there; I cannot say. Certainly Haros had no reason to have someone watch, but by traveling this way, I can keep an eye out for any such sentinel."

He trusted her, yet something rang false in both her words and actions. She would not betray him, but Jeremiah was certain that some of what she did was unnecessary and hindered the two more than it helped. *Maybe she's just afraid of becoming real.* For some, achieving a dream could almost be a nightmare, but Callistra didn't strike him as being that sort. A trace of doubt resurfaced. *She wouldn't betray me…would she?*

He was going to find out soon enough. By this point, it was ridiculous to turn back.

"Hold tight again!"

This time the grocery store became a factory that became a strip mall that became the very familiar sight of a small development of farmlike condominiums, one of which belonged, at least a few days ago, to one Jeremiah Todtmann.

Then, they were standing in his living room.

"There's no place like home," Callistra whispered, repeating his earlier comment.

Home is the hangman, was Jeremiah's own thought. He had no idea where the unsettling phrase had sprung from, but its Greyish flavor did nothing to ease his tensions. That it made little sense only heightened its effect.

By even the most loose standards, Jeremiah would never have considered his home lavish. After his stay in the suite prepared by Haros, even run-down seemed too high a praise for his furnishings. The only thing Todtmann could think of in defense of his home was that, well, he was a bachelor. It was not that the couches or the dining room table were worn or tattered; it was just that in comparison to the opulence of that other place even the most extravagant Lake Shore penthouse resembled something closer to a country shack.

Like much in his life until the coming of the Grey, Jeremiah's home reflected the unremarkable style he had lived by for the nearly thirty years of his life.

"Is something amiss? Is something here out of place?"

"Only the last couple decades of my life." That would change once he returned to the world of the waking. If there was one good thing his excursion into the nightmare that was the Grey had brought about, it was his need to alter his life. There would be more from now on then just eating, sleeping, and Morgenstrom.

Callistra walked around the small domicile, drinking in every object with her eyes. She ran a hand across the one picture he had managed to hang and briefly gazed into the small kitchen where Todtmann microwaved his meals. Without his permission, the dark enchantress journeyed down the short hall to the two bedrooms. One Jeremiah used for work— there was always work to bring home—and also for his collection of books, which he noticed for the first time was threatening to take over the entire room. Callistra studied each shelf, a slight smile toying with her perfect features. The smile struck him as a little odd; it had a bittersweet cast to it.

"So much reading."

Before he could comment, she was out of that room and into his sparsely decorated bedroom. A bed, mirror-chest, and nightstand were all that filled the place. Like most of the other walls of his home, the walls here were all but devoid of decor. Only a small calendar marred the otherwise pristine sides of the bedroom.

"The other chamber first, I think. Your reading is the initial link." The grimace that he had seen so often on the deathly visage of Haros formed.

"My reading?"

"You are what you read…extensively so." She led him back into the workroom, briefly studying the desk as she entered. "You bury yourself in your work. That, too, would be a good start."

Jeremiah glanced at the contents of the room. "I still don't know what you want me to do."

"Touch your past and remember it."

Callistra was pensive and for no reason that he could think of. Was she really that nervous about joining him in the real world?

Could she join him? Had she lied about that? Jeremiah was beginning to wonder. He walked up to the nearest bookcase and ran his finger along one shelf of novels, still more interested in what Callistra might not have told him than in his escape. If she could not go back, then what—

He heard a rumbling. Turning his head, he saw that the doors of the room closet had begun to vibrate violently.

"Callistra! What's going—"

"Time to come out of the closet!" a voice merrily cried. A familiar, mocking laugh followed.

The closet doors blew open.

Jeremiah ducked, but no debris struck him. He looked at the closet and saw that while on one plane of reality the doors were a battered and broken ruin, on another level they were still whole. The peculiar double vision was confusing, but there was no time to wonder about it, for swooping out of the hole was the raven.

Seizing him, Callistra shouted, "Hurry, Jeremiah! Out!"

He started for the hallway, but she swung him around and, to his confusion and dismay, threw him toward the sole window in the workroom. Jeremiah only had time enough to pray that he understood what she was doing before his shoulder slammed against the glass pane

…And went through without even cracking the glass. The hapless Todtmann flew across the development's communal yard and nearly into the street. Unlike the wall, the ground he landed on was very real and very hard. Pain seized the reins and refused to give them up until Jeremiah managed to force himself to a sitting position. Even then, dizziness made the scene swim for several seconds.

Shaking his head, he looked back. A rainbow of light flooded his home and spilled out into the darkening sky. Still Callistra did not emerge. To his surprise, Jeremiah heard excited voices. Several people emerged from various doorways nearby and stared in the direction of his home.

They can't possibly see it…can they?

He had his answer a moment later when the raven came bursting through the window, showering the area with a glass rain and sending his neighbors stumbling back. Some of them pointed at the winged pariah.

But...It was impossible! Wasn't it? *The Grey can't do that, can they?*

One of them, at least, could and had.

The huge bird was almost upon him. The eyes flashed red, then white, then red again. Jeremiah scrambled back. "Get away from me!"

As if striking a wall it could not penetrate, the raven bounced backward, falling into the thin line of bushes that decorated the front of Jeremiah's building.

Did I do that? Jeremiah raised his hands to look at them, only to have the left one seized by a force so strong he was dragged along.

"Hurry! This is neither the time nor the place!" It was Callistra. Where she had come from, he could not say. She had not followed the black bird through the window, but then unlike the raven she lacked such violent substance.

His neighbors still clustered around the area, staring at the shattered pane and mumbling about the raven and what it had to do with Jeremiah, who most of them knew was missing. None of them took any notice of the fact that their missing neighbor was among them, being frantically pulled along by a beautiful, pale woman clad in garments both archaic and modern. A few shadows marked their passage, but they stayed far away, frightened, no doubt, by the presence of the raven.

Callistra had dragged him past two other buildings and now led him toward a small rise atop which existed only the very same train tracks that had so often taken him to and from the city. Beyond was a field that, as far as Jeremiah knew, was frequented mostly by traveling geese, field mice, a raccoon or two, and a family of beavers that had not gotten it into their heads that this was now a suburb and not the wide, wooded plains of old. What sort of aid, he wondered, did Callistra hope to find here? Hiding in the grass would certainly accomplish nothing. From his aerial viewpoint, the raven would have no trouble spotting them. "Where are we going? Why don't we just vanish?"

"Trust in me!" was all she said.

He was beginning to have his doubts again. After all, how did the raven know where to find them so quickly? True, he might have been watching all this time, but would not Callistra have been able to sense that?

As they neared the tracks, Jeremiah heard a long, mournful howl from the west. He pulled up short and struggled with his companion. "There's a train coming!"

"I know."

The single eye of the train was already visible. It was a commuter train heading back to the city. While not familiar with the complete schedule for this line, Todtmann was certain that no train heading east was due at this time. There it was, though, staring balefully and calling out its warning to anyone foolish enough to be playing by the tracks.

"Be ready...and hold my hand tight!"

Be ready? "We're going to jump on the train?" "Let me guide us!"

He glanced back and saw the growing shape of the raven as it darted between the two buildings they had passed. In mere seconds, he would be upon them. Jeremiah returned his gaze to the oncoming train, which was somehow much closer than he thought it should have been. The recalcitrant lord of the Grey recalled then that Callistra had said earlier that if he had known how, he could have joined those riding the bus. When the bus had met him, all Jeremiah would have needed to do was basically think himself aboard. Surely boarding the train would be no more difficult for someone in the realm of the Grey?

Would it?

Jeremiah braced himself. He would just let Callistra lead. She would get him safely aboard the...the ...

He stared in disbelief at the engine.

There was a reason, Jeremiah now knew, why the train's schedule coincided so well with their desperate needs. It had not simply happened along; it had been summoned. Summoned, no doubt, by Callistra.

Like Haros Aguilana's Rolls, it was a memory. A ghost train, as far as Jeremiah was concerned. Whether of one that regularly passed this way or one that had stopped carrying passengers years ago did not matter. The Grey could summon to life memories old and new for their purposes.

Facing the raven no longer seemed so unattractive a choice, but before Jeremiah could lodge his protest, Callistra, with the astonishing strength that her appearance ever belied, pulled him forward.

Jeremiah screamed as they jumped into the side of the train. Ghost, memory, or whatever, a train was a train and no one but a suicidal madman leapt into one. His scream did not stop until he realized the two of them had passed through its side.

Relief was a short-lived thing, for despite his assumptions, Jeremiah Todtmann continued to fall. He called out to Callistra, but no words escaped his mouth. Then, to his ever-increasing horror, she released her hold on his hand and pushed him ahead. The wretched expression on her face as she abandoned Jeremiah left him even more confused. It was the last image he saw before he went bursting out of the other side of the ghost train and into the field.

The ground was as hard as he expected, the tall but wilting plants offering little padding as Todtmann struck the earth. The earth always seemed real and oh-so-solid no matter where he was. Real and very solid. Even the marshy ghost of Chicago's far past had been real enough in its own way. Unable to stop himself, Jeremiah continued to roll through the field. He was certain that the raven was on his back, but there was no way to control his tumbling. If the sinister Grey wanted to take him now, the one consolation Jeremiah would have was that he would at least stop rolling.

The raven did not seize him, however. Jeremiah came to a disheveled halt among the tall reeds and, after allowing his mind to resettle, looked around to discover he was alone. The sky was empty of winged terrors. No shadows even crept through the field. A short distance away, he could hear sirens, but they were no doubt on their way to his home, where the astounding avian had laid waste to the last bastion of normalcy Jeremiah had had left.

It was several seconds before he finally deciphered just what had happened. The raven could have only followed the ghost train and Callistra. He had flown after it on the assumption that it held Jeremiah Todtmann as well as his Grey companion. She sacrificed herself for me? He was still not certain whether a Grey could perish, but the raven, at the very least, threatened her with capture and perhaps even pain.

Meanwhile, what was Jeremiah supposed to do? Sooner or later, the black bird would discover his error and be back this way for him, this time without the interference of Callistra. Jeremiah evidently had some power, as evinced by his last-second defense against the deadly Grey, but he had little doubt that both his power and his skill were at present no match. They probably never would be and even if by some miracle he was given time to become more skilled, the raven would be wary next time. He would allow his human prey no opportunity to utilize those powers.

The sirens sounded much closer now. His thoughts returned to what Callistra had brought him here for. In his home was his only chance of escape from this bizarre, preposterous world that coincided with the one of Humanity. Callistra could only have meant for him to escape while she led the raven on a merry chase.

But if I cross over to the real world, how will she get across? She had been able to touch him before his original crossing to the shadow realm; would she be able to join him even after he discarded the mantle of king—or rather anchor, as Jeremiah was beginning to understand—and became fully human once more? *It must be possible!*

Possible or not, first Callistra had to survive the black bird and Jeremiah had to find the path back. The latter meant that he had to return to his home, chaos or not.

He journeyed back to and over the railroad tracks, eyes ever flickering back and forth as he watched for either the raven or one of his marauding shadows. His thoughts battled with one another. He should be hiding, not coming out in the open. Callistra needed his help; if he cared for her, Jeremiah should have given chase, not remained behind like a frightened rabbit. Callistra had purposely left him behind so that he could thwart both the bird and Haros by crossing beyond their reaches once and for all; therefore, returning to his home was the proper choice.

The last was the one he adhered to, but the guilt continued to ferment within him. It was guilt fed not only by his failure to stand by Callistra, who had given up all else to aid him, but also by his inability to remain with the shadow folk and help them. Jeremiah tried to convince himself that his successor would be a much more appropriate candidate for the arduous task ahead, but the hints he had picked up concerning some of those who had come before him did not promise much. Thomas O'Ryan had sounded decent enough if a bit peculiar, but a few of the others had sounded petty and close-minded. Jeremiah had no doubt that at least one had probably been of a cruel nature. The spell did not seem to care about that; its choices sounded almost entirely random at times, not something influenced even by the anchors. Any influence by the kings had not seemed to have helped, else why would O'Ryan's choice of him have been allowed to happen?

Once I'm back, none of that will matter! Although he tried to convince himself of that over and over as he made his way back toward his home, Jeremiah Todtmann was well aware that the fears would remain with him even then. The fears and the guilt.

He was almost tempted to return to the field when he saw the crowd gathered before his building. Neighbors from all around had assembled and their numbers were further complemented by two squad cars, an ambulance, and two bright yellow trucks from the Bartlett Fire Department. Two police officers were taking statements while two others, followed closely behind by the paramedics, peered through the ruptured window. A few other people wandered about as if dazed. Among them—

They were neither short nor cute. They looked as if they had never built toys or lived in trees and baked cookies. Haros had talked of the Grey as they had been long ago, when men had dreamed of fairies and sprites. Some folk still did and that was why the two darting through the crowd still held the forms of elves.

The cold, pale figures were clad in dark, form-covering cloaks. The hoods of the cloak were thrown back, allowing Jeremiah a more-than-desired view of the long, delicate-yet-cruel visages and the prominent ears that almost made him think of aliens and five-year missions instead of magic rings and hairy-footed dwarfs. These two had a mission of their own and there was no doubt in his mind that said mission concerned finding him. It was doubtful that they served the raven, which meant that they either followed the will of Haros or represented a third group of Grey. The shadow folk were, after all, the products of Mankind's minds, minds that were able to produce conspiracy after conspiracy in the real world.

He found himself shivering again.

His home was cut off from him and with it his only escape from the realm of the Grey. Jeremiah backed around the side of the building nearest him and stared at the field without seeing it. The world faded a little as he turned his attention inward to consider his next move. Even if the power his role gave him enabled him to travel from one place to another with but a thought, there was no guaranteeing that the Grey would not find him. More important, Jeremiah had absolutely no idea where to go next. He had been so certain that his escape was imminent that now it was hard to think of having to go on.

"Hello, Jeremiah Todtmann."

Jeremiah jumped, his first assumption being that the elves had popped away from his home and surprised him here. It was not the elfin Grey, however, who faced him, but rather the apelike form of the shadow creature he had christened Otto. The quivering human slumped against the wall. "You've come to take me back?"

"You gave me a name."

He stared at the murky face but was unable to read any emotion that might have better explained the statement.

"I like you, Jeremiah Todtmann."

Aware that the two cloaked watchers might at any moment be upon him, Todtmann hesitantly asked, "Will you help me?"

"You gave me a name," Otto repeated, this time holding out one oversized paw.

Jeremiah hoped he was guessing right as he stretched forth his own hand. Otto looked capable of tearing off his arm without even noticing. The simian Grey took the human's much smaller hand and clutched it just tight enough so that Jeremiah could not change his mind. There was something akin to a smile in the midst of the vague features.

"I like Haros, too," Otto added when his grip was assured.

"Wait a minute!" Jeremiah shouted, cold certainty creeping over him. He had fallen into one of Haros Aguilana's traps after all!

Then, behind Otto, one of the elves formed. The apelike Grey's eyes flashed and his grip on the human loosened as he swiveled his head halfway around to gaze at the newcomer.

Jeremiah looked from one Grey to another and could only think, *I've got to get away from here!*

He did. Otto, the dark elf, and the field became the much-too-familiar interior of Everlasting Mortgage's Sears Tower office. This time, there was no one in sight. The lights were off and only the dim illumination of the shadow world allowed him to see.

Enough was certainly enough. *I have got to find another focus in life!* He had never realized how much his life had centered around work. It was going to get tedious if every time he fled from somewhere he reappeared in the office. Tedious and dangerous. Jeremiah considered it fortunate that none of the Grey were waiting for him here. Certainly both Haros and the raven were more than familiar with this place.

Thinking of that, the weary monarch returned to the question of where exactly to go now that his home was no longer safe. While it was within his power to travel anywhere, Jeremiah shuddered at the thought of wandering aimlessly around the world. He wanted someplace that would give him at least the semblance of security. Someplace where he could sit and think for a time.

It was several moments before Jeremiah Todtmann realized the answer was before his very eyes.

He had materialized next to his own cubicle, not a surprising thing since it was his second home. The direction he faced, however, allowed him to peer into another cubicle. Hector's. Hector, who was, in his own estimation, as good a friend as Jeremiah had. Why not go to his home? The Grey would never think to look for him there, would they? After all, the two men only knew each other from work. They never mingled much outside of work save an occasional ball game. Besides, Hector would be unable to see or hear him; Jeremiah would be less than a ghost. Since there would be no help for him, hopefully the Grey would not think it worth his while to go there. Not much to hope for, but...

It would give him a place to rest, however, and that was the most important thing. Jeremiah was certain that if he just had some time to plan, he would be able to think of something more than simply running and running and running...

One problem and one problem alone remained before he could transport himself to Hector's; he had no idea where his friend lived. In all the time the two had worked together, the subject of where the other man lived had come up again and again, but never had he really listened. Regret for the lapse urging him on, Jeremiah scanned the top of Hector's desk. Unfortunately, there were no bits of personal correspondence. Of course it could not have been that easy, but Jeremiah had hoped. Just once, it would have been nice to have things go his way.

He could have probably walked through the divider wall, but the notion still unnerved him even after having crossed through solid objects more than once. There was always the nagging fear that he would become stuck. Jeremiah instead hurried around to the other side and began looking over the layout of his coworker's domicile. Much too clean. He needed something, some personal note or envelope. Hector lived in some suburb south of him; that was all he knew.

Trying to open the desk drawers proved painfully futile. There was some trick to working with real objects. The raven could do it and the raven was only a shadow. He was a very solid shadow, but still only a shadow, whereas Jeremiah was human. Not much of one, but nonetheless still falling into the category. If anyone in the realm of the Grey should have been able to open the drawers, it should have been him.

He was almost certain that the raven was breathing, rather figuratively, down the back of his neck. Jeremiah straightened. There had to be something he could do. There had to be some way he could make the methods of the Grey work for him. *Maybe there's something I've forgotten. Maybe if I can remember everything Haros showed me, I'll—*

Remembrance. That was it! Memory was the key. No, not memory, but *memories!* What had Haros said at Wrigley Field or the ruins of Troy? The human anchor stirred the memories of the past to new life! That was not quite what the cadaverous Grey had said, but it was close enough. As chosen king for the shadow folk, he had it in his power to summon up memories of what had been.

Why not memories of Hector? Why not trace his daily routine from the time his workday was ended? Jeremiah grew excited. He did not even have to start at the office. Hector was a commuter the same as him; the other man just did not take the same train.

That would mean going back to Union Station, though. His growing enthusiasm died a swift, fiery death. If he returned to the train station, either Haros or the black plague on wings would catch him. Todtmann was certain of that.

If only there was a phone book, but then, how could I turn the pages? I can't even let my fingers do the walking! It was all very frustrating. When he had been shifting toward the dream realm, he had at least had the strength to push open the glass doors by the receptionist. Now, he doubted he had the strength and substance to pick up the telephone receiver, much less push the doors open even a bit of the way. It was possible, he knew, but how was a mystery he had no time to study.

"Telephone?" he blurted. The lone word was a shout that fortunately no one else would have heard even if every employee were still hard at work. The bedraggled businessman pushed back some errant hair and started for the reception area.

A black shape almost collided with him.

The small shadow he nearly walked through was more terrified than Jeremiah. Where the shapeless, timid creature had come from was as good a question as where it went but a blink later. The Grey vanished even before Jeremiah was able to comprehend what happened. The shadow walker had simply appeared before him, coming around the corner of the wall that separated the foyer from the workers. Then, just before they would have crossed paths, it had faded away.

The presence of the lone Grey could not be a good sign. Jeremiah was very much aware that his presence drew them and that the longer he stayed the more that would come. Sooner or later, one of those newcomers would look like an elf, a raven, or Haros.

Slipping behind the receptionist's station, he surveyed the desktop. If he remembered correctly...

Jeremiah exhaled a sigh of relief. Under the clear plastic cover of the desktop was an array of information sheets the receptionist kept out for handy reference. They ranged in importance from the telephone listings of other branches of the company up to the price lists of the nearest take-out restaurants frequented by the staff. The desktop was snowed under a layer of white, ink-spotted sheets that if lost would have sent the entire office into a tailspin of confusion. Few, if any, of the employees of Everlasting had up-to-date listings of their own.

In the center, glaring defiantly at him, was the employee call list.

"Thank you, Mr. Morgenstrom," Jeremiah whispered. The employee call list was management's way of reminding the staff that the company knew where they lived and would be more than happy to speak to them at any time. It was a threat that kept many from shirking their duties and staying home while they had the flu or some other minor malady. Management, also known as Morgenstrom, was of the opinion that the ill and dying could still consult. After all, they would be home doing nothing anyway.

Jeremiah's anxiety briefly rekindled when he found himself unable to recall Hector's last name. He shook his head, both in disbelief and in an attempt to remember. The man was always

Hector the way Jerry was always Jeremiah despite protests to the contrary. After several attempts, he gave up, snarling.

Still, there was only one Hector as far as he knew and so it was possible to find the proper name with little problem. Jeremiah planted a finger next to the only available choice. *Jordan! I'm an idiot!* JORDAN, HECTOR read the list. The address and phone number were to the right. Jeremiah smiled. He knew the area. Hector, too, lived alone in an apartment.

If only he could see me! If only I could talk to someone human! That was asking too much, however. The most he could hope for was a bit of peace and quiet. They could not know about Hector. Even if they did, he reminded himself, the Grey would have no reason for suspecting his home as Jeremiah's haven. It was a well-established fact that Jeremiah Todtmann was a hermit.

Which was why no one would miss him.

Fighting off the self-pity, Jeremiah tried to imagine the area where the black man lived. It was easy enough to imagine some far-off place like Egypt or China; pictures of those lands were everywhere. Trying to form mental images of suburban Chicago, especially of a place he only drove through on the rare occasion, was a little trickier. Not impossible, though. Jeremiah tried to picture the area.

He blinked...and was at his destination.

It was not Hector's apartment, not even his apartment complex. It was the town, however; Todtmann recognized that much. This was the best he could have hoped for. Jeremiah still did not understand how this method of travel worked and doubted he ever would. What mattered now was that he was close.

Like Bartlett, this town, too, was a parody of what it was supposed to be. The shadows lingered here. The buildings were twisted and reshaped, making it resemble a town out of some low-budget horror film or simply, as he had thought more than once, some surrealistic artist's nightmare. A few shadow walkers flitted around, but none had as yet noticed him and Jeremiah had no intention of staying on the street any longer than he had to stay. It said something for the situation that Jeremiah Todtmann no longer found the sights before him that terrifying. Becoming accustomed to the ways of the dream realm, though, was not something he wished.

Reinforcing his determination, he began the process of finding the apartment complex. The town was not a large one, and if his memory served him correctly, there were few apartment buildings in the area. Jeremiah wished he could have asked directions, but humans would not hear him and while there might have been some merit in trying to question one of the shadows, that would only serve to draw attention sooner than he wanted. Even Hector's apartment would only be safe for a short while, but by then Jeremiah hoped to have some solution to his problem. Hoped.

He would have liked to travel by the same method that Callistra had used when they had arrived in Bartlett, but how she had done that the lissome Grey had never said. All Jeremiah could hope was that none of the other Grey would be waiting for him when he materialized.

Thinking of Callistra made him clench his hands in frustration. He felt like a coward leaving her to play decoy with the baleful bird even though it had been by her choice. Had he been the hero that she seemed to see him as, Todtmann would have pursued the pair back to the city and damn the consequences.

But I'm not. I'm Jerry...Hell!...Jeremiah Todtmann, nonentity, pacifist, and coward.

The galling thought remained with him as he began his first hop.

His first two attempts were without success, but on the third, Jeremiah materialized near a set of apartment buildings off of the main streets. They were well-kept, attractive buildings made of brick and what looked like cedar siding. Jeremiah shifted his position in order to take a closer look at the street sign by the complex entrance.

A nervous smile escaped him. It was the correct place. The gleeful Todtmann fumbled in his mind for the apartment number and almost panicked when the only one that came to mind was his own. Fighting down his fright, Jeremiah took a deep breath and counted to ten. While he was counting, the number suddenly reared to life. He nodded to himself and concentrated.

The scene before him abruptly grew murkier. Jeremiah's first inclination was to assume that a fog had begun to rise, but then the murkiness before him started to move. He stepped back as a Grey formed before his eyes. It was only one of the shadows again. They seemed everywhere. This one had a vague, bent-over shape to it, but not one that was recognizably human in detail. The reluctant anchor stepped back. He had as much time for this one as he had had for the last, namely none. Before the Grey could coalesce further, Jeremiah transported himself to the interior of one of the buildings.

As with Callistra, Jeremiah felt ashamed. He knew it was within his power to help both the Grey in the office and the one on the street to become more substantial, more real, but if he started with one, another would follow and then another and another and another into infinity. They would never stop coming if he permitted it.

The next king will be better, he reminded himself. *He—or maybe she since this was the supposed liberated age—would be able to do what Jeremiah could not face. Anyone has to be better!*

Taking in his surroundings, Todtmann was startled to see that he had managed to actually appear before the very door he was searching for. There was no name listed, however. Jeremiah thought about finding the mailboxes and matching up Hector's name with the apartment number, but his patience was almost at an end. If this was Hector's home, then that would probably become apparent once he was inside. If, for some reason, it was not, Jeremiah would be on his way that much sooner.

Staring at the door, he decided to simply walk through. It would have been just as easy to transport himself into the apartment, but his growing irritation at his own cowardice had risen to a point where he wanted to somehow prove he was brave, daring. The safest and most immediate way was to confront his fear of moving through real objects. It certainly was safer than facing the raven.

Life is a constant series of reinforced notions and one of those is that walking into doors is painful. Even punching one. In the end, Jeremiah Todtmann went through the closed door the only way he could. He stepped back, closed his eyes, braced himself, and started running.

By the time he stopped and opened his eyes, he was almost at the living room window. Another few feet and Jeremiah realized he would have overshot the apartment. It not being on the first floor, he wondered whether he would have fallen. Gravity seemed to have some effect in the realm of the Grey. Gravity or the impressive illusion of it, anyway.

His hopes dampened when he looked over the furnishings and decor of the apartment he had invaded. The furniture was well kept, tasteful, and the entire place was immaculately clean. Not at all like his own and not at all like what he would have expected from Hector. As neat as the black man was with his appearance, he still struck Jeremiah as a more-or-less typical bachelor.

There was nothing at first glance to correct his perception, no magazines, no open letters, no photos. Biding his time in a total stranger's home, even as a silent, unseen specter, somehow felt peculiar to the ghostly monarch. Better if he left now. Perhaps there was another set of apartments he had missed...

He heard keys and someone fiddling with the doorknob. Out of human habit, Jeremiah moved to an out-of-the-way vantage point and waited. The door finally swung open.

Hector entered the apartment, briefcase in one hand and long coat in the other. He looked every bit the sort of man Jeremiah would have expected to see on the front of a fashion magazine, even more so than Todtmann had last remembered him. Suddenly the place seemed very much the sort of home his friend would have kept, bachelor or not. *I don't even know my best friend, do I?*

The tall, dark figure put the briefcase down next to the door and went to a closet nearby. He opened it, removed a hanger, and hung up the coat. Closing the closet, Hector reached for the leather case and carried it toward the kitchen...which happened to be the out-of-the-way vantage point Jeremiah Todtmann had chosen. The smoke-haired phantom stiffened and waited as his friend and coworker turned the corner and stared directly at him.

Jeremiah was barely able to get out of Hector's way before the latter nearly walked into him. The black man continued on, first dropping the briefcase on the table, then opening it. Behind him, Jeremiah eyed his back, crestfallen. He had known that Hector would not see him, had known that only to the Grey and maybe a few mortal folk would he be visible. He was so invisible that the other man had not even tried to step around him, but had simply tried to stalk through. It made Jeremiah feel like less than a Grey. He was no longer even significant enough to be noticed on the subconscious level.

All plans to spend his precious time alone and think of a way out of his predicament fell to the side as he followed Hector around much like a small dog awaiting a treat. Jeremiah tried desperately to think of some way he could contact the only other person who might help him. He was still not at all skilled in touching real objects, as his aborted confrontation with Morgenstrom had proven. The most Jeremiah could do at this point was shout in his friend's ear, but that would only accomplish annoying and puzzling Hector, which served no purpose.

The taller man abandoned both his case and the kitchen and headed toward what could only be the bedroom. Jeremiah tagged along after him, ignoring his surroundings save when he had to avoid a table. He was vaguely aware of a wide bed and a chest of drawers when they entered the room, but that was the extent of his interest in the decor. Only when Hector turned and stepped into the bathroom did Jeremiah pause, desperation giving way to propriety. Then, Hector turned to the sink and turned on the faucet. Jeremiah stepped to one side of the bathroom doorway and waited while the black man washed his hands and rinsed off his face.

The longer he waited, though, the more he began to shake. Now that he was actually here, the fact that he could not speak to Hector, the one person who might listen, was driving Jeremiah mad. He wished there was some way to reach him. Jeremiah needed someone to talk to, someone who could help him.

He slipped in behind Hector, who was still bent over the sink. Hector was reaching blindly for a towel. Jeremiah tried to reach it to him, but managed only to lift a memory, which promptly faded when he released it.

Damnit! Had he been real, Jeremiah would have thrust his fist through the mirror above the sink. *Damnit! Why can't at least he see me? Why can't someone?*

Hector had located the towel on his own. He straightened, then started rubbing his face with it. Todtmann gave up. There was nothing he could do about his friend, but at least he still had sanctuary here. The shadows were not as thick out here as in the city. It would take them longer to gather. One or two would be tolerable and not likely to draw the attention of Haros or the raven…so he tried to convince himself.

Hector removed the towel from his face and returned it to its proper place, carefully folded, of course. He leaned forward and started to examine his face in the mirror. Jeremiah returned to the doorway, debating what to do next. The least he could do in return for his sanctuary was give Hector some privacy.

He was just about to leave the bathroom when the black man straightened, took hold of the mirror, then glanced toward the doorway, eyes wide and unbelieving.

"Jeremiah?"

CHAPTER X

The ghost train wailed mournfully as it raced back to the city. Callistra paid the phantom train and its occupants no mind. They were memories, nothing more. Not like the raven.

At least Jeremiah was safe. He would go back to his home, remember his life, and return to his world. It was better that way. Another would take his place and he would be safe. The raven would have no more use for him and Haros would adjust his plans once his fury diminished.

She did not think less of Jeremiah for his decision. It was not by his choice that he had been thrust into such turmoil. That was Thomas O'Ryan's fault. Why had he picked on Jeremiah? As carefree as Thomas had been, he had still been an intelligent, good man. Why throw someone as unprepared as Jeremiah into the nest of the black bird?

Thinking of the malevolent creature, she searched the misty skies of the border world. The raven kept shifting in and out of sync with the realm of the Grey. How he did it she had no idea, but it made it hard to keep track of him. Callistra no longer really cared what Haros or the bird plotted, but she needed the raven to keep following her long enough to ensure Jeremiah's safe return. By now, he was probably already one with the true world, but she wanted to make certain. For his sake.

"Where are you, thing of evil?" The skies were still devoid of black shadows. "Where are you, bird or devil?" The border world became a burning sun. The shadows melted away like morning dew in highest summer. Callistra screamed and lost her concentration. The ghost train's mournful wail faded away as it returned to memory. She opened her eyes to find herself in an ever-shifting land where the actuality of the waking world vied with the dreams of the sleeping. Buildings sprouted full-grown, but faded into rolling lands that, to the human eye, would have resembled a negative from a photograph. To Callistra, it was all a very natural sight, a thing of no consequence yet of some beauty that was disturbed only by the vast black form swooping down upon her.

The raven pulled up just short of his prey. He cackled merrily and said, "Heaven and bliss, we've got to stop meeting like this!"

She tried to think of some ploy that would draw his notice long enough so that she could spirit herself away. All she needed was a moment. As long as he watched her, Callistra had no chance. His will, his power, dwarfed hers.

Callistra tore her eyes from the black bird and gazed wide-eyed behind him. Her mouth opened wide and she shouted, "Haros! No, don't!"

The trick was old but this was the realm of the Grey, who lived and breathed the old, the tried and true, the clichéd. The raven suddenly whirled around, seeking his adversary. Callistra did not hesitate; the pale enchantress transported herself far, far away from the rampaging raven.

She tried to, anyway.

Circling back, the black bird laughed harshly. "Leaving so soon? I think not. I've got you and I'll get your little king, too!"

With no other opening left to her, Callistra defiantly faced the mocking Grey. "Jeremiah is beyond your reach now! He was never with me! I've shown him how to be free!"

"How human of you. To err is human, you know."

The raven seemed not at all put out by her revelation. She shrank back, suddenly afraid for the mortal she had come to care so much for. Jeremiah had gone back, hadn't he? "What do you mean?"

"You can lead a horse to water but you can't expect him to find his way home on his own."

Even for one of her own, the raven was a confusing creature to speak to, but Callistra was almost certain that she understood the gist of his peculiar turn of phrase. The raven was insinuating that left to his own devices, Jeremiah Todtmann had evidently not taken the path home. Why he would do otherwise, she could not comprehend. He would have known why she had abandoned him. Why would he then remain among the Grey, where only danger awaited him?

Try as she might, the harried enchantress could not help but think that the bird was speaking the truth. If Jeremiah was still lost in the shadow realm, he was prey for the carrion crow. The carrion crow or Haros. He could hope for no other fate, unless... "Let's make a deal!" Openly amused by her impulsive cry, the raven circled lower. For the first time, Callistra noted the shadows forming around them, the deep, dark shadows that Jeremiah had rightly called hungry. They were of the blackest, most base dreams of Mankind and logical toadies to one such as the mad magpie.

The raven alighted onto a branch that was not there and dipped his head low. The eyes switched from dead white to hell-wrought crimson. "Speak. Speak now or forever hold your peace."

"You want…you want the power of the anchor for your own, a puppet, a toy, who will be your running boy." Distraught as she was, Callistra still winced at the rhyme. Forever it would remind her of what Jeremiah was and what she would never be.

The bird cocked his head to one side, but said nothing.

Encouraged, the night-tressed enchantress pressed on. "This is not the king for you. He was chosen by Thomas. What if, instead of having to deal with someone else's choice, you could have one chosen by you? One who will serve your needs and perform your deeds!"

Silence might be golden, but at that moment Callistra would have gleefully traded it for a positive response from the feathered Grey. All he did, however, was remain perched on nothing, staring at her with what she felt was amusement. She did not understand the reason for the intensity of that amusement, either. The raven eyed her as if he knew something that she did not. Still, he had not as yet denied her offer. Hope sprang eternal.

"If, as you say, the human is still among us, let me go to him and convince him to follow your dictates in finding a successor. Choose the one you think best and let Jeremiah Todtmann abdicate in his favor. Then, you will have the king you want, chosen by your claw and molded to your liking."

The shadows began to withdraw the moment she was finished. Callistra was unable to decide whether that was a sign of success or failure. The raven cocked his head the other way and eyed her from head to toe, as if somehow such an examination would help him decide his answer. In the back of her mind, the tall Grey continued to pray that Jeremiah had actually made his escape. Whether such prayers had any say in the matter, she did not care; it was a human thing to pray in times of trouble whether one believed in a deity or not and so it was also a Grey thing to do.

"Love is blind."

She stared at the malevolent magpie, not comprehending. "Jeremiah Todtmann *is* the king of my desire and the last human we shall be forced to call *sire*." He spread his wings and lifted himself back into the air. "All things come to those who wait, little girl lost, and soon I will collect my due."

She still did not understand and cursed herself for that. If Haros had been here, he would have understood. Of course, Haros would have never come to such straits. "Thomas O'Ryan did not pick your king; a whispering in his mind did the thing."

A whispering in his mind did the thing? A whispering? The choice was made by another? Her wide eyes met the sideways, single-orb stare of the raven. He dipped his body in an avian bow.

"No!" She tried again to free herself, but his hold on her was too great. Somehow, she had to warn Haros, find Jeremiah!

"Oh, yes, my little chickadee…" A flutter of wings brought him high above her. The shadows had retreated far back, as if whatever was happening had dampened their eternal appetites. "But I see that you still do not believe."

"You couldn't! It is not possible!"

The raven laughed again. The laughter cut through everything and silenced Callistra. "You are in the dark, my pretty." He fluttered higher. "Let me enlighten you."

A sudden searing brilliance engulfed Callistra.

"Jeremiah?" Hector repeated. He squinted, as if not truly able to focus on the other man.

The stunned Jeremiah walked up to him. "Hector? Can you really see me?"

Hector frowned. "You can't be there. I must be tired." "It's me, Hector! It's Jeremiah!"

Puzzled, the black man leaned closer. "There's no such thing as ghosts. You can't be real."

"I am! I'm very real!" Jeremiah stretched forth a hand, but his friend shied from it. He withdrew the hand with some reluctance, but understood how it must seem from the other side. Would he have wanted to touch the hand of a ghost?

Despite his refusal to touch the phantasm before him, Hector did not try to run. Instead, he looked over the transparent figure and, with much trepidation, said, "If you are Jeremiah, spook, then say something."

"What more do you want me to say?"

The balding mortgage man cocked his head to the side. "If you're saying something, man, you have got the worst case of laryngitis. All I can hear from you is a distant mumble."

That surprised Jeremiah, who until this moment had thought that the two of them had been having a conversation. Evidently their words had just matched fairly well. Still, if Hector was now able to see him, perhaps with a little work Jeremiah could make his coworker hear him, too. Maybe if he concentrated more on that...

"Can you hear me now?" He enunciated the words carefully, trying whatever he could to make his message clear. Hector straightened, stammering, "I...hear...you." Jeremiah was almost ready to hug him, so overjoyed was he at the black man's response.

Jordan, though, looked ready to back away if he tried anything physical.

"Thank God, Hector! I didn't think it was possible! I didn't think anyone would ever be able to see or hear me again!"

"What…what happened to you, man? Are you really…a ghost?"

Todtmann laughed. Knowing he was not alone allowed him to truly laugh for the first time since…since…since too long. He shook his head just in case his response was unintelligible. "No, I'm not. Not quite. Technically, I guess you could say that I'm still alive, but in limbo…listen, you'd better find a place to sit down. This could take a while."

"Sit down?" His coworker eyed the narrow gap between himself and Jeremiah. There was certainly not enough room to allow him to pass unless he walked at least in part through his unexpected visitor's very body. Jeremiah, realizing that, stepped aside and indicated that Hector should pass. The latter did, fairly darting out of the bathroom and quickly making tracks for the living room. Without thinking, Jeremiah transported himself there. He succeeded in materializing almost exactly in front of his counterpart, who nearly tripped as he stopped.

"Man, it's been too rough a day! You can't be real, Jeremiah! There just isn't anything like a ghost!"

"I'm not a ghost." He pointed at the couch. "Why don't you sit down, Hector? You'll need to for this. I mean that."

The befuddled-looking figure did as he requested. Jeremiah had never seen Hector looking so lost. He understood now how he had appeared that day when his friend had found him gazing at the shadow-enshrouded skyscraper. He tried smiling, but doing so did not at all seem to encourage Hector.

"I'm not a ghost," the slightly translucent Todtmann repeated. "I'm just not...just not"—*Just not what?*—"just not quite in the same world as you."

He received a blank stare.

Jeremiah wanted to sit or squat, but he had too much pent-up energy. Now that he had someone else to talk to, he wanted to explain what was happening before the opportunity somehow slipped past him. He was fearful that at any moment Hector might no longer see or hear him. Aware of the idiosyncrasies of human nature, he knew it would not take Hector Jordan long to convince himself that what he had seen had been a product of his imagination after all. If that happened, Jeremiah did not know what he would do.

"Listen carefully, Hector." That seemed easy enough. The more he spoke, the more his words seemed to carry to Hector. The latter no longer had to lean forward to hear him. Jeremiah even felt a bit more solid, although that had to be illusion. He was solid; it was just that he and Hector were in two different places. Two different worlds.

Jeremiah explained what had happened to him, paring the events to their most minimal in order to spare his audience as much of the madness as could be possible. Even still, Hector for the most part simply sat there, barely blinking and not at all willing to talk. He listened silently throughout his coworker's performance. Only toward the very end, when the unwilling lord of the shadow realm described his close encounter at his own home and then his trek to the apartment did Hector begin to stir. The look of befuddlement and denial was replaced by a growing air of determination that allowed Jeremiah to finish his tale with renewed faith.

The dark-skinned man shook his head. "This is beyond belief, but I've got to say, in one sense, it's a relief."

"What do you mean?"

"No need to shout," Hector commented. It was not the first time since Jeremiah had begun his monologue that the other had signaled for more quiet. Each passing moment evidently made Jeremiah more of a real person to Hector. "What I mean is that you vanished without a trace. You could have been dead or dying. Just another statistic. Instead, you're alive and well."

"Alive, anyway."

"You know what they say, 'where there's life there's hope.' I'll do what I can for you, you know, man."

"Thanks." Jeremiah felt his body relax. "God, Hector! Why me?"

"Just lucky, I guess." The jovial Hector Jordan was returning, the one that even Morgenstrom's tirades could not completely bend. The balding figure rose and slowly walked toward his spectral friend. "Y'know, you're a lot more solid-looking now, Jeremiah. Maybe we should see just how solid."

Raising a hand, Hector tentatively reached out. Jeremiah remained frozen, literally afraid that moving would break whatever spell had allowed him this much access to another living soul. As the fingers neared his chest, he began muttering a prayer to whoever might be listening. The fingers came within an inch, then half an inch, then...

They could go no farther. Hector Jordan's fingers pressed against the fabric of Jeremiah's suit shirt, any farther progress prevented by the flesh clothed within.

Jeremiah let out a gasp and would have crushed Hector in a bear hug if the latter had not been quicker and trotted back out of reach. "Easy, man! It's good to see you, too, but let's not get carried away!"

"I'm sorry! Could I at least—" He held out a hand and reached toward Hector's shoulder.

"Slowly, though. I don't want you squeezing the blood out of me." Hector waited silently as Jeremiah touched his shoulder.

"Solid!"

"Thanks, I work out."

Despite his pleasure at coming into contact with someone from the waking world, Todtmann could still not believe his good fortune. It could not be this easy. Callistra had said that the way back involved remembering his life and while Hector was a part of that life, he was peripheral in comparison to Jeremiah's own home. "I don't understand how this could happen!"

"Why worry? Curiosity killed the cat. Be glad you're here."

That should have been sufficient for him, but he still could not find it in himself to trust his luck. Jeremiah began pacing back and forth. "It just shouldn't work this way, Hector! If you'd seen and experienced what I have, you'd feel the same way."

The other man scratched his chin. "You've changed, man. You know that?"

"Too much and too little." The moment he said it, the reluctant king snarled. "God! I still sound like them!" He paused, a disagreeable idea occurring to him. Jeremiah looked around for something with which to test his theory. His gaze fixed on the couch. "I wonder..." he muttered, then shook his head. The couch was fairly large and looked to be a sleeper, which meant it would be extremely heavy. Jeremiah resumed his survey of the immediate area and almost immediately noted the coffee table. A half-read novel lay on top. Not wishing to waste any more time pondering his suspicions, he circled around the couch.

"What are you doing?"

"Testing a theory. I hope I'm wrong ..."

Reaching the coffee table, Jeremiah picked up the book. "I knew it was too good to be true!"

Hector had not moved. "You picked it up. What's wrong with that? Proves you're real, man."

"Look at the book." He held it so that his companion could clearly see the front. It was in immaculate condition, shiny and untouched.

"Looks good to me."

"Come over here and look at the table."

Hector stepped up behind the couch and peered over. On the table, untouched, was the novel. In contrast to the one in Jeremiah's hand, this one was a bit worn at the edges and had a bookmark sticking out the top.

"Haros, I'm sure, would make some remark about the judging of books by their cover...then he'd make a face." Bitterness fueling his strength, Jeremiah tossed the other book away. It faded only a few feet from his hand. "That was nothing but the memory of the book from when it was brand-new. I know that much now for all the good it does me!"

Something just at the outer edge of his vision moved toward him. Forgetting his misery, Jeremiah stumbled away from whatever it was. Hector, reacting to him, flattened himself against the apartment door.

One of the murky shadow walkers drifted through the room. It floated slowly around the apartment. Jeremiah could read both hesitation and fear in its movements. There was only the one so far, but where one appeared, others would soon follow. Jeremiah kept his distance from the creature and began to debate what to do now that his sanctuary had been invaded and his hopes had been torn asunder once more.

It came to him then that Hector was still flat against the door. He looked up and caught the black man glancing surreptitiously at the shadow, then swiftly looking away when he caught Jeremiah watching him in turn.

"You…see…it?"

Hector did not answer.

Todtmann started for him. At the sudden movement, the shadow dispersed. Jeremiah did not care. "You saw that thing, didn't you?"

His friend only continued to match his gaze.

Jeremiah studied Hector closely. Things were at last beginning to make a horrible sort of sense. There was no other answer, though. It had to be the reason.

"Hector, you saw that shadow walker. I know that and you know that, but you might not realize what that means."

At last he had the other's attention. Hector Jordan blinked and finally asked, "What?"

"You won't like this. We've been looking at this backward. I'm not becoming attuned to our world again, Hector.

That book was proof enough, but the Grey that you just saw— that's one of the simplest and most harmless ones, just so you know—was something that you shouldn't have seen. Not directly. That's why you could touch me. It's not me who's becoming human again, Hector…" He swallowed. There was no gentle way to put this. "You're crossing over to the dream realm of the Grey. You're becoming like me."

Some people are said to be made of stone and to his eye Hector could have been one of those. His coworker and now fellow exile simply continued to eye him at first. Then, almost acting as if relieved, he stepped away from the door and slowly walked toward the kitchen. Halfway there, Hector turned around and suddenly blurted, "I thought maybe I'd been overworking or maybe having daydreams. I never thought that they were real."

"You've seen others?"

He nodded. "For the past few days. Since you went missing."

"Haros said that now and then certain types of people cross over to his world. I guess you and I are those certain types."

The shadow or one just like it returned. Both men watched it, Hector with wariness and Jeremiah with expectation. Another joined it and a second later those two were joined by a third. None of them had any semblance to anything Jeremiah recognized. These were as simplistic as the Grey could be. Still, it was not a good sign. The more they gathered here, the more likely that Haros or the raven would be along soon.

A fourth shadow formed.

"Hector, I'm going to have to leave soon."

"Why? Are they dangerous?" He took a step away from the shadows, not a necessary precaution, actually, since the shadows were only interested in the king. They ignored the other man as much as they ignored one another. Only Jeremiah Todtmann was of importance. The anchor of their existence.

"Where the shadows gather, other Grey follow."

Hector nodded in understanding. "The raven and this Haros."

"Exactly. The longer I stay here, the more I risk being found. They don't waste much time, either. I could have only seconds."

"Where do we go, then?"

At first, Todtmann did not catch the different pronoun. When the other man's words registered, he found himself unable to immediately respond. On one hand, he welcomed the company. On the other hand, this was not Hector's fight. It would not be right to include him when there was a chance that his friend at least could return to the land of the living.

"We go nowhere, Hector. I go somewhere. The best thing for you would be to leave here for a few hours, then return. They know I won't come back after this, so you should be safe. Then, you can do what I was going to do. Walk around." Jeremiah indicated the apartment and Jordan's belongings. "Touch things and remember your life. That's what Callistra said. I can't do that now, but you still have a chance. I can't see why it wouldn't work the same for you."

The balding figure crossed his arms. "I won't abandon a friend in need. Two heads are better than one, man. Hell, I wouldn't even abandon Morgenstrom to this. Who else you got?"

"I can't let you do this." His dusky flock was growing; there were almost a dozen of the shadow folk floating in the vicinity of the living room. They had not as of yet gotten up the courage to approach close enough to touch him, but the nearest was now only just beyond arm's length. "I've got to go. There're too many here already. The black bird could come at any moment."

"Jeremiah, you vanish and I'll hunt you down to the ends of the Earth. I can't abandon a friend, man, and you've got no one else to turn to, do you?"

It was true. Oh, there were a few vague names and faces, but he no longer knew where any of those people lived. If he understood his pursuers at all, he was certain that the few relatives he had, all distant, would be under surveillance. As for recent friends... Hector was the closest thing he had to one and Jeremiah had not even known where the man had lived.

He put a hand to his forehead and looked down. "God, I'm a sorry case! Why would Thomas O'Ryan ever pick someone like me?"

"Jeremiah!"

The king of the Grey looked up just in time to see Hector coming toward him, hand outstretched. Jeremiah was suddenly aware of the unsettling fact that the pack of shadow walkers had completely vanished. Before he could draw the proper conclusion, however, Hector Jordan had his wrist.

The apartment became a metered parking lot next to a tiny train station.

He stared at his companion, who had released his wrist and was eyeing their surroundings in rather stunned silence. "What happened, Hector?"

Hector finally seemed to notice him again. Clearing his throat, he explained, "The shadow things vanished. Just like that. You weren't paying attention when it happened. From what I heard"—something caught in his throat, he cleared it again, then continued—"from you—I thought it was the bird coming to get us."

If not the bird, then Haros, Jeremiah thought. Either way, his fellow exile's quick thinking had possibly saved him from one of the two. From Haros he doubted that he was in danger of being harmed, but once back in the gaunt cadaver's fold, Jeremiah was fairly sure that he would never be left unattended again.

"Where are we?"

"My train stop, I guess. I didn't know I had it in me."

"There's no telling what you can do here." He looked around again to make completely certain that they were alone. "We can't stay long." Jeremiah sighed. "You shouldn't have helped me, Hector. It would've been easier for you that way."

"What are friends for?" Hector crossed his arms again. "What do we do now?"

What should they do? He had been hoping that a respite in Hector's apartment would allow him the time to think of a plan, but the only thoughts clear in his mind were the fact of his exile and Callistra sacrificing herself for his sake. Jeremiah reddened as he considered not for the first time his shameful behavior. She had allowed herself to become the raven's prey for his sake and all he had been concerned with was trying to escape.

He slowly began to realize that even if he had made it back into his home, he could not have gone through with the crossover. That was why his thoughts were so muddled, because the cowardly aspect of Jeremiah Todtmann was in battle with the aspect that knew that the right thing to do was to go after Callistra and damn the consequences. Not just the right thing, either. He had been willing to admit to himself that he cared deeply for her and had even been willing to bring her back with him…but on the assumption that she would become human, too. "But I don't care whether she is or not," Jeremiah Todtmann argued to himself. "I don't care!"

"What?"

"I have to find her, Hector. Even if it means facing that damned devil bird. I can't leave Callistra." The grin on his face contained no humor. "Pretty melodramatic, huh? Didn't think I was capable of it."

Hector did not argue. He simply nodded and asked, "What do you propose?"

That was yet another problem. What could he do? The role of king included some power, but he had no idea how to use those powers and what their limits were. Also, Jeremiah did not desire a direct confrontation with the raven. That would be just plain suicidal. Whereas he was not certain if the Grey could actually die, he knew that the human anchor was quite capable of perishing. Thomas O'Ryan had proven that.

"I don't know," Jeremiah finally admitted. "I suppose I could go back to Haros and ask his help. He seems to be the only one the raven respects."

"You don't want to do that, man."

He was surprised by the adamant tone. "Why not?"

Hector gave the area a quick scan. Jeremiah could not help but follow suit. They were wasting more time here than they should have been. "Do you think that Haros will help you? Isn't he more likely to keep you from going after the lady?"

That was all too likely a scenario. Haros Aguilana's only concern was his control over Jeremiah. Callistra was expendable.

He spread his hands in an imploring manner. "I don't know what else to do, Hector. I love her, if you can believe that. I love one of the Grey!"

His comrade was stone-faced, almost as if he did not know what to say in regard to Jeremiah's bald confession. Todtmann could not blame him; he had indicated his interest in Callistra, but Hector had likely not believed that the interest ran so deep.

Hector folded his arms. "I didn't say abandon all hope, man. You can't go to the ghoul for help, that's all."

He looks so calm; 1 wish 1 could be the same. "Then, what can I do?"

"First thing is to remember that it's 'what can we do?' All for one and one for all, y'know. I'm not running off on you no matter how many times you tell me to do so."

He was grateful for Hector's show of loyalty even if he would have preferred that his friend remained behind. There was no use arguing with him, however; the black man's expression was clear indication of his resolve on this issue. One way or another, he would be coming with Jeremiah.

Once again, Jeremiah had to ask himself, *Where are we to go?*

As if pondering the same thought, Hector asked, "Where did you last see her? The train, you said?"

"Yes, it was heading east…with the raven right behind." And gaining. In Jeremiah's mind, there was no way Callistra could have escaped the bird's claws.

The other's face softened. "He's gotta know what she means to you, man. She'll be okay, but I think we've got to go back to the city."

"Back to Chicago?" He knew there was no way to avoid going, but the thought of returning…. While the Grey were everywhere, Chicago appeared to be one of their centers of existence. That might have been O'Ryan's doing, but it continued now because of Jeremiah. Chicago was overrun with the shadow folk, in fact, and the more Grey nearby, the more attention he would draw. Attention meant Haros and the raven.

"Best place to start, from what you've told me."

"But if the raven doesn't notice me, Haros will."

"That's a problem, yeah." Hector's eyes darted this way and that. Looking for shadows, no doubt. It was astonishing to think that the two of them had still not been located. Each moment that passed without detection by the Grey was something of a miracle in the eyes of Jeremiah. "Say…what about your powers? Can't you make some kind of shield?"

"Use them to hide from the Grey? I can't." "Did you try?"

He opened his mouth to reply, but then paused. Mulling over his tenure as involuntary king, Todtmann could not recall a time when he had really tried hard to use his abilities to protect him from the prying of his supposed subjects. In the back of his mind, he had simply assumed that it was not possible to use a spell originated by the Grey against the dream people. What if it was, however?

"Why don't you give it the old college try, Jeremiah? It couldn't hurt."

"I'd have to protect you, too." Could he do it? When the raven had attacked him at his home, he had somehow shielded himself from the marauding Grey. Was it all just a matter of will? Had he been running needlessly?

"I wouldn't take too long deciding…"

"All right." Jeremiah could think of no other way to go about the process except by concentrating as hard as he could. He closed his eyes and tried to picture a sort of invisible barrier around the two of them, a barrier that allowed movement, but would deny the sensitive probes of the Grey.

He felt a sudden tug in his mind.

"Did you do it?" Hector asked the moment his companion's eyes opened.

"I did something. I think it might be what we wanted."

Despite the uncertainty of his success, he felt rather pleased. Perhaps he was not quite so helpless as he had imagined. Of course, it was Hector who had made the suggestion, just as it had been Hector who had managed to rescue him from the apartment. He wished he was as quick a thinker as the dark-skinned man. O'Ryan would have been better off choosing someone like Hector Jordan instead of Jeremiah Todtmann.

There was no time to think about what might have been. He needed to find Callistra. "Where do we go?"

"I've been thinking, Jeremiah. We can't go to the office and we probably shouldn't go to the train station. You know, for all the time we've worked in the city, I can't remember too many places besides the landmarks. Not places we'd be safe, anyway."

That was Jeremiah's problem, too. All the places that he could have transported them to were too well known. Haros, at the very least, would expect him to choose something like the John Hancock Building or Wrigley Field, both places he was familiar with.

Hector suddenly smiled. "Man, I think I've got it. It's a landmark, but the odds are probably with us on this one."

"What's that?"

"Feel like visiting the old water tower?"

Old water tower? He shrugged, not recalling the landmark.

His partner in exile gave him a look of comic shock. "You don't remember the old water tower?"

"Sorry." Actually, Todtmann had a vague impression of some old structure, but what was significant about it he could not recall. That he could not showed just how fog-enshrouded his life had been before the Grey had intruded upon it.

"All the better, then. I think I can describe to you where it's located. That should do, shouldn't it?"

"I suppose it should. I found you with less to go on."

"Fine." Hector Jordan rattled off a short description of the location, the key point being the tower's location on or near Michigan Avenue. Hector admitted that even he was not certain of the exact location, but was certain that his directions would put them within a block or so, which might even be better for the duo, considering the circumstances.

Jeremiah nodded. He had a good idea where the area was that his friend had described. Curiosity, however, would not let him transport them until he asked one question. "Just what is significant about this old water tower?"

"You've been living with your head buried in the sand, buddy." Hector stifled a laugh. "Do the words *Great Chicago Fire* ring a bell?"

CHAPTER XI

"If you want something done right, you should do it yourself!" Haros Aguilana leaned back in the throne originally created for Jeremiah's sake and re-created on the anticipation that the prodigal king would soon be returning. The Wasteland was empty, as it always was when he needed to conduct business, save for the two cloaked figures before him. The two elves glowered but did not argue with him. Their day of power was long past; now Haros and those like him held sway in the world of the Grey. "There are times, gentlemen, when only clichés hold the truth!"

He materialized a cigarette and took a puff from it while he allowed the two to continue to glower. That was what elves did all the time, it seemed. They glowered. When they were not glowering, they were being pretentious and self-centered. Even after falling from power with the advent of the first so-called Modern Age of Reason, they still continued to think of themselves as the driving force of the Grey. *And what have they to show for all those years of driving? A wrong turn that brought the anchor spell and us to this dead-end path!*

They were behind the times, relics, old dogs that could not and would not be taught new tricks.

He grimaced when he realized how his anger had tricked him back into the Grey manner of speech and thought. It was ever a war of will. To be human, to understand them, he had to think human.

"I'm especially disappointed in you, Oberon. You came across him twice and still couldn't lay a finger on him."

The elder of the two elves grunted. Oberon was especially a problem; he could not forget that he had once been king of all. Not enough people truly believed in his sort of elf these days, though, and so his kingdom had all but faded. Oberon and a few others had enough will and human believers to support their continued existence, but the last couple anchors had not cared one bit about them. The only creatures like Oberon who had flourished at all during the reign of Thomas O'Ryan had been the blasted leprechauns and even they had been reduced to comic roles thanks to O'Ryan's humorous nature and modern human literature.

I thought you might be the one, Thomas, Haros found himself thinking. But like the past few kings, *you didn't even last fifty years.* It was probably a good thing that he had forbidden anyone from mentioning or even hinting about the shortening spans of the human anchors to Jeremiah Todtmann. Such talk only served to disrupt things.

He had left Oberon and his companion to their shame for long enough. They still had their uses; the others agreed with that. The others, in fact, were probably more forgiving than Haros, their spokesman, was, but then that was why he was in charge and they stayed in the background. He had the force of identity needed to keep things running smoothly, to be, for all practical purposes, de facto prime minister to the human given the kingship.

"Get back to the hunt," he ordered. "You know that blasted spell better than most. It's changed, but no anchor has ever been able to use the power to mask himself; it just isn't done. Jeremiah Todtmann, our king, is out there and we have to find him before you-know-who does, right?"

His question was rhetorical and the elves knew it. Oberon nodded his understanding of the cadaverous Grey's commands, although his glittering eyes still smoldered at being so ordered about. The next instant, the elves were gone.

"I'm glad that's settled." He rose, allowing the throne to fade back into nothingness until it was needed to impress the human again. Around him, the Wasteland was suddenly filled with Grey again. Haros Aguilana ignored them, especially the shadow walkers, who often swarmed around him almost as much as they did humans.

As he descended the dais, Haros took a step sideways in space. Stepping sideways in space was a bit like stepping forward or backward in time, but not quite. To most Grey, it was a normal thing and much the same as the method by which Jeremiah was able to transport himself from one place to another. The Grey did not have to think about where they wanted to go, however; they simply took the right path. In this case, the path Haros had chosen was a private one to a tiny bit of dream realm that was his and his alone. There he would see to his ace-in-the-hole, his backup plan should Jeremiah Todtmann get himself killed.

A long set of steps formed beneath his feet even as the Wasteland faded from view, a set of steps over which floated a huge, ticking timepiece much akin to an old pocket watch. Haros descended swiftly down the lengthy, spiral staircase. The staircase, like all else that was Grey, was only a matter of perception, but because he was a Grey and desired all things human, Haros followed the steps down rather than simply materialized to his destination. Besides, here time did not matter, so time was not wasted. A human would have found the continually flexible subject of Grey time baffling, but the Grey themselves understood it perfectly. Time flew when you were having fun or when a deadline was near; it also marched on. Time dragged during rainy days. It was as simple as that.

Haros glanced up at the clock. To clock watchers, time seemed to slow down to practically nothing. Here, in this little piece of the dream realm, that was more true than ever. It was also necessary; time still passed for living things that had crossed over, just more slowly. Haros Aguilana's ace-in-the-hole had been here a long, long time and his health had not been good when he had fallen through the cracks of reality. That was the trouble with the real world; it was often the refuse that fell into the dream land.

"Beggars can't be choosers," he muttered, for once taking note of the cliché he had just uttered. Beggars, indeed. The Grey's ace was just that. A beggar and drunkard whose rotting mind had propelled him into the shadow world. The man was a broken shell, but because he was a man and not a Grey, the perverse laws of the universe gave him certain rights over such as Haros. With the proper instigation, he could even become the new anchor. Haros was certain of that. Left bereft of a host, assuming that Jeremiah Todtmann was killed, the spell would have to seek a successor on its own.

The rotting shell that Haros had taken under his wing would be a beacon. The spell could not help but attach itself, if only out of the survival instinct it had appeared to develop over the centuries of contact with the anchors.

At the bottom of the stairs there was a door. Nothing else. The door stood proud and alone, no one evidently having thought to tell it that there should have been a wall around it. Haros glanced at the door as he descended the last few steps. It opened, revealing a doorway that, even more than the door, should have known about the necessity of walls. The gaunt Grey did not stop once he reached the bottom of the staircase but continued on through the open doorway.

Where Jeremiah's suite had been the epitome of excellence, the suite where Haros Aguilana's chosen successor lay was a distorted nightmare of old and rotting things, broken walls and furniture, and shadows almost as dark and hungry as those that served the raven. They were not there by the choice of the Grey, but rather the mired, festering mind of the occupant.

"Rise and shine," Haros called out, staying as close as he could to the door. A Grey had to be wary at all times about the danger of becoming influenced by human thought...or even the thoughts of something only marginally human. "Up and at 'em."

In the soiled, bent bed that his ace-in-the-hole had chosen of his own free will lay a mound of cloth. Somewhere beneath that mound was the room's inhabitant. He made no move to respond, which was fairly typical of him.

Beggars can't be choosers, perhaps, the ghoulish figure thought as he started for the bed, *but I would gladly trade this one for Jeremiah Todtmann.* Any sympathy he had ever had for the beggar's plight had faded the first time the man had taken a knife to him. The knife had passed through Haros, of course, but just the idea that someone would have had the audacity to stab him offended the Grey. Was that any way to treat the one who had offered him shelter? *Once the power is transferred, though, I'll keep you busy until I find a more suitable host.*

That was all this one was good for. A temporary stop-gap to prevent the raven from seizing control. When Jeremiah Todtmann had been chosen, Haros had almost abandoned his side plan. A good thing he had not, he thought now. *Everything will work out in the end.*

Grimacing at the desperate depths to which his thoughts and speech had slipped, he stepped to the side of the bed and gently kicked one of the legs. The leg wobbled, but did not fall apart. The mound also wobbled, but as the bed stilled so did it.

"We have work to do." This time he kicked the bed harder. Haros was quite certain that he was being very obliging; his real desire was to let the bed and its moldering contents plummet a few hundred feet before restoring solidity to the floor. That would wake the fool up.

When there was no response this time, the fastidious Grey reached down and, with a look of growing disgust, pushed the mound with his finger.

The finger went through the cloth unimpeded.

Snarling, Haros seized the top blanket with both hands and flung it aside. He did the same with the second and third, then paused when he saw what was underneath them.

Nothing.

The blankets framed a nonexistent form, a shell of air created by a spell. The beggar was gone...but how and where?

"He wanted to go, Haros. I let him."

"Hmm?" He turned to discover his table companion of old, the apelike one, standing near the doorway. "What was that you said?"

"My name is Otto, Haros. The king gave it to me. Long live the king."

"Don't be absurd, he's—" The gaunt Grey bit off the rest of his statement. It was only now occurring to him what the simian monstrosity's first comment meant. "You did this?" He indicated the empty chamber. "You dared to do this?"

"Jeremiah is my friend, too. So was Thomas." The burning orbs flashed on and off.

"Where is he?" growled Haros, moving closer. He was trying to keep his temper in check, but it was hard to do that when surrounded by so many imbeciles, so many obstacles.

"He is gone, Haros. I like you, too."

"Spare me false, human sentiment, Otto. It's beyond me and definitely beyond you."

"It isn't," was the only argument the other Grey gave on that subject. "You need Jeremiah Todtmann now."

"And he is probably in the claws of the raven by now. Do you realize that your meddling has probably lost the game for us? Do you realize that?"

"This is no game, Haros. This is it."

Haros reached by his waist and drew forth an epee from the essence of the shadow realm. He pointed the long, narrow sword at his counterpart's torso. "It's a good thing for you, Otto, that death comes not easy to a Grey nor does torture solve anything! If you were human, I'd have your head on a pole! You have given the game to the bird! Is that what you wanted?"

"I want what is best," replied Otto in calm tones. The simian Grey shrugged. "Jeremiah."

"I don't have him! The bird does!" When his companion did nothing but stare, Haros lowered the blade. "At least, I think he does…but all's quiet on the western front and the magpie is one who would crow over his victory!" The blade vanished as the Grey scratched his chin in thought. "Perhaps the game is still afoot, after all." He had all but given up hope, even despite having sent those cretins back out to search. Yet, if the raven had won, all the realm would have resounded with the dark announcements of his victory. The fact that Haros himself was still free was a good sign that the day was not yet the bird's.

There was a slight problem, though, even assuming he could find the human. Jeremiah Todtmann trusted him almost as little as he trusted the raven. It hurt Haros to be so unjustly judged; he was only doing what was best for all concerned. That was the price of being a crusader, however. It was a cross he would just have to bear, which in no way helped him solve the problem of how to approach the human. He needed Jeremiah's trust.

No…simply someone else he trusted. There was only one Grey the king trusted, only one Grey he cared enough about. That part of his plan had at least not gone awry, Haros noted with some satisfaction. Actually, it had succeeded far beyond his wildest expectations…much to his chagrin. If not for her, Jeremiah Todtmann would be in the fold, safe and secure from all danger, eager to follow the recommendations of his adviser.

"Callistra…" According to the elves, when last seen, the human had been alone. It was assumed that the bird and Callistra had fought. Haros Aguilana did not have to be omniscient to know what the outcome of such a battle would have been. She had sacrificed herself for the anchor. *How…romantic.*

"Jeremiah likes her," added the simian Grey, eyes blinking.

"Yes, I know…" A plan was forming. She was the only one the human would turn to, the only one whose words he might believe. If those words included talk of trusting Haros Aguilana and looking to the elegant Grey for protection against the pinioned pariah, Jeremiah would listen.

Of course, Haros did not have Callistra, but that was not too steep a hill to scale. If the original was lost to him, a copy would do just fine. He knew enough about Callistra to create a usable doppelganger. The double would be even better than the original in one respect; she would not be half as troublesome. It would not take long to create one, either; there were always shadows begging to be given some purpose, if only as a puppet in a deadly game. Once the anchor was his, the duplicate could be dismissed.

There were always shadows.... He summoned a cigarette, puffed it once, and allowed himself an assured smile. With so much raw material at hand, why not stack the deck? Why not cover all bases, all places?

Why stop at one double when he could make a second...or even a third...?

"I've places to go and people to see," he snarled, "but as for you, Otto, I—"

The other Grey was gone. That annoyed Haros less than the notion that he was no longer as in charge of the situation as he had been. Too many things were happening that he had not orchestrated. He would have to make some changes, but for now, it was time to reclaim his king...and by doing so, his people as well.

Standing before the old water tower, Jeremiah Todtmann had visions of the great fire that had torn through Chicago. Whether Mrs. O'Leary's careless cow had been at fault or not was a moot point; the fire had forever changed Chicago the way another fire had changed Rome. Yet, here was a tiny building, a structure more reminiscent of a miniature castle than a water tower, that had stood against the raging inferno and still stood over a century later. Jeremiah could almost feel the heat and hear the flames licking the city as he surveyed the landmark.

In the dim illumination that seemed to come from nowhere, it glowed like a ghost. The tower was actually one of the most distinctive landmarks in the city and it was embarrassing to think that he had forgotten it. Still, Todtmann was by far not the only one. People drove past the tower every day and the occasional tourist from out of town would take its picture, but most folk preferred to visit the other tower, the modern steel tower where Jeremiah and Hector had worked. That despite the fact that few places in and around Chicago had witnessed as much history as the pale stone structure had.

Across the street and even less noticed by most was the pumping station. Neighbors the two buildings had been since before the blaze, but the pumping station lacked the more imaginative copper-green, domed watch tower of the other landmark and so instead ended up resembling a certain venerable hamburger chain famous in Chicago and beyond for bite-sized wonders. Only the place it shared in history lent it that certain air of majesty.

Jeremiah was coldly reminded of his own history. When he was gone, there would be no monument to mark his passing. A week or so ago, that would have bothered him a little; now, it wrenched at his heart. He would leave nothing behind save perhaps a few unfinished files and an automobile still in part owned by the finance company.

" 'Space, the final frontier,' " a voice behind him whispered. "Are you still with me, man?"

"Sorry. Just thinking."

Hector joined him, but the black man's eyes were on their surroundings. "Well, think about this. We don't even want to stay here very long, shield or not. You want to find Callistra, we've got to get moving."

"You're right again." It was a good thing he had Hector now. Left to his own devices, Jeremiah knew he likely would have transported himself right into a trap. "The only problem is, I still don't know where to find her, Hector."

Once again, it was his partner in exile who came up with an idea. "I'd look for the place with the deepest shadows, the hungry ones you talked about. If he's got your girlfriend locked away, it's in the dankest, strongest part of his domain."

On the surface, what Hector said sounded like the right course, but a part of Jeremiah wanted to argue against such folly. Literally walk into the lair of the raven? Play games with his pets? There had to be a less suicidal way. "We can't just do that...can we?"

"If we're shielded, we can."

"I still don't know if the spell worked."

"Well..." Hector glanced around, then fixed his gaze on something across the street. A couple of jacketed youths were walking along the other side. Jeremiah involuntarily shrank back, thinking of gang members. One boy was white; the other was Hispanic. They were obviously in sour moods.

Behind them followed one of the shadow walkers. It was more than simply a shadow this time, though. This walker wore a humanoid shape, a twisted, clawed thing a third again the size of the two unwary teenagers. Jeremiah reminded himself that the Grey was supposed to be a representation of those it watched. It was what they were deep inside.

"Let's cross the street before they get too far ahead!" Without waiting for Jeremiah, Hector started across. The uneasy monarch followed after. Hector took a path that would cut off the two jacketed boys. To Jeremiah's relief, they did not, of course, see either man.

He understood what Jordan wanted him to do. Jeremiah positioned himself close enough so that the shadow could not help but notice him. Hector crossed his fingers.

The two youths hurried past...and at their heels only a moment later was the shadow. It paid not the slightest attention to either of the two men. Jeremiah watched the odd trio vanish down the avenue, shaking his head in disbelief. The spell had worked.

"What do you say now, man?"

The would-be king's mouth twisted in determination. "Let's find Callistra and get this over with."

"Now you're talking!"

"I know where we have to go, too," Jeremiah added with sudden insight. "We could've gone there right away, now that I think about it."

It was Hector's turn to be puzzled...just this once. "Where might that be? Enlighten me, if it's not too much trouble."

"The other tower."

"You want to go back to Everlasting again, man? There's nothing there!"

It was not the mortgage company offices he wanted. "Where can you get the best view of the city...the whole city?"

Hector did not answer, but he was smiling now. The black man nodded and indicated that Jeremiah could perform his magic anytime.

Which he did.

"Damn!" The king of the Grey and his fellow exile fought to maintain their holds as the floor beneath them tilted and swayed. Hector snagged a handrail, but Jeremiah slid loose and crashed into a glass pane. He took hold of another rail nearby and tried to make sense of the chaos into which he had dropped the pair of them.

On days when the clouds did not enshroud its crown, the Sears Tower observatory gave the voyeur a sight unparalleled by any other man-made structure. From the farthest stretches north to the deepest south, from the western suburbs to the expansive reaches of Lake Michigan, all of Chicago was open to view. Even Jeremiah had come up here on occasion to admire the panorama below and beyond. The observatory was the perfect place to study any part of the midwestern metropolis. All one had to do first was to become accustomed to the slight swaying of the skyscraper.

That was how it was in the real world. Slight as used in the realm of the Grey, however, was evidently a different term altogether.

Like a fire truck water hose escaped from its users, the steel-and-glass monolith shook and shivered in wild abandon. Not once when he had looked up at the twisted Grey versions of the city's leviathans had Todtmann seriously considered that the buildings might actually be like that. He had assumed that it was all just a matter of perspective. To be sure, there would be some touches of the surreal, as evidenced by the rising and falling streets he had more than once noticed, but not to the extreme he and Hector now suffered. They were in great danger of being literally thrown from the tallest building in the world. It was either that or be tossed time and time again against the reinforced glass panes.

If Jeremiah had had any doubts about abandoning the role of king, those doubts were all but dead, tossed, as he was likely to be, to a painful end below.

"Jeremiah!" Hector shouted from his position. He had his arms locked firmly around the rail and looked to be much more in control of himself than Todtmann was. "Jeremiah! Can't you do something?"

Perhaps he could have, but he was finding it hard to concentrate. Being slapped again and again against the windowpane was not conducive to organized thought, he was fast discovering.

"You're part of this world, man! You're king of all you survey! Adjust the picture! Get a new perspective on things!" Half of what the other man said sounded as bad as the raven at his most Greyish. Yet, Jeremiah understood enough to know what Hector wanted of him. He was the anchor. He was here to give the dream world stability. He was here not just for the Grey, but for their world, too.

Maybe I can straighten out matters.... He did not bother grimacing at the phrasing, for his mind was already at work on the threat. This is not the way it should be, he told himself. *This is not the way the Sears Tower should be. It's stable, only swaying a little. Just enough to be safe. It wasn't born a snake, for God's sake!*

The vacillating slowed. Jeremiah was better able to secure his position and finally relieve his body of any more confrontations with the glass wall. The floor slowly became horizontal. Not yet trusting his luck, Jeremiah continued to concentrate, picturing the tower as it was supposed to be.

Stable. Just swaying a little.

He wondered, for a time, why he had never noticed the violent twisting during his sojourns to the office. Finding no answer that would satisfy him, Todtmann finally chalked it down to yet another of the dream realm's inconsistencies. At this point he was of the opinion that the only things of consistency in the world of the Grey were their clichéd tongues and their desire to make his life miserable.

Jeremiah was still clutching the rail when a heavy hand slapped him on the shoulder and a jovial Hector said, "Good trick, man! See what you can do when you put your mind to it?"

"It was your idea, though," he replied as he released the handrail and straightened. Once again, it had been his friend's quick thinking that had saved them from disaster. Jeremiah's only supposed good idea had been to send them blindly into this latest near-catastrophe. Had it been Hector in his place, he was certain things would have gone much smoother. Hector was able to think under pressure, something Jeremiah had yet to learn, apparently.

"Well, now that everything's settled, so to speak, let's take a look for your girlfriend—ummm—just what are we looking for again?"

What were they looking for? Jeremiah did not know. A place covered in deep shadow? It seemed such a simplistic hope now. Had he really thought it would be that easy to find her? He stalked over to one of the windows on the opposite side. "I don't know, Hector. Something out of the ordinary...even for this place."

"You don't expect much, do you?"

"No," he muttered. "I really can't." Peering down upon the city, he thought about the proverbial needle in the haystack. What did he really expect to find? A vast neon sign pointing the way?

From where he stood, Hector gave a sudden whistle. "Ask and you shall receive! Over here, man!"

"You found something?" As he turned, he could not but marvel at Hector's luck. The man had to have the eye of an eagle.

Hector was gazing down on the city when Jeremiah joined him. His companion pointed to the right. "Does that look like what you want?"

A black blot covered more than a city block. The blot was shifting, too, an amoebic form slowly engulfing more and more of its surroundings. Todtmann recognized the hunger.

"Unfortunately, yes."

The two of them stepped away, Todtmann, at least, fearing that the shadow would somehow notice them. Hector, on the other hand, was more impressed than frightened by the sight he had just witnessed. "When you said deep, hungry shadows, you meant it, didn't you?"

"You can stay behind, Hector." Jeremiah tried to ready himself for the quest ahead. "Believe me, I won't have a problem with it."

"I would." The black man held out a hand.

Shaking it, Jeremiah nodded in thanks. It was good to have Hector's adaptability and quick thinking on his side, but he promised himself that should the need arise, he would see to it that his companion was sent elsewhere. He had already endangered the other man more than he had a right to do despite Jordan's words. This was Jeremiah's nightmare and only his.

The shift to the shadowed block was performed almost without effort. As the duo materialized on the street, Jeremiah took note of the ease with which he was utilizing at least one ability of the kingship. It was a pity he did not know enough about whatever other skills remained to practice them. It was a pity that Haros Aguilana had never gotten around to telling him everything, but then that would have loosened the hold the Grey wanted to have on him.

The blot covered everything with a layer of slick darkness. He pictured an oil tanker, a flying one since this was the world of dreams, running aground on one of the sharp radio antennae that perched atop the tallest of the skyscrapers. The tanker would have finally freed itself, but the hole caused by the damage would have let loose a waterfall of black gold. That was what the block ahead resembled, a bit of city drowned under a sea of oil.

Callistra was supposedly in there.

Up close, he also saw that it was not one massive shadow, but rather many intermingling with one another. *A swarm of black ants stripping a carcass....* They did not seem to notice the two newcomers, which meant that the shield he had created still held. Jeremiah felt justifiably proud about that accomplishment, but again reminded himself that it had been at Hector's wise suggestion that he had tried.

They had only taken a few steps toward it when a vehicle pulled out of a side alley and headed directly toward them, headlights ablaze. Jeremiah would have all but ignored it, having finally grown somewhat accustomed to the blindness of other people where he was concerned, but the style of the vehicle caught his attention. It was old, very old, and reminded him of something out of a black-and-white movie from or about...gangsters?

No...he did not want to think about it. It couldn't be what he was thinking.

A figure wearing an old fedora leaned out of one of the rear windows, the legendary tommy gun of the Roaring Twenties in his hands and pointed at Jeremiah's side of the street.

Chicago was the city of big shoulders, the old meat-packing capital, and a sports mecca, but it had also been the home of men such as Johnny Torrio, Dion O'Bannion, and Scarface Al Capone. No one who knew the least bit about the history of the city, Jeremiah Todtmann included, could think about Chicago without once thinking of the days of Prohibition and mob wars. To many, Chicago still was the home of Big Al.

Which, of course, was why these Grey wore the forms they did.

They were definitely Grey and not simply memories raised by Jeremiah's presence. The Grey, for all the shadow that they were, were more substantial and independent creatures than the ghosts of the past. These shadow folk were looking for something in particular and that something in particular could only be the renegade king.

Despite his best efforts to control it, anxiety flooded over him. Jeremiah backed away from the curb as the old car neared. From the other side of the street, Hector silently tried to get him to stand still. Jeremiah, however, could not control his feet; they continued to propel him sideways toward the nearest alleyway. Fortunately, the dark figures in the vehicle appeared ignorant of his presence. They continued to scan the street, half-hidden faces twisted into movie-style snarls. None of them were distinct of visage; they simply represented the legends of gangsters and bootleggers, not any one particular person. Still, Jeremiah could not help wondering if there was indeed an Al Capone somewhere in the city.

The car slowly rolled past. Relieved, Todtmann exhaled. Just as a precaution, however, he remained where he was and surveyed the area in case this search party was not alone. His shield still held, but there was no sense in taking chances. If another car, another anything, for that matter, appeared, he wanted to be ready.

Nothing else materialized, for which Jeremiah was grateful. He finally turned his attention back to the search party. The spectral vehicle continued its snail's pace down the avenue, an annoyance since he did not want to move again until it was out of sight. Jeremiah stared hard, trying to encourage the car to be on its way.

Then, out of the corner of his eye, a figure moved. He recognized just enough to completely forget the search party and turn every bit of his attention to the newcomer.

It was Callistra, just barely visible around a street corner. Even as he started to call out to her, she vanished behind a building. Jeremiah had been unable to make out much, but he was certain that the expression he had glimpsed was one of hopelessness and fear. Fearful of losing the tall, pale enchantress again, he started after her.

"Jeremiah!" spat Hector.

There was the squeal of tires, of a sharp, violent turn.

He looked down the avenue and to his horror saw that the car had come around and was now building up speed as it raced toward him. Why they had not teleported to him instead of relying on the swiftness of the ghost car was curious. Perhaps the constraints their forms enforced on them was stronger than he had imagined.

A small consolation.

Torn between chasing Callistra and trying to reinforce his failing spell, Jeremiah at first hesitated. He still had no idea as to why his decision to follow Callistra had shattered the shield and drawn such unwanted attention to him. Once more the inconsistent ways of the Grey had propelled him into the lion's den.

Throwing all caution to the wind, Jeremiah raced toward the street corner where he had last seen Callistra. Behind him, Hector called his name, but the would-be monarch tried to ignore his pleas. He was certain with him in sight, the Grey would ignore the other man. Hector was inconsequential as long as Jeremiah held the mantle of king.

Sure enough, the car swerved to intercept him. Jeremiah reached the street corner first, but only because of the shorter distance he had had to cross. The Grey were cutting short the gap. He could transport himself at any time, but Jeremiah feared losing track of Callistra if he did. He could not allow that; he could not lose her.

From behind him came the sounds of new pursuit. Someone or something on foot. Jeremiah glanced over his shoulder, wondering what new hunter pursued, and saw instead Hector catching up to him. "You're not a part of this, Hector!" he gasped. It was becoming exceedingly difficult to share his attention between the Grey, Callistra, and now Hector. The last thing he needed to worry about was his friend. "Go away and they'll ignore you!"

The smile on Hector's visage was incongruous considering their dire situation. "All for one and one for all, Jeremiah! I'm sticking to you like glue whether you like it or not!"

Todtmann swore and gave up. He had enough to worry about. Callistra was still not in sight and it was beginning to look like she had transported away.

No, there she was again. This time, the night-tressed Grey waited at a bus stop. Even with the illumination the dream realm provided, it was hard to see her clearly. She was two or three blocks away, much too far away when one was being chased by ghostly vehicles and unearthly mobsters. Jeremiah called out to her, assuming that by this time there was no need for secrecy.

Callistra turned at the sound of his voice, but as she looked at him the street before Jeremiah began to rise like a wave. Asphalt and concrete filled his vision. He was thrust into the air as the street below him blossomed into a hill. Hector shouted then, but even if the hapless king had wanted to respond, he could not have. Riding the impossible wave as best as he could manage, Todtmann sought out Callistra, only to find her gone yet again. His frustration was almost as great as his fear now. She had seen him; he was certain of that.

While Jeremiah tried to sort that one out, the hill receded and with it went what was left of his balance. Jeremiah tumbled forward, too confused and pained to recall what he had done when the Sears Tower had run amok. Behind him he again heard Hector, but the man's voice was faint. There was no sign of the car, perhaps even the skills of the Grey were now at their limits. For a moment he was certain that they had completely given up the hunt; then he saw them moving on foot, two figures on each side of the avenue. Two of them had the infamous machine guns, while the others held conventional handguns. Whether they would really resort to them was not something Todtmann wanted to discover the answer to if he could at all help it.

The answer came quick, nonetheless, for the foremost machine gunner raised his tommy and fired away, cutting a swath of death about a foot over his target's head. Jeremiah was quick to understand that this was a warning shot. They did not want his body; they wanted him. Their warning, though, backfired, for it gave him the impetus he needed to keep going. If the Grey wanted him, they would have to work at it.

He found out how willing they were to work at it when every manhole cover before him exploded into the air, creating a rain of metal. From the open manholes emerged a succession of huge, reptilian figures...alligators. Jeremiah turned in mid-step and headed for one of the side alleys, but a crowd of red, eager eyes made him halt. Rats the size of small dogs began pouring out of not just the alley he had chosen, but every other alley as well.

Jeremiah backed away from the rats and alligators just as a vehicle roared toward him. At first he thought it was the hunters, but then he noticed the distinctive yellow coloring and the sign on top. A cab. Not a ghost, either, but a real cab wending its way through the city. Oblivious to the madness around it, the cab drove up and down the rippling street with no difficulty whatsoever. The alligators did not give way for the vehicle, which cut through their ranks without hesitation and did them no harm whatsoever. It was a reminder to Jeremiah that this was his personal madness; the rest of the world was oblivious to what was happening.

His choices quickly dwindled to nothing. The legions of Grey had him physically surrounded. Todtmann had neither the concentration nor the trust in his abilities to create a viable defense. Shifting to elsewhere was his only chance, even if it meant somewhere like the office.

Perhaps not the office. In a burst of sudden inspiration, he recalled a place that the Grey themselves had used but might have now abandoned.

As simple as that, the chaotic avenue became an empty storefront.

It was the same vacant store where he had attempted to buy a coffee and make a telephone call. This time, no Greyish café run by a refugee from a Lon Chaney, Jr., film graced his view. The store was as closed and empty as it should have been. For once, he had been correct; the Grey were not watching this place. It was not one of the locations to which they would have expected him to return. He had at last managed to outwit them on his own.

Satisfaction turned into bitter self-recrimination. Now he had lost both Callistra and Hector. Both of them might now be paying the price for helping him…and Hector was human. He could die, if the Grey so decided. Jeremiah's only hope was that Hector had made use of his own limited ability to transport himself from one location to another. *I have to find him, though.* As important as Callistra was to Jeremiah, Hector faced the greatest risk. *Things just keep going backward! I'm worse off than before!* Where would his fellow castaway go if he had escaped?

Jeremiah paced the length of the store, wracking his brains for some solution to one of his problems and finding no success. He almost regretted the café not being here; a cup of fresh coffee would have nearly been worth his freedom. There was nothing he could do about that, unfortunately, but at least he was safe for the moment.

"Yeah," he muttered, leaning against one of the walls and staring outside at the empty street. "I'm so safe and everybody else is in trouble because of me."

Shifting his feet, he almost knocked over an empty pop can left by some construction worker. He studied the can and suddenly felt all of his frustration build up to boiling. Straightening, Jeremiah raised one foot and kicked at it as hard as he could. His foot passed through, but at the same time a shape flew across the room. He waited for it to clatter against the opposing wall, but the shape faded just before reaching the other side. A curse escaped him. Kicking around the memories of an empty can was far less than satisfactory, but in retrospect, a lot safer. Only now did Jeremiah think about the din that a real metal container would have made as it bounced around the barren store.

That, he concluded, *was too close!*

He had no idea how close it had been until he looked up and saw the elf standing on the other side of the window front.

His gasp was cut short by the hand that clamped hold of his shoulder, the grip threatening to turn the shoulder into a mass of bruised flesh and broken bone if he tried to move at all. Jeremiah nonetheless tried to transport himself away, but his concentration slipped every time he almost had it.

The elf outside became an elf inside…and only an arm's length from Jeremiah, at that. He was one of the two that had been hunting the renegade king at his home. The elf was much taller than he, with cold, patrician features that reminded Todtmann of the ancient marble statues of the Greeks, only without the warmth of those carved faces. The fact that the elf was stunningly handsome did not at all make up for the inhumanity within.

The elf also had long, ivory hair with touches of green in it and in his overall bearing was the sense of royal authority that the hapless lord of the Grey could never hope to imitate. His eyes focused on the smaller human before him with a peculiar combination of both interest and poorly suppressed disdain.

"You are to be our guest, your majesty."

Slumping, defeated, Jeremiah nodded. "Will you be taking me straight to Haros?"

Just the briefest flicker of harsh emotion crossed the bland, regal countenance. Then, the elf smiled, revealing his perfect teeth. Perfect predatory teeth just like those of Haros. "I think you misunderstand, mortal. Perhaps it would be better to say that you are my guest…now and forever after."

CHAPTER XII

Although she was neither bound nor guarded, Callistra was a prisoner. The murky land she strode upon was not a part of the dream realm that she knew. It was not very large, either, for by her own estimation, she had traversed the entire thing in little more than a thousand steps. The lithe Grey knew this because after the first time she had recognized the place from where she had begun the previous journey. No matter which way Callistra walked, her trek always ended here.

"Happy trails!" the raven had taunted after he had deposited her here. Callistra should have known then that the bird had created something special for her.

Anger was not an emotion she was very familiar with. It had raised its spiteful head when she had discovered that the Marilyn Grey had been in Jeremiah's suite. It threatened her again now, but she had learned enough to know that while a little anger was reasonable, too much would cloud her judgment beyond usefulness. That would never do. If there was a way out of this prison, she would only find it by thinking. Thought was not a process easy for a Grey; the shadow folk by nature were more reactive to their surroundings. Initiative was not common. Most Grey were satisfied with achieving form and substance and even welcomed the personalities those forms demanded of them, regardless of limitations. The Marilyn was one of those.

It had first been Haros, then Jeremiah who had pushed her to such individuality. Haros had done it for all the wrong reasons, but Jeremiah had simply changed her because he liked her. *Yet, right now I would rather have you here, ghoul!* She cared for the human and was almost willing to say that she loved him except for the simple fact that she was not familiar enough with that emotion to verify if the emptiness she felt when he was elsewhere was indeed love. Haros, however, had the strength and cunning she needed for her immediate situation.

It was vital that she escape from this fog-drenched prison. Neither Haros nor Jeremiah knew the full scale of the raven's madcap machinations. Even Callistra was uncertain as to the extent to which the magpie was willing to go.

*Round and round I go…*she thought as her starting point once more came into view. As a Grey, Callistra expended little, if any, energy, so while she contemplated manners in which to escape, she continued to stride about the land. The walk served another purpose. Each time she circled the area, Callistra scanned her surroundings, hoping against hope that some clue would present itself. So far, though, her hopes had been dashed.

Jeremiah, what is happening to you? Are you safe and sound at home? Again, there was no answering any question until she was free.

A new wrinkle abruptly added itself to the monotony of her prison. Now the land curved upward at a sharp angle. Callistra followed the trail with her eyes, soon finding it necessary to bend back to see where it continued. Her suspicions were justified when she caught sight of the path directly above her head. The flat, circular plain had become a wheel in shape, a wheel in which Callistra played the mouse inside, ever running but never getting anywhere. The bird's sense of humor left nothing to be desired, she concluded.

Callistra had just decided that she was not going to walk anymore when she caught a glimpse of something to the side. The pale woman looked, but saw nothing. Yet, for some reason she was reminded of the squat little creature that Haros sat with and who had been given a name by Jeremiah. Otto. That was ridiculous, though, for what would that one be doing here? *One of the bird's tricks,* she assured herself. Her decision was made. She would stay where she was, neither following illusions nor walking in circles.

The wheel of earth promptly began turning. If Callistra had thought herself akin to a mouse before, she had been sorely mistaken. The raven had plotted for her a convoluted series of changes, indeed. She found herself unable to stay in place, for the surface grew slick if she remained where she was for more than a moment. The turning of the wheel forced her to begin running merely to stay where she was. Her only bit of compensation proved to be the fact that she still retained her ability to transform her clothing, including, thankfully, her shoes, to whatever was desired. At the moment, that was proving to be something more practical for running than the heeled boots and skirt Callistra had chosen for Jeremiah's sake.

The pace picked up. The path also began to twist at random. Although not something that would normally bother a Grey, this place was designed for her discomfort. Callistra was as earthbound as any human, possibly even more.

If I could only be human...Not only would it fulfill her desire and shatter the one unbreakable barrier between Jeremiah and her, but as a human, she would have some say over the shadow realm, enough say, perhaps, to free herself. That could never be, though, because she knew that Haros had only hinted of the possibility of humanity for her because he had wanted her in turn to manipulate Jeremiah Todtmann.

A sudden curve in her path nearly sent her tumbling. She dared not let that happen for fear of never recovering her balance. She would be condemned to be tossed and thrown about for however long the black bird chose to let her suffer...and he would let her suffer; it was foolish to think otherwise. Mercy was a word not part of the horrific magpie's distinctive vocabulary.

I must escape from here! As many times as she thought about it, however, not one plan formed. All were quickly discarded in the face of the protean snare in which she was caught.

Another abrupt shift in the path almost tricked her. Callistra managed to readjust her balance just in time. Was she to run this chaotic circuit forever? Likely the black bird would keep her here as a hostage against Jeremiah's cooperation.

No! He's escaped! He has to have! If not, there was no hope for him; he did not understand her world enough yet and the raven would see to it that he learned only what the bird wanted him to learn. A tear escaped her eye, but she disowned it, certain that Grey could not shed real tears for the simple fact that they themselves were not real.

As unannounced as its other transformations had been, the path straightened. The twisting simply ceased and the pace slowed.

She frowned and reduced her own speed to walking. If the trek was easier now, it could only mean a new, more vile alteration was coming. Callistra's gaze shifted continuously as she sought to keep from being overwhelmed by the raven's next move, whatever that might be. She even dared glance back over her shoulder now and then, but saw nothing she could identify as a threat.

The road continued to straighten, even to the point where the wheel it had formed collapsed and became a plain again.

There was still a slipperiness to it, but not enough to cause her trouble. Puzzled and anxious, Callistra pondered this latest change. The feathered monstrosity was planning something terrible; the longer she walked the more she feared that. At the same time, however, Callistra's hopes revived. Maybe, just maybe, the power the kingship granted to Jeremiah was working for her. Maybe… maybe he needed her—her *help*, that is—so much that his desire was reaching out to free her.

Callistra knew nothing about the original design of the spell the elfin Grey had cast, only that it had been reshaped through its contact with the very humans it had been designed to locate. Haros had spoken of the spell as having an existence of its own, making it a Grey of sorts. Perhaps it was reacting to Jeremiah the way any of the shadow walkers would have.

Perhaps she could escape after all. Her pace quickened.

Iron bars do not a prison make, but there was no denying that they often helped. Gates in the true world meant nothing to a Grey, but this was a product of the fertile and fetid imagination of the black bird and so Callistra's heart, or the Greyish facsimile, almost sank when it came into view. Here, she thought, was the raven's secret ploy. He had teased her with hope of escape, only to dash that hope just when it was at its peak.

Yet, inspecting the barrier from where she had halted, Callistra could not see the threat. The gate was not even that high. With a little effort, she could climb it. What was the danger?

Her answer came almost immediately, for at the base of the gate a tiny shadow moved. The size of it did not fool her, for she knew the depthless beasts of the raven quite well. The shadow did not have to be large; it merely had to be hungry…which the demonic magpie's pets always were.

A Grey could not die as far as she knew, not literally, but it could be engulfed and assimilated. Callistra supposed that such a fate was as good a definition of death as any for her. She had no desire to become part of the shadow guarding the gate, no desire to forever be hungry. She was hungry enough for the life that was forbidden her.

The shadow moved from its resting place, sliding along at a slow but even pace. Her jailer's pets were not intelligent in the manner that she was. They lived on some terrible instinct. Any image of intelligence was a masquerade, a façade created by their master. His commands were their actions.

So close. Despite the deadly guardian, this time Callistra could not bury her hope. This was the final barrier to her escape; she could somehow sense it. It almost made her feel human, thinking so. If only the shadow could be led astray, she would be able to conquer the gate and free herself from the raven.

Ask and ye shall receive, she thought, staring wide-eyed at something that chose then to materialize on the other side of the gate. It was nothing more than one of the shadow walkers and a thin, tapering one at that. Little more than the essence of dream and with not much more in the way of intelligence. Compared to it, the sentry shadow was a genius on a par with the greats of human history. Only two things made the walker a superior form of Grey. The first was that it had the potential to evolve whereas the raven's pets were forever black holes of despair, dark thoughts ever hungering to be made real.

The second and in its own way just as important difference was speed. The smaller shadow was swifter. Hunger knows no bounds, however, and so the raven's guardian began moving toward the tinier shadow. Surprisingly enough, its prey did not dissipate as would have made sense, but simply drifted away at a speed only barely greater than that of the guardian. The hungry blot tried to close the gap, but the other shadow remained just beyond it. A tentacle of black ink shot forth, but fell short of the intended victim.

As the sentry allowed its insatiable appetite to overrule its commands, Callistra realized that the shadow walker's arrival could hardly be coincidence. It had materialized here for the specific intention of leading the devious avian's monster away, enabling the prisoner to escape.

"Jeremiah..." His name escaped her lips before she could prevent it, but the guardian did not hear her. Jeremiah could only be the one who had sent it. No one else would have considered her important enough to bother rescuing. She had betrayed Haros, the only other who had any need for her services. He would certainly not waste precious power on her even if he knew where she was.

The protean sentry was completely hypnotized by the morsel floating just before it. Quite aware that it could return to the gate the instant it noticed her, Callistra nonetheless knew that it was now or never. Unable to transport herself, the pale shadow woman ran as fast as the limitations of human legs allowed her. The gate seemed so very far away, but she dared not let herself be trapped by such thinking. If she feared the distance too great, the confounding ways of the dream realm might actually make it so. A wrong thought could make her avenue of escape a remote speck forever beyond her reach. As inconsistent as she had observed the waking world to be, Callistra would have gladly exchanged her realm for the true Earth and all of its own peculiarities.

The gate was almost within reach. A dozen steps. Ten. Eight. Four. Two.

Grumbling, the iron-wrought barrier swung open for her just before her hand would have touched it. A raging wind threatened to carry her off through the gate, but she fought against it, preferring to choose her own course rather than be blindly tossed. The wind might be the work of Jeremiah or then again it might not. The fearsome gust made each step a task worthy of Hercules, but slowly she crossed the barrier between her prison and freedom.

The blot almost had her then.

It was her own resurging confidence that nearly cost Callistra her existence. She slowed just a little as one foot crossed beyond the gate, her thoughts not at all on the possibility that the opening of the iron door would have alerted the guardian shadow. Callistra's mind was on her imminent freedom, not on dangers already passed. Thus, when the shadow formed behind her, it almost succeeded in snaring her without her even noticing its existence. Only the fierce wind saved the Grey, for it made her stumble, causing the foremost appendage of the black beast to miss her.

Callistra gasped and, lacking any use of her abilities, threw herself forward, permitting the violence of the wind to do what it wanted with her so long as it took her far from the guardian. The ever-growing windstorm tossed her about, almost making her regret her quick decision. Yet, there was merit to what she had done, for as she spun around, Callistra caught glimpses of the gate and its furious sentry. The shadow tried in vain to seize her, but for some reason its reach would not extend more than a foot or two beyond the open gateway. This time, it was possible that the raven's plotting had worked for her. Perhaps not wanting his guardian to forget its task and go wandering back into the shadow realm, the overcautious black bird had put boundaries to its hunting ground. Likely its entire domain consisted of the region alongside the gateway its master had created. By succeeding in passing beyond those boundaries, Callistra had won her freedom.

Admittedly, she had hoped for something other than this as her reward.

Round and round and round she went, turning ever in a smaller spiral. It was impossible to focus her will on anything for there was nothing to focus it upon. There was only the gate, its frustrated and hungry custodian, and the wind. Not much to choose from by any standard. Callistra began to fear that she had left one prison for another; that all her work had simply been for the entertainment of the black bird, who at any minute would appear, untouched by the wind, and reclaim her.

A hole opened above the helpless Grey, a hole to which she was drawn regardless of any desire to the contrary. Her speed increased the closer she drew to it. The hole widened, resembling as it did so one of the raven's dogs.

Callistra fell through…and felt her power return to her full-flung. She steadied herself almost instantly, pausing in her flight just in case some other threat lay before her. There was no visible threat, however, and she almost immediately recognized her location. Callistra was back in Chicago, or *perhaps above* would have been a better term.

Below her was the building in which in her domain was housed the Wasteland.

Relieved about her safety but confused by her location, she transported herself inside the club. To her further confusion, the club was empty. Not even the least shadow occupied the place.

No, that was no longer true. Seated at his usual table was Otto. The blazing eyes alternated several times, then remained lit in tandem as he focused on her. The simian Grey said nothing.

"Where is everyone? Why is the club empty?" Lacking so much as they did, the Grey were not wont to abandon what little they had unless it was for a very good reason...or perhaps a very bad reason, depending on how one looked at it.

"The hunt is on. The others are afraid or a part of it."

Her brow wrinkled. "What hunt? They are hunting Jeremiah, aren't they?"

"He's very popular."

"Spare me your witticisms." She shifted to the table, taking up a defensive position opposite the fury figure. "You've become quite knowledgeable of late, Otto. Have you noticed that?"

The eyes blinked, then stiffened into a burning stare again. "I have always been, Callistra. It was just hard to remember. It was hard to remember everything."

The conversation was beginning to bother her. "What do you mean by that?"

In return, Otto instead commented, "Jeremiah needs you, Callistra."

Jeremiah...As much as she wanted to know what the other Grey was up to, Jeremiah was still her priority. If Otto wanted to match wits with Haros and the raven, that was his prerogative. Callistra had had enough of games and plots. The Grey were not as bad as Humanity; they were worse. They were more obsessive and distrusting than those whose thoughts and dreams had formed them.

"Where is he, then? Tell me!"

"I like him, Callistra. So many kings and no name. So long and so much forgotten. I remember elves. I remember much about elves."

"Speak gibberish to Haros! If Jeremiah is your friend, then you'll tell me where he is!"

"It is the elves who have him, Callistra." The apelike creature was as still as stone, only his eyes betraying any activity. They almost seemed to have a need to move about now and then.

The elves. "He's back in the clutches of Haros." Her relief concerning Jeremiah's safety was countered by her distrust of the gaunt Grey. "Where has Haros taken him if not here?"

"Haros does not have him, Callistra. The elves have him."

It was easy for the dark-haired enchantress to see why Jeremiah Todtmann would never desire to remain the human anchor her people so badly needed. Otto's muddled and repetitive responses built up within her a tension so great that at any other time she would have simply stood where she was and admired the so human reaction. "I heard you the first time and start making sense! How can Haros not have Jeremiah if he's with the—"

Otto nodded slowly as the meaning of his words finally sank in. The eyes flashed for a brief time, then steadied again as the simian creature added to his explanation with but a single word, a name. "Oberon."

Oberon. As she matched her companion's maddening gaze, Callistra began to wonder just how much more tangled the game could become than it was already now that the elves had chosen to act on their own. Certainly not much.

The other Grey was watching her closely, as if the next decision she made determined Jeremiah's fate once and for all. The regrettable thing was that her choice might very well indeed determine the outcome. In the world of the Grey, it was almost impossible to reject any notion.

"I think…" She hesitated, not at all desiring to speak what had to be spoken. Yet, for Jeremiah it had to be done. "I think I have to talk to Haros. He is the only one who might help."

Callistra did not wait for Otto's reply. She had to locate Haros and locate him fast. A frown on her otherwise perfect countenance, the tall Grey vanished.

Otto blinked, then stared at the space she had vacated. In an oddly pleased voice he said, "I do remember elves. Elves and spells."

In stories he recalled from childhood, mortals taken into the realm of Faerie would sometimes return to their own world to find that years had passed. Knowing the creatures now to be of the Grey and knowing how time differed here, Jeremiah saw credence in the legends of old. Days had passed since his unsuspecting arrival in the shadow realm, yet he had slept little and eaten less. In fact, he could not recall the last time he had eaten. He had been given a drink or two, but when his last meal had been, the reluctant lord of the Grey could not recall.

That lack was more than being made up for now. The elves were throwing a banquet with him as guest of honor. Jeremiah had almost expected to find himself the butt of the proverbial dinner joke, that he was the main course. Instead, he was an honored guest.

He was also still a prisoner.

"Some wine?" whispered a breathy voice. A slim maiden clad in a tight, gossamer gown the color of morning leaned over him and offered a crystalline decanter. Jeremiah shook his head at both the spoken offer and the one he could read in her eyes. Even had he been interested—more than he was—in the elf maiden, the stories he had read and heard had also warned about becoming too intimate with such. Elves were notorious for playing games with unwary fools, which, in his opinion, put him at enough of a disadvantage already.

Seated at the place of honor, the human had an excellent view of his surroundings. They were impressive in design. Marble columns wrapped by flowering vines. Gold plates and ware. A table made of alabaster or so one of the other guests had claimed. Tapestries marking the feats and victories of elves, especially those of Oberon himself.

The guests were dressed in gowns that even outshone their surroundings. Silks of every color of the rainbow, many multihued. Emerald rings, perfect pearl necklaces, bejeweled daggers. Fanciful tiaras that stretched more than a foot high in some cases, but were somehow so appropriate. The elves themselves were beautiful, even many of the men. Any one of them would have won the hearts and pocketbooks of Madison Avenue advertising and Hollywood filmmaking. They were all eager to make eye contact with him, causing no end to his blushing. What was worse for him was that it mattered not to the elves whether he was male or female. Their tastes went beyond such mundane boundaries, he had already discovered. His, he was thankful, did not.

The hall of Oberon the Fairy King was, to say the least, overwhelming in all things...but one.

It was the tiniest banquet hall he had ever seen. The walls were so close as to make him nearly claustrophobic. Compared to the Wasteland, Oberon's kingdom seemed to be stored in a closet. Why, when the realm of the Grey seemed without physical limitations?

He lowered his gaze from the walls and caught Oberon himself eyeing him. Jeremiah quickly concentrated on his food. He did not want to encourage the elf lord's attention. That might mean the end of the banquet and the beginning of the king's demands.

Elf and fairy meant the same here, he had been quick to discover. Oberon and his subjects were the distillation of many legends. There were slight differences in some of the guests and a few of the servants who came and went looked more like the short creatures from modern children's novels.

Another course was laid on the table, suckling pig complete with the apple in the mouth. It smelled wonderful and despite what he had eaten so far, Jeremiah found himself looking forward to trying it. It occurred to him that here he could probably eat as much as his heart and stomach desired. Even the food was part of the magic of imagination. Everything in the Grey's world was except for Jeremiah.

He had the nagging feeling that there was someone else, someone as real as he was, who was also a part of the dream realm, but for the life of him the king of the Grey could not recall who it might be. Certainly, if there were other human beings here, he would have recalled.

Glancing at the roast pig brought the edge of his gaze back to Oberon, who now conversed with his queen, Titania. Twice Jeremiah had looked at the queen and twice he had come away not quite certain of what she looked like, save that he knew that she was the most beautiful woman here. Risking the attention of

Oberon and his spouse, he tried again to focus on Queen Titania's countenance. She reminded him of someone. Someone close to him, he felt.

He stared too long. This time, King Oberon caught his gaze and kept it snared. The other participants, Queen Titania, and the banquet itself faded as his attention was drawn whole to the elfin monarch.

‘

No! Danger! Todtmann blinked, finding it then possible to completely tear his eyes from the elf. Oberon's face darkened. The tall figure took a wine goblet in one elegantly gloved hand and pounded the base against the alabaster table, entirely oblivious to the damage the golden goblet was wreaking on the surface.

"This banquet is at an end."

The other elves finished whatever bite or sip they were taking, replaced their goblets and forks, and pushed back their chairs. A silent legion of automatons, the banquet participants stepped away from the table and departed in two perfect lines. Servants cleared the table so quickly that it almost appeared that the contents vanished of their own accord. Only Oberon and Titania remained.

"My dear wife is not adverse to the occasional human lover, Jeremiah Todtmann. Especially one of your august station."

He was still fumbling over a response to the unexpected comment when Titania, her voice reminiscent of music in springtime, added, "There are others who are also interested should you desire diversity. I hope you will think of me, first, though."

Don't look directly at their eyes! he reminded himself. That was always how they captured mortals in the books and movies...or was that vampires who did that? Jeremiah decided that Oberon and Dracula were close enough in type to make the distinction negligible. "I thank you for the most…most generous offer, I really do, but not…not at this time."

"Of course," the wondrous queen replied, her every word sending shivers of pleasure through the mortal. Jeremiah wanted to accept her offer—few men would not have—but knowing who and what she was made him pause. Again Jeremiah thought about how familiar she looked, how she reminded him of someone else, someone who meant much to him. Someone…

Callistra! The clenching of his fists was the only sign he made in response to his sudden recollection and even that would have been too much if not for the fact that both hands were hidden by the table. More than ever, he knew he had to be wary. Despite thinking he had matched their will, the elves had managed to play with his mind. They were trying to do it a piece at a time, making him forget one thing and think another. Callistra could not be the only memory suppressed; he still recalled another human, a man, in the dream realm, but the name would not come to him.

Jeremiah also recalled now the face of Oberon when he and his companion had located the human in the empty store. That and the elf's words, that the mortal was to be his guest…forever.

And here I've been sitting calmly through this banquet, a banquet in my honor! Another subtle twist by Oberon's magic, no doubt. Still, now that he knew, what could he accomplish? Under the elfin Grey's watchful eyes, Jeremiah was unable to flee, else he would have escaped back in the store.

"As you desire," Titania was saying in response to his decline of her very generous offer. "And as you desire, I shall be waiting."

Oberon smiled at his bride's small play on words, but there was something harsh in that smile. "Then it comes time to speak of other matters, mortal. Of confounding the bird and the scarecrow and bringing the realm proper back to the glory of old. Of creating a new golden age, when men and fairy lived in harmony and the ills of the present were merely a bad dream."

The elfin Grey did not share the tendency of other Grey of speaking in cliché and rhyme, but their own manner of poetic, lilting speech was in its own way even more a parody of Humanity. Jeremiah would not have been surprised if either Oberon or Titania suddenly spouted Shakespeare.

"We know you would like to return to the mortal plane, Jeremiah," continued Oberon, "but that would play into the talons of the raven. He would dearly love for you to depart, so that there would be no king and, therefore, no control over him."

While there was validity in what his host was saying, Todtmann was not trusting enough of the Fairy King to believe every word. The black bird could have let him depart back at Jeremiah's home, but instead he had assaulted the human anchor and Callistra and forced them to abandon their plan to depart the shadow realm. No, Oberon was either mistaken or lying.

Jeremiah did not think the elf was mistaken.

Oberon took his silence for interest and agreement. He nodded. "You understand that the raven cannot be left to his own devices. Good! By now you must also understand what the word of Haros Aguilana is worth. The conniving trickster is a worthy Puck in his own right, I say to you. Yet, in the end, Haros is only concerned with his own glory. He is as bad as the bird."

Somewhat confused, Jeremiah blurted, "But you worked with him."

"It was necessary. Times change, Jeremiah Todtmann. Ever they do. Once, the world was almost pure, unsullied.

Oh, there were dark shadows and evil thoughts, but their power was slight. In those days, when men believed in elves, fairies, trolls, dragons, and such, there was stability and sanity. We had purpose and lives. From the realm of dreams, we watched over those who had brought us into being, protected them from themselves. Though we are your children, still are men children, too. Under our cautious rule, however, men learned to tame the beasts within them…for the most part."

A servant entered bearing three goblets and a decanter. She curtsied to her lord and lady, then to Jeremiah with almost as much deference. He nodded to her, surprised to find that he enjoyed such a show of respect.

The servant filled the three goblets with a clear liquid. When she sought to bring the first to Oberon, he frowned at her and indicated Jeremiah. The elf girl blushed, an interesting contrast to her pale, exquisite face, and hurried to the human. Jeremiah was about to decline, having felt he had drunk more wine than he safely dared to here, when he realized how parched his throat was. The elf humbly placed the goblet before him, then returned to the two remaining cups, which she quickly served to Oberon and Titania.

When the servant had departed, the elf lord raised his goblet to Jeremiah and drank. Titania followed suit. Todtmann stared at his own drink, then, unable to think of any excuse, took the goblet and sipped. The liquid was cool, tangy, and seemed as potent as orange juice. Nevertheless, he was careful to drink no more.

"We wanted to help men more, though," continued Oberon. "So a few among us suggested a spell that would seek out a wise man among mortals and bring him here to dwell with our kind. With our advice, his own intelligence, and the abilities our carefully crafted spell would give him, we intended to enable our human brethren in part to bypass the dangers and rigors of growing to maturity." The Fairy King straightened, an act that made Jeremiah try to do the same out of sheer inadequacy. Oberon's presence was as impressive in its own way as his queen's was. Where she radiated beauty and desire, however, he radiated determination and strength. "I will not lie to you, mortal, that our own self-interests were not also at stake. Humanity at peace meant our realm at peace."

We know what's good for you, Jeremiah thought. The perspective shift from the story that Haros had related to him was interesting, but he did not believe it. Perhaps Haros had been lying, too, but his tale was probably closer to the truth than the one Oberon was spouting. Todtmann knew where the elf's explanation was heading, but as he had no plan of escape, he decided it was better to let his host talk. Hopefully either Jeremiah would think of something or Haros would come looking for his absent allies. The gaunt Grey was looking more appealing to Jeremiah.

"Haros has told you of the spell, no doubt, and while his lies are ludicrous, I know that his explanation of the basics of the spell we cast were probably nearer the truth than the rest of his telling." Another sip. This time, Jeremiah did not join his hosts in a drink. "Actually, to a point, I imagine his story of what went wrong was also within reasonable bounds of probability. The truth be told, Jeremiah Todtmann, no one knows what happened. Only that with each successive king, the spell became more errant. It chose ones entirely unsuitable for the dedicated task. Madmen and fanatics. Once among us, we could not turn back the tide. The darkness that we had kept in check flowed freely. We grew fearful for that darkness would change not only us, but spread its influence over the waking world." Oberon's eyes flashed. Literally.

"It was the beginning of the end of what should have been the Age of Harmony!"

The words still echoed in Jeremiah's head a breath later when he found himself standing with Oberon and Titania atop a high hill overlooking a lush, rolling landscape. The sun glowed, the songs of birds filled the air, and the thatch roofs of a tiny, peaceful village could just be made out in the distance. It was a picture no artist could have painted to satisfaction. None of it was real, of course. It was simply a recreation of what the Fairy King wanted him to believe in.

Realizing that and realizing that he was not at all taken in by Oberon's stunning vision encouraged Todtmann.

"This is what might have been if not for the spell's itinerant way! It could have all been so idyllic! Yet, instead, each successive king tainted the world, feeding further the darkness in a never-ending cycle."

The fairy-tale landscape dimmed and twisted. The forests and green hills gave way to roads and buildings all distorted and foreboding. The only birds that sang here were the crows and ravens. To one who had not become at least somewhat accustomed to the world of the Grey, it was a garish nightmare. The land smelled of decay and ominous shadows blocked the sky. The lack of any other sound save the black birds' calls summoned up the impression of a dead place. A place without hope. It was harder to ignore the horrid tableau now presented to him than it had been to ignore the previous one, but Todtmann persevered. This was no more real than the idyllic countryside. It was simply another one of the Grey's illusions.

He had been trying to let Oberon's words slide over him, but each time his host talked of Jeremiah's ability to influence both worlds, the words struck him like barbs. Haros had hinted of some subtle influences, but not to the vast extent that Oberon had now twice spoken of in his attempt to win the alliance of the human. Who was right and who was wrong? Were both of them right?

It mattered not either way. The truth was and would always be that Jeremiah Todtmann was a tool. The Grey—Haros, the raven, and Oberon to be more specific—saw him as a way not only to stabilize their mercurial world, but also as a way to put the minds and dreams of the humans under their direction. Why him and not the others before, though?

Perhaps a bit overconfident in himself, Oberon apparently decided that he had all but won his case. "For the first time, we have the ability to turn back the clock! You will have to work slowly at first, but the more our influence spreads back across the dream realm, the quicker and easier will come the results!"

A goblet held by a delicate, cream-colored hand materialized near Jeremiah's mouth. Startled, he discovered that Titania now stood on the opposite side of him, one arm draped around Jeremiah's waist. Her attempts to offer him the goblet were insistent and he almost expected her to try to forcibly pour the liquid down his throat. It was the same wine he had discarded but moments before. If the wine was supposed to be weakening his will, it and the other cups before it had failed. Despite the lapses of memory he had suffered, Jeremiah's mind was as much his own as it had never been. Not that being of his own mind had helped him much in the past.

Hadn't it? *It worked in the tower...and I was also able to shield myself later. Maybe I could—What?* He was no hero. In his hands, whatever powers he had been given were wasted. At least Hector would have had more of an idea what to do in a situation like this.

Jeremiah was fairly certain that his friend would have calculated a way out of this situation by now. *But not me! Never me!*

Oberon's heavy hand clamped onto his free shoulder. Jeremiah could not stop himself from shaking, a reaction that he did not doubt lessened him even more in the eyes of the Grey. The elf lord pulled the human toward him, freeing Todtmann at least temporarily from the temptations, liquid and otherwise, Queen Titania offered him. "It is a great task I ask of you, mortal, and I know that you may think it too great for your skills to handle. Rest assured, though, that I will guide you through it in the beginning."

Oberon glowed with good intentions, which only made them that much more false, although the elf evidently could not see that. Regardless of his lack of faith in himself, Jeremiah Todtmann hardened inside. He could never allow himself to be used by Oberon. What the Fairy King and his kind desired was to turn back to the days of ignorance and superstition, when they had been among the dominant Grey and Humanity had been more susceptible to their influences. Oberon hardly seemed the altruistic type and while he had admitted that his goals would help his kind, his notion, if the Grey truly believed in it, of what was good for humans was quite different from what most humans might have chosen. Under Oberon, there actually was no choice.

"You see what must be done, good Jeremiah?"

He did and Oberon was not going to be pleased. Forcing himself to play a role of enchanted acceptance, Jeremiah removed himself from the grips of his hosts and pretended to be horrifically fascinated by the dark scene stretching forth below him. The elves were quiet, allowing him to drink in the terror of it all. Jeremiah stepped to the edge of the hilltop they stood upon and looked over. Below him was a tremendous drop, probably several hundred feet by his guess. Trying not to show his fear, he leaned forward as if desiring a better view...and leapt.

As Jeremiah went over, he fought down rising panic and concentrated on the image of the old water tower. While possibly no longer the best location to transport to, it was the first one that came to mind. He hoped that surprise and shock would keep Oberon from sending forth pursuit until after he had shifted to his second location, the strip mall parking lot about a mile from his battered home. From there...from there Jeremiah would find somewhere. Callistra and Hector were still lost and until he found them, he could not think about his own safety.

All of this flashed through his mind in the space of the first few maddening seconds after he committed himself. Then, with the image of the parking lot firmly entrenched, the king of the Grey transported himself.

"It would have been better for you, mortal, if you had allowed yourself to be taken in by my more pleasant lures. I fear that I must now enforce our desires upon you and that is truly a pity."

Oberon stood no more than two or three yards from him, a blinding aura surrounding his armored body. The Fairy King was clad like a knight of old, but one taller than a human and clad in thin but glistening armor the color of the forest. A winged helm with nose guard hid the upper half of the handsome but deathly countenance. In one hand, Oberon carried a whip almost as long as Jeremiah, a sinewy black snake with nine spiked heads promising painful bites. In the other hand the elf bore a shield upon which was emblazoned a black unicorn locked in combat with a massive bird...a raven, of course.

The two of them stood not in the parking lot but rather the forested land that Oberon had been displaying to him. The land was now a peculiar hodgepodge of beauty and beast, with pieces of both versions intermingled haphazardly. Twisted roads began and ended in the midst of forest. Songbirds alighted onto dark, bent buildings. A shadow draped the village, but the sun was shining on some of the nearest misshapen structures. Crows cavorted in the green fields, acting more like robins in springtime. Without Oberon's will to guide it, his display was falling apart.

The elf lord hardly cared. He only had eyes for the slight figure who had defied his will. "Take the king and show him to accommodations suitable to his status."

Two warriors that had not been behind Jeremiah a moment before seized him by the arms. While they subdued him, Titania joined her husband. The sweet smell of flowers surrounded her as the queen walked up to Jeremiah and ran a single, perfect nail across his cheek.

She shook her head and tsked at the mortal. "You really should not have behaved so abominably, Jeremiah Todtmann. Your stay with us could have been so pleasant. Now, it will be painful." Titania smiled and playfully tapped his chin. "But have no fear; Oberon will not kill you. I would never permit him to do that."

"Play later, my dear," called the elf lord. "It is time for his majesty to retire."

"Oh, very well," murmured the glittering lady. She cocked her head and smiled daintily to the captive. "You know, you're very fortunate."

Jeremiah could only gape.

"Oh, yes, very fortunate," repeated Queen Titania. "Imagine if you had fallen beyond the boundaries of Faerie! Why you might have run across the black bird or Haros!" She turned away in a swirl of silky, diamond-encrusted skirts, finishing, "I shudder to think what the raven might have done to you! At least you're still safe from him!"

He was still gaping when his guards took him away.

CHAPTER XIII

The raven flew between the waking world and that of the Grey, his eagerness to complete his latest experiment keeping him unusually silent. The raven liked to talk, not only because he adored the sound of his own voice, but because few others, Haros excluded, were willing to dare even a short exchange of words with him. That they did not was no skin off his back, as the saying went. The black bird was perfectly satisfied with his own august company.

The line blurred between dream and reality. Chicago of the true world reared its unsuspecting head at his latest intrusion. The black bird soared about for a moment, defying everything that was living. He was here now and would only leave when he decided to leave. Of course, that would be as soon as his experiment was over, but it would be by his choice.

Then, as he dove among the tall buildings, sending pigeons into panic, the raven saw his target. He altered his course and dropped toward the ground.

The cat rummaged through the Dumpsters behind a building housing one of the elite restaurants of the city, but it was not simply after the half-eaten remains of someone's not-quite-cooked-to-perfection filet. No, the cat was a hunter and its game was what was after those remains. Plump rats, grown lazy from good pickings, were equally good pickings for the brown-and-black predator. The cat only ate what was needed to satiate its appetite. A survivor, it knew what overindulgence did. Only those who kept alert and quick survived long in what was truthfully an urban jungle.

Those traits were what the black bird wanted for his experiment.

The winged fury caught the large cat as it was burrowing after a particularly fat morsel. Talons raked at the feline's backside, but the cat, after its initial start, was veteran of enough battles to react with a slash of its own claws that sent the raven fluttering out of reach.

Spitting, the cat hunched up and slashed again at the upstart avian. Birds were occasional banquets for it, mostly pigeons caught up in their feeding frenzies. Although it was vaguely aware of the larger birds the city had brought in to keep the pigeon population in check, those predators remained in the heavens and this was certainly not one of them.

"Curiosity killed the cat!" mocked the raven even though he knew that the animal could not comprehend his words.

He dropped on the cat again.

As fast as the alley fighter was, it could not keep up with the fluttering and shifting of the raven. Claws cut at air, on occasion almost rending feather and flesh, but ever just coming short. The talons of the black bird, however, scored again and again, ripping fur and leaving streaks of red to stain the brown and black. In seconds, it was no longer a battle, but a rout. The cat realized its danger and tried to flee, but the raven, laughing, forced it back into the fray each time.

The back door of the restaurant burst open and two men clad in kitchen uniforms jumped outside, the sticks in their hands intended for the breaking up of the cat fight they expected to find. When they saw the truth of the situation, though, they stopped where they were and stared.

Perched atop the ragged, lifeless form of his adversary, the raven laughed. He raked his claw over one still-open eye, unleashing a new torrent of blood. Belatedly, the avian killer noted the two humans. He winked at them and, cawing, flew up into the sky. As he ascended, the raven glanced down and watched as one man eyed him while the other pushed at the loser's reddening form with his stick.

He had *killed!* It was enough! He had broken the barrier at last! "Nine lives, indeed!"

It was time at last for the human anchor to fulfill his part. It was time for the raven to fulfill his destiny.

He had *killed!* The seductive taste of blood still lingered. How more sweet it was to be able to strike down the life on his own, then utilize an object, as he had done with the human he had killed! How much more sweet it would be when the final step of his grand scheme was realized!

The raven opened the way to the shadow realm and vanished through it, humming merrily all the while.

"Jeremiah?"

Arms aching, the would-be king of the Grey opened his eyes and tried to focus in the dim light. Out of reflex he tried to reach out, but the chains that held his arms high above his head refused him even the slightest movement in that direction.

"Jeremiah?"

It *sounded* like…"Callistra?"

"Jeremiah!" She came out of the shadows, looking exactly as he had last seen her. The tall, beautiful enchantress hugged him tight, putting him through both pleasure and pain, the latter because her enthusiasm pulled him forward, almost stretching his arms out of his shoulders.

"I'm sorry, Jeremiah!" she whispered, moving him back. "Have they hurt you much?"

"No…I've just been left hanging here."

Callistra stroked his cheek. "Poor Jeremiah! I'm here now. I'll take care of you."

He peered over her shoulder, fearful that guards would materialize at any moment and put an end to any hope of escape. Callistra did not seem at all hurried. She wiped a smudge of dirt from his face.

"Can you get me out of these?" He rattled the chains impatiently.

"In a moment." From somewhere, she managed to produce a cup, which she immediately offered to the captive king. "You should drink this first, Jeremiah. It will help."

He was thirsty, but that could wait. Freedom at the cost of a little thirst was more than worth the price. "I'll drink it after we're out of here, Callistra. Just free me! Oberon might come back at any moment."

"If you want to have the strength you will need for the journey ahead, you should drink this now, dear Jeremiah."

Todtmann stared at her, his eyes narrowing. Finally, he clamped his mouth shut and turned his head aside.

"Jeremiah? What is wrong?"

"You're not Callistra." He continued to look to the side. Staring into her eyes might be dangerous. "If you're not Callistra, then you have to be an elf."

"Well, I tried," Callistra said wistfully, only it was not Callistra's voice anymore, but rather Titania's. Glancing at her, Jeremiah noted that she had returned to her glorious form. The cup was still in her hands. "And here I thought I had performed my role so splendidly."

"You did," he replied, playing on her vanity. In truth, she had ruined her chances the moment she had brought the cup into play. Even barring her insistence that he drink while still chained, her somewhat carefree attitude in the face of danger had already worn thin; another moment or two and Jeremiah would have been certain of her identity even without the poorly played cup ploy.

"I was so hoping you might see it my way and drink. The wine of forgetfulness is so much more pleasant than what dear Oberon will have to do to you. Are you certain that you won't change your mind?"

"I'm sorry, no."

"A pity." Titania smiled and was gone. For the life of him, Jeremiah could still not recall the particulars of her features.

Now fully awake, he glanced around at the "accommodations" Oberon had provided for him. Shadows obscured everything farther than a yard ahead, but at least they were not the deep, hungry shadows of the raven. To each side, roughly another yard away, were simple stone walls. He already knew that the wall behind him would be the same, barring the tiny opening high above that provided what little illumination he had. The chains were made of some metal that was not iron and might have been silver. Whatever their composition, they held and that was what mattered.

Well, your majesty? he mocked, referring to himself and not the elf lord. *What now?*

On the surface, his defiance of Oberon's desires looked idiotic. Now he would spend as long a time in this dungeon as was needed by the ruler of Faerie to convince him of the error of his ways. Even knowing that, though, and being properly dismayed by it, Jeremiah could still not bring himself to acquiesce to his captor's demands. Oberon wanted a return to the Dark Ages and Jeremiah understood enough now to know that he did have the power to influence both the waking and dream realms toward that direction. Under Oberon's guidance, he would turn Mankind away from the future and into the past. For all the problems facing the human race, Jeremiah was of the opinion that it was still better off the way it was than how it had been during the so-called idyllic period to which the elf lord wished to return. Jeremiah Todtmann had no intention of using his powers to those ends.

His powers...They were his powers. Oberon, Haros, the raven... everyone saw great potential in his spell-wrought skills, but always for their own purposes. Everyone wanted to change the world and they were of the opinion that he was the key.

The reluctant monarch wondered just how powerful he really was. If he was so great a force in the dream realm, then should he not be able to free himself from something so simple as a dungeon cell? He had to be. How could his captor expect so much from him otherwise?

"There's only one way to find out," Todtmann muttered. He tugged on the chains again, just to make certain. Yes, they felt very solid. There was no help there. How was he to go about it? Simply wishing them off did not work. Experience told him that. Jeremiah had also tried transporting himself away early on, but that had failed, also, although he did not know why. What was left to him?

How had he used his powers so far? A shield to momentarily block the raven's assault. Transporting himself from one place to another. Shaping the shadow walker. Halting the frenzied twists of the Sears Tower.

The list stopped there, as far as he could recall, but Jeremiah was fairly surprised by the variety. As the human anchor, he had a wide array of abilities, it seemed. There might even be more…there had to be more, he corrected. What was it Oberon wanted him to do? Make the dream realm over into what it once had been. A human in the realm had much more influence on the Grey than the rest of the waking world combined, Haros had passed that much on.

Haros. The cadaverous creature had been fairly honest with him when all was said and done, but had he understated the extent of Jeremiah's power? *If I can change the world, I can change this little bit of the dream realm.*

Licking his lips, Todtmann tried a variation on what he had done to the Sears Tower. In that instance, he had succeeded despite nearly being flung back and forth across the entire observation deck. Here, he had no distractions save the chains and they, of course, were the focus of his experiment.

This time, Jeremiah did not simply try to wish the chains away. Instead, he tried to picture what his surroundings might look like without the bonds. It was an alteration of perspective, a small change in what was to what should be. Jeremiah had no idea if he was on the right track or whether there was even a track at all; it was the best he could come up with under the circumstances.

The same cell, the same building, the same realm, but with the one difference being the lack of chains. He could picture it. It was real to him. Jeremiah saw himself lowering his arms, for if there were no chains, there was no reason to keep his arms in such a painful position.

He then became aware that he *had* lowered his arms.

Raw and aching they were, but his hands and arms were free! Jeremiah brought his unhindered hands close, a stunned smile slowly cutting across his face. It could not have been as simple as it seemed, but the proof was before him. His hands were free! *I've done it!*

What exactly he had done, the unwilling king was still not certain, but it had worked and that was what mattered. A change of perspective. Hadn't Hector made a suggestion hinting something like that during the chaos in the tower? Jeremiah decided he probably had. Hector seemed to have thought of just about everything first. He deserved to be the focus, not Jeremiah. Of course, Todtmann doubted that his fellow exile would want the role, but it was nice to imagine someone as capable as Hector Jordan as anchor. Very nice.

But I'm the one stuck with it! he reminded himself. And as long as I have it, I might as well put it to use! He very well might have been able to affect a complete escape on the first try, but Jeremiah was not one to go rushing into the unknown. He also wanted to avoid the notice of Oberon for as long as he could.

The would-be lord of the shadow lands stared at the darkness as he tried to calculate his next move. If he could adjust the realm of the Grey so that the chains no longer existed, he should be able to adjust things so that he stood in an open field or simply the empty and dimly lit mist that appeared to be the true essence of the dream realm. He did not have to transport; instead, Jeremiah could simply decide that his present surroundings just did not exist anymore. A tight-lipped smile of determination formed. It sounded easy enough.

The smile and his plans were shattered by the jarring intrusion of an elfin jailer who simply walked out of the shadows. The brooding elf froze and took in the sight of the prisoner standing unshackled.

Jeremiah reacted almost on instinct. He did not want the elf to be here; he wanted a variation of this scene, one in which the elf was anywhere but the cell.

Jeremiah adjusted his reality.

There was no elf. The scene was exactly as it had been before the jailer's unannounced arrival. It was as if the intrusion had never been.

Did I do that?

Briefly, Todtmann wondered where he had sent the unsuspecting elf, but then the notion that he might have permanently erased the Grey's existence made him quickly drop the query. True, Jeremiah had been forced to do it, but the elves were certainly not the most sympathetic Grey. They would not take kindly to what he had done.

It frightened him some to think that he, Jeremiah Todtmann, wielded such power. It frightened him more to think that he would have to use it again. There was no other choice; it was his only means of escape. They could block his ability to transport, but not, apparently, this skill. Did it have something to do with being based on the human capability of influencing and shaping the realm of the Grey? It was the only reason he could think of. Perhaps all the other gifts of the kingship were Grey-given.

Whether that was the reason or not, Jeremiah was risking himself by staying here any longer. If all he had to do was imagine his surroundings as, say, an open field, then that was what he needed to do…and do it now.

The earthquake that nearly threw him to the ground was not part of his image. Jeremiah almost ceased his wish, but then he saw the sides of his cell tear free from the floor and fold back much the way the convertible roof of an automobile might. The walls and ceiling continued to fold back, collapsing into themselves. Revealed to him was not the rest of the interior of Oberon's palace, but rather a gray blankness in which he could almost make out the vague images of a grassy field. As the cell closed on itself, the field grew more and more distinct.

Recalling what had happened to the suite Haros Aguilana had supplied him, Jeremiah quickly stepped from the stone floor of his prison onto the forming field. To his relief, the earth beneath his feet held.

The floor fell away but a moment later, perhaps having waited for him to depart before collapsing. He was glad he had not had to test that theory.

Jeremiah watched in astonishment as the kingdom of Faerie folded together. Walls fell into courtyards. A garden dangled over nothing, then fell into oblivion. Birds fluttered up from the higher towers, only to fade away once they left the vicinity of the crumbling citadel.

Then, without ceremony, Faerie popped out of existence.

Caught up in the wonder of the awesome spectacle, Jeremiah only then pondered what had happened to the elves. His mouth opened, but only a hiss escaped. Todtmann's hands shook. He had not meant to erase them. Not at all. He had only wanted to be free.

"What have I done?" he whispered. Supposedly the Grey could not die…but did that hold true for a situation such as this? He stumbled back a few steps and stared at the spot where Oberon's once-mighty kingdom had stood. Not a trace remained that he could see. Everything—castle, gardens, grounds, and inhabitants—was gone.

Gone...and he was responsible. Jeremiah continued to stare, but the sight did not change. He had eliminated the existence of Faerie.

He turned away in self-disgust and started walking. Whether this was the right direction or not, he could not say. It was the only direction he had, though, and the sooner he was away from what had once been Faerie, the better. Perhaps then it would be easier not to think about what he had just done.

Then, as he walked, Jeremiah heard a rumble behind him, a growing rumble that did not sound like thunder, but rather was more akin to a stampede. He slowed, then halted. The sound grew nearer. With great reluctance, Jeremiah returned his gaze to the former resting place of Faerie.

"Oh...my...God!" was what he wanted to say, but the sight before him was so overwhelming that Jeremiah Todtmann simply forgot to talk.

It unfurled toward him, a gargantuan, runaway carpet covered with pop-up landscape. Trees snapped to attention and threw birds into the air. Hills sprouted like bubbles that at the last moment had forgotten to burst. The first of the elfin structures blossomed skyward.

Jeremiah turned on his heels and started running.

"How dare you, mortal? How dare you so callously dispose of my realm?"

There was no question as to whose voice called to him from all around. Jeremiah ran faster.

With little effort, Oberon, followed by a legion of elfin knights, rode out of nothing into the plain, cutting off his escape. The landscape shifted, becoming the hills and woods of Faerie again. The knights paid no heed to the changes around them; Jeremiah was their obsession. They spread across his path, then slowed to a stop several yards away, Oberon foremost in the ranks when all was said and done. Once more the Fairy King wore his elegant armor and carried the shield with the dueling unicorn and raven embossed upon it, but this time in his other gauntleted hand King Oberon held a jeweled sword with a long blade that shone like a star. The point of the magnificent blade was focused on Jeremiah's chest.

"How dare you?" he repeated in the terrible voice that carried despite the distance. *"How dare you when there is so little left?"*

Oberon lowered his sword a fraction.

The glittering elfin knights charged on the hapless mortal.

Todtmann stumbled back, but he knew there was no escape. He could only do what he had done before and pray that it worked better than it had with Faerie itself.

The gleaming row of knights vanished. They reappeared.

They vanished again.

Once more, the row rematerialized, no closer than they had been before their first disappearance.

Desperate, Jeremiah tried something different. If he could not remove their presence, then perhaps he could play with the landscape.

A hill burst into sedentary life in the midst of the elves' ranks. Horses shrieked and riders were unseated. A few, however, maneuvered around each side of the hill and two even made it over.

He reshaped the land to include a river whose banks on one side ended at his very feet and on the other just before the hooves of the racing animals. Unable to halt their progress, the powerful beasts plunged into the water, carrying their armored masters with them.

To his disappointment, Jeremiah discovered that elfin armor floated...or maybe the elves themselves just did. Nonetheless, the attack was broken up.

Almost, that is. Jeremiah had forgotten about Oberon himself.

Snarling out words incomprehensible to Todtmann's ears, the elf lord pointed his sword directly at his mortal foe's chest. Jeremiah braced himself, fully expecting a lightning bolt or some such terrible assault.

Instead, the water frothed, growing higher and higher...A tentacle broke the surface.

Rising from the water was a monstrosity that should have been at home in the high seas, not a river. What seemed a thousand tendrils shot forth to seize Jeremiah. A beak of a mouth opened and closed in hunger and the vast eye that stared his way was cold and inhuman. The body of the beast was the color of blood, Jeremiah's blood if Oberon's desires were granted.

A student of legends and lore would have known it for the mighty Kraken, but it was enough for Jeremiah to think of it as one tremendously large and enthusiastic squid.

With death in the form of a multitude of tight caresses upon him, Jeremiah could devise only one defense against a sea monster gone astray.

Another sea monster.

Focused on its summoner's adversary, the Kraken did not notice the huge, unfocused shape suddenly rising behind it until the second beast was nearly upon it. When it did notice, the tendrils immediately withdrew, to take on the fuzzy leviathan come to Jeremiah's rescue. Timing and angle were on the second monster's side, however. The newcomer roared its challenge and without preamble thrust its maw directly at the Kraken's eye.

Tentacles wrapped around the long neck and wide torso of Jeremiah's champion, but the massive squid's reactions were too little too late. The jaws of the blurry beast clamped on to the eye and tore into it. Ichor flowed and many of the Kraken's appendages went into spasm, freeing up the second monster some. It ripped away the eye and tore in anew, sending gobbets of stench-ridden flesh flying to both sides of the bank.

The Kraken's tentacles tightened around the other monster's neck, but the newcomer refused to give up its assault, its jaws biting down once more on the wounded eye.

The battle was over almost as soon as it had begun. Too much of its bodily fluids flowed free for the Kraken to maintain the counterattack. It began to grow limp and as it did so, the out-of-focus monster Jeremiah had desperately summoned fell upon the body and started to push it under. In moments there was nothing to be seen of the Kraken save for a few loose bits of flesh and a growing pool of darkness befouling the surface of the magical river.

Roaring its triumph to Jeremiah, the Loch Ness Monster joined its defeated opponent beneath the misleadingly quiet surface.

A roar of a different sort escaped Oberon's throat. He hefted his sword and, seemingly ignorant of the distance, threw it at the human before him.

Jeremiah backed up several paces, prepared to defend himself with some other spell, but the sword fell short despite the elf lord's prodigious effort. It landed tip first in the false ground more than two arm's lengths from the man.

A blink of an eye later, King Oberon himself knelt next to it, his face downcast and his position toward Jeremiah Todtmann.

"I yield to you, your majesty."

Jeremiah glanced around, then looked down at the kneeling figure. "What?"

It was clear Oberon greatly despised repeating himself, but he did nonetheless. "I yield to you, Jeremiah Todtmann, King of the Grey."

"I've won?" If it was a trick, it was a peculiar one, but how else to explain it? How could he have defeated Oberon, king of the elves? This was hardly a...a fairy tale! Good did not just triumph over evil, not even here!

Yet, Oberon knelt at his feet in obeisance. Reluctant obeisance, but still obeisance.

"You have won," the elf lord confirmed, daring to look up. "Ignorant as a newborn babe, yet you have won, mortal. Look around you and see my kingdom. Look around you and see that if I fight any longer, there shall be no Faerie for which to fight! I am at my limits."

For the first time since the short battle, Jeremiah Todtmann surveyed his surroundings. At first he was perplexed by the elfin Grey's comments, for Faerie was as Faerie had been before Jeremiah's mis-thoughts had almost rendered it nothing more than memory. The trees, the hills, the castle, all were as they had been and likely would be. All were—

Frayed at the edges?

He noticed it first on the palace of Oberon, a fuzziness on the edges. It was not like the Loch Ness Monster, however. Instead, it was as if the palace were dissolving or fading away at the sides. The unwilling lord of the Grey glanced around at the rest of Oberon's kingdom and began to notice the same frayed edges throughout the landscape. He was reminded of, of all things, fading memories.

"It is my will that now holds it together," Oberon explained, the haughty countenance giving way to sadness and some fear. "My will alone that sustains Faerie. As belief faded, so, too, did Faerie. As my will weakened, so, too, did Faerie. Only my will—the will granted me by so much earlier belief in my kingdom—allowed me to keep it nearly as it was." He shook his head. "None of this is real, mortal, not even in the terms of the Grey. The banquet was smoke and the courtiers mist. There are only a handful who truly recall from the days of power, a handful who work with me to keep the memory of our glory alive."

For an illusion, it had been a pretty solid one, Jeremiah thought. "You mean none of this is real?"

Oberon rose slowly. Todtmann tensed, but the elf shook his head. There was no fight left in him. "Let me show you what is truly left of glorious Faerie."

The scene changed again.

To Jeremiah, it looked as if someone started to sketch the idea for a wondrous fantasy realm but had grown bored and abandoned it halfway through to completion. There were the outlines of trees and hills and a vague notion of their place in the scene. Oberon's palace was a half-glimpsed structure of indeterminate shape and size. Jeremiah felt like a character tossed into the preliminary drawings of a comic book. There was no form or depth. The only things of depth were himself, Oberon, and six or seven cloak-clad figures standing behind the Fairy King. He recognized one from the encounter at his home, but another he expected to see was not among the lowly group of elves.

Oberon's eyes flashed as he realized just who it was Jeremiah was searching for. "Mist, mortal. All we have are memories and mist."

He had never been in any great danger. Jeremiah knew that now. Almost all of Oberon's power was illusion. So long as Jeremiah had believed in that power it had been able to hold him. The moment he had tested it, however, it had faded away as quickly as dreams in the morning.

The elf lord put a hand over where his heart should have been and went down on one knee again, his few followers quickly imitating his actions. There was no anger, no arrogance left. Oberon's voice trembled just a little as he talked. "You have the power of existence over us, Jeremiah Todtmann. Never life, for even you cannot give us that, I see now. You have the power to change things as you like, to mold us as you like."

"I just want to go home," the reluctant king whispered. "I just want to go home!"

Oberon shook his head, seeming very understanding at the moment. "I cannot help you there, your majesty. If anyone knows a way back, it would be either the raven or Haros." He had been afraid that such would be the answer. That left him with no choice. At this point he needed the stick man to help him with everything— Callistra, Hector, escaping the raven's traps—everything. "How do I find Haros, then? Can you show me how to do that?"

"I can show you the path to the border between worlds, Jeremiah Todtmann. Nothing more. Where Haros Aguilana chooses to be only he knows."

It was less than he would have wanted, but more than he had expected. "Show me that, then. There are a couple of friends I need to find first."

Oberon did not stand. "I ask a boon, first." "A boon? That's a favor, right?"

"Yes." Oberon glanced back at his fellows, then at Jeremiah once more. "I ask that you try to believe."

"Believe in what?"

"Believe in elves, dragons, fairies, and unicorns...at least a little."

Jeremiah eyed the pitiful group. This was all that was left of childhood dreams and stories. Perhaps the elves were not that deserving of his sympathy, but what they represented was, he decided. Not just for him, but others. There was a need for Faerie, if not necessarily Oberon himself. "I'll try."

Now the handsome armored figure rose. As he did, the false realm bloomed back to life around them. It was still frayed around the edges, however, as if not enough memory of its glory existed to strengthen the illusion further. "Then come. I will show you how to get back." The armor changed to the traveling garb that Oberon had first worn when Jeremiah had seen him outside of his home. "There is one thing that you should realize, Jeremiah Todtmann, before we part company."

"And what's that?"

The realm of Faerie was already fading around them. Even as Oberon spoke, the last vestiges dwindled to nothing, to be replaced by the misty emptiness that Jeremiah had come to know all too well. "Defeating me was nothing, mortal. I am little more than memory myself. With each passing day in the waking world, I become less and less real...even for a Grey. When you face the raven, that will be a battle on a far greater scale. He is almost as real as you."

Jeremiah shivered, but maintained a calm expression. "I don't intend on fighting him."

His guide studied him, then nodded his head once. "For the Grey's sake, I hope you do not." He glanced beyond the two of them, as if seeing something. "Of course, you still have to convince the raven otherwise, do you not?"

They now stood in a sort of limbo. Not quite here, not quite there. Jeremiah ignored it, for something Haros or someone else had told him earlier had come to mind. "Oberon, was it you who created the spell I bear? Were you one of the Grey who cast it?"

It was as if they had come to a jarring halt. Jeremiah knew that they had ceased traveling even though there was no visible sign.

Oberon's countenance was dark. "No, mortal, I am not one of those who cast it. A fortunate thing, for the strain was too great for those who cast it. They…forgot…themselves, mortal. The greatest horror for one of our kind. They had identity and they lost it." The Fairy King actually shuddered. "There was nothing we could do. Nothing I could do for any of them or the many who followed when humans lost their belief in us."

*Death for a Grey…*Haros had talked of how the Grey changed as the dreams of Humanity did, but this was the first time he had heard of a Grey falling to such a fate. He thought of Callistra, then pushed the horrible image from his mind. To lose her would be unthinkable. "I'm sorry. I am." Jeremiah hesitated. "Will you answer me just a few more questions? They're important."

A grim smile crossed the elfin features. "I no longer have anything to hide, do I?"

"What was the true purpose of this spell? Was there more than just choosing one human to guide things?" He hesitated again, still not certain that his former adversary would not try to hide something. "Why would you give so much power to an outsider? A human? Why would you willingly be ruled by him?"

To his surprise, Oberon nodded in what might have been approval. "A fair question. We had no intention of being ruled, Jeremiah Todtmann. Ever. In truth, the spell was cast so as to choose a malleable person and then focus that mortal's will in a manner of our making."

So the king was to be a useful tool, but nothing more. A powerful slave, even. That sounded much more like what Jeremiah had expected to hear. "But something went wrong."

"Not at first. The first two or three were as we desired, but then each successor deviated more. By the time we realized the extent of the deviation, it was too late. The spell had grown beyond us."

Which was much the way he had heard it the first time. "One more thing, if you don't mind. I know I said I only had a few questions, but—"

"If it will aid you in battle against the raven, then I will answer gladly, mortal."

"That's just it. Where does the raven fit into all of this? Do you know?"

Oberon pondered for a moment, then finally shook his head. "To know where and when a Grey forms is trickiest at the best of times. Often, we simply are. The foul bird, though, has existed almost as long as the spell. Indeed, one might say it drew him as a flower in bloom draws a bee, for he has ever circled near."

"And no one's stopped him in all this time?" "No one has known how."

The answer was enough to silence any other question Jeremiah had.

CHAPTER XIV

Haros Aguilana sat in the back of the Rolls puffing on a cigarette. None of his decoys had as yet lured the prodigal human back into the fold and it was beginning to look like perhaps the raven had him after all. Still, where there was hope there was fire or some such saying. It said much that he could not even untangle a cliché. The raven had him on the ropes.

"Haros."

The other figure suddenly seated next to him did not in the least shock him by materializing there. He was, in fact, becoming quite bored with her face.

"Ahhh, the face that launched a thousand duplicates," he hissed as he puffed on his cigarette. "I thought you lost and gone forever, Callistra."

From the other end of the seat, the lissome Grey frowned. "No thanks to you, Haros."

"You were the one that ran off with our king...who is sorely missing from your company, I see. Pity."

"Puffing on those memories won't bring him back." She leaned forward, anger barely kept in check. "He had every right to leave, Haros, and I had every right to help him!"

The cadaverous Grey ignored her emotional display despite its relative novelty. "And has he escaped?"

"No." Callistra leaned back, just a bit deflated. "But we know where he is…or was…"

"'We'?"

Callistra looked around. "Otto was the one who told me."

"Indeed." Haros cocked an eyebrow. "I am really going to have to have a talk with our simian friend. I have this suspicion that he's been hiding something from us."

She was of a similiar opinion, but Otto was by far one of the lesser worries on Callistra's mind. First and foremost was Jeremiah. "Will you help me find him?"

"By 'him,' I would assume that you mean one Jeremiah Todtmann, mortal and king-errant, human anchor for our kind. Or could you mean Otto?" Haros disposed of the cigarette the way he always did. As it faded to nothing, he smiled at his companion. "Before you start another outburst, I know who you meant. Of course, I'll help you. I'd be a fool, otherwise, wouldn't I? Better Jeremiah in my tender hands than the talons of the black bird, am I right?"

Callistra slowly nodded, hoping deep inside that she would not regret her decision. It would have been better if Otto had remained with her. She wondered where he had gotten to, then decided it was not worth worrying about. "The elves have him, Haros."

"Do they?" The mask slipped, revealing a brief glimpse of anger. The elves were his allies, Callistra knew. Unwilling ones, but allies nonetheless. Haros did not care for betrayals, especially when he was the one being betrayed. Only when the mask was back in place did Haros reply, "We shall have to speak to Oberon. Now, I think."

The Rolls Phantom glided smoothly around the next corner. The darkened streets of Chicago faded, to be replaced by a golden road made of brick. The Rolls-Royce handled as calmly on the brick as it had on the asphalt and concrete.

"It won't be long now." To the car, he added, "A bit slower. Oberon is a touchy sort."

The Phantom, which had no driver to speak of, slowed obediently. Then, to Callistra's surprise, it stopped completely.

Haros Aguilana leaned forward. "I said 'slower,' not 'stop.' "

Callistra looked out the window, studying the landscape. She found she did not like what she was seeing. "Haros…look outside."

He did. "Well now, what do we have here?"

What they did not have was landscape, for even as the gaunt Grey spoke, the brick road and the forest that had just begun to form faded away. The Phantom was left sitting in the midst of nothing.

"Back up," Haros commanded. The Rolls did not respond.

The cadaverous figure sighed. "I'm afraid we shall have to do without comfort, Callistra, dear." Haros reached out and took her hand. "Will you be joining me?"

"As if I have any other choice?"

"Yes, there is that." The Haros smile appeared. "Then I think it is time we were off."

Nothing happened. The two Grey looked at one another.

Haros Aguilana leaned back and conjured up a cigarette. He took a single puff. "At this point, Callistra, I am very much open to suggestions."

She was not listening. With the realization that they were trapped, a name had come to mind. Not the raven, strangely enough, but another.

Why, though, was she certain that it was Otto who had trapped them? Why also was she certain that he had done it, not to harm them, but simply to keep them from finding Jeremiah?

He had said something about remembering elves....

Jeremiah stepped into the shadow reality of Chicago and marveled that it was still night despite his long stay in the land of Faerie. Oberon had assured him before their separation that it would indeed be the same night and not a later one. Time was relative in the dream realm, as Haros would have said, but to Jeremiah it was just confusing.

The dim illumination of the border world continued to bathe the city. More mundane lighting allowed him to study the peculiar architecture of the old water tower in front of him up close, something he had not bothered to do last time. Some thought the edifice ugly, but Todtmann decided he liked it after all. He also felt a kinship with it and the pumping station across the street. The three of them were refugees out of time and space with little connection to their surroundings.

Sighing, Jeremiah looked around. He had hoped to find Hector here, but even to himself he was willing to admit that it had been a long shot at best. Oberon had been no help at all; he did not know Hector and therefore could not locate him. The elf lord had been mildly apologetic but had offered no alternatives.

Hector had to be his first priority. As the only other human, he should have been easy to detect, but Jeremiah had no idea how to go about searching for him. Oberon had also seemed to think it possible for Jeremiah to detect his friend's presence, but once again had offered no solution. Todtmann was rather glad to be rid of the elfin Grey; Oberon's lack of enthusiasm toward the end had been sapping his own much-depleted reserves. It was all Jeremiah could do to keep himself from just giving up even despite his recent triumph against the Fairy King.

If there was no sign of Hector, at least there was also no sign of either the raven or his shadows. There were not even any of the mistlike shadow walkers, although the last would surely change. They had a sixth sense when it came to his presence.

"No sense hanging around here waiting for them, though," he muttered. If Hector was not here, then that simply meant that he was elsewhere, which meant that it was time for Jeremiah to move on.

Which he did.

He materialized in the parking lot of Hector's apartment building, then, finding nothing, transported himself inside. At first glance, Jeremiah saw nothing. The apartment was as he had last seen it. He scanned the living room, but found nothing to indicate that his friend had been back. Then, just as he was about to depart, something at the edge of sight caught his attention and made him turn toward the kitchen.

"Hector?"

There was a stirring. "Jeremiah?"

The black man came barreling around the corner and nearly collided with him. Hector managed to draw back just at the last moment. Jeremiah, who had been about to throw a bear hug around his friend, held off, aware of Hector's dislike for such close contact.

"Man, I thought you were lost and gone forever!" Hector did pat him on the back, but that was the extent of his greeting. "I was afraid that the raven had gotten you!" "Everybody just ignored me after you vamoosed! I felt like a fifth wheel, man!" Hector sobered up. "So where were you? What happened?"

Jeremiah took a deep breath and described both his escape attempt and his run-in with Oberon and Titania. " 'The King doth keep his revels here tonight,' " Hector started without warning. " 'Take heed the Queen come not within his sight. For Oberon is passing fell and wrath...' " "What is that?"

"Shakespeare, oaf! A Midsummer Night's Dream. Oberon and Titania rule the fairies."

Jeremiah grimaced. "That's what I thought. I should've known." He ran a hand through his hair. "That's all that happened— hmmph, that's *all*?—to me. What about you?"

Leaning against the wall, Hector shrugged and replied, "Like I said, nothing. I came back here after you disappeared and waited. Figured you'd be along at some point. If you didn't show up after a while, I was going to go search for you."

"I'm glad you didn't have to."

Hector folded his arms. "Yeah, me, too. So, I know I've asked this question before, but what now?" "What now?" Jeremiah blinked. What now? He sighed. "It's time this thing came to an end, Hector, but if it's going to, I have to do two things. The first is find Callistra." "I've got no problem with that, man. I'd like to meet this woman just to see if she's everything you make her out to be."

Todtmann managed a smile. "She is. The second thing I have to do is find a way to rid myself of the mantle of kingship...or the anchor, which it really is."

The other man's eyes narrowed. He shifted. "How do you hope to accomplish that miracle? Don't you have to give them up to somebody?"

"I was hoping I could just abandon the role. Callistra seemed to think that possible. The spell or whatever you want to call it would just float around until it found someone else. Hell, it probably has someone in mind already." Under his friend's suddenly alert gaze, Jeremiah found he could not look up. The more he talked about the notion of simply abandoning the spell to fate's whims, the more he felt like he was taking the coward's way out.

"Sounds risky. You could get some lunatic."

"What other choice have I got?" he asked, forcing his eyes to fix on Hector's. This time, his friend looked away, but Todtmann felt no great moral victory. Rather, he felt like a coward and a bully. It was not right for him to thrust the decision on to Hector. This was Jeremiah's problem and no one else's.

"That's something that can wait," he finally said. "Right now, I need to find Callistra."

"Yeah, but with better results than the last time we searched, buddy."

"I know. The only problem is that I'm not at all certain that the raven even has her. You saw what—" Jeremiah froze. Something tickled at his mind. Somehow, he knew what it was.

"What's up?" Hector tensed and looked around. "We're about to be attacked!"

The apartment became awash in shadow. Dark, deep, hungry shadow.

"Look out!" Hector shouted, pushing Jeremiah in the chest. A tendril of darkness cut between them, narrowly missing either man.

"Hector! My hand!"

The black man hesitated, then, as another ebony tentacle rose above them, he stretched out and took hold of Jeremiah's offered hand.

The scene shifted around them, becoming the overly familiar sight of the Sears Tower in the background. Jeremiah glanced around and immediately regretted his decision. The shadows were everywhere and over everything. Even as he adjusted to his new surroundings, the nearest began reaching for him.

"There's nowhere to run, nowhere to hide, man! Use your stuff to hurt the bastards! Send them running with their tails between their legs!"

He had not wanted to do that. He had not wanted to face the raven's monstrosities head on, but the choice was not his anymore. There was no longer anyplace for him to hide. Jeremiah either had to take the battle to them or simply give up.

Cornered, he found he could not even think of the latter as any real choice.

"I remember what this place is supposed to be like," he muttered to no one. "I remember a place without shadows, a place with *life*." Jeremiah stared at the oncoming shadow. "*You* don't belong here."

The shadow did not vanish, but it did recede.

"I *said* that you don't belong here! None of you do! You're aberrations! Bad dreams!"

Now the other shadows receded as well. In their absence was the city as Jeremiah Todtmann had known it, but with something added. A glow, almost a life, that seemed to fill in whatever spaces the foul shades abandoned. He still saw the world through the eyes of the Grey, but now he was seeing it as it was meant to be, not what the raven desired it to be.

"Go for broke, Jeremiah! You've got 'em on the run!"

Enthused, he nodded and started toward the retreating shades. They were really nothing to fear, he saw. Without the raven to guide them and the fear of their victims to feed them, the shadows were as powerless as Oberon had turned out to be. They were cowardly things, bigger cowards than even he had ever been. Jeremiah tried not to let overconfidence overwhelm him, but it was hard not to in the face of his impending victory. It felt good to be the one in charge, the one making the demands.

As he walked, Jeremiah continued to picture the city as he desired it to be. The shadows of the black bird could not face him and retreated as fast as he advanced. Jeremiah knew that they were not simply backing up, either. His images of Chicago, of the Chicago of his dreams, were pushing at the shadows from all sides and forcing them into a smaller and smaller pocket.

Where was the raven, though? That was the one thing that nagged at him. The raven should have been here. "Victory is at hand, buddy!" Hector shouted, his words cleansing away the uncertainty. Jeremiah nodded and, his confidence renewed, struck again at the shadows that had dared to invade the city, his city, and try to make it some twisted parody.

The inky shapes receded farther. Just a little more and they would be trapped. Chicago would be free of the raven.

Then, he saw her.

Callistra stood in the midst of the shrinking darkness, her arms outstretched and her mouth open in a silent shout. Then, she was pulled away by the shadows and a familiar laugh rang through the night. Jeremiah spun in a circle, but could not find the source.

"Button, button! Who's got the button?"

"Where is he?" There was no trace of the black bird and his voice seemed to resound from everywhere and nowhere.

"Easy, man!" Hector's eyes darted here and there. "We'll find him! Don't let him taunt you!"

Once again, he was thankful for his friend's stabilizing influence. The mere sight of Callistra in danger had nearly been enough to send Todtmann running blindly into the waiting shadows. Not so, Hector. The only way to defeat the winged menace was to keep a cool head. If they failed to do that, then the black bird would win, Callistra would be lost, and Jeremiah would likely be dead.

And I would've charged in like a mad rhino! Again he wondered what Thomas O'Ryan could have possibly been thinking about when he had chosen him. A sense of humor was one thing, but to set the outcome of everything on the shoulders of someone as inept as Jeremiah…O'Ryan had to have been even a bigger fool than the man he had picked as successor.

Yet, Jeremiah was fairly certain that his predecessor had been anything but a fool.

That, of course, did not help his present situation.

Well, I wanted to bring an end to all this! Guess I'm going to get my wish!

"Any suggestions, Hector?"

The black man gave him an evil smile. "Hell, if it were me, I'd call him out and proceed to pluck his feathers! You got the power, man!"

He did have the power. He was certain of that. However strong the raven was, he was a Grey and subject to the limitations of his kind. Jeremiah was human.

"I'm going to do it."

"I'm behind you all the way!"

"And that's where you'd better stay, Hector! I mean that this time!"

His companion almost argued, then evidently thought better of it when he stared into Jeremiah's darkening countenance. "All right, but I'll be ready, just in case!"

Todtmann nodded, then turned back to face the shadows. Before he called out the raven, he wanted to ensure that the black bird's pets would trouble him no longer.

He need not have worried. The shadows retreated even without his encouragement. Their fear was so overwhelming, Jeremiah could almost taste it.

That left only the raven. "Where are you?"

The mocking chuckle made him falter, but Hector put a hand on his shoulder and whispered in his ear. "Don't let him play mind games! That's the only hand he's got left to play!"

"You're good at leaping out of shadows and catching people by surprise," Todtmann shouted at the city, trying to ignore the sweat pouring down his forehead. "How good are you at facing someone on equal terms?"

"Some of us," came the voice, "are more equal than others!"

A patch of darkness formed before the two and coalesced into the flapping form of the raven. Despite his bravado, Jeremiah wanted nothing more at that moment than to turn and run away. He did not, however. Not only for Callistra's and Hector's sakes, but also because he doubted that he would get more than a half a dozen steps before the raven tore him apart. Besides, there was a part of him that truly did want to finish with the raven, to see the maddening magpie brought down.

"Chin up, Jeremiah!" hissed Hector.

"I'm okay." He really was not, but it would serve no purpose to tell anyone otherwise.

"You asked for it, you got it!" laughed the raven. "Time to put up or shut up!"

"I want Callistra!"

"Something to sweeten the pot? Offer me something better for the woman I've got?"

A bargain? Did he dare bargain with the raven? Impossible! It was not as if he could trust any deal this particular Grey agreed to. The raven was duplicity itself.

"No deal. I'm telling you."

The eyes changed from blazing red to frost white. The ebony terror laughed loud...and Jeremiah's world turned...upside down.

The two men tumbled over. Jeremiah grabbed hold of a street post and Hector a fire hydrant. The raven seemed unhindered by the topsy-turvy world and simply continued to fly in place.

"And now, if I may have someone from the audience?" At the bird's summons, Callistra appeared. Like the two mortals, she was upside down. She was also chained to a wheel.

"Callistra!"

The raven had deigned to leave her ungagged, no doubt with the intention of adding to Jeremiah's strife by allowing the two of them to talk but not touch. "Jeremiah! You should never have come here! You cannot defeat him!"

Cannot? Callistra thought he had no chance? Jeremiah's hopes sank.

He tried to drag himself forward, but there was nowhere to go that did not first require releasing his grip on the post. If he did that, he was liable to fall up to the heavens.

"Round and round she goes," announced the black bird, sounding exactly like a carnival barker. As he spoke, the wheel began to rotate. Callistra screamed. "Where she stops, only *I* know!"

"Jeremiah!" Hector twisted his grip on the hydrant in order to bring himself a little closer to his companion. "Come on, man! You can think us out of it!"

Distracted by both Callistra's words and screams, it was a monumental task for Jeremiah, but with terrible effort he at last succeeded in picturing the world as it should be. Everything in its place and turned right side up. That was the way it always had been and the way it always would be.

The world returned to normal. Hector, close to the ground already, struck the street with a grunt. Jeremiah, hanging higher, swung against the post, nearly knocking all of the air out of his lungs.

The black bird was no longer laughing.

"Will wonders never cease," he muttered. With a glance, he froze the wheel in place, leaving Callistra upside down. "Let's have a little light on this subject!"

"Jeremiah!" the panicked Grey called. "Look out!"

He recalled the thing of light, a thing as hungry as the shadows. It was a creature of brilliance, a thing so beautiful yet so terrible. The raven had twisted its purpose somehow, for Jeremiah could not believe that this creature had been born a monster like the shadows. It should have been their antithesis, not their twin.

Even more terrible than the first time, its mere presence was almost enough to blind him. Jeremiah shielded his eyes as best he could. Nearby, Hector cringed under the intensity of the overwhelming illumination.

"Have you seen the light?" roared the black bird, the mockery back in his words. "Do you see the light?"

"Is there any way to shut him up?" Hector asked. "Or shut that light bulb off? Shouldn't you be impervious to that thing? It's only a bright shadow, isn't it?"

Was it? Was it truly that much like the other shadows? Slowly Jeremiah recalled the last time he had faced this thing. It had hesitated in his presence, hadn't it?

He took a step toward it. The light ceased its advance almost instantly. Jeremiah took a second step. This time, the light creature retreated a pace, exactly as its darker counterparts had done earlier.

"Once more into the fray!" the raven commanded, but the light instead retreated. The bird flew in a frantic circle, his eyes reverting to bloodred. He seemed at a loss for a moment, then his gaze went back to the presumptuous mortal. "Sometimes, it's the little things in life that get to us! So foul and fair a day I have not seen!"

"You've got him, man!" the black man called. "Now it's your turn to hit him where it hurts!"

Hit him where it hurts... Jeremiah had no idea where that was, but he was ready to do whatever he could to the black bird. The malevolent Grey had hounded him unmercifully, torn his life asunder, and threatened the ones Jeremiah cared for most. Where earlier he had qualms about erasing the existence of the elves, he had no such qualms now. If it was possible to make the raven not, then so he, king of the Grey, now desired. He focused on the source of all his troubles ...

And the bird...did not cease to exist.

That was not to say that the raven did not suffer. The black bird shrieked and cawed and his shape twisted, becoming a gnarled smoky thing more akin to the shadow walkers than anything avian in form. The light creature vanished and the shadows dwindled to near nothing as their master crowed his defeat.

Jeremiah gasped at the effort. Despite his will, the bird would not fall. Oddly, it was as if Jeremiah himself were hampering his own efforts, for his will felt diffused, as if he were trying to destroy two different things, one the wrong target.

The wrong target?

Mouth agape in horror, he suddenly looked Callistra's way.

Her mouth was gone, wiped clean away at some point by the infernal avian. Nevertheless, she was trying to scream and scream as loud as she could, for as the raven suffered, so, too, did she.

Desperately, Jeremiah Todtmann tried to adjust his attack, to make the bird the only focus, but the raven, even in defeat, held sway. The more he tried to direct his power, the more it seemed the mouthless Callistra tried to scream.

She started to melt. She started to melt and Jeremiah's best efforts seemed to do nothing but speed the horror along.

Then, coming from behind him, a stick the size of a baseball bat in his hands, Hector charged the writhing bird. He waited until he was within arm's reach, swung the heavy stick back...and hit as good as a home run as Jeremiah had ever seen.

The battered form of the raven went tumbling back into the dark recesses of the street, where the shadows quickly enveloped it. It struck the ground with a rather insignificant sound all things considered. Jeremiah would have almost expected something more like an explosion. He *wanted* an explosion. Anything to put a final flourish on the destruction of the demonic bird.

" 'Quoth the raven,' " Hector whispered, dropping the stick which faded out of existence before it even touched the ground. " 'Nevermore.' "

Nevermore...Reality slapped him hard, reminding him of the fate of another. "Callistra!"

The wheel—and its captive—were nowhere to be seen.

Stumbling forward, Jeremiah searched the ground. She had to be there! It had to be a mistake! A Grey could not die, he told himself. A Grey could not die!

"Jeremiah ..."

He shook off Hector's hand. She had to be here! It was a trick! The spell had simply transported her elsewhere! He ran his fingers across the section of the street where the raven's mad wheel had floated. Jeremiah found no sign of her passing, but he also found no sign of her departure. A creature of shadow, Callistra would have left nothing behind in either case. But...

"Jeremiah...buddy ..."

Again, he shrugged off the hand. "We've got to find her, Hector!" He stalked toward the remnants of the dark shadows, which virtually cringed before him. "He must have transported her somewhere!"

"She's gone, man."

"She's not gone.!" There was no way she could be gone! He would have seen that! Jeremiah tried to recount the last moments, when Hector's sudden initiative had broken the stalemate. Surely, the surprising physical attack had broken the link between the raven and Callistra! Surely the black bird had not somehow dragged her down with him?

Had he?

From the streets came the echoes of the raven's laughter.

Jeremiah swore. Was there no destroying the winged Grey? Yet, if the raven still existed, then perhaps so did Callistra. "Where's that coming from?"

Hector looked around. "Sounds like everywhere, man, but mostly...I think..." He pointed to his right. "That way!"

"Come on!" The king of the Grey ran in the direction his companion had pointed, his vision red and slightly blurred. He was tired of the raven's games, tired of the whole damned thing. Jeremiah wanted to finish with the bird and then finish with the Grey. He wanted to go home and take Callistra with him.

If she was still alive…

"Once more into the fray!" called the black bird.

A crack formed in the line dividing the center of the street they were on. The crack swiftly ran the length of the street for as far as Jeremiah could see, then began to widen, creating a gully.

"Two roads diverged in a yellow line and sorry I could not travel both…but one or the other will suffice!"

The two men leapt onto one side of the now truly divided street. Jeremiah continued toward the sound of the voice but kept an eye on the growing crevice. So long as he stayed where he was, he should be safe…

Evidently the bird was not to be satisfied with that, for when the crevice had grown wide enough, the street began to tilt inward. Trash cans and loose refuse tumbled from the curb, across the street, and into the dark abyss. Although he knew on one level that everything that happened only happened in the realm of the Grey, it was difficult not to think that Chicago itself was in the midst of the catastrophe.

This time, Jeremiah did not waste his effort. He stared at the tipping road and recalled it as it should be. Cracked, with potholes, but still very serviceable and, for all practical purposes, as flat as could be expected.

The world rippled.

The street was level again and all sign of the raven-wrought abyss had vanished. Even the crack was gone.

Jeremiah gasped, the mental effort taking its toll. He was only just beginning to understand the strain the changes caused. His first attempts in Faerie had seemed so easy in comparison, but now he understood that there was an accumulative effect. Perhaps with time he would be able to manipulate things better, but the raven was not giving him that time.

"Jeremiah! You okay?"

"Just...worn out a little."

The other man leaned close. "Listen, buddy, I think you've got him if you can just get him to stop playing games! He's stalling you! You hurt him bad! Just give him your best shot one more time and you've got him beat!"

"I've got to find Callistra first! I...I've got to find out whether that was her before or just some trick!" Jeremiah straightened. The street had become much too quiet.

"What you've got to do, man, is take the initiative." Despite all that had happened to them, Hector Jordan still looked presentable. Jeremiah glanced down at his own garments, which looked rumpled and twisted at best. "Get him before he gets you again. You almost had him last time, but you let him get away!"

Let him get away? The only reason he had held back was because the black bird had used Callistra as a shield. If he had continued to attack, she might have...died. There was no other word that fit. Erase...cease to exist...they were all euphemisms. A Grey who no longer was, was dead.

"Tired?" came the maddening voice. "Then rest in peace!"

A darkness started to overwhelm the street, but Jeremiah, finding strength he did not know he had, stiffened and shouted, *"No!"*

The darkness was gone. Just like that.

In its wake it left one very befuddled bird.

" 'No'? 'No'?" squawked the raven awkwardly, as if trying to regain control. "Although you may try, my will you *cannot* deny!"

"Go get 'em, Jeremiah!" Hector whispered, patting him on the back for encouragement. "No letting up, this time! Show him who's boss!"

"I said 'no.' " Todtmann stalked toward the black bird. There was no sign of Callistra. "I've had it with you!" "How sharper than a serpent's tooth, a thankless child! I made you what you are today!"

That made Jeremiah laugh bitterly. "You only destroy. You can't make anything. You destroyed my life."

The raven fluttered back as Jeremiah came within arm's reach. "A shadow of a shadow of a life! A living ghost you were, your mortal life nothing but a blur!"

There was truth in what the black bird said, enough truth to strengthen Todtmann's resolve. "But you had nothing to do with that. You didn't choose me, did you?"

He reached for the raven, but the black bird was swifter. It darted just out of his reach and laughed.

Furious, Jeremiah lost all control. He snatched at the raven again and this time caught the feathered monster in his hand.

The raven cawed loudly and pecked at his hand, but Todtmann would not let him go. The claws scratched bloody grooves in his wrists, but Jeremiah overcame the pain and brought his other hand around to seize the black bird by the throat. He wanted nothing more than to twist the Grey's neck until it snapped, but the raven was made of steel. It was all he could do just to hold on to the frantic creature.

Then, the raven began to melt. First he stretched in Jeremiah's grip, then started to sag like heated wax, Fearing a trick, Jeremiah readjusted his grip, but the raven was like quicksilver. Less and less he resembled any creature at all. Todtmann found his arms and hands full of a twisted mass of black feathers and liquefying flesh.

"Hold on tight, Jeremiah!" Hector called. The black man stayed back, however, evidently uncertain as to how he could aid his companion. Jeremiah could not blame him. The raven's form shifted constantly, making the use of another pair of hands more a hindrance than help. Besides, the battle was his. The raven owed him.

"A captive!" roared the oily, ghastly mess. "A captive! My kingdom for a captive!"

Captive? "Callistra? Where is she? Tell me!"

"Too late!" A pair of accusing eyes, one scarlet, one ivory, looked up at him from the horrific burden in his arms. "Too little, too late! An eye for an eye and a death for a death!"

The raven laughed one final time, then abruptly erupted into smoke.

Gasping, Jeremiah finally released his captive. What was left of the black bird poured to the street, the inhuman orbs still staring in accusation. The raven tried to laugh, but this time it was more of a pitiful gurgle than a mocking chuckle.

"An eye for an eye..." the nauseating form rumbled.

"Where is she?"

He would receive no answer. Even as Jeremiah repeated the question, the black bird passed beyond speech. With growing swiftness, the smoke engulfed the liquefied Grey. The dark form shriveled. Stunned, Jeremiah watched as his foe finally evaporated, leaving no trace but a few wisps of smoke that gradually faded away.

"God, Hector! What have I—"

He heard Callistra scream. Jeremiah knew that it had to be her; the timing was too precise. Just the way the raven would have plotted it, even to the end. The black bird's misty corpse forgotten, he ran toward the sound of the scream, Hector close behind him. Callistra screamed again, which both cheered and horrified him. That she suffered tore at his heart, but that she still screamed meant that there might yet be time to save her from the raven's final revenge.

Somehow, Todtmann was not surprised to find himself facing the Sears Tower. The bird had a fondness for the gargantuan edifice that went beyond his interest in Jeremiah. Perhaps it was because it was the tallest structure around or perhaps there was some reason that Jeremiah did not know. It only made sense in retrospect that here was where the raven had chosen his revenge to take place.

The shadows of the black bird still enshrouded most of the structure and these did not flee at the sight of the human anchor. They had good reason, too, for bound by some invisible bond, Callistra was attached to the tower. The shadows surrounded her and while they had not touched the imprisoned Grey, they toyed with her as cats toyed with their prey. Tentacles of darkness touched her, then withdrew. A circle of safety surrounded her, but it grew smaller with every passing breath.

He could almost hear the raven's laughter.

"Damn!" Hector muttered, looking up at the sight. "What are you going to do?"

"I don't know...they won't retreat! The others always retreated!"

"You've gotta do something, Jeremiah! They look ready to eat your lady!"

Todtmann started to turn to his friend. "I don't know what I can—"

"You've got no more time to think, buddy!" Hector's eyes went wide as he stared past Jeremiah. "One of 'em's going for her!"

Jeremiah whirled and pointed at Callistra, thinking only that she should be with him, safe from the menace of the foul magpie's pets. Her safety was all that mattered. If he was truly the chosen anchor, the one to whom the stability of this dream realm had been given, then it should be within his powers to recreate this scene and cheat the black bird of his final ploy.

The Sears Tower shimmered. His hopes rose. The shadows faded, then deepened, then faded. Callistra seemed to float toward him.

What sounded like the flutter of wings and a soft, mocking chuckle broke his concentration. He blinked and the sounds vanished, but by then the damage had been done.

The shadows of the raven began to move...and the nearest reached for the still-captive Callistra.

He screamed denial, but it was too late. Callistra had time enough to realize her fate, time enough to open her mouth in terror.

The shadow enveloped her.

Jeremiah called out her name, then fell to his knees. He shook his head, trying not to believe what he had just seen. He had failed her, failed her twice. Fate had given him a reprieve but moments before and he had made nothing of it. Before his very eyes the late, unlamented raven had torn the woman he loved from his grasp. Never mind that she had been one of the Grey; Jeremiah knew that the shadows were death for another Grey. She had ceased to exist the moment it had swallowed her.

He could not even vent his pain on the murderous blots, for with their dirty deed completed, the shadows fled, vanishing in little more than the blink of an unbelieving eye. Unable to do anything to assuage his turbulent emotions, Jeremiah simply beat his fists against the hard, cold street.

After a few moments, a voice cautiously whispered his name. It was Hector, he realized. Jeremiah tried to ignore his friend, but the black man would not let him bury himself in pity. Jordan put his hands on Jeremiah's shoulders and leaned over him.

"I'm sorry, Jeremiah, I really am…I thought you had her, man! I really did."

"Thomas O'Ryan," he muttered. At first, even he did not know why the former anchor's name cropped up, but the more he thought about it, the more Jeremiah realized the aptness. "What the hell did he see in me, Hector? I've done nothing right since I was thrown into this! What the hell was he thinking?"

Hector just shook his head.

All this power and 1 can't save the one person important to me! I would've been better off staying a guest of Oberon! Even he would have known better what to do!

Hector Jordan looked around. "Place looks calm, but it might be a good thing if we went elsewhere, man. Somewhere more private so that you can sort things out at your leisure."

"I don't want to do anything except get rid of this albatross on my back, Hector. Without Callistra, there's nothing that I want from the Grey. I don't care what happens; I just don't want to be 'king' anymore. King! Anchor does make more sense, you know. It drags you under, takes everything you care about with it! If I could just toss it all away, I would."

A look of uneasiness passed over the other's handsome features. "Be careful what you wish for, man. You may get it. Remember what I said before? You don't know what sort of person the next one might be. Could be someone the raven would've liked."

At the moment, Jeremiah could have cared less. The Grey and, yes, even Humanity could go to hell in a hand basket for all he cared. *Hell in a hand basket?* He swore under his breath at the Greyish phrase. The dream world had invaded his very being and he was sick of it all. "Well, what should I do?" he snapped. "Do you want it?"

Hector scowled, but, after a moment of silence, finally nodded. "If pot luck is the alternative, yeah. Better the king you know than the one you don't."

Jeremiah snorted. "You'd fit right in, talking like that."

When his friend did not smile, he stared at him. "You can't be serious!"

"Never been more serious in my life."

"You don't know what you're getting yourself into."

"I think I have a hunch. Can't be any worse than today."

To be relieved of the kingship…It was too good to be true, yet… he did not feel right about it. Hector could not possibly know what taking on the role of anchor entailed. "You really don't know what it means, Hector! We're talking about living among creatures out of your worst nightmares…literally! It means forever being able to see life but not be a part of it! To live among things created by the darkest dreams of Mankind! To never touch another…person… again!"

"You must like it a lot to be trying to talk me out of it."

Couldn't he understand? "I'm trying to talk you out of it because you don't know what it's like!"

Hector stood, his eyes never leaving Jeremiah. "You won't change my mind. It's either me or whatever madman that spell might find."

It was an argument that Jeremiah was admittedly happy to lose. If there was one man he felt safe in turning the mantle over to, it was Hector. Hector had handled this entire situation with more ingenuity and confidence than Jeremiah had. Thomas O'Ryan had been close in his choice; he should have simply looked into the next cubicle at Everlasting before making his decision. *Who knows,* Todtmann thought, *maybe this had been the Irishman's plan all the time.* Give the spell to Jeremiah to throw the raven off the mark and then have him pass it on to the black man.

The notion was ludicrous even to him. He had been chosen on a lark by a fool and even though he had managed to destroy the raven, Callistra was also dead. If Hector Jordan wanted to take his place, then so be it. Hector could have all the headaches and the pain, all the fears and the suffering.

Then, it occurred to him he did not know exactly how to pass on the spell. He started to laugh hysterically. When Hector asked him what was wrong, he told him.

His companion did not find it so amusing. "You must have some idea!"

"The only method I know involved remembering my life, but that would let the spell drift off on its own. There's no guarantee it would choose you."

"This is a fine kettle of fish!" Hector snarled. "You don't know!"

Somewhat taken aback by the other's vehemence, Jeremiah became defensive. He stood up and confronted his would-be successor. "I've been a little busy…you may have noticed that!"

Hector grew apologetic. "You're right. Sorry. Just guess I'm on edge."

His friend's willingness to admit his mistake calmed Todtmann down, too. "I wish I did know, believe me."

"You know…maybe you do."

"What's that mean?"

His expression hopeful, Hector pointed at his forehead. "It's all in your mind, Jeremiah, buddy. O'Ryan saw you, decided you were his successor, and—poof—you were!"

"But he had to die for the spell to actually come to me!"

"You don't know that." The black man's expression was crafty. "You're always assuming everything has to be done the hard way. Maybe if you just will your abilities to me, that'll be good enough."

"I want to pass the spell onto you!"

"A part of you isn't willing." Hector thought about it some more. "I bet physical contact would help push it along, though. Maybe we should both sit down and hold hands. Seems to work in the movies."

"That's—" Jeremiah had been about to tell him that the idea was absurd, something only a B-movie would use, but then he recalled where he was. If it was cliché, it had a good chance of running true in the realm of the Grey. "Maybe you've got something there. I'm willing to try anything. Where do you want to do it?"

"Might as well sit down right here."

"In the street?"

"It's now or never, man. We go elsewhere, your friend Haros might find us before it's done."

Haros…"I'd completely forgotten about him." "I haven't."

Once more, Jeremiah was reminded of how better equipped Hector was for the role the Grey had thrust upon him instead. He was more alert and quicker to react, yet able to analyze a situation at the same time. The Grey and Humanity would be better off with someone like Hector Jordan than with a misfit like Jeremiah Todtmann.

"Let's get on with it, then," he told Hector.

They sat down on the street, which, being a Greyish variation on the true one, was neither cold nor wet. It simply existed unless Jeremiah—and soon Hector—willed it otherwise.

Hector reached out with both hands, which Jeremiah seized in his own. He felt a little funny, but since he had no other idea, his companion's would do for now. If it failed, then they would have to find some other solution. For some reason, however, Jeremiah felt fairly certain that Hector knew what he was doing. In a few moments, Jeremiah would be free of everything...except the memories of his failure to save Callistra. Those were shackles he knew he would never be able to free himself from.

He found he really did not want to, either.

"Ready when you are," Hector commented.

Jeremiah nodded and closed his eyes. He really, truly, wanted this to work. The spell had brought him nothing but pain. Hector wanted it and he could have it. Jeremiah no longer felt guilty about passing on his troubles. His friend would be much better able to handle the situation. Hector Jordan was no Jeremiah Todtmann.

He felt a tug at his mind.

A terrible darkness tried to overwhelm him.

Jeremiah lashed out with all the power at his disposal. He lashed out blindly and only after did he realize who it was who took the brunt of his fear-driven strike.

Hector.

Jeremiah's eyes opened wide. The scene he witnessed played out in slow motion. Caught unaware, Hector was flung back without a sound. The black man went crashing into the wall of a nearby building. Surprisingly, it was not Hector but the wall that gave some. Jeremiah's companion slid to the ground a crumpled heap.

"God! Hector, no!" he whispered. Stumbling to his feet, Jeremiah started toward his friend. If he had killed Hector...

He had taken no more than three or four steps when the dark figure rose. Jeremiah started to exhale in relief, but that relief gave way almost immediately to confusion and then fear.

Hector Jordan was shimmering in and out of focus like a poor television image. Only once before had Jeremiah seen that happen and that one time had been when he had been questioning the Marilyn doppelganger about Thomas O'Ryan.

Hector was a Grey.

CHAPTER XV

"What's the matter, Jeremiah?" the wavering Hector asked. "You look like you've seen a ghost."

Now that he knew, Jeremiah was amazed at the number of clichés, quotes, misquotes, and rhymes that the false Hector had tossed at him. It seemed impossible that he had not realized it sooner. How far back did the masquerade go? As far back as he could remember, he suspected. Likely all the way back to the first time Hector had appeared to notice him.

He had been played for a fool.

"Man, some cat got your tongue, buddy?"

Jeremiah stepped back. "You're not Hector. Keep away from me!"

The false Hector smiled. He could really not hide the truth now. "No, I guess I'm not."

"Where is he? Where's the real Hector?" Todtmann was certain that he knew, but despite his suspicions, he had to ask.

"Hector Jordan had rocks in his head," the doppelganger replied. "Or maybe just one *heavy* one."

Dear God, Hector...not you, too!

"Oh, well," laughed the dark figure, glancing down at his torso. "Easy come, easy go!"

Hector Jordan began to come apart.

The sides of the black man's face peeled upward. At the same time, his skin darkened to pitch-black and took on a ruffled appearance. Feathers sprouted on his cheeks. The torn flesh reshaped itself into long, then longer wings. Hector's nose and mouth stretched forward, melding together. From the muscles in his throat a pair of taloned legs grew and separated. To Jeremiah's mounting dread, his friend's head broke free from the torso and floated above. The rest of Hector's body collapsed in a stomach-churning mass of boneless flesh that thankfully faded away only a breath or two later.

The last vestiges of Humanity shriveled away from the flying head. Rising to a height nearly twice that of Jeremiah, the resurrected raven laughed at his adversary's horror-filled expression.

"I'm not half the man I used to be, am I?"

Jeremiah just stared. Even without the raven's words, he would have known that Hector was dead. The raven could not have counted on his friend to not be around at an awkward moment. Worse, he was certain that to have maintained such an elaborate hoax, the winged demon would have had to have taken more than a simple memory ghost of Hector. Despite the lapses in his speech, the false Hector had been very close to the real one.

First Callistra and now this. Jeremiah had no idea what it was the black bird wanted from him, but he knew what the raven was going to get.

The king of the Grey adjusted the raven.

The sinister shadow rippled and Jeremiah's heart beat faster. This time he had the monster! This time the raven would pay for both deaths!

A tremendous force shook the street and knocked him off balance. Jeremiah fell, the shock of his back striking the hard pavement shattering his concentration.

"You cannot unmake me, Jeremiah Todtmann! I am too much of you! You are my strength! You could no more unmake the sun, the moon, and the stars!"

The raven dove at him with such swiftness that Jeremiah's only thought was to protect his face. His hands went up just in time to block razor-sharp talons as long as his fingers. He grunted but did not scream as the claws scarred the back sides of his hands. The black bird came at him again, but this time stopped short of touching him.

As the raven returned to his prior position, Jeremiah lowered his bloody hands. They looked worse than they felt. He knew that the sinister avian had merely been letting him have a taste of what he could do. "What do you want from me?"

"Just everything."

"But why?"

"Why, indeed?" The raven fluttered to a street sign and alighted. He groomed his wings for a moment, then stared at his prey with one gleaming red eye. "To dream the impossible dream, of course. To live life to the fullest. To boldly go where no Grey has gone before! To go to this island Earth for more than a few snatched minutes!"

"You want to go to the real world?"

"I want to be a part of the true world!"

A part of the true world. Jeremiah envisioned the raven as part of Humanity's world. The vision was a grim one. It was highly doubtful that the raven would be satisfied with merely existing there. He could not be allowed to cross the threshold, yet the only one who was standing between the black bird and his goal was Jeremiah, who felt totally ineffective against the winged Grey.

Despite that, despite knowing his chances, he said, "I can't let you do that."

The raven, as was his wont, laughed. "Can't? Must! I have whispered in ears to kings through the years! I have cajoled and cursed, for this final day is well rehearsed! Kings through the ages have I steered through the stages, until your coming! Now the time has come, the walrus said, and the hour is nigh! You are the culmination of my plan, the power of the kingship to pry! I guided you and guided your friend, until the necessity of a stone led to his end!"

The black bird's whimsical manner of speech in no way dulled the horror of his revelations. How long had the raven plotted all of this? From his own words, it had been a plan that had seen anchor after anchor manipulated, choice after choice made without the realization that it was the raven who twisted the path the spell was taking. He had somehow even killed Hector so that he could wear a form that would fool Jeremiah into turning the power of the human anchor to him. The long-term planning was convoluted yet crafty. What had he wanted from each human host? What traits or skills had the raven sought through the various pawns? Why did it have to culminate now, with Jeremiah?

He tried to stall, despite being unable to think of any way that he might be able to permanently deter the inevitable. "But you already go to the true world, don't you?"

"A minute here, a minute there. I must return eventually or turn to air! Either way, not full life!"

Not life. It always came to that. As real as they were, the Grey were not living by human standards. In the real world, they were complex ghosts, dream folk who evaporated or changed at the whims of the truly living. Even the raven— who had killed—was not real enough. There was more, though. The raven was not telling all…and why should he?

It did not matter in the end. Again, despite his sagging spirits, spirits still in tatters because of Callistra's death, Jeremiah found it within himself to deny the black bird once more. "I can't let you have what you want. I'll stop you…" Even he had trouble believing his threat. The fear was strong within him. "…any way I can."

"Now who dreams the impossible dream? Know you not yet what I am, Jeremiah Todtmann? The Grey are the dreams, the fears, the wonders, and the tears! Each human touches the world of the Grey in his or her little way. Yet, of all who touch this realm, it is the king, the anchor, who does most. Here dreams become reality, wonders become the fact…and fears are given substance!" The baleful magpie allowed his words to sink in before continuing, "*I* am the culmination of the fears and terrors of each human anchor brought here since almost the spell was cast! I have grown with each madman and built my strength further by playing on their paranoia and inner darkness! Each king has fueled me with his basest fears; each anchor has added to my strength with his frightened tears!"

It made a horrible sense, especially after Oberon's explanation. If the humans brought here influenced the realm of the Grey far more than all of their brethren in the true world combined, then it was only reasonable to assume that their own faults, their own conscious and subconscious terrors, would likewise be amplified. The spell, designed to focus the powers of the anchors, had further amplified those terrors, giving them substance.

In the world of the Grey, that meant giving shape and strength to those horrors. That meant giving shape and strength to a winged abomination.

The raven flapped his wings and chuckled at the way the action made the human jump. He leaned forward and focused a now ivory eye at his pawn. "Yes, Jeremiah Todtmann! I am indeed quite literally your worst nightmare come true!"

Then it was that the world became flame.

It was not by the black bird's doing, that much was obvious. The raven, perhaps even more startled than Jeremiah, fluttered up into the sky in a panic. Jeremiah, meanwhile, eyed the sudden inferno in dazed wonder. All of Chicago was a raging storm of fire and heat.

The Great Fire...

A heavy paw came across his mouth, preventing any chance of a shout. A furry arm wrapped itself around his chest, nearly cutting off his ability to breathe.

"You are my friend, Jeremiah," whispered the gruff voice of Otto.

Friend or not, it hardly mattered, for the simian Grey virtually lifted Todtmann from the street as he dragged him back from the flames and the winged fury. His vision partly obscured by the massive paw, Jeremiah glimpsed the black bird struggling against the fire. The inferno's scarlet tongues sought out the raven with unerring accuracy, but somehow the deadly Grey avoided them. Still, the raven was so harried by the flames that he could not pay attention to his former prey, which was likely as Otto had planned it.

There was another puzzle. When last he had met the apelike creature, Jeremiah would have been hard-pressed to describe Otto as crafty. In fact, he had barely seemed able to hold a short conversation. Now he was plotting rescues.

The world shimmered. Chicago's leviathans faded, to be replaced by the marshy field that Jeremiah knew had existed before even Fort Dearborn, the city's predecessor, had been built. Finding himself half dragged through the wet grass, his thoughts turned to Callistra, who had been his initial guide here.

"Rise and shine!" barked Otto, shaking him a bit. "Now is not the time to sleep, perchance to dream!"

The simian Grey had finally removed his paw from Todtmann's mouth. Jeremiah spat what appeared to be real hair from his lips and asked, "Where are you taking me?"

"Somewhere over the rainbow, Jeremiah Todtmann. Where skies are blue and birdless. Somewhere...I had forgotten."

Chicago chose that moment to reform. There was no transition; it simply happened. Once more the flames surrounded them, but this time they seemed less guided and more like flames should be. Prepared for a trek through a muddy, uneven field, Jeremiah tripped and fell. Only his rescuer's powerful grip kept him from striking the pavement face first.

"He is stronger. Your fear is too strong."

"What"—gasped the would-be king as he rose—"does that mean?"

"He did not lie, Jeremiah Todtmann. He is the deepest fears of the anchors, the kings like you, come to life. He has worked to make you fear him above all else; his food is your strife."

"You're saying that he gets stronger the more I fear him." "Truer words were never spoken."

"Then I've really lost, haven't I?" Jeremiah searched the dark sky for the darker blot that was the raven. "I can't just shut off my fear. It's too ingrained in me."

"He has worked his wicked ways well," Otto agreed. One of his eyes twisted skyward, a sight that almost disconcerted Todtmann as much as any thought concerning the raven. "We must go elsewhere, Jeremiah Todtmann."

Chicago vanished again, this time to be replaced by the panoramic scene of hill after woodland hill. The beautiful countryside extended for as far as he could see. Small, simple homes dotted the landscape here and there, but not enough to give any sense of crowding. As entrancing as it all was, however, it reminded Jeremiah too much of another place and time, one with few fond memories. "This looks like Faerie, where Oberon rules."

"Oberon."

There was something about the way his companion pronounced the name that made Jeremiah look at him closely. Otto was still a creature of rather indistinct features and so it was hard to be certain what expression he wore, but Jeremiah was fairly positive that the apelike Grey was struggling to recall something concerning the elf lord.

"Are we in Faerie?"

"No," replied the other slowly, "this is jolly old England."

England? He had always wanted to travel to the British Isles, but not under such circumstances. "Why are we here?"

Instead of answering his question, Otto said, "I remember Oberon. I remember elves."

"You—"

"I remember the spell." The crossing-gate eyes flared. "I remember the casting."

"You remember the casting of the spell?" Oberon had talked of how the Grey who had cast the spell had forgotten themselves, had lost their hold on their identities and, for lack of a better word, fragmented. No longer elves, they had probably reverted to something akin to the shadow walkers.

One of them had apparently not forgotten everything, however. The Grey he had half jokingly named after one of the local zoo's more famous simians had once been one of the proud and powerful rulers of the twilight realm.

The more he spoke of remembering the smoother Otto's speech became. Yet, it was still more like listening to someone talk of an old acquaintance rather than their own past existence. "The spell was difficult. They tried to tie shadow to reality, Grey to Mankind. It failed at first. If at first you don't succeed, though, you must try again. The suggestion was made to tie the life and power of the spell to the mind of the bearer. It would feed on the anchor's thoughts as it also focused them. It seemed perfect. Crystal clear."

Otto was no longer looking at him. The Grey was caught up in a rush of old memory.

"The mind is a terrible thing to face," he said matter-of-factly. "We tied the spell's working to the first chosen, but we were shadows and he was human and the strain proved too much. Success bred failure." The apelike creature blinked. "I could not hold myself together. The identity I had nurtured collapsed. A house of cards it became. I was strong, though, Jeremiah Todtmann. I remembered a little and held on to that little as hard as I could. As long as I could."

From master to nearly nothing. As little he had to show for his own life, Jeremiah knew how important it was to him. He had done next to nothing, but he had an identity. He was someone. Otto, on the other hand, had existed in a sort of limbo, remembering bits but unable to do anything else for fear of losing those tiny fragments. Only when given a new name had he begun the journey back.

"Is...is the raven really what he says he is?"

"Yes, Jeremiah Todtmann. I know that now."

The elves had, in a sense, laid the groundwork for the raven's creation. The spell had brought him into being and, with the black bird's own aid, had strengthened him.

The first glimmer of a notion formed. Ravens and spells. He tried to draw it out, but the idea slipped back into the realm of the subconscious. Another question popped into his head. "Otto. Could I have really passed on the powers of the spell to him?"

For a time, the simian Grey was silent. Then, he blinked and said, "Yes."

Again, the notion tried to fight its way out of his subconscious. "But wouldn't that—"

"You must not give it to him, Jeremiah Todtmann. He would be most powerful. He would be able to touch the waking world."

A gentle breeze rocked the lightest of the tree branches, but being part of the shadow world, Jeremiah was himself untouched by it. At the moment he would have welcomed even a storm, if only it came from the real world. "This is all crazy! Makes me wish that Haros were here, after all."

Otto's eyes flashed in a peculiar alternating pattern, a sign, the human realized, of agitation. "Haros can do nothing. The raven would make him forget himself. Callistra, too. They are—"

Jeremiah almost grabbed the Grey and shook him. "Callistra? She's...she's alive?"

Now the simian shadow was truly anxious. "You must *not* think of them, Jeremiah Todtmann. You must not. For them. For—"

He was beyond hearing warnings. "Callistra!" he whispered in near-reverence. "Callistra!"

"You must not think of them."

It was almost possible for him to see her. Callistra, tall, ethereal, and perfect. A pale goddess with silky hair the color of midnight. The more he imagined her, the more real the image in his mind became. To his surprise, he also found himself picturing Haros Aguilana. The gaunt Grey stood next to Callistra, leaning on his cane.

"No!" Otto swung a meaty hand at him. Jeremiah had no time to react; the flat-handed strike caught him on the chin, sent him spinning around in a circle, then collapsing to the ground. He shook his head and stared in horror at the monstrous Grey.

"That really was not cricket, my old friend."

Otto turned at the sound of the voice. He sighed. "Too late. Too late."

An ebony-tressed dream rushed past the apish creature and nearly fell on the stunned Jeremiah. "Jeremiah! Are you all right?"

"Callistra!" he finally managed. "What has he done to you?"

He rubbed his jaw. "I'm…okay." Considering Otto's remarkable strength, the slap had been little more than a light tap. "I don't think he meant to hurt me."

Otto swung his head back to the human below him. "Knock a little sense into you, but too late. Haros should not be here. He, like you, draws the bird. Now the raven is certain to find you, Jeremiah Todtmann."

"The black bird will never attack with all of us here, especially me," Haros insisted. "He is no fool to run in where angels fear to tread." The cadaverous Grey frowned at his rather clichéd statement.

"He has never feared you, Haros. He has used you. You have prepared the way."

"Absurd!"

Otto shrugged. "Best is the puppet who does not see his strings. Every time you moved, the raven knew."

"We're wasting time!" Callistra snapped, helping Jeremiah to his feet. "Jeremiah's only hope is to escape our world!"

His head at last stable, Todtmann finally decided it was time he said a word or two of his own about his future. "Listen, I think there might be something that I can—"

"Well, well, the gang's all here!"

The sloping hills and enchanting woods of the British countryside became the shadow-encrusted giants of Chicago. Giants that burned.

"Too late," Otto muttered again. "Too late."

"And the Red Death held illimitable dominion over all!"

The ghost flames of the Chicago Fire danced, but their dance was no longer either a hunt for the raven or the random movements of a wild blaze. Instead, they danced with eager glee toward the small band. The raven had seized control of Otto's trick and now sought to use it against his adversaries. Scarlet tentacles flickered back and forth, ever drawing closer to Jeremiah and his companions. If there was any question as to whether the fire would harm him, the awful heat answered that swift enough. It alone would kill him if he was subjected to it for very long.

Around him, Callistra and the others suffered as well. The flames were Grey-wrought and so they could touch the shadow folk. Even if the fire could not kill them, it would certainly hurt. He had seen enough to know that.

Otto chose then to seize him by the collar. Before either Haros or Callistra knew what was happening, the simian Grey pulled Jeremiah to him and shifted them elsewhere.

Chicago became a high, snow-covered mountainside. Below the twosome stretched a desolate valley.

Jeremiah turned on his rescuer. Otto had seen fit to take him, but he had abandoned the other two Grey. "What did you do? You can't leave them!"

"You must be saved, Jeremiah. At all costs."

He was just about to argue with his would-be rescuer, when the chilling voice of the raven echoed throughout the mountains.

"Yeah, though you walk through the valley of the Shadow of Death!" the winged fury snapped. "You shall fear my evil!"

Shadows? Jeremiah knew what was coming, but all he could do was raise his hands in warning and shout, "No!"

One of the shadows behind his companion moved.

It moved with a swiftness remarkable even for one of its kind, swallowing the apelike Grey before he could react. Otto was simply enveloped. There was no sudden realization, no scream. It was quite possible that the Grey never understood what was happening. Jeremiah hoped that was true.

Once again, fire-wracked Chicago formed around him. If not for Otto's terrible fate, it would have almost seemed tedious. The sensation of being some sort of living yo-yo once again crossed his mind.

The scene before him did not raise his hopes of escape. Haros Aguilana, cane pointed headfirst at the flames, was attempting to fight both the fire and its master, but it was clear that he was losing ground. Callistra stood behind him, her expression indicating that she, too, was a presence in the combat. Despite the strength of the two, however, the fire was gaining ground. As for the sinister magpie, he fluttered merrily above the heads of the threesome, taunting Haros again and again.

"Stand still and fight like a man, bird!" snarled the skeletal figure. He pointed the cane's wolf's-head tip at the raven. A lupine form larger than a man sprouted full-grown from the cane and leapt at the black bird. At first the raven continued his fluttering, but as the wolf closed on him, he suddenly glared at it.

Haros Aguilana's wolf froze in mid-flight and tumbled to the street. As it struck the pavement, the still form shattered like fine china. Pieces of petrified wolf rained on the two defending Grey and Jeremiah. Bombarded, Haros and Callistra were evidently unable to maintain whatever shield they had created to hold back the flames. The blaze rushed toward the trio.

Retreating from the onrushing fire, the two Grey at last noticed his return. Callistra ran to Jeremiah's side and held him tight. Haros, his attention in great part still on the fire and the raven, was a little slower in reaching the human.

"Where is Otto?" the gaunt Grey snapped. "Why did he bring you back here?"

"He didn't!" The crackling of the flames was making it necessary to shout now. "The raven got him! A shadow...a shadow fell on him! The raven was the one who brought me back!"

Consternation twisted the Grey's already angular features. "Impossible! I have at least been keeping our feathered fiend occupied here!"

"He was there, too...wherever that was!" "He cannot be that powerful!"

" 'Cannot'?" The raven hovered directly above them. Haros again pointed his cane at the black bird, but if he expected something to happen, he was sorely disappointed.

The raven shook his head, admonishing his foe. "Cannot, you say? Ahh, but seeing is believing, is it not?"

There was a shimmering in the flames. Jeremiah saw nothing else, but Haros and Callistra looked horrified.

"Haros!" Callistra was, if possible, even more pale than normal. "He couldn't have, could he?"

"Coincidence." Despite the flippant answer, he was obviously as distraught as she was.

Jeremiah, who could still see nothing new to fear, leaned close. "What happened? I didn't see anything!"

"You are looking at our version of the world, of course," Haros explained, still staring ahead. "You must desire to see into the waking world."

Not understanding but willing to attempt the Grey's suggestion, Jeremiah thought about the world he had come from and what it should look like.

The shadows faded and the twisted structures straightened, yet they also did not. He was seeing both versions, the true and the shadow, of this portion of the city. As he concentrated, the dream realm version grew faint but did not entirely disappear. The fearsome inferno that surrounded them faded, although the heat was still oppressing.

Yet, one small portion of the fire did not fade.

"Do you see it?" Callistra asked. "Do you see the fire in your world?"

"In...*my*...world?"

"He has started a small blaze in the true world, Jeremiah," Haros explained. "A small but significant blaze. He can touch your world, my friend. Touch it and *infect* it with his evil."

In truth, it was not so great a shock to him as it was to his comrades. He had already seen the raven's handiwork where the world of Humanity was concerned. Hector had died because of the black bird. That the baleful Grey could light the city on fire was just another example. What did worry him was the effect this knowledge had on Haros, the one being he had hoped might keep the raven from victory. All defiance was gone from the elegant figure. The raven had revealed just how pitiful the gaunt Grey's own powers were. Even Haros could only affect the waking world in tiny ways.

"All hail the conquering hero!" roared the black bird. He eyed them all with one blood-colored orb. "Kneel before your better!"

Haros and Callistra did fall to their knees, but it was clearly not by choice. They struggled all the way to the pavement, yet could not halt their degradation in the slightest. For good measure, the bird made them bow to the ground.

Jeremiah looked from his companions to the raven and then to himself. He had felt no compulsion to kneel. The raven laughed, but it was a laugh a bit too late, as if meant to cover something rather than echo his triumph.

"Now where were we before we were so rudely interrupted? Ah, yes! Time to give the devil his due!" The true world had faded away yet again and now the ghost flames sparked heavenward, accenting each word the pinioned pariah uttered. "Time to give up the mantle you have so ineptly worn! Time to fulfill my destiny!"

There were times that were said to try men's souls and for Jeremiah this was certainly one. His mind frantically raced, trying to go over every—any—option he had. There would be no aid from his companions. It was up to him. He could either give up the power thrust upon him or he could fight the raven.

The black bird's victory was not complete, that much Jeremiah Todtmann knew. Had his power been as great as he pretended, the deadly Grey would not have needed Jeremiah's spell-wrought skills.

Again, he wondered about the spell. The notion that had tried at least twice to command his attention resurfaced. What had he been told about it? The spell fed off the anchors. The raven had likely been created by the very spell he now sought to control. He was the culmination of the fears of every human tied to the Grey magic with strength enough to manipulate his reality, as the human anchor was supposed to be able to do…

Then it was that for Jeremiah Todtmann, king of the Grey, everything fell into place. He knew—or hoped that he knew—what had to be done.

Jeremiah knelt before the raven. He pointed at his companions. "The spell in return for their freedom."

The deadly shadow laughed, then dipped his head. "I am nothing if not magnanimous!"

Todtmann doubted the raven's sincerity, but that was not important. What he had to do now was give the winged Grey what he desired…and hope that it was the correct thing to do.

"Render unto me that which is mine!" commanded the avian. He did not drop to the ground, but rather stayed where he was. This time, there was apparently to be no contact. If it was possible to do this without having to actually touch the raven, that suited Jeremiah just fine.

He braced himself for the monstrous avian's invasion.

The touch was as foul and alien as before, but this time he did not fight it. Body shaking from fear, fear that the black bird had planted and nurtured for so long, he allowed the raven to link with him, the better to pass the legacy of the elfin Grey on. Jeremiah doubted the elves or any of the shadow folk would have recognized the spell as it existed now. It had become too much of a human thing and he had been right to think of it as something almost like a Grey, with a mind of its own. His greatest fear turned out not to be the invading presence of the raven, but that the spell would resist his intentions and fight to remain a part of him. If it did, he was uncertain as to what he could do. For all the power he had, Jeremiah did not have the talent to make proper use of it. The raven knew that, too.

He tried to think only of the transfer from that point on. The raven did not seem able to actually read his thoughts but he could certainly sense them. Linked, the sinister magpie might be able to delve deeper. Jeremiah had tried to think up some sort of mental shield, like they often used in movies, but he was at a loss as to whether he had succeeded. He felt no different...

Quite without warning, the raven shattered the link.

"Done!" The jubilant Grey performed circles in the sky. "V for victory! I am complete!" He trailed off into triumphant laughter.

Here goes nothing, Jeremiah Todtmann thought.

He struck the celebrating Grey with the only power that was his by right of his humanity, the one thing that perhaps the raven did not understand belonged wholly to Jeremiah and was not part of the spell.

Jeremiah struggled to alter the world from the one the raven controlled to a choice of his own. In that choice, of course, there was no raven.

The flames died. The shadows retreated. Skyscrapers became docile and solid. Again, it was a Chicago filled with life, not the decay and darkness that the raven represented.

"Children will be children!" tsked the raven.

The murky, fire-drenched vision of Chicago, complete with the twisted buildings out of some surrealistic painting, returned with a vengeance.

Jeremiah gritted his teeth, the pressure of the deadly avian's counterassault pressing at his mind. Still, he fought back again, reminding himself that if he was correct, it was only a matter of time. The important thing was to not let the raven have time to understand what was happening.

He pushed for another tableau, one drawn from his experiences here. The city began to fade. Having been tossed back and forth so many times himself, Jeremiah had some sympathy for its plight, but he could not stop now. As Chicago gave way, a small settlement sprouted among the grass and woods that were taking its place. Fort Dearborn. Possibly not the exact historical fort, since Jeremiah had no idea how to summon that particular ghost, but at the very least his perceptions of what it had looked like.

Unlike his first attempt, he was unable to complete the shift. The raven slowly pushed his own choice back to the forefront, but the effort was slower than his previous counterattack. Jeremiah took heart even as his head pounded from the strain.

"Enough games!" roared his avian adversary. With ease he expanded to several times his normal size. A chilling eye caught Todtmann's gaze. The raven began to draw him in, utilizing the fear that he had built up in the human. "To know me is to fear me! I grow strong as you grow weak! Your strength will wane; mine will peak!"

He felt himself losing ground. The raven, even without the spell, could still draw from him, if not quite as much. Jeremiah cursed himself for underestimating the demon bird even as he fought back the fear.

Soft fingers took hold of his right hand. Callistra's voice cut through the pain and raven-induced terror. "Courage, Jeremiah! You have him! He could not hold us any longer and still fight you! You mustn't let up now!"

"Two heads are better than one," Haros whispered from the other side of him. "Three are even better than two. Let us join your effort. Guide us and we will add to your strength."

"One, two, or three; all the same to me!" The raven, however, was no longer laughing.

The fear receded and with it some of the pressure. New strength did flow through him. Callistra and Haros, having seen his limited success with the black bird, were content to let him lead.

Again Jeremiah attacked the raven's reality. This time, he struck only at the bird himself, testing the winged terror's remaining strength. The huge raven cawed and met his attack. Briefly the avian Grey shimmered, but that was as far as the assault succeeded. The raven's laugh once more held a mocking edge to it.

Gasping, Todtmann shook his head. His thoughts were becoming muddled from the extensive effort, even with his two companions to aid him. The fear threatened him again. How could he hope to defeat the undefeatable?

"You have him on the run," whispered Haros, his tone one of growing encouragement. "No counterattack has he done!"

No counterattack. It was true. Despite Jeremiah's momentary lapse, the raven had not pressed his advantage. Compassion was not a part of the bird's makeup; his lack of action could only mean that he was beginning to struggle.

Now it was a question of which of them would fail first.

Jeremiah stood, his companions following his lead. He could still feel their own will backing his own. Yet, the fear that they, like the elf who had become Otto, would overextend themselves and lose their identities kept him from pressing the way he truly desired.

They must have felt his hesitation and understood a little of it, for Callistra squeezed his hand and whispered, "Do whatever is necessary, Jeremiah, or we will all pay the price."

"Pluck the pigeon," Haros added rather baldly.

He eyed the black bird, who still fluttered above them, but at not so great a height as before. The wings beat slower and the raven himself was smaller, almost his original size again.

"You're nothing," he told the avian menace. "A bad dream! A child's fear! Nothing with substance."

With each declaration, he attacked the raven anew. The black bird fought off the assaults, but no longer struck back. Pushing himself, Jeremiah once again imposed his own vision on the city. The fires died, the heat dwindled, and the shadows withdrew. To his surprise and pleasure, this time they did not return.

Leading his companions, the king of the Grey took half a dozen steps toward the malignant avian. The raven fluttered backward.

"I live now!" he insisted. "The sweet mystery of life I have at last found!"

Jeremiah shook his head. "You've been wrong from the start. You've been living nothing but a bad dream."

"I have looked upon the waking world and touched it!"

The truth hurts, they say. Let's see. "You built your reality around me and my fear, but the *spell* is what allowed you to feed so well off of me. Now that I'm no longer a part of it, you can't draw enough. The only one you can draw from is yourself, because the spell is now attached to you."

"To be or not to be, that is no question now!" The raven was fairly aglow with pent-up power. "I will be; you will not!"

The world became a true nightmare.

Buildings shifted like quicksilver. The streets rippled and sagged. The sky was red, then purple, then orange. Lampposts struck out at the trio but fell short. Jeremiah looked down at his own body and confronted a twisted, angular form that at first he seemed unable to control. Beside him, Haros and Callistra fought to maintain their grips. They, too, stretched and turned and Jeremiah realized that the Grey suffered more than he did, possibly because they had been strengthening him.

That last allowed him to shake off the confusion the raven's desperate attack had caused. Jeremiah braced himself. It could not be long now, he hoped. All he had to do was harry the raven enough.

Jeremiah jabbed at the black bird again and again. Small alterations, but all designed to harass the black bird where he was weakest. The avian countered them as he had done before, but slowly the madness he had summoned faded...until the only thing that remained of his vile power was the magpie himself.

This was it. Jeremiah forced himself to copy the same mocking tones the raven had always used and said to his adversary, "All or nothing now! Time to go for it or give up!"

The raven cawed his fury and spread his wings wide as if ready to dive upon the insolent human. He focused on Jeremiah.

The cry of fury became a gurgled cry of surprise.

Wings suddenly wrapped around him like a shroud, the malevolent raven shimmered. The black bird blinked in confusion. A blue halo formed around the avian body.

He began to fade.

"He's burning himself out," Jeremiah whispered, almost afraid that any word spoken louder would reverse the raven's fate. That was not to be, however. With every passing moment, the raven grew more transparent and although his fate must have been obvious even to him by that point, he would not give in. Spreading his wings one last time, the sinister Grey glared at Jeremiah Todtmann and opened his sharp beak as if to talk.

Whatever last witticism the raven had intended on spouting, Jeremiah was mercifully spared it. Before he could utter a sound, the winged pariah froze in place...and was no more.

Chicago became the Chicago Jeremiah knew and loved. Todtmann exhaled, then nearly collapsed. Callistra took hold of him and squeezed and Haros said something congratulatory, but at that moment Jeremiah Todtmann hardly noticed either of them. He simply stared at the last place he had seen the raven. There was no trace, no sense of the black bird being anywhere.

Jeremiah stared for a breath or two more, then finally turned to the others and asked, "Is it really over?"

The expressions on their faces finally permitted him to smile.

CHAPTER XVI

He would never go home, but now it was by choice.

Haros had insisted on a celebration, for that was a human thing to do and therefore it behooved the Grey to imitate it. Jeremiah had reluctantly agreed. All he wanted to do was take some time and seclude himself, perhaps with only Callistra as company. He needed time to think about what he had to do next. That, regrettably, would have to wait. In this one thing, his companions had been truly insistent.

The Wasteland was a place of merriment and while it might have been to a great extent false merriment, Jeremiah thought that perhaps there was a hint of true hope mixed in with it. He already knew that it was possible for a Grey to be more than a reflection of Humanity's conscious and subconscious. What the Grey could not become, he had realized after the raven's dissipation, was human. That was their mistake; they thought that they had to be a part of the true world. They could never truly be alive, not in the human sense, but why was it necessary to follow that path? They were simply another sort of life whose origins were as ambiguous in their own way as that of Mankind. Jeremiah was trying to convince them that even though they were related to Humanity, their future lay along a different path. The Grey could create a different world, one that still touched the minds of men, but also had its own say in what was to be.

Of course, there would always be the shadow walkers and their like. As long as Humanity dreamed, they could not help but create them. The key was that many Grey could move on, as Haros and Callistra had done. Haros had moved on long ago, driven by something that Jeremiah might never discover, for even the gaunt Grey was uncertain as to his origins. Todtmann suspected the elves somehow, even though they were not as advanced as Haros. Oberon and his like had had the potential, but having taken on the forms and identities they had, those particular Grey had stagnated. They had been locked into the regimented ideals their shapes had demanded. For the Grey form too often did dictate function.

"Jeremiah?"

Callistra, seated beside him, wore a look of concern. He smiled at her. She, too, was more than she had been when they had first met. His belief in her had paved the way, but Callistra had pushed ahead much on her own ability. She had told him of her belief that he had freed her from the raven's prison, but he was of the opinion that she had done it herself. Like the raven, she had become real enough to affect her world. The black bird's mistake had been thinking that he could go beyond that.

"I'm okay," Jeremiah finally replied. "Just tired."

Had the raven really believed him in the end? Had he even understood that as real as the minds of the human anchors had made him, he had still been a Grey and always would be?

When Jeremiah had explained it to Haros, the chalky-faced ghoul had smiled and said, "So we really should not have worried all this time? He was destined to fail?"

They both knew better. The fire the raven had started, which fortunately had been extinguished rather quickly by the Chicago Fire Department, was proof enough of the danger he had represented. Even condemned to ever be a Grey, the raven would have been a threat that would have touched not just the dream realm but indirectly the waking world as well.

Around Jeremiah and Callistra, the shadows danced. There did seem to be an undercurrent of something actually approaching pleasure. Preyed upon in the mind by the raven, none of the other kings, not even Thomas O'Ryan, had ever come into their potential. Yet, some few had had some influence, including O'Ryan, which was why Grey like Haros and Callistra existed. Now, with the past behind them, as the Grey would say, Jeremiah hoped that things would change. The Grey deserved that much.

Haros Aguilana, clad ever as the courtier, bowed before Jeremiah and said, "Eat, drink, and be merry, your majesty, for the raven is dead and may long live the king!"

It was impossible for Jeremiah to keep from smiling at the twisted clichés, which was what he suspected Haros had intended. They both knew, however, that the raven was not literally dead. He had ceased to exist, true, but what he personified would always be a part of the Grey realm. Yet, now that it was understood what he had been, the danger of another like him had been lessened considerably. Those who followed in Jeremiah's footsteps—and that would be some time in coming if he had his way—would always be prepared.

"It will all be over soon enough, Jeremiah," Callistra whispered, misunderstanding his silence. "Haros has promised. You know, I think he's a little afraid of you after the way you handled the black bird."

"Which won't stop him from trying to do a little whispering of his own in my ear, will it?" The cadaverous Grey had already made a few suggestions. Jeremiah was on guard now, however. He would listen to Haros Aguilana, but make no promises without thinking matters through. Now that he had decided to stay here and help the shadow folk, any decision he made affected him as well. That alone was almost enough reason to take care.

Callistra handed him a goblet that she had conjured from somewhere. Jeremiah glanced at her, took the goblet, and peered inside.

"Don't worry. This vintage won't be quite so dry as the last."

"Just checking." It was, in fact, quite tasty.

She leaned closer. "You know I am happy that you've chosen to stay, but I worry for you, too. You've given up your world, your life, for us."

Jeremiah Todtmann, human anchor, king of the Grey, contemplated his life before the summoning. He then scanned the interior of the club, studying the beings that he would spend the remainder of his life among. They came in all shapes and sizes. They were both the imaginable and, in some cases, the almost unimaginable. Yet, for all the fascinating array of forms the Grey consisted of, they were all dependent on him.

Returning his gaze to the beautiful, pale figure beside him, the one Grey whose existence ensured that he never dare fail in the monumental task set before him, Jeremiah took another sip from the goblet and replied, "My life's just *begun*."

ABOUT THE AUTHOR

New York Times and USA Today bestselling author Richard A. Knaak's works include The Legend of Huma, WoW: Stormrage, and nearly fifty other novels and numerous short stories, including works in such series as Warcraft, Diablo, Dragonlance, Age of Conan, and his own Dragonrealm. He has been published worldwide in many languages. He currently divides his time between Chicago and Arkansas.

BOOK

IS COMING

PERMUTED
PRESS

PERMUTED PRESS
needs **you** to help

SPREAD (THE) INFECTION

FOLLOW US!

f | Facebook.com/PermutedPress
𝕏 | Twitter.com/PermutedPress

REVIEW US!

Wherever you buy our book, they can be reviewed! We want to know what you like!

GET INFECTED!

Sign up for our mailing list at
PermutedPress.com

PERMUTED
PRESS

14

Peter Clines

Padlocked doors.
Strange light fixtures. Mutant
cockroaches.

There are some odd things about
Nate's new apartment. Every
room in this old brownstone has
a mystery. Mysteries that stretch
back over a hundred years.
Some of them are in plain sight.
Some are behind locked doors.
And all together these mysteries
could mean the end of Nate and
his friends.

Or the end of everything…

PERMUTED
PRESS

THE JOURNAL SERIES
by Deborah D. Moore

After a major crisis rocks the nation, all supply lines are shut down. In the remote Upper Peninsula of Michigan, the small town of Moose Creek and its residents are devastated when they lose power in the middle of a brutal winter, and must struggle alone with one calamity after another.

The Journal series takes the reader head first into the fury that only Mother Nature can dish out.

PERMUTED
PRESS